# A DARK QUEEN RISES

The Burnt Empire Saga

Book 2

# A DARK QUEEN RISES

Ashok K. Banker

A John Joseph Adams Book
MARINER BOOKS
HOUGHTON MIFFLIN HARCOURT
Boston New York
2021

hmhbooks.com

*Library of Congress Cataloging-in-Publication Data*
Names: Banker, Ashok, author.
Title: A dark queen rises / Ashok K Banker.
Description: Boston : Houghton Mifflin Harcourt, 2021. |
Series: The Burnt Empire saga ; book 2 | Summary: "Returning to Ashok K. Banker's brilliant #ownvoices, epic fantasy world of the Burnt Empire first introduced in Upon a Burning Throne, A Dark Queen Rises features Krushni and Karni, two women on quests to protect the innocent and bring down tyrants" — Provided by publisher.
Identifiers: LCCN 2020023907 (print) | LCCN 2020023908 (ebook) |
ISBN 9781328916297 (trade paperback) | ISBN 9781328916730 (ebook)
Subjects: GSAFD: Fantasy fiction.
Classification: LCC PR9499.3.B264 D37 2021 (print) | LCC PR9499.3.B264 (ebook) |
DDC 823/.914 — dc23
LC record available at https://lccn.loc.gov/2020023907
LC ebook record available at https://lccn.loc.gov/2020023908

Book design by David Futato
Map by Carly Miller

Printed in the United States of America
DOC 10 9 8 7 6 5 4 3 2 1

*for bithika,*

*yashka,*

*ayush yoda,*

*helene,*

*and*

*leia.*

~

*this gift of words and swords,*
*this forest of stories,*
*this ocean of wonders,*
*this epic of epics.*

# *Dramatis Personae*

## Gwannland

| | |
|---|---|
| Gwann | Ruler of Gwannland; husband of Vensera |
| Vensera | Queen of Gwannland; wife of Gwann |
| Guru Dronas | Enemy of Gwann; legendary teacher of warcraft |

## The Wagon Train

| | |
|---|---|
| Aqreen | Princess of Aqron; daughter of Aqron; estranged wife of Jarsun |
| Krushita | Daughter of Aqreen and Jarsun; cousin of Shvate and Adri |
| Bulan | A Vanjhani; master of the wagon train |
| Muskaan | A Vanjhani; Bulan's second in command |
| Subed | A Vanjhani; colonel of the wagon train militia |
| Vor | A shvan |

## The Reygistan Empire

| | |
|---|---|
| Aqron (deceased) | King of Aqron; father of Aqreen |
| Jarsun | Descendant of Kr'ush; nephew of Shapaar; brother of |

| | |
|---|---|
| | Sha'ant and Vessa; husband of Princess Aqreen; father of Krushita; God-Emperor of Reygistan |
| Darinda (deceased) | King of Reygar |
| Drina | Queen of Reygar |
| Dirrdha | Brother of Queen Drina of Reygar |
| Prees | Daughter of Jarsun; wife of Tyrak |
| Tessi | Daughter of Jarsun; wife of Tyrak |
| Seratova | Son of Jarsun; the architect of Grarij |

## Followers of Jarsun

| | |
|---|---|
| Bahuka | Jarsun's agent |
| Bane | A Morgol chieftain and general in the Imperial Arrgodi Army |
| Musthika | A Morgol chieftain and a Khobadi fighter |
| Ladislew | Maha-Maatri of Reygar; a Morgol chieftain; wife of Pradynor |
| Uaraj | A Morgol chieftain and associate of Tyrak |
| Pradynor | Tyrak's chief of guards; husband of Ladislew |

## The Arrgodi and Mraashk Nations

| | |
|---|---|
| Tyrak | A legendary urrkhlord |
| Arrgo (deceased) | Founder of the Arrgodi and Mraashk nations |
| Kensura | Queen of Arrgodi; wife of Ugraksh; mother of Tyrak |
| Ugraksh | Husband of Queen Kensura; legal father of Tyrak |
| Tyrak | Crown prince of Arrgodi and Mraashk; son of Kensura and Ugraksh (legally) and Tyrak the Urrkhlord (biologically) |
| Kewri | Princess of Arrgodi; half sister of Tyrak; wife of Vasurava |
| Vasurava | Prince of Mraashk; brother of Karni; husband of Kewri |

| | |
|---|---|
| Kirtiman | Eldest son of Kewri and Vasurava |
| Drishya | Son of Kewri and Vasurava |

## Subjects of the Arrgodi and Mraashk Nations

| | |
|---|---|
| Alinora | Wife of Eshnor; adoptive mother of Drishya |
| Eshnor | Husband of Alinora; adoptive father of Drishya |
| Rurka | Friend and ally of Vasurava |
| Arrgo | A groom |
| Shelsis | Chief advisor to Tyrak |
| Eredon | Tyrak's demon elephant |
| Gaurika | A cow blessed by Drishya |

## The Gods

| | |
|---|---|
| Jeel | Goddess of water; former wife of Sha'ant; mother of Vrath |
| Artha | Goddess of land; the Great Mother (a.k.a. Mother Goddess); protector of the mortal realm; sister of Goddess Jeel |
| Shima | God of death and duty |
| Sharra | God of the sun |
| Inadran | God of storms and war |
| Grrud | God of winds and birds |
| the Asva twins | Twin gods of animalia, health, and medicine |
| Shaiva | God of destruction |
| Coldheart | Spirit of mountains and high places; forebear of Jeel; grandfather of Vrath |
| Brak | The Stone Father |
| Gnash | God of auspicious beginnings, remover of obstacles |

| | |
|---|---|
| Jaggernaut | A stone god |
| Lankeshva | A stone god |
| Vakaronus | Architect of the stone gods |
| Shaputi | Amsa of the stone god Shaiva |

## The Burnt Empire

| | |
|---|---|
| Kr'ush (deceased) | Founder of the Krushan dynasty and the Burnt Empire |
| Ashalon (deceased) | A Krushan forebear |
| Shapaar (deceased) | Descendant of Kr'ush; emperor of the Burnt Empire; king of Hastinaga; father of Sha'ant and Vessa |
| Sha'ant (deceased) | Son of Shapaar; emperor of the Burnt Empire; king of Hastinaga; father of Vrath, Virya, and Gada; husband of the goddess Jeel and of Jilana; cousin of Jarsun |
| Vrath | Son of Sha'ant and the goddess Jeel; uncle to Adri and Shvate; prince regent of the Burnt Empire |
| Jilana | Dowager empress of the Burnt Empire; dowager queen of Hastinaga; wife of Sha'ant; mother of Vessa, Virya, and Gada; stepmother of Vrath |
| Vessa | Seer-mage; son of Jilana; biological father of Adri, Shvate, and Vida |
| Virya (deceased) | Son of Sha'ant and Jilana; husband of Umber |
| Gada (deceased) | Son of Sha'ant and Jilana; husband of Ember |
| Ember | Wife of Gada; mother of Adri; sister to Umber |
| Umber | Wife of Virya; mother of Shvate; sister to Ember |
| Amber (deceased) | Sister of Ember and Umber |
| Adri | Prince of the Burnt Empire; son of Ember and Gada (legally) and Vessa (biologically); grandson of Jilana; nephew of Vrath; half brother of Shvate and Vida; husband to Geldry |
| Shvate | Prince of the Burnt Empire; son of Umber and Virya (legally) and Vessa (biologically); grandson of Jilana; |

| | |
|---|---|
| | nephew of Vrath; half brother of Adri and Vida; husband to Mayla and Karni |
| Vida | Son of Vessa; half brother to Adri and Shvate |
| Mayla | Princess of Dirda; wife of Shvate |
| Karni | Princess of Stonecastle; wife of Shvate |
| Geldry | Princess of Geldran; wife of Adri |
| Kune | Prince of Geldran; brother of Geldry |
| Yudi | One of the Five; Karni's daughter fathered by the stone god Shima |
| Arrow | One of the Five; Karni's child fathered by the stone god Inadran |
| Brum | One of the Five; Karni's child fathered by the stone god Grrud |
| Kula | One of the Five; Mayla's daughter fathered by the stone gods the Asvas; Saha's twin |
| Saha | One of the Five; Mayla's daughter fathered by the stone gods the Asvas; Kula's twin |
| Dhuryo | Eldest son of Geldry and Adri |
| Dushas | Son of Geldry and Adri |
| Duhshala | Daughter of Geldry and Adri |
| Kern | Foundling son (adopted) of Adran and Reeda, firstborn son of Karni by stone god Sharra and consigned by her to the river Jeel |
| Sauvali | Maid in the royal palace, lover of Adri, mother-to-be of his unborn child |
| Prishata | Captain of the imperial guards |
| Adran | Charioteer of Adri; husband of Reeda; adoptive father of Kern |
| Reeda | Wife of Adran; adoptive mother of Kern |

# ARTHALOKA

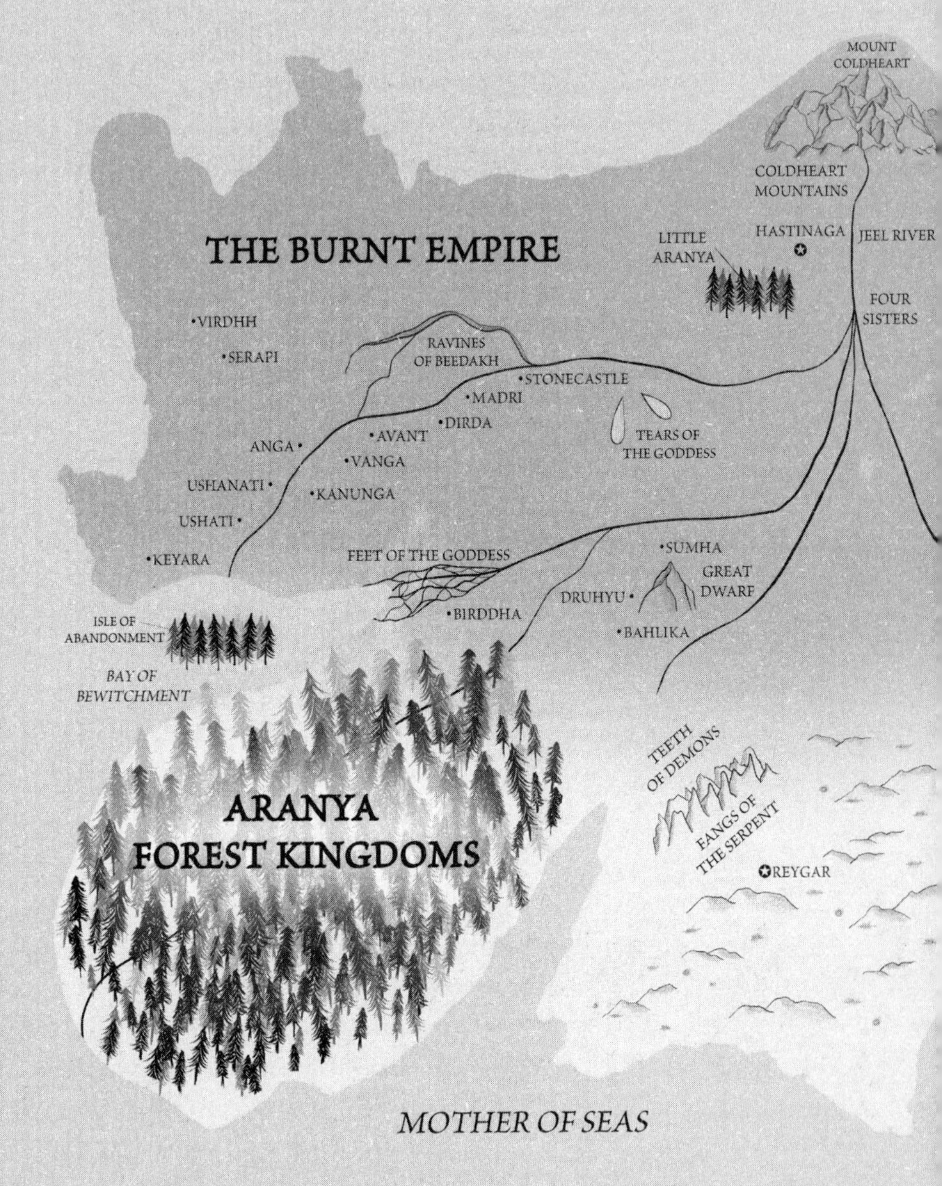
THE BURNT EMPIRE
MOUNT COLDHEART
COLDHEART MOUNTAINS
LITTLE ARANYA
HASTINAGA
JEEL RIVER
FOUR SISTERS
VIRDHH
SERAPI
RAVINES OF BEEDAKH
STONECASTLE
MADRI
DIRDA
AVANT
ANGA
VANGA
TEARS OF THE GODDESS
USHANATI
KANUNGA
USHATI
KEYARA
FEET OF THE GODDESS
SUMHA
GREAT DWARF
DRUHYU
BIRDDHA
BAHLIKA
ISLE OF ABANDONMENT
BAY OF BEWITCHMENT
TEETH OF DEMONS
FANGS OF THE SERPENT
ARANYA FOREST KINGDOMS
REYGAR
MOTHER OF SEAS

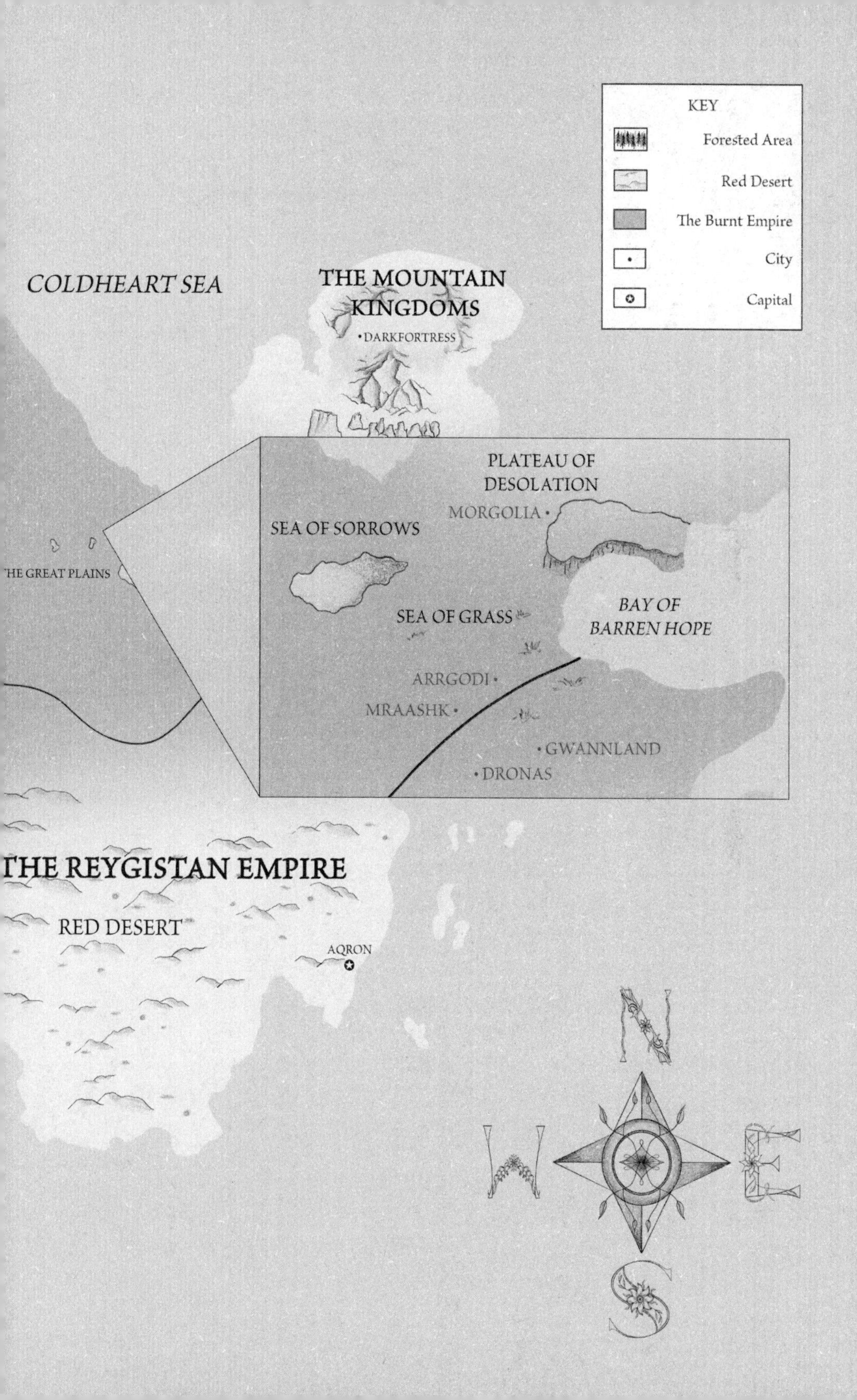
KEY
Forested Area
Red Desert
The Burnt Empire
City
Capital
COLDHEART SEA
THE MOUNTAIN KINGDOMS
DARKFORTRESS
PLATEAU OF DESOLATION
MORGOLIA
SEA OF SORROWS
THE GREAT PLAINS
SEA OF GRASS
BAY OF BARREN HOPE
ARRGODI
MRAASHK
GWANNLAND
DRONAS
THE REYGISTAN EMPIRE
RED DESERT
AQRON
N
W
E
S

# PROLOGUE, EPILOGUE

## *The Given Avatars*

YEAR 207 OF CHAKRA 58

# *King Gwann*

## 1

BURN.

King Gwann's kindly eyes widened.

The single word had not been uttered by the high priests chanting sonorously in classical Ashcrit. It had come from the altar itself.

The stonefire had spoken.

He stared at the fragment of rock that lay in the center of the large white pentangle. The altar was five times the normal dimensions — twenty-five yards on each of its five sides, instead of the normal five yards. The tiny pebble of stonefire was a mere black dot in the center of the ash-carpeted ground. The silverwood barrier that formed the five lines of the pentangle provided further protection to the priests, ministers, nobles, and servants who sat on the periphery of the sacred space.

The priests had insisted on this precaution, and Gwann had agreed gladly. His desire for a successful ceremony was outweighed by his inborn terror of stonefire. To a Krushan, it was a great source of power, the searing fire a response to the call of their ancient blood. But to any non-Krushan, it was evil incarnate.

It had cost several scores of lives just to obtain the precious, cursed thing itself. Stonefire was not officially banned, because the Krushan knew that there was no need to ban it. The wretched substance could take care of itself, and then some. Scores of Gwann's bravest and boldest had sacrificed their lives to acquire and smuggle it across the Burnt Empire and into Gwannland. A few had been betrayed, others were killed fighting bandits as well as smugglers who had caught wind of the enterprise, but the vast majority of those brave warriors had been killed by stonefire itself. Despite all precautions — special yards-long silverwood tongs to handle it, a silverwood casket to contain it, and even two silverwood shields, all devised at great cost — the wicked thing had found opportunities to lash out at its abductors and burn them to ash during the long, perilous journey.

Among them was Jonasi, Gwann's late wife's brother and his most trusted champion. With him and most of his elite king's guards lost in the desperate quest, Gwann was left with nothing more than a few platoons of untested recruits and broken veterans. His capacity for war, or even defense, was gone. Gwannland's coffers, bare. Gwannland's natural resources, taken. The war against Guru Dronas had cost him everything, and the price he had paid for mere survival had been the better half of his entire kingdom. Gwannland was now Gwannland only in name.

All he had left now was this final, desperate gambit.

The Ritual of Summoning.

## 2

And what did Gwann hope to achieve by this arcane ritual?

Vensera had asked him the question when he first spoke of it several months ago, after the war with Dronas ended.

A means of survival, he had answered.

She had looked at him for a long moment, her grey-green eyes searching his face the way one might look at a man to ascertain his sanity.

"This is Krushan sorcery," she had said, and there was an edge of fear in her tone. She had not sounded so fearful even when they had stood on the field of Beha'al, looked out at the vast host arrayed against their own forces, and realized that they stood no chance of victory against Dronas. "These rituals are meant to summon the stone gods. And the stone gods recognize only the Krushan. We mortals were never meant to meddle in such matters."

Gwann had drawn in a deep breath and released it slowly. "Neither were mortals meant to live alongside Krushan. Yet here we are. All together on a single continent. Thus has it been ever since they arrived here from wherever they came from. That is the way of our world, Vensera; it is what we are given. We can only survive by whatever means are available to us. If using Krushan sorcery is the only way to repair our fortunes, then so be it. We have no other choice."

She had looked into his eyes and seen his despair, his ache at the forfeiture of territory his ancestors had fought so bitterly to win and hold for generations. "We will endure this loss," she had said then. "It is what we do. And one day, when we have rebuilt our strength . . ."

She had not needed to continue. She was the greater warrior of them both, the superior strategist and tactician. His skills were those of administrator, jurist, and city planner. He had always taken her word when it came to martial affairs, just as she took his when it came to domestic ones. But he need not be a military genius to know that they stood no chance of ever rebuilding; he knew economics, and the fact was, Gwannland had nothing left to rebuild with. Everything their kingdom had possessed — people, farms, mines, trade stations, everything and anything that could fetch income, now or in the future — was now controlled by Dronas. He had carved out the heart of Gwannland and left them with the bare, broken bones.

Gwann had put a hand on her cheek, gently. She was still handsome, the scars adding to her rugged appeal. What most mistook for hardness, he knew to be a carapace; she was as soft on the inside as she was hard on the exterior.

"You know that will never happen," he had said softly. "This is the only way."

"It is one way," she had admitted. "There are others."

"It is the only *sure* way," he had said. "If this succeeds, we will stand a chance of retaking Gwannland and ousting Dronas."

She had fallen silent then. She could have countered with the argument that ousting Dronas, even if such a thing was possible now, would come with a heavy price: the wrath of the Burnt Empire. And if they had not been able to defeat Dronas at their strongest, to attempt to resist the empire at their weakest would mean total destruction. Not even the fealty oaths of his ancestors would protect them. But she said none of these things.

Instead she had said the one thing Gwann had never expected.

"Gwannland was my dowry," she said at last. "Given to me as the price for taking you in matrimony."

He had stared at her, not sure how to respond.

Yes, the realm was endowed to her, and she was its supreme commander.

That was the tradition: stree, being the stronger gender and built for war, received a dowry from the manush's family at the time of nuptials. In this part of the world, the tradition called for the manush to gift a dowry to the stree, and Gwannland had been Gwann's to Vensera. His only claim was a heritage, to the history of his ancestors whose bones were embedded in the foundations of every town and city across its breadth. She owned it, and it was hers to do with as she pleased. If she wished, she could command him not just as his sovereign but also as the commander of the domain.

But that was not at all what she meant.

"Yes, it is yours to dispose of as you will," he had said.

"And I would willingly lose all of this and more," she went on, "but losing you is a loss I cannot bear. That is all that concerns me now. Your well-being."

*She's afraid the ritual might backfire and cost me my life,* he realized with a start. Fool that he was, he had only thought of the political capital to be gained from the ceremony, without a care for his personal safety. She had reason to fear, after all; her own brother had been incinerated when he was occupied with fighting off bandits, one of whom had sprung open the silverwood casket like an idiot. The chip of stonefire had lashed out instantly, the tongue of white-hot flame turning Jonasi — and several other men within its reach — to ash and cinder in a flash. It was only natural that she should fear losing him as well.

Tears had sprung from his eyes. He had embraced her and touched her feet, the traditional sign of submission and respect to one's betters, or in this case, a husband to a wife. "I do this to save Gwannland, and us," he replied fiercely, "all of us. It is the only way. If I must die trying, so be it. I would rather be seared by stonefire than live in helpless thrall to Dronas."

She had caught him by the shoulders, her powerful arms far stronger than his own, and raised him up, pressing her lips to his roughly. When she released him, her eyes were hot with love and fear.

"Do what you must, then. I will stand with you."

# 3

Vensera sat beside him now. The silverwood barrier that formed the pentangle was sufficient only to protect them when seated. And deceptive though it was, sitting passively in that large ash-grey space, that vile thing would lash out faster than a viper's fangs if so much as an inch of mortal flesh showed over the top. She was seated beside him, their hands clasped together tightly, dressed in their finest regal attire, waiting to be called upon to do their part.

It had taken a great deal of convincing to get the priests to conduct the ceremony at all. In the end, it was their own reduced circumstances that had brought them around. When the liege was defeated, so were all those dependent on her munificence. The priests had experienced loss of luxury and the looming specter of abject poverty, even starvation, if something was not done, and quickly. The ban on any citizen, high or low, crossing Gwannland's newly redrawn borders, ruled out any chance of fleeing or seeking succor elsewhere.

*Dronas has done everything possible to destroy us without actually sentencing us to death,* Gwann thought heatedly. *That way, he can have his revenge and stay within the letter of Krushan law.*

Krushan law, as arcane and antiquated as their ceremonial rituals, forbade the killing of any bloodline oathsworn to Hastinaga. The forebear of the Kuin had taken the sacred oath before the first of the dynasty, the mythic Kr'ush himself, in the misty prehistory of the world. Dronas's campaign of vengeance prevented him from harming any Kuin directly. He had done the next best thing: invited them to pitched battle, wiped out their army, taken everything of value to them, and left them with nothing but this desolate patch of fallow territory with no water source, no farmlands, towns, cities, or means of trade. He may as well have taken them to the middle of the Red Desert and abandoned them without food, water, or transport. That would have been a speedier death.

Vensera felt Gwann's grip tighten and sensed his anger. She squeezed back, her much stronger grip curbed to avoid hurting him. He let the anger dissipate slowly, determined to keep his head clear through this ritual. It was dangerous enough without being distracted by his own emotions.

This *must* work.

He had to believe that now, and so did Vensera.

The priests had warned them beforehand: they must come to the altar with genuine need, holding back nothing. And if granted their given wish, they must accept it without question.

That was the way of the stone gods. You took what you were given, and you thanked stonefire.

Or stonefire would eat you alive.

The high priest was approaching a peak in the chanting. His face was limned with perspiration. Despite its deceptive appearance, the tiny pebble was exuding heat more intense than any bonfire. Yet it remained stolidly black and inert, just a little bit of black rock. The heat was penetrating enough that Gwann felt the palm that gripped Vensera's grow slippery with sweat, even though they were seated some yards behind the high priest herself.

How far did the damned thing's reach extend? Gwann had heard varying reports from the surviving soldiers who had returned from the expedition: some said it could extend any distance it pleased, which was impossible; others, that it could burn flesh from no more than ten yards away. But apparently the heat could be felt much, much farther than reported. Gwann estimated that he was well over sixty yards away, and still beads of sweat were breaking out on his forehead.

What was stonefire, anyway?

No one had a definite answer. It was forbidden to speak about it, let alone question, study, or record its properties. What little was known about its qualities was the stuff of myth and legend.

This much was certain, though: stonefire *burned.*

Not merely the burning of an ordinary fire. It consumed its prey whole, like a demonic thing armed with teeth, fangs, and a maw of living flame. The story went — whispered in private — that it consumed your very soul, from the inside out. And once it devoured you, you were trapped inside the stone itself, your essence digested and contained within its oily, alien surface. It was also said that though it looked like a stone, it was in fact a viscous thing, a dark substance that was not truly black, but appeared so because it erased light itself. That was the reason you could look at it but not truly see it. You only saw what it wanted you to see. Stonefire was no mere rock. It lived, it ate, it grew. And most of all, if you were Krushan, it empowered you. That was the reason why those who sat upon the Burning Throne, the highest seat of power in all Arthaloka, ruled the world.

It was that empowerment that Gwann now sought, in his time of desperation.

It was that which this ritual was supposed to summon.

The high priest's sonorous voice droned on, reciting the Ashcrit mantras by rote, as priests before him had done for thousands of years. These particular mantras were rarely if ever used. The high priest had told Gwann that to the best of his knowledge — which was considerable — they had not been used by a non-Krushan in at least three sausaal, a sausaal being a unit of 108 Arthaloka years. And on that last occasion, the ritual had ended in disaster.

Gwann had heard the priest's tone of disapproval and ignored the implicit warning. He would not be dissuaded from his chosen path. It was desperate, yes, but it was the only way. The magic mantra which would, if all went well, provide him with the power to overthrow Dronas and take back the kingdom that was rightfully his. He would have Gwannland back once more, and this time, he would have the power to hold and defend it.

A sudden silence alerted him.

The chanting had ended.

The high priest and all the purohits had completed the recitation of the mantras.

Gwann blinked, staring at them. They appeared to be frozen, staring blankly at the center of the pentangle.

The baking heat from the stonefire had increased in intensity and was increasing still.

He felt the sweat pouring down his face and back. Vensera's palm was slick with sweat against his own. He glanced at her and saw her sweating as profusely. The white kushtas of the priests, though loose and flowing, had dark sweat patches as well, and he could see beads of perspiration gleaming on the upper lip of High Priest Namanraj. The man looked terrified, his eyes fixed on the stonefire. Everyone was staring at it, except Gwann himself. He glanced around and saw that even the sentries several yards behind him were shifting uneasily, their knuckles white around their pikes. The air was thick with a dry, searing heat. He had never been to Reygistan, but he imagined this must be what it felt like in the Red Desert.

*Burn.*

His head snapped back to the altar, eyes finding the stonefire.

This time that sinister, tongueless voice was louder, filling the space. He saw from the reactions on the faces around the altar that the others had heard it too. He had no recollection of this from the myths. Could stonefire . . . speak?

*BURN.*

The word felt like an ember igniting inside his brain.

He clutched his head as the heat seared him from the inside and was aware of the others holding their heads and exclaiming as well. The heat from the altar increased. Now sweat poured freely down his body, drenching his silk robes. He tugged off his turban, feeling as if his hair and skull must surely be on fire.

His hands felt only the normal warmth of skin and bone, but his head felt as if it would combust at any moment. An apprentice rose screaming, hands clutching his shaven pate, babbling that he could not take it anymore. Gwann saw High Priest Namanraj swear at the novice, gesturing wildly with one hand, something he had never before witnessed at a ceremony.

But it was already too late.

A spear of red hot flame, as slender as a scarlet thread, flashed out from the stonefire. The tip connected with the skull of the babbling acolyte, and Gwann watched, aghast, as the life left the man's eyes and his limp body dropped bonelessly to the ground. He fell onto the silverwood barrier, sprawled partially over it, head and limbs extending into the ash-covered pentangle. One hand struck the ash-covered surface, and a grey puff rose in the air. A thin thread of blood dripped from the tiny perforation in the man's head, falling onto the ash.

And in the instant it took that drop of blood to fall the remaining few inches to the ground, the stonefire claimed the body.

The head and upper torso of the acolyte evaporated in a liquid explosion. A small dark cloud hung for a moment, then even those fine particles of bloody ash were incinerated to near-invisible motes. The rest of the unfortunate victim's body burned steadily, fiercely, like a corpse committed to the funeral pyre.

A howl of lament rose from the scores of gathered priests, clutching their heads and shaking from side to side as they mourned the loss of one of their own while calling upon their gods to protect them.

Vensera's voice forced Gwann to look away from the ghastly sight of the destroyed apprentice.

She was staring with a stunned look on her face.

In her pupils, Gwann saw the red heat from the altar reflected. The light glowed upon her face. He saw that the entire gathering was illuminated by the stonefire's glow.

And still the heat grew.

*BURN!*

The voice of flame screamed inside his skull now, making rational thought impossible.

It was the heat of naked, raw emotions, unfettered by moral considerations or civilized concerns.

Was this what it felt like when demons — urrkh — raged? Perhaps this was what they felt when they went into battle against mortals.

A blazing fire that shredded sanity, drove out all awareness, thought, even the need to ensure one's own survival.

Only the flame itself remained, seeking to burn, to destroy, to ruin.

*BURN!*

The stonefire cried out one final time, the heat in Gwann's head beyond endurance.

He was aware of more priests thrashing about, rising, sentries tearing off their helmets. He glimpsed one woman's helmet, the metal melted to the texture of soft wax, sticking to her hair and scalp, ripping them away as she flung the headgear to the ground.

Stonefire blasts blazed out in all directions at once, seeking, finding, incinerating any and all flesh that came within range. Bodies exploded. Helmets and armor melted, then exploded outward in a deadly spray. Screams filled the air, vying with the stench of scorched flesh, burnt blood, and the iron taste of molten metal.

Gwann began to lose consciousness. He felt as if his brain was melting inside his skull. He found himself hammering at his own head with his fists, punching himself hard enough that the bruises would surely show for days afterward, as if seeking to break open the cage of bone and free the fire within.

The awareness of Vensera starting to rise distracted him. Some deep part of him, overwhelmed though he was by the terrors unfolding all around, made him lunge out and grab her waist, yanking her down hard. She stumbled back, and he fell upon her as a blast of red rage passed through the space they had occupied only a fraction of an instant before. He would find later that the hair on the back and top of his head had been burned off, leaving a blistering red patch that would never heal completely, but his speedy action saved her life.

The altar and the space around it was a festering place of hellish heat, smoke, and burned flesh.

Lying on his back now, head ringing from the burn and from the impact with Vensera's armor, Gwann saw only thick grey smoke boiling above and around.

Slowly, by degrees, he came to understand that the heat was dissipating, the searing agony in his brain receding, the glow from the stonefire fading.

Something was happening in the pentangle.

Vensera sat up carefully, helping him up to a sitting position as well. Her arms and strength comforted him, helped ease the return to full self-awareness. He regained rationality, remembering who he was and why he was there. All the mundane, mortal miseries of existence that the stonefire had seared out of his head returned.

The Ritual of Summoning.

He grew aware of something moving within the cloud of smoke.

Within the pentangle.

In the altar.

Had the ritual succeeded?

He felt a blast of wind. For an instant, his skin registered it as intense heat. Only when he saw Vensera's breath condensing as she exhaled and saw a matching puff from his mouth did he realize it was icy cold, like the blow from a blizzard in the Coldheart Mountains. Gwannland's coldest winter nights never came close to freezing, so whatever this was, it was no natural phenomenon.

A portal had been opened.

Even through the grey haze, he could see movement and a light. A cold dark blue light the size and shape of a large cave, perhaps four yards high and five or six yards wide. Around it was whiteness, utter whiteness.

Whatever that place was, it was frigid, covered in snow.

Within the darker bluish hole in the whiteness, a shape was moving.

He strained to see through the haze.

The ritual had succeeded.

Something or someone was coming through.

The shape moved out of the darkness and into the pentangle.

The world shifted for an instant. Like a single tremor in an earthquake. A sliding of reality.

He felt the lurching sensation within himself, as if all his organs had shifted a fraction to one side, then settled back in their original places. Vensera exhaled, and one of the surviving priests faltered, hands raised as if to exalt a divinity.

The other priests rose as well.

None were being burnt. It seemed the threat of stonefire had passed.

Vensera rose to her feet. Gwann's heart skipped. He flinched in anticipation of a blast from the stonefire.

Nothing happened to her.

She stood erect, staring at the dark shape that had emerged from the portal.

Slowly, cautiously, Gwann rose as well.

The figure moved through the swirling haze.

It stood before them, magnificent, terrible, darkly beautiful.

"Who . . ." Gwann swallowed, took in a breath, then tried again. "Who are you?"

The figure stood silently for a long moment.

Around them, the priests and sentries—those few who had survived—were standing with arms raised in salutation. The priests were chanting the Mantra of Gratitude. As they finished, they lowered their arms all the way down, bending from the waist until the tips of their fingers touched the ground. They remained that way, eyes cast downward, in the traditional gesture of submission.

Gwann realized he was in the presence of a stone god—or at the very least, a demigod.

The ritual had worked.

His wish had been granted.

A savior was given unto them.

"Are you a god?" he asked now, when it appeared that no reply to his first question was forthcoming.

A delicate tinkling and susurration came in response. It was followed almost immediately by the sound of a feminine voice.

"No."

Another figure had emerged from the portal.

Gwann blinked in surprise.

A pair of delicate ankles adorned with tiny silvery bells were the first thing he saw. While not actually supplicating himself as the priests and sentries were doing, he had instinctively lowered his gaze. He didn't know the protocol for greeting a stone god or demigod, but his own faith required one to be humble in the presence of divinity.

So it was that the first thing he saw was her feet.

"We are not," she said in a voice as silvery and clear as the bells on her feet.

He raised his eyes, surprised by the answer, and the use of his own tongue. He had expected high Ashcrit, the antiquated language of the scrolls, or at the very least the Old Tongue used in the Burnt Empire. Not his own common dialect, spoken only by the people in this godforsaken part of the world.

She was young, handsome, with a regal bearing. Her skin was the color of burnt wood. Her eyes, banked fires. Her limbs, her body, as lithe and toned as Vensera's warrior physique, but also with a feminine softness about it. Her eyes were rimmed with kohl, her lips glossed with rouge, her hair wild and untamable, a beautiful beast unto itself.

She smiled at him. There was something mischievous about her smile, as if she was considering a private joke.

"We are something more," she said simply.

Then she came forward.

Gwann sensed Vensera flinch, her hand instinctively falling to her sword hilt.

The stranger noticed and included Vensera in her smile.

"Mother," she said.

Vensera's hand left her sword hilt. Her mouth opened in surprise.

Gwann stared openly now, unable to look away from the woman's compelling gaze.

"I am your daughter," she said now, first addressing herself to Vensera, then to Gwann.

She spread her arms, including them both in a figurative embrace.

"I have answered your summons."

Then she joined her palms together and bowed low from the waist.

"I am here now. From this day on, you will fear nothing and want for nothing."

Gwann heard a choking sound.

It came from his own throat.

He was crying. With joy, with disbelief.

The ritual had worked!

He held up his palm in the traditional parental gesture of blessing. "Live long, live well," he said, uttering the words parents and elders had said to their youngers for millennia in Gwannland, as well as across Arthaloka. Some traditions were universal.

He heard Vensera echo the words, her own palm held out beside his own.

The young woman straightened, her palms still joined, eyes lowered, and inclined her head to acknowledge their blessings.

Then she turned and acknowledged the rest of the gathering.

Raising her voice, she said aloud, "We are the Given Avatars."

A reverential response rose from the priests and sentries around the pentangle. The smoky haze had cleared now and Gwann could see everyone once again. He noted distractedly that the stonefire was gone, leaving only a tiny reddish-black mark on the ground. So too was the portal.

All that remained was this young woman and the young man standing behind her silently.

The Given Avatars.

"Have you names?" he heard Vensera ask hesitantly. "Or shall we provide them for you?"

The woman — *our daughter,* Gwann thought, through his dazzlement — inclined her head and said, "I shall choose for us."

Her tone was gentle and pleasing, but also decisive.

She turned to indicate the young man standing beside her, tall, proud, as magnificent as she herself, fully armored and armed, like a warrior ready for battle. His own steely eyes met hers. He stood impassively as she raised a hand to touch his face affectionately.

She paused, tilting her head a fraction of an angle. Again, that sense of inward consideration, as if searching for a way to explain the inexplicable in an idiom comprehensible to mere mortals.

*We are something more.* What could be more than a god?

"He is a portion of myself," she went on, "a part of me yet apart from me. I shall call him brother in this life. It is close enough. I speak for both of us. All that he hears, I hear. All he sees, I see. Everything he tastes, I taste. Anything he smells, I smell. Any and everything he feels . . . everything he experiences, I experience as well. We are as one, though he thinks for himself as well and can act independently if he desires. Always, I am the voice that speaks for us both."

She raised her arms, raising her gaze as well, to the sky.

"I name him Drishya."

The priests chanted the Ashcrit word of acknowledgment: "Sidh! Sidh!" It was one of the few Ashcrit words Gwann knew himself, and was the traditional way of showing respect for an excellent choice. It also meant "auspicious."

The young woman smiled, acknowledging the priests, and turned a full circle, letting everyone present see her clearly.

"I am Krushni," she said.

# Part One

## *The Dagger from My Heart, The Fury from My Eyes*

YEAR 166 OF CHAKRA 58

# *Aqreen*

~

## 1

AQREEN AND KRUSHITA LEFT Aqron in the company of a trade caravan headed for Reygistan. Aqreen's heart cried out as the white spires of Aqron fell behind them, and she hugged Krushita tightly.

*Am I doing the right thing?* she asked herself repeatedly. *He will come after us, I know he will. Is there any point to this attempt?*

Another voice, her late mother's voice, said quietly, *If you had stayed, he would have killed you sooner or later. Is that what you want—for your daughter to see her mother killed by her own father because of his greed and cruel ambition?*

No, she had made her choice. Whatever came next, she would deal with it.

Soon the trundling uks wagon had left the coastal city far behind, and the only thing in sight was desert. It was too late for second thoughts now. There was no going back.

"Why you go Reygistan?" asked Bulan, the train master, when she had applied for passage. "You no trader or merchant." Their two independent heads swept her with a quick, expert glance. "You no mercenary too. Why for go such long journey?"

She hesitated. Although the train master was speaking Aqrish for her benefit, Bulan was Vanjhani, and she knew the Vanjhani were honorable to a fault. Despite being literally two-faced and four-armed, they had a hard-won reputation for being the most reliable, loyal, and fair of all the many races that roamed the Red Desert. But she didn't know whom she could trust, and she wasn't ready to start just yet.

"I have nobody left in Aqron," she said. "My sister lives in Reygar. My daughter and I will start a new life there with her."

The train master was silent. Their massive eight-foot-high hulk towered above Aqreen, but despite the formidable muscled body and intimidating double gaze, there was something reassuring rather than threatening about Bulan.

Vanjhani were dual-bodied. Two massive legs sprouted a torso that split, like a tree trunk, into two upper bodies, each with its own arms, neck, head, personality and gender. Vanjhani were famed for their unique physical appearance, their prowess in battle, and their fierce character and integrity. The fact that the master of this wagon train was one had been a significant factor in her choice.

She felt safer in Bulan's presence. She had grown up around Vanjhani, was familiar with their unusual eating habits and customs, and had learned that like many of the largest and strongest races, they could be surprisingly gentle and kind. Bulan's reputation as a train master was considerable.

"Something about you," Bulan said now, considering her thoughtfully. One head, the one with the scars on the side of its scalp, sniffed curiously, then whispered something in the ear of its companion. "Yes, definitely something. You are running from something. Or someone?"

She swallowed nervously. "I am no criminal," she said cautiously. "I have done nothing wrong. I am simply taking my daughter to see my sister."

One of Bulan's heads laughed softly. The other frowned disapprovingly. "Who say anything about criminal? Why guilty so?" The head that had laughed shook from side to side, unconvinced. "Who travel with small child twenty thousand miles across Red Desert for seven years just to visit sister? Something more than you say to us is behind your trip. Bulan smell it on you, the fear."

She almost broke down in tears. A part of her was still trembling inside, in constant dread of being found out, of being exposed and dragged back to Aqron, to be brought before the burning eyes of her husband. To face his punishment. If he had treated her so brutally at the best of times, imagine what he might do after such a betrayal. No. It didn't take any imagination to know the answer. He would kill her, plain and simple.

"Please," she said at last, forcing her voice to sound as normal as possible. "I will pay you more. Don't ask questions."

Bulan sighed with one mouth and pursed the lips of the other. "Coin. Is coin only thing in world? Everyone talk coin, coin, always coin. It not solve all problems. It mostly worsen them."

She was silent then, afraid she had said too much, sounded too desperate. Were they angry with her? She couldn't take their anger. She had become so sensitive to the very possibility of anger. Jarsun had done that to her. She could only hope she had taken Krushita away from his presence in time, before her daughter could be corroded with the same anticipatory fear.

Something in her face made Bulan pause. Their faces softened as they looked down at her. "Easy," said one head, the nicer-looking one. "No get panic. You want passage on train? I give you passage. Ten thousand wagons — one more not make any difference. I only ask because . . ." The face hesitated, glancing at their companion, who nodded subtly. "Because you look like you need friend."

She stared up at them, looking from one to the other. Bulan's four arms were by their sides now, quite still, but their massively muscled shoulders and trunk-like legs left no doubt about their formidable strength and fighting ability. But what use were muscles and bulk when pitted against black sorcery? She had seen Jarsun dispose of entire regiments of armored cavalry without drawing a sword. She had no right to put the Vanjhani's life at risk. Besides, she could not tell anyone, not for any reason. That was the solemn promise she had made herself before leaving in the dead of night.

She decided to settle for the truth within the wrapping of a lie.

"My husband," she said hesitantly, choosing her words carefully, "was . . . not a good man. I was afraid what he might do to me, and to our daughter someday. I left him. I don't intend to go back. Ever."

Even admitting that much put a knife of pain through her heart. Saying it aloud made it real. Yes, she was leaving Aqron, the city of her birth, of her ancestors, the city built by her family, the greatest, proudest, most beautiful city-state in the world. It hurt to admit it, but it was the truth. She could never go back home.

Bulan looked away, all four eyes scanning the evening sky. The sounds and commotion of the train settling down for the night provided a discordant backdrop of normalcy. The train master seemed suddenly embarrassed.

"I thought something like it," they said at last, still not meeting her eyes. "It is sadly common story." All four of their fists clenched, and both jaws hardened. "Such men do not deserve to have families." They sighed and loosened their fists. "Yet that is world. Such men are."

They stood in silence another moment. Then added gruffly, "You did good to leave. You have lovely daughter. You deserve all good. You will be safe here in train. Bulan will see to it no one bothers you. Go with Goddess."

They turned abruptly away, and Aqreen realized with a start that the interview was over. Bulan was already striding toward the campfire that was being stoked by their assistants. She was filled with a sudden burst of elation. She had done it! She had gained passage on the Wagon Train. Now, she and Krushita could travel safely all the way to Reygar.

But by the time she woke the next morning, the elation at being accepted under the Vanjhani's protection had faded. It was replaced by a more familiar sense of dread.

There were other dangers to consider.

It was one thing to be fleeing Jarsun; taking his daughter and heir was not something he would forgive. The die was cast, and she must simply endure what lay ahead. He would come after them sooner or later, she had no doubt of that. All she could hope was that he would not find them, cloaked in the anonymity of a large desert caravan as they were now.

While the White Desert was policed by Aqron desert marshals, once they crossed over into the Red Desert, there was no authority, no cities or towns, nothing to protect one from the elements, the bandit raids, and the fearsome creatures hardy enough to survive in that deadly wasteland. At least with a large caravan, there was safety in numbers.

Aqreen had considered going with one of the small merchant groups. The White Desert was safe, and their destinations were picturesque coastal cities which were safe and prosperous places. But it was only a matter of time before Jarsun's megalomanic obsession consumed them too. They were much too close to Aqron for comfort. In the end, she decided to stay the course, feeling a twinge of doubt as she watched the splinter groups trundle away.

Over ten thousand wagons remained on the Red Trail. Larger caravans would leave at peak trading season, but she could not wait that long. Ten thousand wagons was a small caravan in the vastness of the Red Desert, but not too small to make the crossing. If they were lucky, perhaps seven or eight thousand would actually survive. The odds were better than staying in

Aqron and risking the fate that had befallen her father and uncles. She could no longer bear to watch Jarsun destroy her family's legacy and turn Aqron into a despotic tyranny.

Reygistan was her only hope.

Jarsun's poisonous reach had not yet extended that far, and Queen Drina of Reygar, the capital city of the Queendom, had made it clear that an alliance with him was not worth contemplating. For that matter, Aqreen could choose to take her daughter to any city in Reygistan. Each of the separate nations in the Queendom was fiercely loyal to Drina and capable of withstanding any assault from Aqron, were Jarsun to be so brazen as to try to take it by force.

So Reygistan it was, and she stayed with the main caravan.

She believed — no, she hoped — that she and Krushita would be safe there.

This was when she still dared to hope. Before the terror began.

## 2

At night by the communal campfires, Aqreen listened to the merchants talk freely over their cups. None believed that all-out war was a serious possibility. She knew better. She understood most of what was said, though at times the myriad foreign accents and dialects made it seem like they were speaking in broken syntax. She had been tutored in the old high languages, supped with great kings and ambassadors from around Arthaloka, but had rarely been exposed to the commonspeak of working folk. These were mostly merchants and traders, accustomed to speaking freely among their own, and they took her for a veiled widow fallen on hard times, not quite one of them but close enough to be treated as one.

"Jarsun is not fool! No war for him with Burnt Empire. Nor can he!" A bristle-bearded wine merchant from Aquina finished his roasted meat and stabbed the skewer into the sand. "Insufficient are Aqron's forces. Hastinaga standing army alone outnumbers Aqron's by twenty to one."

"With Reygistan, maybe he has chance." An androgynous silk trader from Asatin sipped their brew. "Queendom fights fierce."

"Ha! Reygistan never! Queen Drina spits to Jarsun." This from an itinerant baccan-chewing sand-builder with a Reygari accent. She put two fingers to her lips and spat a bright purple stream into the fire. The yellow flames turned green and sparkled. "Thus!"

"He could always invade Reygistan and take over by force," said a heavy-set jewelry trader with a mournful jowly face. "He will not simply ignore the insult given him by Hastinaga. What Dowager Empress Jilana and Prince Regent Vrath did was against Krushan law. Pure hypocrisy! Princess Krushita passed the Test of Fire and has seniority over Princes Adri and Shvate. She deserves to sit upon the Burning Throne, with Queen Aqreen governing the Burnt Empire as regent until the girl comes of age."

At the sound of her and her daughter's names, Aqreen shifted uneasily. She had taken care to dress down, alter her speech, veiled herself with a hibij; no one in the caravan knew her true identity, and they were all foreigners unlikely to recognize Queen Aqreen even if they saw her face. But her daughter was small enough to respond to her given name instinctively. Aqreen glanced toward the back of the wagon where Krushita was sleeping.

"He never dare invade Reygistan," said the Reygari sand-builder. "Queen Drina and the Queendom easy defeat him, leave remains to eaten alive in Red Desert!"

"Jarsun not so easy to kill," said the Asatin silk merchant, stroking the velvety head of their shvan. The animal was one of tens of thousands in the caravan. Every wagon had at least one, many had entire packs. Easily domesticated, shvan were loyal watchers, guards, and protectors. When they sensed a threat, their attractive soft fur hardened into a brindled coat of needle-sharp spines.

On her travels with her late father, Aqreen had seen an infinite variety of shvan breeds in different lands, each suited to their local climate and environment. These were desert-bred shvan, capable of surviving on little water and even less food for long periods, capable of resisting the devastating firestorms that swept the Red Desert. At night, they patrolled the boundaries of the wagon train in large packs. Their roars and howls in the night were unnerving and kept Krushita awake at first, but once she got used to them, she found them comforting; so did Aqreen, who had been forced to leave her beloved shvan, Ackee, back in the palace — he was an aging, ailing, coastal shvan, ill-equipped to survive the long desert journey or the Reygistani climate. Now she felt comforted knowing they were out there, watching the caravan's perimeter. If Jarsun did track her down and catch up with the caravan, they would be the first to announce his presence. Even Ackee had never taken to the demonlord's presence; there was something about his aura or odor that infuriated all animals.

Right now, the shvan dozed peacefully by the warmth of the campfire. The White Desert could be freezing cold at night, often receiving a light dusting of snow before the sun rose and burned it away. Desert shvan loved the warmth, and as they grew older, preferred to stay close to the hearth rather than venture out into the cold. The shvan's indulgent owner continued to stroke the animal affectionately as they went on. "We hear stories on our travel. Jarsun immortal, some say. Cannot be killed. Others say he dies and is reborn each night."

"Uks-shit!" The Reygari spat another bright purple jet of baccan juice into the fire.

"No, no, is some true. I heard stories also." The silk trader glanced around nervously, as if worried that Jarsun might appear at any moment. "Strange talk. Say he is born of urrkh father who rape mortal woman."

"Uks-shit!" repeated the Reygari, looking disgusted. "He just man! Cock between legs same like you. How else have child by Queen Aqreen? See to Princess Krushita—she is perfect mortal child. How urrkh can produce such child?"

"They say he chooses to take mortal form for such purpose," the jewelry trader replied. "He only shows his true form when he attacks. He can change back and forth at will."

The small group was silent for a moment, as if contemplating the idea of Jarsun shifting from mortal to another form and what that form might be. From several hundred campfires burning along the length of the caravan, the sounds of laughter, conversation, music, and singing carried on the still desert air. The plaintive seductive notes of a sehni flute trilled, counterpointed by the rousing backbeat of a tabal drum; loud whistles and lusty cheers encouraged the professional skin dancers to strip off the last of their skimpy adornments. It had been a profitable season, and the traders and merchants were in a celebratory mood. These were people unapologetic about physical appetites and indulgences. She did not mind it, though her conservative Aqronian upbringing did cause her to blush at some of the more orgiastic goings-on by the campfires.

Running shadows flickered beyond the wash of the firelight, startling her back to herself; Aqreen knew they were only the caravan's shvan packs, setting out on their nightly circuits, but the scurrying shapes still put her on guard. She was the only one trying desperately not to think of Jarsun, and failing.

*Yes, he has a cock between his legs like any man,* she thought, despite herself. *And yes, it looks like any man's, but there are times when he is in a rage and starts to change involuntarily . . . At such times, that cock, along with the rest of him, splits into —*

"You from Aqron. What you think?" asked the Reygari. "You must hear stories from palace. Maids, wet nurse, guards, cooks, servants, all talk. Every city knows gossip of palace, yes?"

Aqreen realized with a start that the person was addressing her. She put a hand up to her face, relieved at the anonymity of the veil.

"All kinds of rumors," she said, trying to adopt an indifferent tone. "You never know what to believe and not to believe."

The silk trader also addressed her. "But some must be true. How you say in Aqron? 'There never snows without cold skies'? Some truth there has in rumors also."

Aqreen shrugged. "I wouldn't really know. The only thing I do know for sure is that it was Jarsun who killed King Aqron, not the Krushan."

The Reygari made a disparaging sound. "Everyone know that!"

"Not the people of Aqron," said the jewelry trader. "They believe Jarsun's story that Aqron was murdered on orders of Prince Regent Vrath and Dowager Empress Jilana while they were on the road home from Hastinaga to Aqron after attending the Test of Fire. He says the Krushan elders were loath to allow any rival suitor to live who might someday challenge their own chosen heirs, Prince Shvate and Prince Adri. So they sent assassins disguised as bandits to waylay the convoy in the Ravines of Beedakh."

A shvan's long dark snout twitched as the animal picked up an odor. They were known for their sense of smell more than their sight or good sense. Its rheumy eyes flickered, and it sniffed audibly.

The Reygari made scoffing sounds. "Beedakh is not even on Great Trail, it too far off! Beside, if Krushan send assassin to kill, why they only kill King Aqron? Why leave Princess Krushita and Queen Aqreen alive?"

The shvan's nose twitched again, more vigorously this time, and the pale grey eyes stared into the night.

The wine merchant shrugged. He had risen to pull another skewer off the fire. The roasted meat dripped juices into the flames, which crackled and sparked. "Because Jarsun protect them. Aqron killed while helping fight off attackers. Do not challenge me. I only repeat rumor I hear!" He resumed his seat, too absorbed in biting into a lobe of spicy roast to notice that the shvan had disappeared from its place.

An argument broke out about the rumor. Though it had just started here in the camp, it had been raging ever since Jarsun, Aqreen, and Krushita had returned home to Aqron and word of the terrible disappointment at Hastinaga had spread through the kingdom. There were takers for both versions of the story, and each felt strongly about their version. Over time, these had hardened into firm fact according to their believers, though in truth, neither version was wholly accurate.

Aqreen heard none of it.

She was transfixed by something she saw in the desert.

Ignoring the campfire, the conversation, the safety of the caravan, Aqreen rose and began walking unsteadily into the darkness beyond the flickering shadows. It took the others several moments before they noticed. They began calling out to her, using her assumed name, Fauzi'al, but they might as well have been speaking in foreign tongues. She was deaf and blind to everything but what her eyes saw out there — or what she thought they saw.

## 3

"Father?"

The white-robed figure did not respond.

King Aqron continued staring up at the pitch-dark moonless sky. His aquiline profile, the long white beard, the regal brow, the crown poised on his forehead, all evoked a powerful sense of grief in Aqreen's heart. He appeared exactly the way he had looked the day of the Test of Fire.

What a day of hope and expectation that had been! A world of infinite possibility had loomed before her. It had never been her dream to rule the

Burnt Empire, even as a child. After all, Aqron was not a part of the Burnt Empire: the vast hostile geography separating them made it physically impossible. Besides, her father had raised her to regard all people as equals, had taught her that the monarchy served the people, not the other way around; he had never allowed her to take her privilege for granted. But her marriage to Jarsun and the birth of her daughter had seeded the idea. The very thought that her daughter would sit upon the fabled Burning Throne and be empress of the Burnt Empire was a powerful inspiration. Krushita was Krushan after all; Jarsun was the brother of Emperor Sha'ant, the late husband of Dowager Empress Jilana, which made Krushita the eldest direct heir to the Burning Throne.

On the route from Aqron to Hastinaga — the impossible twenty-five-thousand-mile journey reduced to a few thousand miles by Jarsun's magical portals — she had begun to dream of Krushita seated atop that fabled seat of power hewn from the dark, deadly stonefire. Krushita would end the perennial warring and violence that was a product of the Krushan family's iron-handed methods of governance. She would be a kind, generous, well-loved monarch who would unite the warring nations and tribes and bring about an era of lasting peace. It was a beautiful vision that came to her night after night, impossibly real in its details and texture. She had begun to feel that this was no dream; it was a form of prophecy.

Prophecy, dream, or vision, it had been crushed — nay, burnt to ashes — when Jilana had denied Krushita's claim and Vrath had seconded her. Nor had any of the assembled lieges and nobles dared to question their decision. Aqreen and Jarsun had watched her daughter's claim of legacy razed to the ground. Both were devastated by the decision, but Jarsun had embarked on a campaign of war against the Burnt Empire, unleashing hell and fury against his own kith and kin.

His warmongering had begun almost the instant they left Hastinaga; Jarsun wanted to visit the most powerful kingdoms that were reluctant allies of the Krushan and solicit their support at once. His goal, to tear down the throne that had been denied his heir.

Aqron had refused outright. The kingdom, named after its founder — her father's namesake — a thousand generations ago, had been a peaceable land for almost all its history, its geographical isolation and plentiful resources enabling it to thrive and prosper on its arts, crafts, local resources, and a flourishing trade. Her father had no intention of turning the safest, most peaceful kingdom in all Arthaloka into a war machine to serve Jarsun's desire for vengeance.

An argument had ensued which then escalated shockingly into a physical altercation. Aqreen had intervened — her daughter had grown increasingly agitated by the violent voices. Jarsun had backed off with visible difficulty, barely able to contain his rage.

What happened next was still a matter of debate in almost everyone's mind, except for Aqreen's, and the cause of the argument was still being debated — albeit good-naturedly — by the caravan campfire right now.

The Aqron entourage had been attacked by bandits in the Ravines of Beedakh — a detour Jarsun had insisted on taking — and they'd had no choice but to defend themselves. Jarsun had placed Aqreen and Krushita into a protective circle of Aqron's finest, while he and Aqron led the rest of the accompanying marshals against the bandits. That had troubled Aqreen. She knew that Jarsun was more than capable of dealing with a few hundred bandits. But she could hardly ask her father not to do his duty as a parent, grandparent, and commander of the marshals. Alas, Aqron had been killed in the brief but bloody skirmish.

That had shocked Aqreen. The only way Aqron could have possibly come into harm's way was if Jarsun had intended it to happen. Whether it was a crime of negligence or commission, she never learned, but after her father's death, Jarsun had gotten his way: she and Krushita had been sent home through a portal at once, while Jarsun began his war campaign, just as he'd desired.

Until then, Jarsun had never acted violently in front of her. She'd heard rumors but had chosen not to give them credence. The outburst against her father had shocked her and upset little baby Krushita. But Aqron's sudden death in the ravines had stunned Aqreen thoughtless. Later, she would have many questions, but at the time she was too numb to think, let alone speak. And, of course, she had Krushita to care for.

So she had willingly gone through the portal, the palace marshals traveling with her and carrying their late king's corpse back home, and as the dutiful daughter, Aqreen had tended to the funeral arrangements. The nation went into mourning, equally shocked at the violent end of their beloved liege, and it fell to Aqreen to oversee the affairs of the kingdom as well as nurture Krushita through that difficult period. Though just a baby, Krushita had loved her grand-da dearly and asked for him constantly, insisting he was still "there." By the time the dark tide of grief had receded and Aqreen could think clearly again, Jarsun had returned to the palace, crowning himself king of Aqron and declaring war against the Burnt Empire, which he claimed was responsible for their late liege's murder.

From that day to this one had been a straight, inevitable line.

Jarsun's rage at his daughter being denied the Burning Throne had escalated into a fury. He instituted martial law and then drafted every citizen of the kingdom, able or disabled, old or young, into his army. Incredibly, he had succeeded in provoking several powerful allies of Hastinaga to join his cause, and in the months after his return, Aqreen saw firsthand the manipulative, authoritarian way he compelled pacifist Aqron to prepare for the first all-out war in the kingdom's history. Those who dissented or even protested were killed without trial.

Aqron changed almost overnight. The prisons and dungeons were emptied, their occupants either recruited or executed summarily. In a few short months, her beautiful, peaceful homeland, once deemed the "safest space in all Arthaloka," had turned into a despotic tyranny. Jarsun ruled with an iron hand, using his powers as well as playing on the people's own desire for revenge for their king's murder and the denial of their princess's rightful claim. Jarsun vowed that once he'd installed Krushita on the Burning Throne, Aqron would be the new capital of the Burnt Empire, which would encompass all Arthaloka.

Jarsun's treatment of her worsened, his outbursts escalating and bordering on physical violence. Aqreen began to fear for her life and even, Goddess Jeel protect her, her daughter's. Every day in that palace became an insufferable agony. Finally, she was faced with a stark choice: stay and be complicit, or escape and fight.

And now, only a few short weeks westward out of Aqron, she found herself standing in the darkness of the White Desert, looking into the eyes of her dead father, whom she had last seen as he rode away from her and Krushita, promising to return as soon as he dealt with those "miscreant bandits."

He looked exactly the same.

Yet it could not possibly be him. Could it?

King Aqron was dead.

She had spilled hot tears over his bloodied body, seen him given to Jeel, watched his funeral ship floating away on the clear blue ocean marked by the national flag as well as the personal colors of the House of Aqron. Jeel, in her avatar as the Mother of All Waters, would carry him safely to the Unknown Lands, as she had borne a thousand of his ancestors and would one day bear Aqreen herself. Aqron was gone forever, and that was at least partly the reason why Aqreen had had to leave her homeland; without him, Jarsun was unstoppable and ungovernable.

But right now, here was King Aqron, her father, standing right before her in the White Desert gazing up at the star-studded sky, and her heart desperately wanted to believe it was really him.

# 4

"Regulus and Magellus are ascendant," he said in his soft, musical voice. "The seasons are about to change across Arthaloka. Soon it will begin to snow."

"Father?" she repeated in a wavering voice.

He went on without acknowledging her. "Of course, here in this part of the known world, we have only two seasons to speak of: balmy hot summer and icy cold winter! Your mother would complain to me, saying if we were not monarchy, we could spend more time enjoying the different seasons of this great continent. I used to tell her, if we were not monarchy, we would never have had the opportunity to go on those royal tours that allowed us to experience those different seasons. Like all else, they were the privileges of royalty."

Aqreen took another step closer.

"Da, is it truly you?"

She had always called him Da in private, even as a grown woman. That was how it had been between them.

At the use of the endearment, King Aqron turned and looked at Aqreen.

She felt a ripple of emotion pass through her.

"Aqreen," he said with familiar pleasure, the exact same tone he had always used when she came upon him unexpectedly. "What are you doing here?"

"I might ask you the same thing," she said. "Are you . . ." Her thoughts swam. "Are you with the caravan?"

He looked at her with the same remote expression that he had when gazing at the stars. "You know where I am, Aqi."

Her breath caught in her throat. Aqi was his private nickname for her. He hadn't used it in a year or three, perhaps because they'd had few private moments together once Jarsun came into her life and swept her up like a whirlwind.

He glanced toward the lights of the caravan behind her. Even from here, she could feel the cadence of the tabal drums like distant heartbeats pulsing in the background. Somewhere, a shvan bayed and was answered by a thousand more.

"You are doing the right thing, taking Krushita away from that evil man."

She listened without speaking. Just the sound of his voice, the sight of him, the presence . . . she had needed it desperately. This was a precious gift, even if it was only a desert mirage.

"Your instinct was true. The bandits outnumbered us, but Jarsun could easily have destroyed them all unassisted. Before it happened, I saw him glance at me, venom in his eyes. He moved aside to allow them to attack me, while he pretended to help the marshals. Two of them witnessed this, so he killed them. I tried to fight back, but he had done something to me when I wasn't looking — my arms and feet had turned numb and cold. It was like being snakebit. The bandits struck the killing blow, but Jarsun watched as they did so, not moving a finger to help."

Aqreen felt a tear spill down her cheek.

King Aqron saw the tear and shook his head.

"Enough of that," he said. "It was important that you be sure of it, but that is not the reason I left Mother Jeel to come speak with you."

"I am glad you came, Da," she said, almost choking on the words. "I need you so much."

His eyes crinkled sadly. "Aqi, you must be strong now. You have taken a great step, but even now you are not safe. That is why I came to warn you. He is coming after you and Krushita."

Her palm came away damp when she wiped her cheek. "I know. He will send marshals after us. That is why I joined the caravan. They will never find us here. We are two among tens of thousands. Once we reach Reygar, we will begin a new life. We will be free of him forever. Krushita will be free to live happily, far from his poison."

His gaze hardened. He took a step forward. "You do not understand. He comes tonight! Not his marshals. Jarsun himself!"

# 5

Her heart froze. "But . . ."

"Yes, yes, I know. You waited till he was away before you left. But you remember his powers. He knew of your escape almost at once. He had other business to tend to — the business of war — which delayed him a few days. Tonight he returned to Aqron through one of his infernal portals. As we speak, he is killing the last of the palace marshals for letting you escape. When he is done, he means to come after you."

Her hand rose to her mouth. "By Jeel."

She spun around, her heart going to the wagon where her daughter slept. From here it was faintly visible as a faint dark silhouette against the glow of the campfires. "Krushita!"

"She is safe for now. He will not harm her. She is his blood, an heir to the Burning Throne, his only chance of regaining control of the Burnt Empire and claiming his legacy as a Krushan. He is right about that much; she is the rightful ruler of Hastinaga, and Vrath and Jilana must pay for denying her the throne. But even had she been accepted, he meant to use her as an excuse to control the empire himself. He has terrible, unspeakable plans, Aqi. He means to commit genocide on entire nations. To take over the entire world, known and unknown. That is the very reason he was banished by his own brother. Sha'ant was true to the Ashcrit meaning of his given name: Peace. Although he had inherited a legacy built on war and violence, he had no intention of continuing that legacy. He was content to rule the empire as it was, resorting to battle only as a last resort. Jarsun wanted to use war as a stick to beat the world to its knees and lord over it. He believes in the ways of the first Krushan, Kr'ush himself, who was more stone than mortal. It was the cause of their falling-out and the reason Sha'ant eventually banished him. Jarsun will not rest until he regains the Burning Throne. He needs its power to enable his campaign of conquest. That is the way of the Krushan. Only when empowered by the throne can they ascend to true godhead. Sha'ant was careful not to seat himself upon it too long and was redeemed by his mortal love for his wives, Jeel and then Jilana. If Jarsun sits upon it, he and the throne together will unleash a reign of rage and fury such as Arthaloka has never before known. And to achieve the throne, he needs the legitimacy of Krushita's claim."

Aqreen felt her face harden. Her tears dried, her hands clenched into fists. "I will die fighting before I let him take her from me."

Aqron shook his head. "That is exactly what he wants. Except it will not be a fight. Though a brave, strong woman, you are mortal, as was I. Jarsun is a demigod, a direct descendant of one of the original stone gods. When cojoined with stonefire, his powers are unstoppable. Even Mother Jeel fears the terror that he will unleash. She loves all things that live and breathe upon Arthaloka, just as she loves the dwellers of her oceans and rivers. She it was who woke me from my endless sleep, that I might come here and warn you in time."

Aqreen felt her head swim again. "What should I do, Da? Tell me!"

"You—"

Aqron broke off abruptly. He looked away, into the darkness.

A pack of shvan—a very large pack—began shrieking suddenly. That brain-penetrating sound was their way of issuing a warning that something dangerous was approaching. Not merely a stranger or a threat, but a predator. Suddenly, tens of thousands of the watchbeasts were shrieking shrilly at once, filling the desert night with the piercing siren alert. From the caravan behind her, Aqreen heard the music and laughter cut off as people began shouting and yelling to one another, and she knew even the most sodden drunks would be reaching for their weapons. In the desert, all fellow travelers were family; the group she was with would defend Krushita's life with their own if anything dared threaten her. It was the only thought that kept her from racing back to the wagon.

"He—" her father began as he looked up.

A portal burst open.

A whirling maelstrom of blinding white light exploded into existence in the air yards over Aqron's head. A blast of icy glacial wind raised a cloud of sand mingled with flurries of snow, forcing Aqreen to take several steps back and shield her face. The veil guarded her eyes and enabled her to breathe, but the fury of the gust drove sand and snow at her like a thousand pinpricks. A furious howling filled her senses, drowning out the shrieking of the shvan packs.

She struggled to see through the dust and snow.

Aqron stared up as twin dark shapes fell upon him. They thrashed, entwining him like a pair of scourges whipping in concert, as if seeking to cut him to shreds. But his seemingly mortal form, so solid and real until a moment earlier, dissipated into a cloud of hissing steam, like water evaporated by a sudden blast of heat.

Even through the blinding, deafening maelstrom, Aqreen could not mistake the tall, stick-thin form of the father of her child, the husband of her body, the assassin of her father.

Jarsun Krushan.

# 6

His face was clotted with rage as he scanned for his intended prey. Two snaking tongue tips flickered out of the corners of his mouth. He hissed his frustration.

"Send back your mortal devotee to face me, Water Goddess!" he shouted. "I will kill him a thousand times over."

As abruptly as it had appeared, the portal winked out of existence. The steam evaporated, the sand settled. Only a faint smattering of snow underfoot, indistinguishable from the white of the desert, and a brisk chill in the air lingered.

So too did the shrieking of the shvan cease.

Jarsun turned his gaze upon his wife.

"Aqreen," he said.

"You will never have her," she said, standing her ground. "I will not let you make her the instrument of your evil."

His slitted eyes squinted to thin lines. His pursed lips were a curving slash across his face. His bunched fists rose, baring the folds of the flowing red-ochre robe. He wore no jewelry or adornments. When they met, during those first breathless nights of passion, Aqreen had marveled at how smooth, unbroken, unblemished, he wore his skin.

*I have never known a prince to be without tattoos or jewels,* she had murmured.

*You have never known the likes of me,* he had replied.

Now she shuddered with revulsion at the very sight of him.

How had she ever found this man attractive? Not even a man . . . a *thing.* What must her poor father have thought? It was a great credit to Aqron's tolerant nature that he had never questioned her choice of mate, merely listened quietly as she had expressed her determination to wed him. Aqron was a matriarchal society where males could rule only with the permission of women. Not quite a strict queendom like Reygistan, where men were considered fit only for reproduction and laborious tasks, but different only in custom and grace. She could not comprehend what madness had caused her to give her heart and body to this animal. Was it only three years ago? It seemed a lifetime.

Jarsun hissed plaintively, but there was amusement in the sound now.

"I should have put you down the instant you birthed me an heir." The sibilant syllables carried on the still air. "As my mother did my father after he seeded her. All she'd needed from him was his Krushan blood. His link to stonefire and her Serapi power combined to make the most powerful being that has ever existed. It was his awareness of this fact and jealousy that made my brother Sha'ant resent me. He deprived me of my birthright when I was still unformed and lacking my full strength. Now Sha'ant's remains have been absorbed back into the throne, and none who remain possess the power to challenge me."

"You are not the only demigod that walks the world," she said scornfully. "Vrath is the son of Jeel herself, birthed by her mortal avatar and fathered by Sha'ant. Your nephew alone is sufficient to put you down, monster!"

A snapping of the air, a rush of wind, and he was in contact with her, his hands clasped tightly around her throat. She choked, gasping, and flailed as her feet left the ground. His fingers slid around her windpipe, squeezing the life out of her. She struggled, but it was futile. He could have snapped her neck instantly but was instead choosing to make her suffer.

"Your foolish escapade has cost these travelers their lives," he hissed in her ear, his breath cold and musky. "I will slaughter every last one, mortal and beast. Just as I slaughtered the last of your pitifully loyal palace marshals. All you did was delay the inevitable and hasten your own end. I was willing to let you live to tend to the child's needs until she was grown. It would have saved me the use of slave nurses. I shall not even show you the mercy I showed Aqron as I put him down in the grey dust of Beedakh. Him, I numbed with my venom so he would not feel the cuts and hacks of the bandits as they chopped him to death. You will feel every last instant of pain and terror before the life leaves your pathetic mortal form."

Aqreen felt the darkness rush into her and knew she was dying. Struggle was impossible.

Her last thoughts were of Krushita, of all that could have been and, horrifically, all that now would be.

# 7

Jarsun howled with pain.

A hurtling shape collided with his rakelike form, clenching razor teeth onto his deceptively skinny arm. Other shvan flew at him from all directions, gripping different parts of his body. Instead of finding their teeth gnashing on bone, as would have been the case for a mere mortal, they sank their sharp fangs and talons into thick, juicy meat. Utterly boneless meat.

At the moment of contact, their bodies stiffened, and they dropped dead, the potent venom in Jarsun's body stopping their hearts instantly. Their bodies thudded to the white sand. But more replaced them, giving up their lives to assault the Krushan. More and then still more, endless hordes of them leaping at him from every side. Although Shvan bayed to call out to one another, chuckled at their human companions, and shrieked at predators, when attacking, they were silent as snakes.

Barely alive, Aqreen staggered back, breath trickling into her abused windpipe. Regaining consciousness with slow, ragged breaths, she dimly glimpsed the writhing sea of dark four-legged furry shapes surging around her would-be assassin and erstwhile mate. Unable to speak, she thanked Jeel for their presence.

But even as she struggled to recover, Jarsun bellowed with a sound that was more thunder than animal cry. His tall form burst alight with the bright viscous blaze of his stonefire. In most Krushan, stonefire burned blue at birth, but each individual developed their own unique shade as they grew.

Jarsun's had a greenish-reddish hue with swirls of yellow, a mottled diamantine pattern that glistened like the skin of a deadly serpent. It made him appear as if he were surrounded by a shimmering shield of power, which wasn't far from the truth.

The shvan began shrieking again. Their kind had never encountered stonefire in several thousand generations, thus they did not know what to make of this alien threat. All creatures feared fire, but stonefire was more terrible than ordinary flame. The wave of fur receded, eyes glittering like a scattering of rubies in the desert as they held their distance. Aqreen's heart fell in dismay. She should have known better than to count her stars too soon.

Jarsun's stonefire reduced in intensity until Aqreen could once again make out the man shape within the unearthly blaze.

He strode toward her, his features a mask of rage and murder as he raised his hand to unleash a blast of stonefire that she knew would destroy her. Already her hair and brows were being singed by the unbearable heat, her veil starting to smoke as the fabric caught fire.

"You will—" he began.

But he never got to finish his threat.

An invisible force struck him in the face, knocking him sideways like a rag doll. He flew several yards to one side and landed in loose sand, skidding and tumbling, his stonefire suddenly extinguished.

The shvan were still keeping their distance in a large circle, safe from the searing stonefire. They were baying now, passing on the word of the attack to their fellows.

"Ma."

Aqreen turned her head to see, several yards behind her, a small shape on two legs. "Krushita!" she cried, and stumbled toward her daughter, who ran to meet her, barreling into her with the fierce possessiveness of a loving child.

"Da hurt Ma!" she cried indignantly as Aqreen wrapped her arms around her. "Da hurt Ma!"

"Oh, my child," Aqreen said, tears spilling freely from her sore eyes. "You should not have come after me. It is not safe."

Krushita hitched in a tearful breath. "Krushni know. Ma in trouble.

Krushni come." Unable to pronounce her own name fully, she had settled on Krushni. For once, Aqreen went along with her self-given nickname.

"Oh, my baby." Then it occurred to her. "What did you do to Da? How did you —"

Krushita's head snapped around. She made a sound Aqreen had never heard from her before: a kind of growl that was less animal than flame. Like a forest fire feeding on a thousand trees at once.

Aqreen turned to see Jarsun striding toward them.

His eyes glowed in the darkness.

"So my daughter has begun to demonstrate her power. Early even for a Krushan. She is strong, stronger than I was at her age. But still a child."

The crackling growl built in Krushita's belly.

Aqreen could see the glow faintly visible through the slim gap between her daughter's teeth; she could feel the rising heat; the banked power of stonefire in the little girl's core. *But she's only a baby,* she thought. *It was only a few weeks ago that she began to form words!*

"Come to me, girl," Jarsun said with the smooth oily tone that passed for affection in his lexicon. "Come away from that woman. You will be raised by your father now. We have no need of mere mortals, you and I. Together we will be unstoppable. I will train you to use your powers to —"

Again, he never got to finish.

A tongue of fire flashed out from Krushita's mouth, disappearing almost instantly as it flew toward her father. No, not disappearing, transforming.

Jarsun staggered back as an invisible fist struck him in the torso. He hissed with outrage. "Ungrateful wretch!" he cried as he clutched a palm to the struck region. "You dare attack your own forebear!"

"Da hurt Ma," Krushita said from beside Aqreen.

Aqreen stole a glance at her daughter. Krushita's eyes swirled with curlicues of power. Within them, she could see distant stars and entire worlds. It was not a reflection. It was within Krushita. She stared. She had never seen this side of her daughter before. It was awe-inspiring, but not in the repulsive way that Jarsun's power could be; it was like looking up at the night sky and realizing how minuscule mortals were and how even the entire world of Ur and the great supercontinent of Arthaloka were insignificant in the vastness of the cosmos.

In the desert around them, the shvan bayed happily, converging again on Jarsun, who was staring at Krushita. Abruptly, he turned his gaze aside to Aqreen.

"This is not over," he said. "I will find you again, and I will destroy everyone you touch. She is mine! Mine!"

An explosion of light and wind, and a dark empty space opened behind him. This time, Aqreen felt the musky wooded scent of an ancient forest. She caught a brief glimpse of a dense wood at night, smelled exotic flowers and herbs, then Jarsun stepped through and the portal snapped shut behind him.

The shvan bayed in exultation, celebrating the retreat of their enemy.

They crowded around Aqreen and Krushita, licking the little girl's hands and softening their fur so she could stroke their heads. They stared at her adoringly.

Aqreen watched her baby daughter with the animals and felt a powerful mixture of motherly pride and renewed hope.

*Now,* she thought, *we have a chance. We can do this. We can survive. Perhaps even more than that.*

She rose to her feet, taking her daughter's tiny hand, and together they walked back toward the caravan, followed by a river of tail-wagging shvan.

# *Tyrak*

TYRAK RODE GRINNING THROUGH the smoke and chaos of a burning village.

His Marauders were busy ransacking the remaining houses for anything of value before setting them ablaze. He would give them time to enjoy themselves and relish the spoils of war. Stopping on a high verge, he watched with amusement as the settlement was razed to the ground. It amused him that these govala could be so easy to kill, their villages so defenseless, their women and children so unprotected—

A high-pitched scream exploded from behind. He turned to see a young Mraashk boy charging at him with a shepherd's crook, of all things.

Tyrak laughed and deflected the point of the crook easily with his sword. A twist of the reins drew the bit tightly enough into his horse's mouth to make the beast sidestep. The boy lunged past and sprawled on the ground. His turban, the same bright saffron color as his dhoti, fell into a muddy puddle and was sullied.

Tyrak sheathed his sword and pulled the reins up short, making the horse rear. There might have been blood on its mouth, as he had a habit of whipping his mounts on their mouths if they failed to respond quickly, but he hardly noticed it. He was the crown prince of Mraashk. He could have any number of mounts he desired.

The boy moaned and struggled to his elbows. As he turned and looked up, he froze at the sight of the massive Morgol stallion rearing up before him. Tyrak brought the horse's forehooves down with a loud thud. The boy cried out and moved his legs out of the way just in time to avoid them being smashed.

A gust of breeze from the village carried the voice of a woman screaming pitifully for her children to be spared, followed by three short, sharp cries that cut off abruptly as each of her wretched offspring were dispatched by Tyrak's efficient soldiers. The boy turned his head to listen, his pain and empathy marking him out as either the woman's son or a close relative. In a moment, the desperate woman's voice rose again, now launching into wailing cries of grief and self-pity as the soldiers turned their attention to her.

The boy glared up at Tyrak with hot brown eyes filled with hatred. "Urrkh!" he cried. "Only urrkh would attack unarmed shepherds protected under a peace treaty!"

Tyrak grinned. "Then why don't you call upon your stone gods to protect you? What good are they if they can't defend their own devotees?"

The boy shook a fist. "They will come. Our stone gods always hear the prayers of the righteous. Lord Vish himself will come down and make you pay for your crimes!"

Tyrak roared with laughter. "Lord Vish himself! I must be very important, to attract his attention!"

While talking, the boy had managed to get hold of a fist-sized rock. Now he flung it hard at his aggressor, his aim good enough to hit Tyrak a glancing blow on the temple. Tyrak's right ear rang, and warm wetness instantly poured down the side of his head. He stopped laughing and grinned down at the boy, who was scrabbling around in search of more missiles.

"It's a sad stone god who arms his devotees with only stones to defend themselves," he said as blood trickled down his neck.

The grin stayed on his face as he yanked back on the reins and forced the horse to rear, bringing down both forehooves on his intended target with a bone-crunching impact — again, and again, and yet again, until what remained on the ground was no more than a crumpled bundle of shattered bones and leaking flesh.

"Lord Vish can't be here today to help you," he said to the corpse. "He has more important things to attend to."

A contingent of riders approached at a brisk canter, slowing as they arrived.

Bane was in the lead, Uaraj beside him. Both exclaimed as they saw Tyrak's head streaming with blood.

"Lord Tyrak, you are injured," said Bane. "Uaraj, call for our Lord's vaids at once."

Uaraj barked an order, sending two riders back to the Arrgodi camp a mile or two upstream. Tyrak and his Marauders tended to ride ahead of the main force, leaving the sluggish supply caravans trailing in their wake.

"It's just a scratch," Tyrak said absently, gazing out across the village. The woman's screams had just stopped, although other equally terrible cries could be heard across the ruined settlement as other women and victims suffered at the hands of the Mraashk. To Tyrak, the screams were sweet music acknowledging his superiority as a military commander and soldier.

"Tell me," he said to Bane, who knew at once what he wished to know.

Bane began recounting the tally of the dead. The ratio of enemy dead to their own was ludicrous. They had killed or left for dead some two hundred enemy and lost only three men. "Because we take them by surprise and after the treaty, many have returned to herding and farming, so they rarely have weapons close at hand." He smirked, licking his lips. "And the women and children are almost always alone and defenseless in their homes."

He recounted the spoils of private treasures they had appropriated as tax — Tyrak had forbidden the use of the term "looted" on pain of death — measuring up to a substantial amount.

Bane chuckled as he finished the tally. "A good day's work, my lord. These herders and farmers make for easy prey. Almost too easy. We roll across the landscape like chariots across millet, crushing them underfoot."

"Yes, well, that won't continue much longer," Tyrak said. "Word must be spreading already about our campaign of liberation. We should expect to meet some resistance soon."

He raised a clenched fist, adding, "I pray we do. I am tired of hacking down feeble herders caught unawares and boys with sheep crooks!"

Uaraj grinned slyly. "It has its advantages." He jerked his head in the direction of the village, where the screams of dying women and the crackling of briskly burning straw-and-mud huts filled the smoky air. "The men enjoy it too."

Tyrak didn't respond. He stared into the distance. Bane and Uaraj exchanged a glance. Tyrak fell into these moments when he would just stare at the horizon, brooding. They almost always preceded some new plan or strategy.

Finally, he said, "We shall swing north and east," he said. "Toward Harvanya."

"Harvanya?" Bane repeated. Even Uaraj gaped. "But, my lord, that is the heart of Mraashk territory. King Vasurava will not brook an assault on his heartland silently."

"Brother Bane speaks the truth," Uaraj added cautiously. Tyrak did not always appreciate being corrected or having his plans critiqued. A scar on Uaraj's own cheek testified to that fact, as did the rotting corpses of Tyrak's two previous advisors. "Until now, we have only, uh, taxed outlying villages and border territories of the three nations. Our actions could be defended as legitimate actions against border crossings and water or cattle thefts. But if we ride that far into Mraashk, it would be a clear violation of the peace treaty and a declaration of open war against Vasurava himself. The Mraashk nation might respond with an all-out war. And the Arrgodi also might feel outraged enough to get involved as well."

Bane cleared his throat, also careful to couch his suggestions in cautious terms. "Besides which, Vasurava does happen to be the betrothed of your sister Lady Kewri, my lord."

Tyrak gestured them both to silence. They subsided at once. The wind changed, bringing a heavy odor of smoke and the stench of burning corpses along with the fading screams of the last suffering victims.

"I am sick of this peace treaty," Tyrak said. "My father did not consult me before signing it. Why should I be compelled to uphold it?" At the mention of his father, his eyes glinted — both Bane and Uaraj noted this with growing nervousness — and a gleam of naked rebellion shone there. "It is time to put it to the test. Let us see how long Vasurava upholds his end of the treaty when I come galloping into his lands and lay waste to his townships."

Both his advisors glanced at each other uneasily. Yet neither dared speak a word. It was one thing to offer a suggestion or two, but quite another to defy his gesture ordering them to be silent; anyone who spoke now would find his own corpse piled upon one of the several dozen burning heaps that were all that remained of the village.

"They call me urrkh," Tyrak said, unmindful of the blood still streaming down the side of his head. "They call upon Lord Vish to protect them from me. Let us see if Vish has the courage to descend to Arthaloka again in yet another avatar, this time to confront Tyrak. It will be good to have a worthy opponent to sink my sword into for a change! I am tired of stabbing cowherd flesh and slaughtering hairless boys."

He raised his head to the smoke-filled sky and bellowed, "You took an avatar on earth to battle the urrkh demonlord Ravenous. They say whenever your people are unable to defend themselves, you descend to protect them. Now descend to face me, Tyrak of Arrgodi! I challenge you!"

Bane and Uaraj exchanged startled glances. Even the soldiers looked shocked at Tyrak's bold blasphemous pronouncement.

As if in response, a deep rumbling sound came from the smoke-stained sky, followed by an angry crash of thunder. Uaraj winced, and his horse neighed. The smell of imminent rain filled the air, along with a damp coldness. Thunder crashed again far away to the distant horizon.

Tyrak listened, head cocked to one side like a curious hound. Then he threw his head back and laughed long and hard. The sound echoed across the razed settlement, silencing the last desperate cries of the hopeless and the dying.

# *Kensura*

## 1

QUEEN KENSURA LISTENED WITH mounting horror as her spy recounted the many atrocities and war crimes perpetrated by her son. At last, she shuddered and interrupted him midsentence.

"Enough! Enough! I can hear no more."

She rose from her lavender seat and went to the casement, fanning herself. Summer had come down upon Arrgodi like a hot brand, and even the coolest chambers in the palace were barely tenable. The whiff of wind from the window was like steam off a boiling kettle.

She turned away to see maids watering down the flagstone floors to cool them. Her spy waited, head bowed. The sight of him made her stomach churn. If she had not already heard rumors and other snatches of news corroborating parts of his report, she might have ordered her guard to drag him away to be executed instantly. As it was, she was tempted to give the command, if only to prevent him from recounting the same horrific things to others in the palace. But, she reasoned with herself, what good would that do if these things were already known? In fact, it appeared that she was the last to learn of her own son's misdeeds — or the extent and severity and sheer volume of those misdeeds. No, it was no fault of the spy; the poor man had only done his job as she had commanded.

Even the scent of the fragrant water being sprinkled on the floors, drawn from the deepest well and infused with roses from the royal gardens, could not calm her nerves. Her son, doing such terrible things? How had it come to this? Oh, that she should have lived to see such a day.

Suddenly, she lost her patience. Trembling, she shouted at the maids, the spy, even her personal guards standing at the doorway.

"Out! Everyone out! I wish to be alone."

A moment later, she sat in the privacy of her chamber and broke down, sobbing. She thought of little Tyrak, a pudgy fair boy with curling hair and a fondness for young animals of any breed. He had always had a kitten, a pup, a fawn, a cub, or some other youngling in his chubby arms, cradled close to his chest.

She remembered calling out to him on numerous occasions, "Tyroo, my son, give the poor thing room to breathe. You'll smother it with love!" And both Ugraksh and she laughing as Tyrak had blushed, his milky fair face turning red in the same splotched pattern every time as he ran away in that shambling hip-swinging toddler's gait, his latest acquisition clutched close to his little chest.

She smiled, wet-eyed, remembering how adorable he had been, how proud Ugraksh and she had been of their son, their heir. What dreams they had spun, what plans, what ambitions . . .

But then she recalled something she had almost forgotten, a seemingly insignificant fact suddenly made significant by the spy's report.

All those tiny kittens, puppies, fawns, squirrels, calves, and other younglings . . . where had they gone?

Tyrak had always had a different pet every few days or weeks. At first, they had stayed for longer periods, she thought, with one or two even growing noticeably larger and older. But over time, they seemed to change with increasing rapidity. Until finally, by the time he was old enough to play boys' games, he seemed to have a different pet every time she turned around, at least one every day, until it had become a matter of great amusement to his parents. She even recalled Ugraksh's joke about Tyrak being an avatar of the Asva twins, the gods who ruled over the animal kingdom.

What had happened to the earlier pets?

A cold sword probed her heart, piercing painfully deep, her feverish blood steaming as it washed upon the icy tip.

Where indeed?

And there, with a lurch and a start, her memory gave up the recollection of a day when she had found Tyrak crouching in that peculiar toddler way over something in the recesses of a corner, something wet and furry and broken that had once been a kitten, or perhaps a whelp. Tyrak standing over a pile of burning rags and a tiny charred corpse in the back corridor, eyes shining in the reflected light of the flames. Tyrak carrying a stick with a sharpened tip sticky with fresh blood.

There were more memories. Many, many more.

At the time, she had dismissed all those incidents as accidents or the passing phase of a young boy's normal growth pangs.

But now they sent the point of that icy sword deep into her bowels, raking up a terrible guilt and regret.

There had been signs. Tyrak had never been quite like other boys, other princes. Even when older, he had not made friends easily, had gotten into fights that ended with terrible consequences for at least some of the participants — almost always those who defied or failed to side with him — and there had been incidents with servants, serving girls, maids, a cook's daughter . . . A minor scandal over a young girl found dead and horribly mutilated in the royal gardens, last seen walking hand in hand with Tyrak the night before his twelfth naming day.

Yes, signs.

Many signs.

But nothing that had prepared her for this.

A mass murderer? A leader of marauders, ravagers, rapists, slaughterers of innocent women and children?

Her Tyrak?

Her little boy with the fair pudgy face and curls grown up to be the Urrkh of Arrgodi, as they were calling him now?

It wasn't possible! There had to be some mistake.

She stormed out of the chamber and went striding through the palace, her guards and serving ladies in tow. Curious courtiers and minister's aides watched her sweep imperiously through the wide corridors with the marbled statuary, brocaded walls, and exquisite paintings.

She stopped outside the sabha hall only long enough to ask the startled guards if the king was inside.

He was, they replied with bowed heads, not daring to meet her agitated eyes. A dhoot had just arrived bearing news, and the king was in private session.

She cut them off abruptly, ordering the sabha hall doors to be opened.

They obeyed at once without protest. Like most traditional societies, the Arrgodi nations had long been a matriarchal culture. Women owned all property, from land to livestock, right down to even the garments on everyone's back. Inheritance was by the matriarchal line, as was lineage. Every stone, brick, and beam in Arrgodi was quite literally the property of Queen Kensura.

She strode into the sabha hall, past the startled guards and surprised courtiers. There were not very many. Only Ugraksh himself and a few of his closest advisors and ministers sat listening keenly to a road-dusty courier — a dhoot — who broke off and peered fearfully over his shoulder at her unexpected entrance as if afraid it might be someone else.

Kensura strode up to the royal dais. Ugraksh frowned down at her, openly surprised.

"Kensura?" he said, lapsing into informality.

"My lord," she said, "I have urgent private business to discuss. Kindly send away these honorable gentlepersons of the court."

Ugraksh looked at her for a long moment. In the guttering light of the torch, she saw how he had appeared to age in the past weeks. The wags around court were saying that the peace treaty had taken a greater toll on him than the troubles of the preceding years.

*No, not the peace treaty, our son's devilry.*

"It is about Tyrak, then," he said, with no tone of inquiry in his words.

She did not answer, not wishing to say anything impolitic before the others.

He nodded as if he understood.

"Come, my queen," he said kindly in a weary voice. "Be seated and let us discuss the latest tales of derring-do of our beloved son."

## 2

Ugraksh and Kensura sat on the royal dais. Except for the mandatory royal guards by the doors at the far end of the hall, they were alone. The dhoot had finished his report in Kensura's presence, recounting further episodes of Tyrak's vileness. From the sighs, head shakes, shrugs, and other gestures and reactions of the others, she had understood that these reports were commonplace. She had shuddered at that realization: innocent lives destroyed by her own son, and even Arrgodi's wisest heads accepted it as commonplace. She did not know which was worse, the fact that he had committed and was still committing such terrible acts, or the fact that they were tacitly accepted and tolerated by those governing the kingdom.

She turned to Ugraksh now, her mind raging.

"We must curb him," she said. "This cannot be allowed to go on."

He sighed, rubbing a hand across his face, looking terribly weary and old, a pale shadow of the man she had wedded, loved, and shared her life with for over two decades.

She now understood why he had taken ill these past several weeks, why he had not come to her bed at nights, why an endless procession of royal vaids seemed to always be coming from or going into his chambers, why the annual festival had been canceled, why no entertainers or artists were invited to the palace of late . . .

Her father had once told her that no matter how comfortable and luxurious it may appear, a royal throne was the hardest seat to sit on. And to remain seated on it meant forgoing all comfort forever. *All these things,* he had said, gesturing expansively at the rich brocades, luxurious adornments, gem-studded furniture, statuary, art, *all these exist to pay homage to the seat itself, to the role of king or queen. For the man or woman who occupies that hard spot, there is no luxury, no comfort, no rest.*

She saw now the truth of those words. Truly, Ugraksh, at the peak of his reign, at the helm of the greatest Arrgodi nation that had ever existed, had no comfort.

"Yes," he agreed at last. "This ought not to be permitted to continue."

She waited, knowing that he was not merely echoing her words but qualifying them.

"Ought not," he repeated, still rubbing his forehead, "yet what can we do to stop him?"

She felt her throat catch as if she had swallowed a dry prickly thing and it had stuck in her gullet. "We can speak to him."

He laughed softly. There was no humor in the sound, it was merely an acknowledgment of the inefficacy of her suggestion. "Yes, of course we can. And he will talk back. And then go out and continue doing what he is doing now. And then what shall we do?"

She licked her lips. "We will have him confined to the palace. To his chambers. Prohibit him from leaving Arrgodi. Take away his privileges."

He removed the hand and looked at her. There was no anger or irritation in his face, merely sadness, perhaps even sympathy. "How shall we do that? Tyrak is commander of all our armed forces. It is he who is in charge of even the city's security, the royal guard. You recall I vested him with those powers when I crowned him heir and king in waiting."

Yes, of course he had. And he had done so precisely because they had felt at the time that once he was given power and responsibility, and all the administrative and other burdens of state that entailed, he would be compelled to cease his adolescent antics and settle into a more serious state of mind. Instead, he had simply progressed to a whole new level of adolescent rebellion.

"There must be somebody you can depute with the task." She glanced around, looking at the empty seats, trying to remember the faces and names of various courtiers. "What about —" She named a senior minister, formerly a general in the King's Guard, the most prestigious regiment of all. "Or . . ." She named several others.

Ugraksh shook his head. "He has grown too strong. He commands the loyalty of the troops now. They would mutiny to support him if we act overtly."

She was shocked. "But surely they know of his brutalities?"

Ugraksh looked away. "He gives them freedom to enjoy the spoils of war as they please. He plays cleverly upon the natural rivalries between our Arrgodi clans and the Mraashk clans. He uses past enmities, petty feuds, tribe conflicts, anything that serves his purpose . . . Recruitment is at its highest mark ever. Every eligible boy old enough to hold a weapon is lining up to join Tyrak's army. That is what they call it now, by the way, Tyrak's army. Not Arrgodi's. Or Ugraksh's. Or even just the army. Tyrak's army."

She looked around for water, wishing they had not sent away the serving staff. There was wine everywhere, as always, but no water to be seen. Water was too precious to be kept lying around; it was always brought fresh, untainted, and closely checked on command. And only royals and the wealthiest courtiers could afford to have clean potable water served at will. The vast majority of their people still had to draw it from wells or drink it from rivers or pools when they desired to slake their thirst. Water, after all, was the main bone of contention of the troubles of the past decades. Although, like all causes of war and violence, it was merely the most visible evidence of the deeper social dissatisfaction. If she understood Ugraksh right, it appeared that Tyrak had cleverly tapped into that deep groundwater source of discontent, using it for his own devious purposes.

"When did he become so savvy?" she wondered aloud. "Where did he learn statecraft?"

Despite her horror and disgust at his misdeeds, she was impressed at his ability to command such loyalty and adulation. Tyrak's army? And for years, Ugraksh had always grumbled to her that Arrgodi were good for fighting in brawls over stolen cows, but utterly useless when it came to disciplined armed combat. Apparently, all it had required was someone like Tyrak to come along and promise them the pleasures of unlawful spoils and the setting aside of the laws of warrior *Auma* that forbade a soldier from doing anything other than defending his nation under duress.

"That is what troubles me the most, my queen," Ugraksh said, leaning on the armrest of his throne. "He must have advisors, and they must be wily ones to enable him to gain so much power and loyalty so swiftly."

She frowned. A part of her was loath to accept this view, for it undercut the last vestige of motherly pride she could hope to take in her son's dubious achievement. But she knew at once that Ugraksh was right in his assessment. However brilliant Tyrak's political skills might be — and she had seen no great evidence of any such skills in his growing years — this achievement was too great for him to have accomplished it entirely on his own. There was another hand at work.

"Whom do you suspect?" she asked with growing dismay, now trying to remember the faces and names of all those who might qualify as opponents of Ugraksh's rule and harbor sufficient ill will to plot outright treason against them. Her throat felt parched, as if she were in the deserts of Reygistan. She could almost taste sand.

"Jarsun, Bhauma, Trnavarta, Baka, Arista, Prambala, Putan, Agha, Musthika, Dhenuka, Bane, Uaraj, Dvivida, Kesi," he said, reeling off the names as if by rote. "But most of all, Jarsun. He is clearly the lynchpin. There have been reports from all these places of curiously similar developments to those in Arrgodi."

He paused thoughtfully. "Almost as if some great plan was being executed and Tyrak is only playing out his part in the scheme."

Kensura's mind had frozen cold at the sound of the first name itself. "Jarsun," she repeated fearfully. "The king of Aqron."

"Yes, and a demon in mortal form if the tales of his misdeeds are to be believed. Some even say . . ." Again, he hesitated.

"Tell me."

He looked at her, eyes clouded with a trace of fear. "There has been talk that he massacred his own family."

She shivered. "Rumors. Vile gossip."

He shook his head sadly. "Perhaps more than that. They say he had his own father-in-law assassinated. That was why his wife took his daughter and fled Aqron, across the Red Desert. But they say he caught up with them and killed them too. Massacred an entire wagon train in the process."

She stared at him. An entire wagon train? That would mean tens of thousands of lives. "Why?"

He sighed, looking very old. "To punish them for harboring the fugitives and to send a message to anyone else who seeks to oppose him or align with his enemies."

She tried to make sense of this news. "Why?"

"It is his way. They say Jarsun has been encouraging all exiles, outcasts, criminals, deserters, anyone who resents or rebels against their own, to come to Morgolia and join his empire."

"Empire?"

"He calls it the Reygistan Empire. He intends to unite all Eastern and Southern Arthaloka, from the Sea of Grass down to the desert kingdoms, even the islands, and combine their strengths to go to war against the Burnt Empire."

She stared at him. "That is . . . impossible."

He shrugged. "He is Krushan. And ambitious."

"So what happened at this meeting?"

Ugraksh glanced to either side, as if checking for hidden spies. "They say he took control of Morgolia."

"Took control how? The Morgol have roamed the Sea of Grass as free riders for thousands of years. They will never ally with anyone."

Ugraksh nodded. "That is precisely why they say Jarsun used his Krushan power to take control of them."

Suddenly, she felt as if her throat was filled with sand. "He can do that?"

"That and much more, it seems. He is determined to stake his claim on the Burnt Empire, and he is using the kingdoms of the East, which include our own Arrgodi clans and the Mraashk of course, as well as Gwannland and the Eastern seaports, as well as the entirety of the White and Red Deserts."

"Such a thing is possible?"

Ugraksh shrugged. "Had you asked me only a year ago, I would have laughed. Now . . ." He shook his head wearily. "Jarsun is exceedingly powerful. Powerful enough to crush us in an open war. But also shrewd enough to know that if he declares against the Arrgodi nation, the Mraashk and Arrgodi will set aside all our differences and stand by us, shoulder to shoulder to the end. Add to that Morgolia's considerable resources, and he would own almost all the East, except Gwannland, which still holds out for the present."

"King Gwann would never join him. Gwannland owns the seaports. Their trade and power come from the Isles of Hope."

Ugraksh looked at her. "Then Gwann will lose all his power and the seaports, perhaps his life as well. I told you. Jarsun will not be stopped. He is a juggernaut that has already been set in motion."

"And if all of us were to agree peacefully to align with him?" she asked, anxiously now. "Then surely he would not war against us? Much as the notion sickens me, it may be worth it to prevent a war with such as he."

He nodded. "I am of the same mind. My age for warring is long past. After the peace accord with Mraashk, I would not see blood spilled on grasslands ever again in my lifetime. But I am old, and soon that decision will not be mine to make."

She stared at him intently. "You mean . . ." She swallowed hard, putting into words the thought she could scarcely bear to hold in her head for a moment. "Tyrak might be deluded into following him? Surely not!"

The thought itself made her feel sick to the stomach. But Ugraksh's response made her feel sicker yet.

"My queen, I fear that has already come to pass."

# *Tyrak*

## 1

TYRAK COULD SCARCELY BELIEVE his eyes as he approached the uks cart. He slowed before it, feeling his mouth twist in a leering grin.

"Vasurava? Clan chief of the Mraashk? Riding only an uks cart?" He laughed, and his men, tired and satiated from another successful and richly rewarding raid, laughed as well. "Does your nation have no chariots for a king? No entourage, royal guard, nothing?"

He turned to his men, grinning and winking. "At least they could have sent a few milkmaids along to protect you!"

A loud round of guffaws greeted that comment. The camp's attention was centered on their leader now, and word spread quickly up and down the cantonment of Vasurava's presence. Many off-duty soldiers and other workers crowded around to catch a glimpse of the great Mraashk king, whose prowess as a general as well as a ruler was legendary. Tyrak saw their surprised reactions as they took in the rusticity of Vasurava's transport and his simple cowherd apparel.

He also noted the absence of visible weaponry.

Vasurava replied in a disarmingly good-natured tone, "We are like this only, Prince Tyrak. Simple cowherds, shepherds, and farmers — we are not sophisticated castle dwellers like you Arrgodi. We live close to the soil and love the smells of earth and cattle."

There was a buzz of amusement. Some of Tyrak's men even clapped and cheered at the response. He glared around in sudden fury, losing his good humor instantly.

Conscripted soldiers though they were, even the most hardened Arrgodi veteran was at heart a cowherd. Cowherds with swords, Tyrak called them contemptuously during drill practice, working his whip arduously "to beat out the traces of milk from your bloodstream."

Never having worked a field or milked an uks, growing up in the lap of luxury in his father's palace, Tyrak had a deep, enduring resentment toward rustic men. The resentment came from envy, from hearing other boys and men talk of crop cycles, soil types, the effects of climate on harvests, bird migrations, uks feed, cattle ailments, and such matters.

These were things from which he had always been excluded, and his lack of knowledge had often been greeted with laughter and derision in the early years, giving him a powerful sense of inferiority. His first fights had been over this very difference between him and other Arrgodi, and he had never truly gotten over being an outsider to such things.

Now he sneered at Vasurava: "Yes, well, we seem to be stamping your fellow countrymen back into the soil they love so much, mingling their blood and brains with uks shit. I'm sure they're very content now."

At once, the gathering grew grim. Tyrak's men, knowing his peculiarities and nature, immediately began to focus on their respective tasks. Curious to a fault though the Arrgodi were, they knew better than to incur the wrath of their lord. Tyrak was given to throwing maces randomly at his own men, killing anyone unlucky enough to be standing nearby. His sensitivity at being reminded of his lack of rustic skills or knowledge was equally well known.

The sight of Vasurava's face — and that of his companion — helped restore much of Tyrak's good cheer.

"Then you admit to killing innocent Mraashk," Vasurava said in a level voice.

"Mraashk, certainly. Innocent, no."

Tyrak shifted his horse a few steps closer to the cart, putting the head of his Morgol stallion almost nose to nose with the uks, who made unhappy sounds and tried to retreat. Tyrak's horse snickered and snorted hot breath down on them contemptuously, showing his superiority. "They were about to transgress onto our territory, some even in the act of crossing the river, others illegally diverting channels from the river for irrigation. My soldiers and I were merely upholding the terms of the treaty."

Vasurava's companion glared at Tyrak with a cold rage that promised blood and mayhem if only he had a sword in his hand. He was clearly controlling himself only under duress. Tyrak tilted his head and smiled cattily at the man, tempted to toss him a sword just to see how well his self-control held.

"And you can prove these transgressions?" Vasurava asked.

Tyrak shrugged. "There were several witnesses. Hundreds. Take your pick."

He gestured vaguely at the mounted contingent behind him, still seated astride their horses until their leader dismounted.

Vasurava kept his eyes on Tyrak. "And if I question your word and produce witnesses of my own?" He added sharply, "Survivors of your 'treaty' raids. Who will counter your claims and give witness that you were the transgressors, entering unlawfully onto our lands, giving no notice of your approach, grossly violating all rules of warrior *Auma,* slaughtering unarmed innocents, including children and the old and infirm, and abusing our women . . . If I provide this countermanding evidence, what say you then?"

Tyrak shrugged, looking away. For a milk-sodden cowherd, the man had a manner that was unquestionably kinglike and commanding. He could see how the Mraashk had developed a reputation for leadership. Vasurava reminded Tyrak of his father when Tyrak was young and soft and Ugraksh was one of the hardest military commanders in all Arthaloka, notorious for his campaigns of conquest.

"You can drag out anyone you want, claim anything," Tyrak said. "As crown prince and heir of Arrgodi and military commander of her armies, I am answerable to no one. I pass summary judgment based on my observations and conclusions. No so-called 'witness' or 'survivor' can question my actions."

"But I can." Vasurava spoke simply, with no trace of challenge or defiance. Yet the steel in that statement was undoubted. His face was a granite carving, his eyes cold lights shining like beacons in darkness. "I am king of the Arrgodi nation, lord of the Arrgodi. It was I who signed the peace treaty with your father, King Ugraksh. I stamped my seal to the terms and conditions of the treaty. I have every right to question your actions and intentions."

Tyrak raised his eyes to meet Vasurava's. The atmosphere on the grounds had suddenly changed. Not a sound could be heard anywhere along the length and breadth of the clearing: every single man was watching and listening.

"Are you calling me a liar, Lord Vasurava?" Tyrak asked softly.

Vasurava looked at him with an unblinking gaze. He seemed to be considering, weighing, debating. Though his face remained outwardly calm and composed, it was evident that a great battle was raging within his soul. Even his companion turned to glance quickly, searchingly at his lord, as if wondering what his next words might be. Finally, a truce was declared — as one side won out over the other.

"I am asking you to uphold the peace," Vasurava said. "To return to Argodi at once with all your forces and leave the policing of this side of the river to me. This is my territory to control, not yours. You are here without my authorization or permission. I request you kindly" — he raised his hands and joined them together in a sincere greeting — "I beseech you, as one king to another, to let me control and police my people myself. Go now, at once, and kindly give my eternal love and best wishes to your father and mother as well. The Mraashk nation and Arrgodi nation are now allies and neighbors. I beg you, let us stay in peace."

There was silence after this pronouncement. Vasurava remained standing on the cart with his hands joined in greeting, head bowed.

Tyrak heard the distant calling of birds across the clearing and glimpsed a flight of kraunchyas out of the corner of his eye, rising from the forest and taking to the skies in a long, wheeling half circle.

Every last man on the field had heard Vasurava's unequivocal command couched in humility, and was now waiting with bated breath for Tyrak's response.

## 2

Tyrak's first instinct was to draw his sword and lunge at Vasurava. A natural-born warrior with an athletic disposition and an easy, instinctive familiarity with the physics of combat, he knew that by spurring his horse with a quick jab of his bladed heels, he could leap forward, slash at a diagonal upward angle, and take off Vasurava's head with one powerful stroke.

It would require control of his shoulder to avoid straining the muscle, and he would have to stand in the stirrups to extend his reach and force, but it could be done. He had done it before — often. The companion would be no trouble at all. The moment Tyrak acted, self-preservation would force his men to follow suit. The man's torso would bristle with arrows in an instant.

But something stayed his hand. Something he had never encountered before in his young experience: for despite his long history of cruelties, Tyrak was barely more than a boy, hardly eighteen summers of age. Apart from magnificent physical strength and robustness, he was also gifted with extraordinary insensitivity to what others around him were feeling at any moment. Yet on this occasion, he could not but help sensing something highly unusual.

His soldiers were favoring Vasurava.

He saw, to his astonishment, that the vast majority of them actually desired that he concede to Vasurava's request. They avoided meeting his eyes when he scanned their faces, and many looked away from him, openly gazing with admiration and awe at the cowherd king. He also sensed their respect and admiration for this simple cowherd who, even though king of a nation no less rich and powerful than his own, could still dress and travel and speak with simplicity and fearlessness.

Had Vasurava come here with a contingent of heavily armed warriors and all pomp and ceremony, he would not have commanded such respect. But by riding in on a simple uks cart with a solitary companion, unarmed and unshielded, and by daring to address Tyrak in such definite terms — "Go now, at once" — he had won their respect and love.

This was courage, Tyrak realized with seething resentment: *true* courage. To go unarmed before an army and still make one's demands without fear of consequences. In that instant, he hated Vasurava bitterly enough to want to see him trampled underfoot by his horse's hooves until every bone in his body was no more than splinters in the dirt.

He knew that were he to attack Vasurava, he would only heighten the hatred his own men felt for him, for his ways and actions. Yet he felt he had no choice. He could not back down from such a clear pronouncement. Either he did as Vasurava said and lost face forever, or he argued and debated like old men at council until Vasurava reeled out more arguments and witness accounts and facts and figures to prove him a liar.

Or he'd do what he always did: prevail. By any means necessary.

He unsheathed his sword and pointed it at Vasurava. A held breath greeted his action as every man watching and listening prepared for the inevitable violence that must follow.

But, instead of attacking as he usually did — always did, in fact — he only said, in a tone that masked the rage and resentment simmering inside, "By threatening me and casting aspersions on my righteous actions, you violate the terms of the treaty, Vasurava. As of this moment, I declare the peace treaty to be broken by you! The Arrgodi nation is now at war once again with the Mraashk nation! All cooperation extended to you thus far is rescinded. You are enemies of our state, and your presence here is an affront to our nation's self-respect. I command you to surrender yourselves as prisoners of war or face the consequences!"

For the first time, Vasurava seemed to lose his composure. "This is preposterous," he said, frowning. "You do not have authority to cancel the treaty, nor can it be canceled thus summarily. It took years to broker that peace accord, and no amount of bluster or threats will affect its sanctity. The peace accord stands. If you wish to move against me, then that is your choice. But note first that I carry no weapons, nor have I come with armed companions. I mean you no harm. I wish only to speak with you and request you to leave in peace. Once again, I beg you, do not misinterpret my words. Only leave us in peace and let us live together as neighbors, as allies, as brothers."

At that moment, as Tyrak stared at Vasurava, feeling pure hatred surge through him for his glib talk and smooth speeches, he saw a peculiar phenomenon. A circle of white light appeared around Vasurava's face, glowing like a garland of white blossoms against a black backdrop. The light was tinged with blue at the corona, and he could not discern its origins or nature. Tyrak rubbed his eyes, frowning and grimacing as he tried to clear his vision. But the ring of light remained.

He was about to speak, to demand of Vasurava if he was attempting to use sorcery against him, and to remind him that the use of maya was forbidden in Arthaloka, when suddenly the world around him went black as night, and a deafening silence descended on the world.

His horse whinnied, reacting to the phenomenon, and he realized with a shock that whatever it was, even the steed could see it as well. It was not just his imagination.

He looked around.

The night-black darkness surrounding him and his mount was not an absence of light. It was the presence of some dark force. He could feel its power singing and thrumming as he looked around, reverberating at the edge of hearing, flickering at the periphery of vision. He could sense his soldiers on the field around him, or their presence at least. But the blackness hummed and buzzed like a dense swarm of bees, blocking clear sight.

The only thing he could see was Vasurava's face, ringed by that bluish white light, as if disembodied and detached from everything else. It floated before Tyrak, looking down, and in the eyes he beheld the same bluish tint, as if the same eerie light glowed within Vasurava!

It took all his effort and skill to hold his horse steady, patting his neck to calm him, keeping the reins in check, pressed low against his mane. Months of hard treatment and regular whippings had taught the stallion not to risk angering his master, and he subsided reluctantly, still nickering nervously and rolling his eyes as he tried to make sense of the unnatural change that had come across his vision.

Then a new, unfamiliar voice spoke. In contrast to Vasurava's calm, assured tones, this voice was deep, vibrant, booming. It echoed inside Tyrak's head, the richness of its bass quality hurting his auditory nerves. He could feel it reverberate inside his chest. It spoke a single word that filled his world entire.

**Tyrak,** said the strange voice.

Tyrak looked around fearfully. There was nothing to be seen. The voice was coming from everywhere, from nowhere, from beyond the world, from within himself.

**Kill him. Kill thine enemy, or he will destroy you.**

The thrumming of the darkness enveloped him, and the horse suddenly grew more frenzied, like a wind whipping itself up to gale proportions.

*This* cowherd? Tyrak thought scornfully. *He couldn't destroy a calf born with three legs.*

**Do not underestimate him. He is no simple cowherd.**

Tyrak stared at the floating face of Vasurava, ringed by blue light.

**He is the means by which Vish incarnate will enter this world and destroy you.**

Tyrak swallowed. *Me? Why would the Great Preserver bother with a mere prince of Arrgodi?*

**Because you are no mere prince. You have a great destiny. Yours will be the hand that will lead Mraashk and Arrgodi together to supremacy over all Arthaloka.**

*If so, then what do I have to fear from a mere uks—*

Even before he finished, the gale around him increased to storm intensity. The horse began to buck, terrified now. He held the reins firmly, forcing his mount to remain in place.

**Destroy him. Or be destroyed! The choice is yours.**

And as suddenly as it had appeared, the phenomenon vanished. One moment, a black wind raged around him like a storm on a monsoon night. The next, he was sitting on his startled horse in the midst of the clearing, surrounded by a thousand of his best soldiers and Vasurava on his uks cart. Nobody else seemed to have witnessed the extraordinary event, although he saw Vasurava's companion staring at him curiously, as if wondering if he was mad.

Tyrak's mind turned as clear as a fresh pool in sunlight. He knew now that no amount of talk or wrangling would suffice. It all came down to one simple choice: either he gave in to Vasurava or he opposed him.

Since when had he ever given in to anyone, let alone a mere cowherd?

He grinned, and at the sight of those brilliant white teeth flashing in the afternoon sunshine, his men stirred uneasily, already knowing his mind.

Tyrak unsheathed and raised his sword in one swift action, the ringing of the steel loud in the silent afternoon. He roared loudly enough to be heard from one end of the clearing to the other, before spurring his horse the few yards to Vasurava's cart.

"KILL THEM BOTH!"

# *Vasurava*

VASURAVA SAW SOMETHING OCCUR to Tyrak, though he was not sure what it was. For an instant or two, it was as if the world went dark and a black storm surrounded himself and the Arrgodi prince. He saw Tyrak staring around, wild-eyed, struggling to control his panicked horse. So. The horse could see the black storm as well! But no one else could, not even Rurka, Vasurava sensed. What did it mean? When the booming voice began to speak, he was startled. It was clearly directed at Tyrak, yet he heard it too, quite distinctly. Nothing of this sort had ever occurred to him before . . .

Or perhaps it had.

He recalled the sensation that had struck him when Tyrak flung the barbed spear at him in Arrgodi. The way the world had seemed to reduce to only a few yards, only the two of them contained within an oval, surrounded by roaring, rushing wind. Beyond the roaring wind, he knew the world still existed, but within that space, there was only Tyrak, himself, and the flying spear. And then a white force had flashed before his eyes, tinged with blue at the center.

The spear had struck home hard, as if hitting flesh and bone, and for a moment, Vasurava thought it had. He looked down at his chest, certain he would see the spear protruding, his life blood spilling out onto the marbled floor of the Arrgodi palace. Instead, he had seen the tip of the spear captured by the white-and-blue light, as securely as a dragonfly in amber!

Then the roaring wind had receded, bringing back the sound and cacophony of the mortal world, and Tyrak had attempted to dislodge the spear, to twist and pull and turn it — without success. And Vasurava had known instinctively that were he to reach down and grasp the pole of the weapon, it would come free of the insubstantial light easily.

He had done so and been rewarded with success. As he took hold of the spear, the white-and-blue light dissipated. He saw motes of blue drifting away, sparkling like starlight on a moonless night, then they were gone.

Now something similar had occurred. Tyrak and he were once more detached from the mortal world by some supernatural force, and once more he had seen that blue light glow around himself. Fear flashed in Tyrak's hot red eyes as Ugraksh's son also recognized what was happening. Then the voice spoke, urging, commanding, demanding . . . and Tyrak's fear was replaced by malevolence.

The world crackled back to life.

The sound of a thousand soldiers roaring with shocked emotion struck him like a wave. They were roaring not out of battle rage, for this was no army they were facing on a field of war. They were roaring with outrage at their own prince's actions. Yet mingled with their outrage and shock was the warrior's throaty rasp of blind rage. Theirs not to question why; theirs but to kill or die. Their prince, their commander, had spoken his orders, and with Tyrak, it was either follow and obey without question or be killed without question.

And so all leaped forward, encircling the two unarmed and defenseless men on the uks cart.

A thousand against two.

Had slaughter ever been this simple?

Vasurava heard Rurka's cry of outrage and frustration. His friend had warned him against precisely this event. He had expected no less of Tyrak. Vasurava felt sad that Rurka had been proven right.

Yet he knew that he was not the one who was wrong. It was Tyrak who had chosen to act against *Auma,* the flow of benign, empowering energy that connected all living beings. His actions were more suited to a Krushan than an Arrgodi. Tyrak's actions here would be condemned by warriors everywhere, and after Vasurava's and Rurka's deaths the story itself would serve to unite the Mraashk against the Arrgodi.

The war that would follow would be to the bitter end, for no Mraashk could stomach such tyranny. Tyrak would be destroyed in time by his own precipitous folly. And Vasurava and Rurka would be martyrs forever, held up as shining examples of courage and *Auma* for millennia to come.

*But I do not wish to be martyred,* Vasurava thought sadly. *I came not for death but victory. All I desired was to triumph peaceably rather than through bloodshed. Is this your justice, Lord? Is this how you would treat your children who desire peace? Then why should not every mortal raise a sword and let a steel edge speak instead of his tongue?*

And then Tyrak came at him, standing in the stirrups of his horse, sword raised at an angle, the slashing blade aimed at Vasurava's neck.

Vasurava raised his hand. It was a reflexive action, and he had no more conscious awareness of raising the limb than he was aware of the intake and release of each breath.

He was also unaware that he held his crook in this hand, the cowherd's crook that he took everywhere when traveling. It had been lying across his lap on the journey here, and once or twice he had used it to swish away flies from the haunches of the uks. Other than that, it merely lay there, virtually forgotten.

Now he raised his hand, and the crook rose with it.

Tyrak's descending sword blade met the length of the crook. Two broad inches of finely honed Arrgodi steel, sharp enough to split a silk scarf in two, struck an inch-thick yew stick, veined and cracked with age — for it had been Vasurava's father's crook before him, and who knew when he had cut it and shaped it and how many decades it had served both father and son.

The warrior's sword met the cowherd's stick.

And the sword shattered.

For a moment, the world was still. The roaring of the thousand died away to silence. Every pair of eyes was transfixed. Every voice stilled.

As if time itself had slowed, the earth stopped its turning, the sun and wind and heavens paused as well, the sword struck the crook and splintered into a thousand thousand parts. Not pieces or shards or even splinters . . .

Dust.

One moment, a beautifully lethal Arrgodi sword, capable of slicing easily through Vasurava's neck, or halfway through the trunk of a yard-thick sala trunk in a single stroke, was descending to its butcher's work.

Next instant, the sword's blade struck the crook . . . and shattered to powder.

Only the hilt remained in Tyrak's hand, and the battle cry in his throat.

The cry died as well, as he swung the bladeless hilt, the lack of impact and his own considerable strength almost toppling him off the horse.

He held his seat, then stared at Vasurava as his horse, spurred on, trotted past the uks cart a yard or three, turned smartly, and turned another complete circle before coming to a halt beside the cart. Tyrak stared at Vasurava's neck with stunned incomprehension.

Then he turned his eyes to the hilt of the sword in his own fist. Bejeweled, intricately carved with the sigil of the Mraashk, finely worked by the most illustrious craftsmen of the kingdom.

Now merely an objet d'art, to be displayed in a museum, useless as a weapon.

He gazed at the hilt in disbelief, blinking.

All around him, his soldiers peered as well.

Then he looked up again at Vasurava, who was lowering the crook to his lap.

A few motes of silvery dust were still swirling in the air, and as Tyrak stared at Vasurava — along with a thousand Arrgodi soldiers — the motes swirled around, rose up, and were carried away by the wind. They were tinted blue, and sparkled as they dissipated.

# *Tyrak*

## 1

FURY ROSE IN TYRAK like bile in a drunkard's gorge.

He reached down and yanked a javelin from its sheath. Like his sword, it too was finely wrought and bejeweled at the grip, his sigil carved into the metal band. He always left one such javelin at the site of any place he attacked, standing from the chest of the chief or leader of the enemy, as a symbol of his conquest.

He raised the javelin, hooked it in his armpit, like a lance, and kicked his horse forward. He charged at the uks cart, aiming the weapon at Vasurava's chest, screaming as loudly as he could.

This time there was no answering roar from his soldiers. They were still too stunned by the shattering of the sword.

But as the point of the javelin plunged directly at Vasurava's chest, the cowherd chieftain raised his crook again, barely a few inches, and countered the powerful lunging weapon with barely enough force to push back a gnat.

It was force enough.

The point of the javelin shattered, the pole splintering into a dozen shards. The pieces toppled, some knocking woodenly against the forward right wheel of the uks cart before tumbling to the churned ground. Only the base remained in Tyrak's armpit, a jagged edge poking out, and a small piece in his fist. He stared at it in disgust as he rode past the cart, turning his mount again, then tossed it aside. It was good for no more than starting a fire now. He had brought down elephants with that javelin, men by the dozen. Now it was kindling.

And yet his arm and body thrummed as if he had struck a stone wall. His fingers were numb, his armpit and shoulder sore from the force of the impact. He had pierced armored shields with lances at top riding speed and experienced less resistance than this.

He stared at Vasurava in fury. The Mraashk had an expression of frank wonder on his face, as if he too could not understand what was happening. Tyrak desired nothing more than to smash in that face, demolish that expression.

Tyrak turned to look around. He saw a mace in the hands of one of his soldiers, a burly, muscled fellow who had been exercising with the weapon as his men often did, swinging it round over their heads to build upper-body bulk and strength.

Without a word, he snatched the weapon from the man's hands. The soldier stepped back to avoid being knocked down by Tyrak's horse, lost his balance, and fell into the mud. Tyrak hefted the mace in his left hand — the right was still numb from the javelin impact.

Roaring with rage, he rode straight at the uks cart again. He saw the whites of the eyes of Vasurava's friend, who was as shocked as Tyrak's soldiers, but with a notable difference. The soldiers were merely watching as spectators; Vasurava's companion was in the firing line of Tyrak's assaults. Tyrak saw the man flinch as he rode forward, swinging the mace overhead in a classic attack approach, then, instead of striking at Vasurava's body, he flung and released it.

The mace flew barely three yards.

It ought to have caught Vasurava in the chest, neck, and jaw, shattering bone, smashing flesh, battering the heart to pulp. It was a death blow. The mace weighed no less than a hundred pounds. Flung with that force from a cantering horse, it would have struck Vasurava with ten times that weight in impact.

Vasurava raised his crook just in time to meet the oncoming mace.

The mace turned to pulp.

Tyrak heard the sound of the metal being crushed, and saw the mace wilt like a flower sprayed with poison. It thumped to the ground, no more than a piece of twisted metal.

Tyrak roared his fury.

Then he turned and pointed at the company of archers, who stood staring in disbelief at these extraordinary sights.

"Archers! Raise your bows!"

He had to repeat the order twice more before they obeyed; even so, they moved sluggishly, like men underwater. One of them remained gaping open-mouthed, and Tyrak vented his fury by pulling another javelin from its sheath on his saddle and flinging it at the man. The javelin punched through the archer's neck and out the other side in an explosion of blood and gristle, almost decapitating him. His corpse fell, shuddering and spitting blood with a wet, gurgling sound as the air in his lungs was expelled from his severed throat. After that, the archers' years of training and relentless discipline took over from their numbed minds.

"Aim!" Tyrak cried. The target was obvious.

The officer commanding the company of archers called out in alarm. "Sire, if we miss our mark, we shall hit our own!" The danger was obvious: In a field crowded with their compatriots, the arrows were bound to overshoot their mark and strike friendly bodies.

"Loose!" Tyrak cried.

White-faced and blinking, the archers loosed.

Over three dozen longbow arrows flew through the air at Vasurava and his companion. This time, Vasurava did not even bother to raise the crook. There was no way to block forty arrows with a single stick.

Vasurava faced the barrage calmly. His expression had progressed from the wonderment Tyrak had seen earlier to acceptance. It was almost beatific in its calmness.

The arrows shattered in midair as if striking an invisible wall.

Blue light sparked where their points struck nothingness.

Vasurava's companion flinched, then stared in amazement, as splinters fell around them in a harmless shower.

Tyrak screamed with frustration.

"Again!" he cried. "Loose again!"

Another barrage. The same results.

Tyrak lost his senses completely then.

He pointed at the cart, yelling, "Attack! Kill them both!"

But not a soldier moved. The archers lowered their bows, ashen. Those nearest to the cart gazed up in wonderment. Several joined their palms together in greeting, as if paying darshan to a deity in a temple.

Tyrak rode forward, striking these men down, crushing them under his horse's hooves.

He whipped others, roared again and again. "Attack! Attack!"

But not one man of the thousand moved to obey.

In a red rage, unable to get them to respond to his commands, Tyrak took a fresh sword and hacked them down where they stood. He slashed at random, not bothering to check if the man was dead. Many were mortally wounded, but none cried out, none protested. All gazed at Vasurava and joined their palms in wonderment, dying without argument.

# *Vasurava*

FINALLY, WITH DOZENS OF his own soldiers lying in bloody splotches on the field, Tyrak's anger dissipated.

He leaned over the mane of his horse, sword blade dripping blood.

He looked up at Vasurava at last.

"I accept," he said in a voice unlike himself. "I will respect the terms of the treaty."

He gave the command to break camp and return to Arrgodi. This order his soldiers obeyed happily, glancing back with fearful respect at the uks cart as they gathered up their implements and weapons and other materials and prepared for the journey home. Throughout their ranks, men spoke with hushed voices of the miracle they had witnessed, of the will of the stone gods, of the great hand of Vish that had protected Vasurava from Tyrak's adharmic attack. For Vasurava's devotion to *Auma* was legendary, and who else was the supreme embodiment of *Auma* but the stone god Vish, of whom Vasurava was a dedicated devotee? There were many who whispered that Vasurava was no less than Vish's avatar on Arthaloka, descended to restore *Auma* to the earth.

By dusk, Tyrak's battalion was riding homeward.

Vasurava and Rurka sat in the center of the empty field, scarcely able to believe what they had accomplished.

The last stragglers disappeared from sight, their passing lit by the fading saffron glow of the setting sun.

Vasurava turned to Rurka. "When we set out this morning—" He stopped.

Rurka looked at Vasurava with brimming eyes. They shone in the sunset like golden orbs. He joined his palms in humility and bowed his head.

"My lord," he said. "Forgive me for having doubted you. I did not recognize you in this mortal guise."

Vasurava clicked his tongue impatiently. "Come now, Rurka. You have known me since we were both boys with snotty noses. I am no avatar or amsa of Vish. I am merely a mortal man, like yourself."

Rurka shook his head. "What I witnessed today, no mortal man could accomplish."

Vasurava nodded. "I confess I cannot explain how or why that happened. But even so, I would credit my conviction in the power of *Auma* and my unwavering faith. I came here determined to convince Tyrak without resorting to violence, and I succeeded. Today's victory is a triumph of *Auma*."

Vasurava was speaking of pacifism here. *Auma* was also the doctrine of nonviolence, since the flow connected all living beings, making coexistence essential to the balance of life. This cooperative coexistence was central to the Mraashk faith.

Rurka shook his head, grinning. "We all believe in *Auma,* brother. Yet I cannot see what you did to Tyrak and his Arrgodi Marauders as merely a peaceful solution. Whatever name you give to it, brother, it was a miracle. Call it a miracle of *Auma* or Vish's hand intervening. Either way, you are proven a stone god among men. Of that, there is no doubt at all."

Vasurava smiled ruefully. "From your lips to Vish's ears. If my sense of *Auma* pleases the stone gods above and helps me serve my people, so be it." He looked around at the empty field. "And I think now that Tyrak will not come again to these parts to do his wicked work."

Rurka made a sound of disgust. "Urrkh. The way he butchered his own men! I wish that you had killed him."

Vasurava had taken the reins from Rurka. He clucked his tongue, driving the uks forward, starting the journey back home. "Had I done so, I would have been no better than he. Nay, Rurka. I think what transpired today was a shining example of the power of peace over the path of violence. Violence only begets more violence. Peace ends violence. Had I slain Tyrak today, his people would have had just cause in attacking my people again, and the cycle would have continued endlessly. By not raising a weapon or causing anyone harm, I proved my point more effectively than a dozen battles could ever have done."

"This is true," Rurka acknowledged. "I do not think we shall see Prince Tyrak again this side of the Jeel!" He laughed. "Who knows. He may even have to retire from warmongering forever. I do not think his men will follow him with any modicum of respect from now on, what do you say?"

Vasurava chuckled. "He might have some difficulty in that regard."

Their laughter rose above the treetops as the uks cart clattered and rattled down the bumpy path, mingling with the cries of birds seeking their nests for the night. The news they carried back that night would occasion celebrations across Mraashk, jubilation at the departure of Tyrak's Marauders and the prevention of what had seemed to be certain war with the Argodi.

Sadly, they were mistaken in their assumptions.

The worst was yet to come.

# *Tyrak*

## 1

TYRAK SEETHED ON THE ride homeward.

He could not believe he had been bested by a milk-sodden cowherd armed with nothing more than a crook. His head still spun from what he had witnessed. He rode alone, even his Marauders avoiding him for fear that he might take out his frustration and bitterness on them: those he was closest to he tended also to treat most harshly at such times. The rows upon rows of cavalry and foot soldiers straggled on toward Arrgodi, attempting to keep their voices low to avoid incurring their commander's wrath, but not wholly succeeding.

He heard snatches of talk everywhere, always about Vasurava and the maya they had witnessed. He knew that the incident would become a great legend over time, and that it had already damaged his leadership badly. He had held together his army by brute force and fear of his own viciousness. They obeyed him because he was their lord and because they believed that none other could stand up to his brutal belligerence in battle. Now that someone had stood up to him and triumphed so extravagantly, they had no reason to fear him anymore. Arrgodi were too independent minded to enjoy the rugged discipline and command structure of a standing army; if he could not hold these men together, they would soon drift back into their traditional occupations. And if he could not keep his core contingent together, the army at large would lose morale as well.

What had happened was an unmitigated disaster. There was no other way to view it. He was still badly shaken by it. Outwardly, he succeeded in keeping up appearances. Inwardly, he was trembling with shock. How had Vasurava done it? It was impossible. Yet it had happened before his very eyes.

But if not sorcery, what?

The other explanation, the one his soldiers were bandying about, was too preposterous to consider for even a moment. Hand of Vish, indeed! As if almighty Vish would reach down from Stone Heaven and protect a simple Mraashk clan chieftain!

But what else could have accomplished such a feat?

He was still lost in his own morose thoughts when his horse came to a halt, stamping his feet.

He looked up to see what was obstructing his way.

It was a sage. A hermit clad in trademark tattered red-ochre robes, resting his weight on a rough staff. But unlike most such hermits and sages, he did not have a flowing white beard or the stick-thin body of one who had wasted away through prolonged fasting and self-deprivation.

Tyrak's horse whickered and shied away from the man. Tyrak squeezed his already tight grip on the reins, yanking the bit hard enough to cut the stallion's mouth and remind him of the consequences of acting up. The mount settled reluctantly, but his eyes looked off to one side, rolling to show their whites, as if he was afraid of the man who stood in his path.

Tyrak frowned down at the sage. "Old man," he said impatiently. "Get out of my way. Do you know who I am?"

The sage looked up at him with that supremely arrogant look of superiority that Tyrak had loathed ever since he was a boy.

**Son of Ugraksh, son of Kensura, your end is nigh.**

Tyrak's horse reacted before he did, bucking hard. It took a few sharp applications of the stick and some mouth twisting to keep the stallion from bolting. Only then did Tyrak allow himself to feel the shock that had struck him the instant that booming bass voice had resounded in his mind.

*It's the same voice, the one that spoke to me on the field before I attacked Vasurava.*

He was overcome by a powerful urge to spur his mount on and run the priest over. But the horse was acting very strangely now; despite his warnings, still the stallion persisted in shying and whickering incessantly, trying desperately to twist his head away from the man. Tyrak raised his stick and was about to administer a harsh reminder of his mastery when he saw something that further chilled his heart.

The man cast no shadow.

The sun was off to their front and to the right, low in the sky, casting long shadows behind them. The hermit's shadow ought to have stretched from where he stood down toward Tyrak, leaning diagonally to the left. That was how the shadows of the trees and passing soldiers on either side were falling, moving and distorting as they intermingled. But where the man stood, with everyone leaving a clear berth for Tyrak, there was not so much as a whisper of shadow.

"What are you?" Tyrak cried out, suddenly feeling apprehensive. The encounter with Vasurava had shaken him to the core, disturbing him more deeply than he had realized. He knew that now, when he saw his horse's reaction, the lack of a shadow, and the obvious way his own passing soldiers were paying no attention to the man standing just a few yards ahead — as if they did not see anyone standing there at all.

**I am Vessa,** said the man, **one of the Seven Sages who walked the mortal realm when it was newly made, before men and urrkh and amsas and avatars and all other manner of beings. We were giants then, and we lived inside the earth.**

Tyrak found himself unable to speak.

The sage peered up and nodded, his face creasing in what might have once passed for a look of amusement.

**You are not as feeble-minded as some think. You have already fathomed that I am here only in spirit, not flesh.**

"Ghost," Tyrak said, the word emerging as a croak from his throat, "ghoul."

Sage Vessa's face wrinkled in that almost-smile again, taking on an almost sinister cast.

**Neither ghost nor ghoul. Merely transporting between planes on an errand. Usually, I would use a portal to pass from one world to the next. But today's errand required a different means.**

"Portal," Tyrak repeated mechanically. He seemed incapable of saying anything original. A band of his Marauders passed on the left, their chatter dying out as they registered their lord standing in the middle of the clearing staring and apparently speaking to no one.

**A manner of portal that enables one to travel between worlds. But por-**

**tals require a physical movement from one universe to the other. They also have specific laws governing them, such as the Law of the Balance.**

"Balance," Tyrak croaked. The stallion had subsided and now hung his head to one side, eyes white, mouth frothing, as he seemed to resign himself to a certain death or perhaps even some far worse fate.

**So I used a Mirror.**

"Mirror," Tyrak whispered, barely audible.

**What you see here is merely a reflection of my physical form. That is why I cast no shadow and why, if you were to ride forward now, you would pass through this image of me as easily as through a cloud of smoke. My voice is projected astrally into your mind, which is why you can hear me and none else can.**

"Astrally," Tyrak said, starting to feel afraid, very, very afraid.

Vessa's face grew somber. **Enough preamble. The reason I am here, Tyrak son of Ugraksh and Kensura, is to impart valuable knowledge and advice to you. I know of your failure against Vasurava, despite my exhortations to kill him. That is why I have resorted to this method to deliver my message to you. Heed my words. For what I am about to say will serve you well in the days and years to come. It may even save your life and enable you to accomplish the great ambition you harbor in your heart. The ambition to be emperor of the entire world. That is what you desire, is it not?**

This time Tyrak could not speak even a single word. He merely nodded vigorously.

**So heed me well. I shall tell you that which shall change your life entire and make the impossible possible. Pay close attention to every word I say, for I am about to hand you your future on a golden tray. The world shall unfold before you like a lotus in water, offering itself freely. You shall be king of all Arthaloka as you desire. Every dream shall be realized, every enemy destroyed, every ambition fulfilled.**

Tyrak was surprised to hear his voice ask hoarsely, "Why?"

Vessa looked just as surprised. He raised his head, frowning.

**Why, you ask? Impudent fool. I am about to gift you the secret by which you will rule the world, and you question why I do so?**

He seemed about to display the legendary epic temper of sages. Both Tyrak and his horse cringed, but Vessa visibly regained control of himself.

**It does not matter. Someday I shall return, in person, and demand of you the priest price as is my right, and you shall grant me my demand without hesitation or question. Does that answer your "why"?**

Tyrak, eyes wide with shock and fear, nodded several times more than necessary. Passing soldiers glanced at him curiously, then looked at each other. Their commander was known for his eccentricities and extreme behavior, but this was unlike even him: standing in the middle of the woods, staring white-faced at nothing, and making absurd gestures! Perhaps defeat at the hands of Vasurava had loosened the last hinge on his door.

**For now, all you need do is listen and do as I say. Exactly as I say. Precisely as I say. Do you follow my meaning?**

Tyrak nodded vigorously again, his chin striking his breastplate more than once.

Vessa nodded, satisfied.

**The first thing you will do is go to Morgolia.**

"Morgolia!" Tyrak's voice rose in disbelief. "That's . . ." He tried to remember exactly how far the northeastern city was from Arrgodi, but memory failed him. No Arrgodi or Mraashk chose to travel to that stonegodforsaken wildland. Only barbarians and savages dwelled there. Even the hardiest pioneers had abandoned the region, proclaiming it unfit for human habitation. "A long way off!" he finished.

**Indeed. It will take you well over a year's travel, if you do not linger anywhere along the way, as you are wont to do. No indulging hedonistic pleasures, no diversions or tarrying, you must go directly to Morgolia, and do not stop until you arrive at your destination.**

Tyrak's lip curled in a sneering complaint. "I won't go. I have no companions, no supplies, and this horse . . . he won't carry me all the way to Morgolia, over the stone ridges and whatever else is on the way. No man traveling alone can survive such a journey."

**I will guarantee your survival. I will be your guide, showing you where you will find food, shelter in inclement weather, and even fresh mounts as required. But you must endure the journey itself on your own. Consider it a test of your determination to succeed.**

"Succeed at what? I am already prince of Arrgodi. Even my own parents won't disown me. My father, curse his sainted heart, may want to, but my mother won't let him. What can you offer me that's worth going all the way to Arrgodi and getting boils on my ass and feet, old man?"

**So you no longer desire to be king of the world? To unseat your father and command the Arrgodi and Mraashk nations, among others? Do you no longer seek revenge on Vasurava for the humiliating defeat he meted out to you? You are the laughingstock of your own soldiers, Tyrak. If you return thus to Arrgodi, you will be the laughingstock of the entire city and nation. If you are content with that condition, then I shall take my leave now and return no more.**

"Wait!" Tyrak said. "I didn't mean I wouldn't go. I was just asking, what's so great about Morgolia that I have to go all the way there? Why can't you do what you promise right here in Arrgodi? These grasslands are my homeland, I like it just fine here."

**And you will return to the Sea of Grass and rule both your nations. You will achieve great fame and renown throughout the known world. But to achieve all that and more, you must go to Morgolia. For only there can you meet with the Krushan.**

"Krushan?" At the mention of the most powerful name in Arthaloka, even Tyrak felt a twinge of unease. "Which Krushan do you mean? The Krushan are too powerful. I don't want to align with them. They'll swallow up Arrgodi and Mraashk and consider them little ticks on the fat behind of the Burnt Empire. Then we'll spend the rest of our days paying taxes and owing allegiance to Hastinaga and following their damned Krushan law."

**The one I speak of is not in Hastinaga, nor is he part of the Burnt Empire.**

This was interesting. All the Krushan Tyrak knew of were in the empire's capital, the great city-state of Hastinaga. Who was this Krushan in Morgolia, then?

**His name is Jarsun, and he is building a new empire, one to rival the Burnt Empire. Morgolia is only his present starting point. Soon he will hold sway across the length and breadth of Arthaloka.**

"Jarsun?" Tyrak frowned. Where had he heard that name before? Some news out of the South, wasn't it? Something that happened in Aqron.

**He is the one you must journey to meet. He is powerful, a conqueror of empires, a destroyer of worlds.**

Tyrak liked the sound of this Jarsun fellow.

"All right," he said at last. "I will go to Morgolia. Is this Krushan named Jarsun expecting me?"

**He is expecting someone like you. You might even say he is to ravagers like yourself what honey is to bugs.**

Tyrak wasn't sure if that was a compliment or an insult, but he decided not to press the matter. He was curious about this Jarsun. Besides, Vessa was right. Tyrak didn't want to go back to Arrgodi with his tail between his legs. A year or three away sounded like a fine idea. It would give people enough time to forget about his humiliation, and if things went well with this Jarsun, Tyrak could return with a new military alliance at least. After all, he was prince of Arrgodi. Maybe Jarsun could help him defeat Vasurava and take over Mraashk. It was worth a try.

"You will guide me on the way?" he asked again, turning his horse northward.

**I will ensure you reach Morgolia and tell you how to approach Jarsun Krushan and how to deal with him. The rest will be up to you, Tyrak of Arrgodi.**

"Very well, then," Tyrak said, starting forward. "I will go to Morgolia."

## 2

A full year and a season later, Tyrak stood on a rocky escarpment and looked out toward the distant spires of a great city.

Morgolia.

A kingdom so rich and powerful and strong at arms that the thought of overrunning it by force had never even occurred to him. Yet, because of its strategic position, Morgolia was a crucial player in the imperial politics of Arthaloka.

Ever since his father Ugraksh's days of warmongering, Tyrak had heard its name uttered with respect, fear, or frustration, often all three in the same breath. He had fantasized of standing on this very rise with a great army behind him, legions of chariots spread out for tens of miles, a host so vast as to strike terror into the heart of any king, large enough to fall upon the great city like a bear upon an unsuspecting prey, crushing it before it could utter a single cry. For that was the only way that Morgolia could be taken: by an enormous force and completely by surprise. Anything else would result in failure and ruin.

Now here he was, alone, exhausted from the long ride. He had told no one where he was going. Several of his Marauders, the few still loyal to him, had somehow followed his trail and caught up with him at the start of his journey to Morgolia. He had been warned of their approach by the sage Vessa and turned to wave them back furiously. When they still followed, he had shot arrows at them from his shortbow, aiming at the ground before them. They had understood then and had slowed to watch him ride on. Their faces betrayed their dismay and confusion, perhaps even loathing — they thought he was turning tail and running away like a coward — but he refused to let himself dwell on that.

Had the encounter with Vasurava not occurred, they would almost certainly have tailed him despite his violent objection, if only because it was their sworn duty as well as their *Auma* to protect the life of the king-in-waiting. But the encounter had unnerved them, and his behavior probably made them assume he needed some time to himself. He suspected they would have made camp and would be waiting for him to return, and might even have sent out regular patrols to see where he went and to observe from a distance. But any patrols had been left behind within the first weeks. By now they would have assumed he had gone into self-imposed exile, which was not far from the truth, and would have reported this back to his parents in Arrgodi.

Alone. He realized now that he had succeeded in making the journey without the omnipresent entourage he had been accustomed to since childhood. On his own. Well, not entirely on his own, since the old man had been true to his word and appeared from time to time, guiding him to water, food, shelter, places where he could find fresh mounts, but that old fool hardly counted as company.

And now he was truly alone. Before he had disappeared the last time, Vessa had said, **Ride into Morgolia and find Jarsun Krushan.**

"And what then?" Tyrak had asked, with some irritation. He was leaner and fitter than he had ever been in his life, but also tired of his own company and desperately in need of good wine, food, and warm bodies to slake his needs. He was at the point where he was questioning his own sanity at having undertaking this long, arduous journey to a strange land notorious for the hostility of its environs as well as its inhabitants.

**The rest will follow,** the sage had said cryptically before disappearing. He hadn't shown his face since.

The thought of riding into Morgolia on his own, without anyone to back him up, was so far removed from anything Tyrak had ever thought or dreamed, it seemed absurd now. And foolish. He literally feared for his life. The shifting politics of the northern kingdoms made it difficult to be certain of one's relationship with one's neighbors at all times — without a specific treaty or alliance between Arrgodi and Morgolia, he had no way of knowing if his unannounced, unaccompanied arrival would be regarded as an act of hostility or perhaps even an insult. Grassland society thrived on tradition and culture, and both demanded many preparations before a royal visit — the pomp and ceremony of the visit itself was an important ritual which enabled both lieges to observe, prepare for, judge, and measure one another. The royal procession through the streets of the city was, in effect, a parade for the citizens to view and measure their neighboring king's net worth and military strength. A holiday was given to enable all to view a royal visit. Stone Father alone knew what these northerners did to welcome visiting dignitaries: They might roast their heads on spits and serve them up with gherkins, for all he knew.

So here he was, alone, bearing no gifts, unannounced, and with unclear politics. He knew almost nothing about the ruler of Morgolia apart from the fact that he must be a strong and violently decisive ruler, because he wouldn't be able to hold the reins of a kingdom this strong and unwieldy if he was not. But that was like saying a warrior could use a sword.

Yet Sage Vessa's instructions had been crystal clear:

**Find Jarsun Krushan . . .**

He shivered as that echoing voice reverberated in his memory again. Kicking his horse, he drove it down the slope of the escarpment.

## 3

Beast and rider stumbled downward, leaving a curling trail of dust that rose lazily into the clear light of afternoon. At the bottom of the slope, they broke into a shambling trot that soon turned into a canter, heading toward the city.

Their progress was noted and then marked by slitted eyes shielded below curved visors.

As they approached, the tips of arrows nocked in strung bows followed the head of the rider, eager to be loosed and embed themselves in his skull.

But the orders were clear and had come from the highest level, down through the ranks:

"A single horse and rider will come. They are to be permitted to pass into the city unharmed, untouched. None shall speak to the rider. Anyone who attempts to speak with him or slow his progress is to be killed on the spot."

Orders were obeyed without question in Morgolia. Men were executed for looking too sharply at their commanders, let alone questioning or disobeying them.

At the city gates, a pack of dogs strayed into the rider's path, barking at the stranger, but soon rolled over, yelping, then lay still in the dust, their thin bodies riddled with arrows.

People in the streets gave the rider a wide berth, windows were shut hurriedly, doors barred, livestock brought indoors, children shushed.

The soldiers in the street who kept the curfew — Morgolia was constantly under curfew, around the clock, all days and nights of the year — glanced briefly at the dusty, saddle-weary man of obvious royal bearing and garb, careful to look away instantly, without meeting his eyes. Their horses shied away from his mount, which was frothing and almost at the end of its strength.

His horse collapsed on a public street, eyes rolling back to reveal their whites completely before shuddering one final time and lying still. The rider kicked it several times, too tired to flay it as he usually would have back home, then walked the rest of the way. It was obvious that he had received neither food nor drink, and had not rested or slept for several days.

He wandered through bazaars bursting with produce and wares, an explosion of color and commerce. He was too exhausted to marvel at the richness of goods on display or the profusion of choice. As princes were wont to do in those times, he had lived mainly within the circumference of his father's power, the risk of assassination or attack being too great outside his own kingdom for him to travel far. In his childhood years, his father had been at war with most of the world, his ferocity tempered only by age and prudence as he had finally given up the campaigns, the conquests, and finally even the rivalries and clashes with neighbors to sign the recent peace treaty. Those long decades of war had made it unwise for Ugraksh's young to be permitted to stray far from Arrgodi. The end result of all this was that Tyrak had seen little of the world, and almost all that he had seen he had either owned or had some power over.

Here he had no power, no protection, no friends or servers.

Had a thousand pairs of eyes not watched him every step of the way, he would have been waylaid a dozen times, killed well before he came within sight of the vaulting palace gates. Thieves, crooked merchants, corrupt guards . . . Morgolia seethed with dangers and threats as difficult to spy out as its rich market wares and goods were easy to see.

Finally, he reached the palace and was not too tired or dehydrated from travel to note that he was neither questioned nor stopped. Spears were turned away, gates opened before him, shields lowered, eyes looked aside . . .

At last he stood in an inner courtyard of the king's own private palace, by a great fountain.

Behind him, the enormous carved doors inlaid with precious gems and decorated with a great sigil worked in battered gold sheets so fine as to be imbedded in the grain of the wood itself through great artisanship, swung noiselessly to, and were shut and barred with booming echoes.

**Ride into Morgolia and find Jarsun Krushan.**

He had done as the great sage had instructed.

He was in the private palace of one of the most powerful kings of present-day Arthaloka.

Now he waited to see what happened next.

# 4

After a fair amount of time, during which the sun passed from one side of the courtyard to the far end, a giant of an eoch appeared, treading slowly, as if stepping on sharp stones, and stood before him.

In a shockingly boyish voice, the eoch said, "Come," then turned and walked away in large strides, legs wide apart.

Tyrak understood he was to follow and passed through to another courtyard, this one festooned with silks of every color and other lavish decorations. The nature of the adornments suggested that he was entering a queen's or concubine's chambers, and he was soon rewarded with glimpses of women.

Hundreds of concubines sat, lay, stood, and reclined in various poses, some on seats or beds, others on marbled floors, several cavorting in pools and fountains. Tyrak had never seen such variety and range of feminine beauty gathered in one place before in his life. He had heard of seraglios of course, and it was said that once even Arrgodi's kings had possessed their own palaces filled with beautiful concubines.

But that was in ages past. Now his own father, Ugraksh, was loyal to Queen Kensura to a fault, and had Tyrak himself not been born, it was Kensura who would have been permitted to cohabit with a priest in order to produce offspring. The men of Arrgodi were brothers, husbands, sons, lovers . . . never patriarchs. All bloodline and inheritance was through Arrgodi women, and they were too proud to ever permit themselves to be used as mere objects of pleasure.

Tyrak felt a surge of disgust for this wanton display of womanly flesh. He had no doubt he was deliberately being taken through these parts of the palace in order to be shown the wealth and power and luxuries of the king, and he resented it every step of the way.

Tyrak passed through the palace of women and then through a number of passageways and corridors and courtyards. It seemed to take forever. He was exhausted from the journey and, even after all this time, still deeply resentful at his humiliation at Vasurava's hands. He wanted nothing more than to eat and drink himself senseless and sleep for days. But that very humiliation and defeat also drove him on, for he was not accustomed to losing, and Vessa's extraordinary words had intrigued him and awakened hope in his breast. He felt that his salvation lay here in Morgolia, for surely a ruler this powerful and wealthy could be of use to him.

Finally, the giant with the boy's voice brought him to another courtyard. This one was bereft of any decoration or sign of luxury. It was little more than an enormous rectangular space with overlooking balconies and what appeared to be doorless chambers on every side. He smelled the rank stench of man sweat, blood, piss, shit, and the other unmistakable odors of death and battle, and knew at once that he was in a place where soldiers trained, fought, lived, and died. In a sense, this was home to him, for he lived and breathed war, and such places were as natural to him as a mother's breast to an infant.

He stood, blinking in the bright sunlight, and tried to see who was sitting in the shadows of the balconies watching, but he could see only outlines and the gleam of eyes, telling him that several persons were watching from above.

The giant eoch turned to face him, bending down and grabbing a fistful of powdery dirt, rubbing it into both palms to prevent slippage during combat. Then the eoch charged directly at Tyrak.

Tyrak had not been taken by surprise. He had been expecting something along these lines ever since he had entered Morgolia's city limits. Indeed, he had been surprised that no one had accosted or challenged him until now. This attack came almost as a relief.

He sidestepped the giant's onrushing advance, turned, and cut at his opponent's larger legs with his own feet, dropping the eoch to his knees, then sending him sprawling with a cry of outrage. The giant landed face-down in the dust, and Tyrak was on his back instantly, grasping hold of his shaven head. The sweaty oil-slicked scalp slipped his grip the first time, but he crooked his elbow around the eoch's neck and took firm hold before yanking his arm upward. The biceps strained then as the giant gasped and struggled, feet and arms drumming in furious protest. A cracking resounded, and Tyrak felt the massive neck give way. The large body went limp as the eoch's excretory organs depleted themselves involuntarily. He lowered the head to the dust slowly, extracting his hand, and rose to his feet.

He stood, gazing up at the shadowed balcony, shielding his eyes from the sun, which was directly over the balcony and in his face.

"Morgolia lord!" he shouted. "How many more of your eoch champions do you wish me to kill before you grant me an audience?"

First there was silence. Then a soft chuckling came from the shadowy balcony. Tyrak saw movement, and a man's shape took form.

"My lord," a clear midpitched voice replied. "I thought to offer you only a small snack to remove the dust of the road from your palate. Now, if you desire, you may enjoy a fuller repast by feasting on my concubines, whom you passed on your way here. They will feed any hungers of the belly you have as well as slake other needs, bathe and wash you in scented oils and waters, and provide you fresh anga-vastras. Then, when you are rested and refreshed, we shall meet again and have words."

The shadowy silhouette turned away, returning to the darkened recesses of the balcony.

Tyrak saw movement nearby and turned at once to see another eoch, also a giant but darker skinned than the first, standing by the archway through which he had been brought to this training area.

"If you will come with me, my lord," said the eoch obsequiously.

Tyrak heard the sound of something heavy scraping on dirt and turned again, just in time to see two other eochs dragging away their fallen comrade.

"My lord," repeated the eoch by the doorway. "If you will accompany me . . ."

Tyrak ran to one of the pillars that supported the roof of the training house. He caught hold of the pillar in a crouching monkey action, landing with all fours, then pulled and kicked himself upward, propelling his body with practiced ease. In a moment, he was on the upper level and vaulting over the railing of the balcony. He landed with a gentle thump on the wooden plank flooring and grinned at the several armed men turning toward him with expressions of surprise. They drew swords and daggers instantly, but he raised his arms carelessly, grinning.

"I wish only to exchange words with the lord of Morgolia," he said, reassuring them.

None of them lowered his blade or moved an inch.

The man who had spoken earlier stepped forward, eyes glinting as he examined Tyrak over the shoulders of his men. "I have heard of your impatience, son of Ugraksh," said the king of Morgolia. "But by your rashness, you deny yourself the pleasures of women, wine, food, and rest."

Tyrak shrugged, ignoring the many blades pointed at him, though one wrong move would cost him his life. "I care not for the pleasures of wine, women, food, or sleep. Time enough for all those when I have sated my first hunger."

The king of Morgolia looked at him speculatively. "And what would that be?"

"To rule the Arrgodi and Mraashk nations," Tyrak said simply.

There was a long pause during which Tyrak could hear the sound of bows stretching as the archers on the far balconies pointed arrows at him. They took aim at his head, neck, heart, liver . . .

Then the lord of Morgolia laughed softly and came forward, brushing aside his men as if they were wheat stalks in a field. They lowered their blades, eyes averted to avoid threatening their master.

The king clapped his hands on Tyrak's dusty shoulders and grinned broadly. "You are a man after my own tastes, Tyrak son of Ugraksh. I think we shall get along very well together."

And he grasped Tyrak's hand, the traditional greeting of warriors, in a grip like a vise, so hard that Tyrak thought his forearm would snap.

"I am Jarsun."

## 5

Jarsun rode with Tyrak through Morgolia. The streets were devoid of people. Even the merchants and bazaars, traders and whores, and people scurrying through the lanes on urgent errands were gone.

Tyrak asked Jarsun why this was so. The men accompanying the king glanced sharply at Tyrak as if expecting his host to order him cut down on the spot for daring to question their master.

But Jarsun only smiled and told him that the citizens had cleared the streets on his orders.

Tyrak marveled at a king who could shut down the business of an entire city simply so he could ride through the streets. He thought of mentioning that such regal arrogance would never be tolerated in Arrgodi or any other grassland nation. Then he recalled that Morgolia was not a republic like most other grassland kingdoms and kept quiet.

"Do you know anything about Morgolia?" Jarsun asked as their horses picked their way along narrow cobbled streets packed on either side with hovels so close to one another that they seemed to share common walls. Some were piled three and four stories high, and they made Tyrak wonder if they might fall at any moment.

He answered his host's question as best as he could: "Only that you take in those who are outlawed and banished by the Burnt Empire."

Jarsun did not nod or acknowledge Tyrak in any way. But there was no mistaking the power of his grip, or the casual yet supremely confident way he spoke, and the sense that he saw, heard, and knew everything there was to know. The sheer power that he exuded was magnetic. Tyrak had never met anyone whose physical appearance so belied his inner power and strength. Pole-thin, tall as a flag post, apparently all skin and bone, yet that grip was an iron vise. He wondered idly how difficult it would be to kill Jarsun in hand-to-hand combat. He assessed every man he met the same way; it was the reason he had been able to dispatch the eoch so quickly — he had already noted the giant slightly favoring one knee during the long walk through Jarsun's palace.

Jarsun's voice was neither deep nor high-pitched; it was pleasant to the ear and clear enough to be understood even when he spoke quietly, which was almost all the time. In fact, he spoke so quietly that Tyrak kept feeling the need to come closer, lean closer. He found himself having to resist this urge several times as they descended the winding hillside road. It would take him a long while to realize that this was precisely why Jarsun spoke thus, compelling others to be quiet in order to hear what he said. Powerful men exerted their power in such ways.

"Unlike most other city-states in Arthaloka, Morgolia was never the name of a kingdom. It was the name given to the place where exiles and outcasts converged."

Tyrak caught a note of deep bitterness in this last announcement. He listened with interest. It seemed Jarsun had a more personal stake in this impromptu lecture than Tyrak had realized at first.

"So where do these exiles and outcasts — *Morgol,* to use the ancient Ashcrit word — go, if they wish to survive, let alone thrive or prosper? Where can they seek employment, residence, enrichment, mates, companionship, and all the rest that life has to offer?"

Without waiting for Tyrak's answer, Jarsun raised a wiry, muscled hand and gestured at the city. "Morgolia."

Tyrak blinked. "You mean . . . these are all outcasts?" he asked, astonished.

"Indeed," Jarsun said. "There is an unspoken rule among Morgol everywhere. When asked point-blank what their affiliation is, they must always answer 'Morgol.' For if they deny even this title, then what do they have left to cling to? You will find that they will always answer 'Morgol' and that they will do so with great pride, even if it means imprisonment or penalty of death." He gestured again at the houses they were passing, less overcrowded than the ones on earlier streets, evidently a slightly less impoverished section of the city. "This is their last refuge. Those who become Morgol understand that the title is more than a caste or a nationality. It defines a person."

Tyrak mused on the implications. "Your entire kingdom is made up of criminals, exiles, outcasts?" He was more than a little shocked: he was, after all, not merely a warrior but a warrior king. It was bred into his blood.

Jarsun laughed. "Yes. That is what I have been explaining to you, my Arrgodi friend. But do not fret, we shall not make you impure through contact with us. Remember, the code of the warriors tells us that we are united despite gender, stature, class, or nationality of birth."

So it did. Tyrak tried to work through the politics of this situation, then gave up. It was too complicated. And as a prince brought up at the helm of power, he was as self-assured about his superiority by birth and entitlement as any highborn Arrgodi; the very notion of being surrounded by an entire city full of outcasts made him . . . queasy.

Something else occurred to him, something that his war-oriented mind found easier to grasp: geography. "But then how did you build this city?"

Jarsun raised a finger, correcting him. "You mean to say, Where did I build this city? For the how is self-evident — it was built as cities usually are. But the location was the main issue. For where do outcasts go? What place is given unto them? The short answer: none. Nowhere. That is why I had to take this land and carve it out of the neighboring states to make my own."

Jarsun turned his horse abruptly to face Tyrak. "Until now, we have had to fight and fend off the repeated attacks and attempts by those same neighbors to take back what they consider their land. Long have I waited patiently, building my strength, expanding my forces, gathering more and more Morgol to me, anticipating this day. Now, at last, I am ready to put into action the next phase of my great plan. To prove Morgolia itself as not just the great city it already is, but as the capital of a great kingdom, the greatest, most powerful kingdom that ever existed in Eastern Arthaloka. This city that you see around us will be only a minor township in the great kingdom of Morgolia that I am about to build, my friend. A minor township!"

Tyrak nodded, impressed. "A great ambition."

Jarsun laughed. "Far more than just ambition. A reality, awaiting the right moment to be unleashed. And that moment is now."

He pointed at Tyrak. "All that remained was for one final piece of the plan to move into place. And that piece arrived at my doorstep today."

Tyrak frowned, trying to understand what he meant. Piece? Arrived?

Jarsun laughed again, this time echoed by his entourage. "Now that you have arrived, I can put into motion my campaign to build the greatest empire the world has ever seen. And you, Tyrak son of Ugraksh, shall be its chief architect!"

# 6

Before Tyrak could say a word, Jarsun turned the head of his horse and rode the rest of the way up a steep winding road to the top of a high hill — the highest point in Morgolia, he realized as he followed.

On his approach to the city, he had seen that it was built on a virtually desolate plain, with sharp crags and dips. He assumed that Jarsun wished to go to the top of this rise to afford him a bird's-eye view of the city. He wanted to tell his host not to bother. He had seen enough of Morgolia. Its squalor and filth, the crowded narrow lanes with houses almost falling over one another, the stench of human lives, the poverty, the lack of public sanitation . . . It had taken every ounce of his willpower not to turn his horse and ride back — or away.

He had obeyed the sage Vessa's orders, he had come to Morgolia and met with Jarsun. But apart from big claims, the king did not seem to have much to offer him. How could a lord of outcasts do anything to further Tyrak's prospects? How could Tyrak take help from such a person, no doubt an exile himself? It pained his sense of self-worth and highborn stature.

No. This was a mistake. He would listen to a little more, then slip away at first opportunity, seeking alliance and assistance elsewhere. There were other enemies of the Arrgodi, other political forces seeking to further their own causes and careers. Eastern Arthaloka was a seething hotbed of politics and ambition. It would not be difficult to find allies.

Then he topped the rise, close behind Jarsun's mount, and caught his breath.

The king of Morgolia laughed as he turned and took in Tyrak's stunned expression. He used his reins and his feet to expertly reverse his horse, making her back away at a steady clip so he could continue looking at Tyrak, who came forward, unable to help the dazed look on his face.

"Well, Prince of Arrgodi, whatever you were expecting today, I do not think this was it!" And Jarsun turned and said in a louder tone to the large gathering awaiting them on the hilltop: "What do you say, my friends?"

A resounding chorus of *nays* and gruff laughter greeted his query.

Tyrak stilled his horse and as he looked at the crowd on the promontory overlooking the city. Some he recognized at once from various concords of Arrgodi nations; others he identified by a sigil stitched onto a breastplate or garment; and others he could not identify at all but knew at once, from their posture, attire, and bearing, to be rulers or lieges of some standing. There were about two dozen people collected at that spot, and his head reeled as he gazed at each one in turn, their diverse faces grinning or smirking in response to his stunned expression.

Monarchs.

They were all kings or barons, every last one of them.

They dismounted, and their horses were led away by waiting hands.

"Yes, Tyrak," Jarsun said, as if reading his mind. "You see gathered here today the most powerful caucus of Morgol in all Arthaloka. These are all leaders of various groups of outcasts who have sworn allegiance with me. Together we propose to build the greatest empire this mortal realm has ever seen."

"With you as emperor, of course," Tyrak said cunningly, showing he had not been completely disarmed by Jarsun's well-mounted surprise. He grinned boyishly to undercut his sarcasm.

Jarsun laughed. "I like this boy more and more. Yes, of course I shall be emperor. For not only do I control a substantial fighting force now, but every exile and criminal — even those who feel unwanted or unassimilated in any community in the Burnt Empire — will gladly ally with me at a moment's notice. Do you know how many of Arrgodi's communities are made up of such people?"

Tyrak nodded, conceding the point. Castes were not ironclad and were never intended to be so. But sadly, those who fell between them or did not satisfy the requirements of their peers were often shunted aside or openly shunned by their own, leading to discontent and inequity. He had often used these inequities to serve his own selfish purposes. Jarsun was doing the same but on a much, much greater scale. He sought to recruit every exile in the world! That would give him the greatest army ever assembled, not to mention spies and allies secretly embedded within every court, every community, every army.

"And where do these fine chieftains come in?" he asked, indicating the collection of Morgol royalty assembled around them. "What do they get in return for supporting you?"

Jarsun smiled. "Each has his own motive for allying with me. Everyone gets his fair share. As will you. For instance, you want to rule the Arrgodi and Mraashk nations, do you not?"

Tyrak swallowed, trying not to show his eagerness and almost succeeding. "I could do that on my own," he said, trying to act nonchalant.

Jarsun chuckled and beckoned someone forward. "I think not."

Tyrak started as Bane and Uaraj appeared, smiling cautiously in greeting. "Well met, Lord Tyrak," they said in turn. "We have always served you loyally, and will continue to serve you."

"In exchange for their own fiefdoms, of course," Jarsun added slyly.

Tyrak stared with growing rage at his war advisor and second in command. "You are both working for Jarsun? And you spied on me all this while?"

Their faces lost color, and they stepped back, wary of Tyrak's temper. Jarsun interceded.

"Calm down, my young friend. Were you to try to root out all my spies from your midst, you would be left with a very poor fighting force indeed. Speaking of which," he said, smartly changing the topic and diverting Tyrak's attention, "I believe you have almost no fighting force left now. Is that not so, Bane?"

Bane nodded nervously, keeping his eyes on Tyrak and his distance from his former master as he spoke. "Aye, sire. The army has disbanded. The Marauders are falling apart, losing men daily. And Vasurava has been given charge of Arrgodi's security."

"Vasurava?" Tyrak's anger was instantly diverted, his outrage roused. "How can Vasurava be given charge of my forces? He is not even an Arrgodi! He is Mraashk!"

He moved toward Bane as he spoke, his first impulse as always to batter and punish the source of the news that caused him discomfiture.

Jarsun stepped forward smoothly. While lean and lithe, he moved with a pantherlike grace that spoke of powerful oiled muscles and a wealth of experience in close combat. Combined with his intense, pinpoint eyes and quiet tone, this marked him as a lethal predator who had no need of showing off his strength in order to subjugate.

Tyrak instinctively took a step back. It was the first time he had ever done that for any man.

"All is well. This is to our advantage. You can claim that he deviously insinuated himself into your father's good graces . . ." Jarsun paused, keeping his eyes fixed on Tyrak's, unblinking. "Or your mother's bedchamber . . ."

Tyrak flinched, his fists coming up at once. Ever accustomed to expressing his anger at the instant it flared, he was not able to master it quickly enough. Jarsun's insulting insinuation coming immediately on the heels of Bane's disturbing news was too much for his limited self-control. He exploded.

Jarsun caught his fists in grips as tight as iron vises, pinning them to his sides without so much as a downward glance. He moved closer, close enough that Tyrak could smell the pungent, sweet odor of tambul nut on his breath. "A king uses whatever he must, whatever he can, in order to further his cause. I speak not of violating your mother's body, merely sullying her name. The accusation would be leveled at your enemy. Is it truly so hard to swallow?"

Tyrak stared at the piercing grey eyes that looked down at him from a height at least half a foot taller than his own. He recalled an old battle master cuffing him as a boy and telling him that the greatest warriors needed not height or great musculature or even elaborate weaponry, that in fact they were almost always short, lithe, small-built, and deceptively childlike in appearance. *'Tis not what you have, 'tis what you do with it that counts,* old Vendook had said, before hawking and spitting a gob of phlegm in the dust of the practice field, beside Tyrak's left ear. Tyrak had learned everything he knew about hand-to-hand fighting from that old master, before he had finally bested him on the wrestling mat and broken his neck. He had been fourteen years old and had never had a fighting master thereafter.

Now it seemed he had one.

He looked into the eyes of Jarsun and understood what this new master was telling him.

He was not truly insulting his mother. He was merely laying out a strategy. One that would help him achieve the first step in his road to dominating the Arrgodi and Mraashk.

Jarsun was telling him how to become king.

# 7

"Dvivida, Pundra, Dhenuka, Karava, Baka, Kirata, Preshnak, Ladislew, Musthika, Karusha, Akriti, Meghavahana, Bhauma, Ranga, Dantavakra, Bane, Arista, Paundraka, Uaraj, Bhishmaka, Bhagadatta, Purujit, Kesi, Trnavarta, Agha . . ."

The list of names of Morgol chieftains reeled off the tongues of Jarsun's aides, Henus and Malevol, in quick succession like honey off a bear's tongue. Even Tyrak was impressed. He guessed that such a show of royal strength was rarely seen outside of a grassland summit. They must represent an army of outcasts equivalent to the whole of Eastern Arthaloka. His pulse quickened. If Tyrak could in fact take over Arrgodi and Mraashk, then add Jarsun's Morgol army of criminals, quarter-castes, and other embedded supporters awaiting his command to rise up, they could easily overtake the grasslands, or all Eastern Arthaloka, or even, perhaps, all realms not yet controlled by the Burnt Empire. Tyrak felt a rush of joy and power such as he had never experienced before — not since the days when he had discovered the joys of slaughter on the battlefield.

Henus and Malevol, each speaking from what appeared to be a carefully rehearsed and orchestrated script, spelled out the domains each king or queen would govern as part of the agreement signed jointly before Jarsun. Tyrak, unable to write his name clearly in Ashcrit or even commonspeak, had let one of the aides put his name to the accord and pressed his thumb into it, ignoring the pretty calligraphy of the others. What use did a king have for writing, art, music, and all that nonsense? He desired only power. And for what Jarsun was offering him, he would have given the Krushan king his own mother's corpse if he desired, not merely her name sullied by rumor. What use was a mother who did not stand up for her son, after all?

He had hardened his heart to all back home on hearing the news from Arrgodi. They were carrying on as if he had been an oppressor and tyrant, not the liberating hero he truly was. The fools! Allowing Vasurava to run Arrgodi! Were they utterly blind and brainless?

After the formalities were done, Jarsun rose again.

"My friends," he said. "We are all of an accord. Time now to cast the die. To start out upon the long path that will take us to our shared destiny."

He gestured to his aides. Malevol, the larger and stronger-bodied of the two, picked up what appeared to be a sigil on a pole. He raised it high above his head, muscles heaving, and waved it to and fro. The red flag flashed in the evening sunlight, probably visible across the length and breadth of the city below.

At once, in response, a great roar rose up from below.

Jarsun gestured to the assembled allies. "Come, see for yourself the launch of our great juggernaut."

Tyrak joined the rest at the edge of the promontory, careful not to step too close to the rim. He did not trust any of his new allies enough not to suspect them of trying to shove him over. After all, the fewer of them there were, the greater each one's kingdom. But there seemed to be none of that petty rivalry here. Seeing how politely and graciously they moved and made space for one another, he instantly felt ashamed of his churlish behavior. These were real rulers already. He was merely a rough boy who liked killing and power so much, he wanted no one above him to tell him what not to do.

He caught Jarsun watching him with that sly knowing gleam in his cat-grey eyes. He nodded curtly, but he knew that Jarsun had caught his moment of self-loathing and weakness. The Krushan seemed to see deep within his soul with those eyes.

The next moment, he looked down, and forgot everything else.

Morgolia was being set ablaze.

Riders were racing through the city, riding like madmen with flaming torches in hand, setting light to houses, rooftops, hayricks, wagons . . .

Already a dozen fires were blazing furiously. After the heat of the day, the close-packed houses were lighting like tinder sticks. Soon, the whole city would be a morass of smoke and ruin.

"But why?" he said, before he realized he was speaking aloud. "Why do you do such a thing?"

Heads turned to glance at him. Several faces wore sardonic, sympathetic expressions for the young novice who had yet to learn so much about politics and kingship. Others glanced scornfully at him before turning away with a shake of their heads. He knew that there were some who questioned if he even deserved to stand among them in this alliance. After all, he was the only one who was merely a crown prince, and a shamed and self-banished one at that, not a ruler or baron in his own right. But Jarsun had no such contempt or scorn on his smooth features.

"I told you, Morgolia is not a city or a kingdom, it is a word that means exile. They who do not belong anywhere. This gathering of hovels you see below" — he gestured expansively — "was merely a temporary refuge. Not a permanent abode."

"But still . . ." Tyrak wrestled with words, trying to frame his thoughts in a way that would not make him seem too ignorant and naive. "How could you burn your own houses? Your own people?"

Several of the gathered rulers snickered. Tyrak turned red with anger and embarrassment. Jarsun put a hand on his shoulder, reassuring. "The people are safely away, all the warriors and fighters in our forces."

Tyrak swallowed and turned his head, listening. "But . . . I can hear them screaming . . . on the wind." He glanced down. "You can see them too. There are people there . . . dying in the fire."

Jarsun shrugged. "Only the very young, the very old, the infirm."

One of the older kings, Bellicor, grunted and quaffed a large goblet of wine, the spill staining his white beard crimson. "Noncombatant women, children, old 'uns, infants, sick men . . . of no use to an army on the move."

Tyrak stared at Jarsun, who nodded. "From now on, we are an invading force. Ever moving, unstoppable, undefeatable. Like the great stone god Jaggernaut, who was a relentless force of nature moving ever onward. By killing their families, their loved ones, burning their houses, leaving them nothing to come back to, I remove every distraction my soldiers might have in the campaign ahead. Now they have nothing left to do but fight, win, destroy, and if they triumph, rebuild a new city, raise new families. This is the Krushan way. First destroy. Then rebuild."

"One must burn the grass in order to grow it anew," said a younger, sly-looking monarch named Meghavahana who kept fingering a large emerald ring on his heart finger.

Jarsun continued speaking quietly.

"Once the city is burned, we shall descend again and take our places at the helm of our forces assembled outside the gates of the city. My army will lead, with the others bringing up the flanks. We shall cut a swath across Arthaloka like the greatest herd of uks ever seen, bulls rampaging across the land, and when we pass, we shall leave none standing. We shall take what we please, do as we will. We are warriors, one and all."

Tyrak nodded, understanding. And now that he understood, he could even take pleasure in the sound of the screams, the cries and wails of the dying, desperate abandoned ones. As the smoke rose and the city burned, and the kings around him drank and jested and bickered and talked, he felt a sense of pride and accomplishment. To burn his own city, put his own weak and infirm to death, what an epic warrior and commander was Jarsun! He had never known his like before. He looked at his new friend, admiringly, fondly, and felt proud that he had made such an ally. He found himself unable to take his eyes off this magnificent man, this incredible leader.

Jarsun glanced at him from time to time and smiled slowly.

When it was time, they descended the hill, brushing aside the stench of burned corpses and houses. Horses bore them through the ruined streets. Tyrak gazed in morbid fascination at the sights that met his eyes: mothers and infants clutching one another in the last throes of agony, burned black. Old men sprawled across pavements, infants curled into fetal balls in the agony of burning. Everywhere he looked, he saw a charnel house, burned corpses leering down at them from the scorched remains, twisted bones and cracked skeletons oozing putrid juices. The kings rode on carelessly, the hooves of their horses crushed the scorched skeletons underfoot, sending up a terrible percussion as they galloped through the devastated city. The Morgol chieftains laughed.

Tyrak thought it was easy for them to laugh. These were only low castes to them. He wondered how they might feel if it had been their cities burned, their women and children and old 'uns trampled underfoot. He thought they might not be laughing as generously then. He caught Jarsun glancing at the backs of the heads of the other kings and knew that the Krushan was thinking the same thing.

*He does this to prove that he will go to any lengths to succeed,* Tyrak thought with a flash of insight. *For only through his own cruelty and example does a leader command the fealty of his followers. By showing how far he can go, Jarsun has outmatched them all before the war has even begun. Now they know that they dare not cross him. For what might not a man do when he is willing to slaughter his own in order to succeed?*

He smiled secretly to himself, pleased to have glimpsed this aspect of Jarsun's strategy.

He spurred his horse and rode on, following his new teacher and guide. To the ends of the earth if required.

# 8

Tyrak bellowed a warning as he galloped forward and threw himself off his horse.

He fell upon the pair of assassins, bringing them to the ground, where all three of them sprawled, the two murderers struggling, twisting, vying furiously to stick their knives into him as they rolled in the dust. He tasted blood and knew one of their knives had slashed his lip and cheek. He ignored it and grasped the assassin's neck.

With some surprise, he found it was a girl, her head shaven and disguised with a scarf. She bit into his forearm, drawing blood. He roared and threw himself back, slamming himself onto the ground as he used the force to jam her head in a deathlock. He felt her neck crack satisfyingly and released her just as the second assassin flew at him with a dagger curved like an old bull's horn.

This one was barely a boy. They struggled in the dust for moments, then Tyrak swung him down with a sudden jarring impact, smashing his shoulder and loosening his grip. With a second swift action, he rammed the hilt of the curved blade backward, through the assassin's own chest, punching through the bone and into his heart. With a moan and a gurgle of blood, the boy died.

Tyrak rose to his feet, looking around warily, ready for more attackers. But there were none. Jarsun dismounted from his horse, examining the dead assassins quickly. Behind him, the city they had just ransacked echoed with the clash of fighting and the screams of the dying. Tyrak leaned against a brick wall broken by a downed elephant. The beast's tusks lay close enough for him to touch. The house into which it had fallen lay exposed to the sky, filled with muddy water from a city cistern that had broken and spilled nearby. Chaos reigned.

"Garaharis," Jarsun said, even as Henus and Malevol came up at a gallop, dismounting and joining their master. They stood with swords drawn, ready to fend off any further enemies, but it appeared that there were none left. After a three-day siege, the city had betrayed itself: Jarsun's Morgol rose up on the inside to slay their lords and neighbors before opening the gates to let in the emperor to whom they had secretly sworn allegiance. "Do you know what this means?"

Tyrak shook his head, busy breathing. He was almost too tired to stand on his own. He had no recollection of when he had last slept, and only a hazy memory of eating some kind of roasted meat the previous night, or was it two nights ago?

His body ached all over, bleeding from a dozen or more superficial wounds, and his hip felt as if it had been dislocated and reset badly.

He had lost count of how many he had slain, and he knew neither the name of the city they had just ransacked nor the kingdom. There had been too many cities and kingdoms these past several days. Life had turned into one battle after another, siege followed by battle, battle followed by skirmish, rally followed by attack . . . War was his only food and drink, rest a forgotten friend, sleep a lost lover.

"It means my fame has spread to the farthest corners of Arthaloka," Jarsun said proudly, taking the scarf of the assassin as a souvenir. He tucked it into his waistband, along with the curved dagger, after he had wiped it clean on the dead boy's garments.

Neither boy nor girl looked older than ten years, and their striking resemblance made it obvious they were siblings. It was their apparent frailty and youth that had enabled them to approach this close to Jarsun, clutching one another and stumbling along, pretending to be weeping survivors. But Tyrak had not been fooled. He trusted children least of all. After all, had he himself not been a butcher of a boy, remorseless in killing?

"If Garahar wants me dead badly enough to send assassins this far south," Jarsun mused, "then it means our campaign is making them quake even across the Coldheart Mountains. They fear that once I am done subjugating the subcontinent, I will turn my eyes further northwest." He grinned, displaying blood-flecked teeth. "And indeed I shall. But I shall not stop at Garahar. I shall go farther, to the limits of the civilized world. Beyond Garahar lies the Burnt Empire and the cities of Jashin, Karchi, Farmush . . ." Jarsun reeled off a litany of names.

Tyrak frowned at the unfamiliar foreign names, though he recognized many of them from poring over his father's old maps as a boy. Geography had always been of great interest to him: he understood the concept of land and the fact that he who dominated the land owned all that stood upon it. That was true kingship, not this munshi's business of taxation and levies. *What good is it to call a place your own if you cannot walk the land and command the obedience of those who live upon it?* his father had growled once at his advisors, back when Ugraksh had been a warrior king, not just an old man governing a dwindling domain.

He swayed slightly, lightheaded and disoriented. Jarsun looked up at him and said gently, "My friend, you deserve a rest. You have saved my hide for the third time in as many days."

Tyrak shrugged self-deprecatingly. "Someone has to keep an eye on our future emperor."

Jarsun smiled his quiet smile. "And you have done that very well. So well, in fact, that I think it is time for you to rest those tired eyes on something more comely."

Tyrak frowned, unable to fathom Jarsun's meaning.

Jarsun clapped his hand on Tyrak's shoulder, making him wince: he had been slashed there by a passing spear. "Come, let us leave my Morgol to enjoy the spoils of war. It is time I showed you what we are fighting for."

They rode away from the ransacked city, the orchestra of cries and screams dying away in the distance. Tyrak was too tired to even ask where they were going. He let his horse follow Jarsun's, noting that except for the omnipresent Henus and Malevol, no one else came with them. That was unusual in the extreme.

After three days' hard riding, they rode over a final rise and Jarsun unfurled the vastra he had wrapped around his face to protect his visage as well as conceal his identity, on his aides' advice. "Behold," he said.

Tyrak stared at the city below. Incomplete though it was, little more than a skeleton partly fleshed and barely clothed, its epic ambition, architectural magnificence, and sheer audacity was breathtaking. He had seen nothing like it, nor heard of such a city. Arodya, Mirilus, all the mythical cities paled before the freshness and beauty of this city rising up from a desolate wilderness. *He has built the heaven of the stone gods here in the mortal realm,* Tyrak thought. And then, dazed, he spoke the thought aloud: "It is Swargaloka."

Jarsun laughed and clapped him on his back. "I call it Grarij. It shall be the new capital city of the new Harvanya. Center of the world."

They rode together through the wide avenues of the city, Tyrak marveling at how precisely each broad road ran from north to south, east to west. He gazed up in wonder at the vaulting towers, the great mansions, the superbly carved facades, the sculpted pillars and arched windows, the sheer opulence and luxury of the place. Every street was a beehive of activity. They passed workers carrying materials, hammering, sawing, cutting, planing, polishing, raising pillars, carving . . .

"Vakaronus himself must have designed it," Tyrak said, referring to the architect of the stone gods. He had never seen such house designs or patterns before.

Jarsun pointed out the hills rising around the city, upon each of which watchtowers were being built, connected by a great wall that formed an enormous circle. A forest of Lodhra trees overran the hills and surrounding countryside, making the city itself near invisible unless one approached within a hundred yards of the tree-protected wall, while the towers could spy anyone approaching from many miles away.

The hills were almost high enough to be considered mountains. Jarsun explained that although this meant that once an enemy broke through the walled cordon, they would be able to look down upon the city itself, the deft manner in which the architects had used the natural wood cover and rock formations afforded numerous defensive points for the city's defenders. And of course, no enemy could ever come close enough in the first place.

Moreover, because the city was at the site of the ancient hermitage of Stone Priest Gotram, he of great fame, it was a highly auspicious location as well. "After all"—Jarsun grinned—"even we criminals do care about such things."

Finally, they came to a hamlet nestled in the very center of the city, with an artificial lake and a great palace under construction overlooking the lake, with gardeners already hard at work laying out sumptuous gardens around the building complex. Here the construction was busiest, and the richest materials were in evidence.

They dismounted as Tyrak looked up at the richest palace he had ever seen. It made his father's palace at Arrgodi look like the oversized cowshed it had once been.

"Home," said Jarsun, gesturing in a manner that suggested that it was as much Tyrak's as his own.

# 9

Tyrak was wonderstruck by the beauty of Jarsun's palace and his rising capital city.

The Krushan had been right. It was one thing to be fighting a vicious war campaign for supremacy of the subcontinent; it was wholly another thing to see some of the fruits of that campaign already being polished and prepared for one's repast. After the brutality and relentless bloodshed of the battlefield, this was like coming home.

Tyrak wished he could pick up this entire palace and city and carry it on his back all the way to distant Arrgodi. How the Arrgodi would ogle and exclaim. Clansmen would come from thousands of miles away to gape at such sights. The simple shepherds and cowherds of the Arrgodi nation had no comprehension that such luxury and beauty could even exist, let alone be possessed by such as they.

*And here am I,* Tyrak thought, *allied with the emperor of the civilized world.*

For he had no doubt that Jarsun's campaign would succeed. Already their victories were legendary, their onslaught relentless and unopposed. Or, rather, they were opposed but feebly, futilely. No army could stand against the juggernaut-like progress of Jarsun's great coalition.

Even he had no idea exactly how many numbers his friend and ally commanded; where the king of Morgolia was concerned, truth and rumor commingled freely to produce that inseparable compound one could only call legend. All that was certain was that the juggernaut rolled on, and day by day the greatest empire the world had ever seen was being stitched together like a patchwork quilt held tightly by Jarsun's brilliantly conceived network of affiliations and alliances.

Many Arrgodi kings had held great war ceremonies, going forth with stone priest rituals to lay claim to larger tracts and kingdoms. In time, they had lost all the ground they acquired when other Arrgodi kings did the same. None had ever before had the foresight and political mastery to pull together such a superb coalition of vested interests, each supporting the other in a seemingly impossible yet unquestionably sturdy web of solid structures.

Tyrak had begun to realize that Jarsun's brilliant plan might not just see him seated emperor but keep him on that hallowed throne for generations to come. "Political alliances are the bedrock, military victories the foundation, and the loyalty of the people the structure of a house," Jarsun had said to Tyrak one night over a meal. "An emperor must have all three to stay an emperor."

He did not need to add, *And I do.*

In a sense, Tyrak mused as they reclined on welcoming satin-cushioned seats and were served wine and fruit by comely servants, Jarsun's campaign of conquest was being waged much the same way as his magnificent new capital city was being built. Brilliant architecture executed with painstaking craftsmanship and artistry, by loyal and dedicated workmen.

Tyrak's thoughts were diverted momentarily as two of the most beautiful women he had ever seen approached demurely, clad in luxuriant garments and jewelry that clearly set them apart from the palace staff. Assuming they were Jarsun's wives or concubines, Tyrak averted his eyes. Never one to be shy at ogling another man's women, nevertheless he would never transgress upon the territory of his friend. For the first time in his life, Tyrak had a true companion, the first man he truly respected.

"Tyrak," said Jarsun, "meet Tessi and Prees. They are the jewels of my heart."

Tyrak murmured a rough greeting, sketching a polite namas instead of the formal bow from the waist with palms pressed against each other. He was startled when the two women knelt beside him and began bathing his dusty, chapped feet with warm fragrant rosewater.

"What . . . what are you doing?" he asked.

They looked up at him with doe eyes, openly flirtatious yet politely demure. "Washing your feet, Lord of Arrgodi," they said together in a single singsong chant. Then giggled.

Tyrak looked at Jarsun for explanation. Jarsun grinned. "My daughters speak as eloquently with their eyes as most women do with their tongues. Their eyes are saying that they like you very much. They would be pleased to have you as their husband."

"H-husband?" Tyrak had not stammered since he was a little boy. He sat upright, staring first at the two beautiful girls, then at his host.

"Yes, a legally wedded husband. I would be honored if you would consent to accepting the hand of one of my daughters in marriage and becoming my son-in-law. Tell me, which one do you prefer?"

Jarsun frowned as he tried to evaluate his daughters' assets objectively. "Prees has the best child-bearing hips and lushest body. But Tessi has the sweeter nature." Finally, Jarsun shook his head. "I dote equally on them both. It is impossible for me to choose. You must decide for yourself. Which do you prefer?"

Tyrak swallowed nervously. Both women had finished the ceremonial washing of his feet and were awaiting his answer.

He saw from their pointed glances that while immaculately mannered, they were not shy in the ways that counted. There was mischief in the warm brown eyes of the one with the riper body. And a promise of sweet nights in the more slender girl's cool grey eyes, reminiscent of her father's own steely irises.

He bit his lip, trying to find the right thing to say without causing offense. "Both are so beautiful," he said hesitantly, "I cannot decide . . ."

Jarsun spread his hands. "Then you shall marry both. So be it. It is decided. You are a man of large appetites; my daughters will be more content with one Tyrak than two of any other man. The wedding shall be tonight itself." He clapped his hands, summoning Henus, who was only a few yards away. "Make the arrangements."

"*Tonight?*" asked Tyrak, astonished. This was all happening much too quickly for him to keep pace.

"We do have a war to wage," Jarsun said apologetically, peeling a grape with expert fingers. "After we finish the first phase of our campaign, you shall have leave to enjoy the company of your new wives, I shall see to that myself. But for now, one night will have to suffice. We return to the frontline tomorrow morning. A good commander cannot leave his forces unsupervised too long."

The wedding was a blur of color and pomp and pageantry. Despite the incompleteness of the city, Jarsun was able to put on a display of royal extravagance more fantastic than Tyrak could ever have imagined. The night that followed was mercifully short, rituals and ceremonies taking up most of the moonlight hours. He barely had an hour alone with his new brides, although they wasted no time in making good use of it. He was yawning when he stepped out of his bedchamber at dawn to follow Malevol through the winding corridors.

At the wedding, Jarsun had introduced Tyrak to his son Seratova. Tyrak had barely begun to wonder why, if Jarsun had a son, he was not on the battlefield with them when Jarsun explained that the entire city they had seen, with all its beauty and splendor, was Seratova's doing. "Some are warriors on the field," the father said. "Others build empires out of wood and stone." The implication was self-evident, but there was not a trace of irony or disappointment in Jarsun's tone. He had clearly accepted his son's choice of vocation and was at peace with it.

Even so, Tyrak could not help feeling a surge of jealousy when he clasped hands with the handsome, almost girlish Seratova, whose hands were softer than any man's he had met before, whose hair curled in delicate twirls around his features. He had not known Jarsun had a son at all. Good that he was only an architect, a builder, and an artist, not a warrior.

In his heart and mind, Tyrak had come to think of himself as Jarsun's true son. For the Krushan was in every sense the father he had always desired and never had. The father he respected and loved, and who acknowledged and praised him in return.

*I would give my life for him,* he thought fiercely as they rode out from Grarij the next morning. He loved the man he was following more than he had ever loved anyone or anything before.

He had not protested or debated when Jarsun asked him to marry his daughters, who happened to be beautiful and everything a man could desire, but he would have done so even had they been wart-ridden and unpleasant to look upon. Jarsun had only to ask him to ride his horse off a cliff and Tyrak would have done so without question, trusting that either there would be a river below to break his fall, or that the sacrifice of his life was necessary for his friend's cause. No act was too gruesome, no sacrifice too great.

In the days and weeks that followed, his resolve was put to the test and only strengthened and tempered further, as steel is tempered by fire followed by ice over and over again until the layers of beaten metal bond permanently.

Even Henus and Malevol, perpetual protectors of the emperor and eternally by his side, were hard-pressed to match Tyrak's ability to spot assassins and deflect assaults. No warrior in the coalition fought as fiercely, no warrior risked as much, no leader achieved as many victories.

As ruthless in meting out violence as he was in meeting it head-on, Tyrak grew from the hotheaded Arrgodi prince who first rode into Morgolia into a finely tempered commander of men in battle. Mraashk iron, never known for its temperance, now as solidly bonded as Mithini steel.

Finally a day came when Jarsun turned to him and said, "It is time for you to go and stake your claim to your own domain."

Tyrak knew at once what his father-in-law meant but pretended he did not understand. "*This* is my domain. By your side."

Jarsun slapped him lightly on the cheek, a gentle admonishment. "You would be an emperor's lackey all your life? You are destined to be a *king*, and a king of your own domains. Remember what you asked for when you came to me. The reason why you formed this alliance, signed the accord. All the others have carved out the kingdoms they desired. Only you remain by my side. Now, it is time for you to go home and command the Arrgodi and Mraashk nations."

Tyrak hung his head unhappily. "Please let me stay a while longer."

"If you stay a day longer, you will stay forever," Jarsun said gruffly. He cuffed Tyrak across the ear, too gently to hurt but firm enough to convey his insistence. "Go. Show me your face again only when you have become lord of all Arrgodi. Put what I have taught you to good use. Make me proud."

Tyrak went, his heart aching, and feeling as if he were leaving home to go out into the wilderness, while in fact it was the other way around.

Jarsun watched him go and said softly to Henus and Malevol, who flanked him as always, "We have watered and nourished and nurtured enough. Now let us see whether the seed we sow in Arrgodi shall bear sweet fruit."

# Part Two

## *A Fistful of Arrows,*
## *A Heartful of Dread*

# *Krushita*

~

## 1

KRUSHITA WOKE TO THE shrill keening of a shvan and was instantly alert. The shvan was warning all within range that there was danger approaching.

The call came from far away, too far for anyone else in the caravan to hear. Beside her, Vor stirred and raised his head, ears prickling and fur bristling. Girl and shvan exchanged a look and shared the awareness of imminent threat.

Krushita sat up and looked over at her mother. Aqreen was fast asleep.

Krushita watched her mother sleeping for a moment. She always thought at such times that this was what her mother must have looked like when she was younger, when all her life was still waiting to be explored, her heart filled with the infinite possibilities that lay ahead. In sleep, all her lines and creases eased away, her face smoothing back into the innocence of youth. Aqreen never looked like that by waking light: the past five years had been hard on her, harder by far than on seven-year-old Krushita.

In the early days on the trail, Krushita had often woken to the sound of her mother suppressing muffled sobs as she cried herself to sleep. She had gone to Aqreen and comforted her as best as she could, but pain had a way of working itself through the heart and mind, taking its own winding course. In time, Aqreen had recovered, but a part of her still bore the scars of the betrayal and loss she had suffered. Those were the lines of care that marked her face, like the lines on the well-worn maps carried by the wagon masters, marking the years as surely as those lines marked where people had died in the past. Her mother's face was a map of all the times parts of her had been killed.

Vor had waited patiently. Now, as she started to rise, the shvan rose too, shaking the sleep out of his long, sleek body. The fire had died out sometime in the night, and the air lay cool and still upon the campsite. Krushita rolled up her bedding, knowing she would not find sleep again till she knew why the shvan had cried out. She stepped carefully past her mother to their wagon. Vor was a dark grey shadow beside her in the predawn gloam. The camp was still mostly asleep. The shvan owned by the other drivers were sent out every night to roam free through the desert, traveling in packs and keeping lookout against any dangers. To the best of her knowledge, Vor was the only one who slept in camp.

They stood before the wagon, gazing out into the dark desert. Krushita placed her palm against the side of the wagon. The wood was worn smooth from the gritty desert winds. It had been almost new when Aqreen bought it from a merchant in the traders' market in Western Aquila, exchanging one of her jeweled rings and their two fine horses for it.

Krushita remembered crying at being parted from her horse, which had been barely a foal when her grandfather had surprised her on her first birthday, but the wagon and the team of uks that drew it had become as familiar to her now. This pile of wood had been home to her and her mother these past five years.

The wagon was one of a circle of a hundred other similar vehicles. There were seventy-one such wagon circles in the train. In the five years they had been on the trail, the drivers had fallen into predictable patterns. Those foolish or reckless enough to disregard the rules had been culled out in the first few months. Krushita had witnessed more deaths than she could count. They had left Aquila with over one hundred twenty circles of a hundred wagons each, over twelve thousand wagons in all. After almost two thousand split off to go northward along the eastern coast of the White Desert, they had been left with over ten thousand wagons, all headed for Reygar. Almost a third of that number had been lost en route.

"A train that arrives with half its original number is one that had a good trail," Train Master Bulan had said, turning their two heads to spit twin streams of purple baccan out onto the red sand. They were master of this circle and master of the entire wagon train. Aqreen had paid extra to be in Bulan's circle. The master had a reputation for being honest to a fault, tough on drivers but fair, and for bringing their trains home with minimum loss.

Bulan had insisted on the nightly talks with their circle, and after a few weeks, the other drivers in the circle grew accustomed to them; some, like Krushita, even looked forward to hearing Bulan's nightly trail stories. They had quite a few to tell, and nearly all of them involved fighting and death, both of which Krushita knew a great deal about by now. Some of the other masters delivered the perfunctory cautions required by law, then permitted their circles to feast and party as they wished, even joining in the debauchery themselves. Bulan was always at pains to remind their drivers that the trail was not an adventure, that it was a journey between points, the most perilous journey most of them would ever make in their lives, and they would have the rest of their lives left to feast and party when they reached their destination.

"A little nip at the bottle to help ease the aches of the trail, a few shenanigans from time to time, those are understandable," Bulan had said in their dual voices, each head addressing one half of the circle. "We're all only mortal, after all. To drink yourself into a stupor, or to roll in the back of a wagon with someone else's partner, those are things that might just be indulgences or vices back home in Aquila. But out here on the trail, fifteen thousand miles from Reygar, with all manner of beasts and natural phenomena hungry to do us in, it's plain suicidal. You need food, you need rest, you need some relaxation, within reason. Anything more than that, and the desert does you in."

When some of the drivers had asked, somewhat skeptically, how a single master could expect to maintain such discipline on their own, far away from the laws and enforcers of Aquila, Bulan had offered two separate grins.

"The magisters back in Aquila may convict or forgive, the prisons will feed, clothe, and shelter you, the marshals may be fair or harsh. But out here, the desert never forgives, never relents, never fails to punish. It isn't Bulan you need to fear, me dearies, it's *that*."

They jerked both their heads, indicating the endless darkness beyond the spill of the campfires. "The trail is hungry, ever hungry. It feeds on your urges, encourages them, and when you give in, it reaches out and snatches you up, dragging you out into the darkest part of the desert, where even the shvan fear to go. There is no appealing to the king, or posting bond, or second chances. Just cold, hard death."

The skeptics quieted after that. A few who had still looked arrogantly unconvinced were long gone by now.

That had been sometime in the first few weeks on the trail. Krushita was still just a baby, then, barely two, and everything was still new and foreign to her. She had sat in her mother's lap and, along with the drivers of the one hundred other wagons in their circle, listened to the train master's nightly talk.

Bulan had told the people of their circle that in times past, entire wagon trains were known to have been lost on the trail. Of course, that had been back in the days when the Red and White Deserts hadn't been mapped as thoroughly and the most treacherous regions were still unknown.

The train master had poked a finger of one of their four hands at the map that they had nailed to the side of their wagon. "Back in olden times, they din't have no modern maps like this, all water sources and whatnot marked out so nice and properlike." They gestured. "Oh, they had *maps,* mind you. But they was barely sketches, showing only the biggest landmarks and cities. You could travel *years* without knowing if you were headed in the right direction or not. Olden times maps, if you could call 'em that, would just have the word *BEWARE* written across them. Whether that meant savage beasts, firestorms, or desert dragons . . . that was for *you* to find out."

Krushita recalled those nightly lectures by the trail master with fondness. Tough and overbearing as they had seemed in those early weeks to her wide-eyed, more innocent younger self, she knew now that Bulan was only trying to keep them safe and alive. The months and then the years that followed had proven the master's nightly advice, rulings, and warnings to be invaluable. Those who had ignored Bulan — or worse, scoffed — had paid the price. The Reygistan Trail was littered with their remains. Others who had listened only halfheartedly, failing to follow their rules or panicking when the moment of danger came, were long gone too.

*The trail claims its price,* as Bulan often said. *The Red Desert forgets but never forgives.*

The train master was also awake. Krushita had sensed their presence but had given them time to make their own assessment. She knew they had sensed, rather than heard, the distant warning cry of the shvan that had awoken her.

Now she moved toward their wagon.

## 2

Bulan was standing outside the circle, facing outward. Krushita ducked under the interlocked swingletrees of two wagons, both the property of the train master, and stepped outside the circle to join him.

One head swiveled on the master's knotted neck to look at her. The mouth grunted by way of greeting. One enormous hand reached out to greet Vor as the shvan sidled up to the master's trunk-sized legs, sniffing with interest. Another hand patted the beast's head. Shvan allowed only a few select individuals to touch them, something most people were loath to do: that plush fur could transform into needle sharp spikes in an instant. Bulan was one of the accepted ones, like Krushita. They were pack.

In a third enormous gnarled hand, Bulan held a battered bowl, which steamed lightly in the chill morning. Krushita wrinkled her nose at the awful smell. She had grown accustomed to the unusual eating habits of the myriad species and cultures that traveled in the train by now, but she would never be able to understand how some dishes and concoctions could be consumed by anyone.

"Won't offer ye some," Bulan said as one of their mouths took a sip, "but you know you're welcome to help yeself."

Krushita resisted the impulse to shudder at the thought of actually drinking that vile-smelling fluid. "Thanks," she said.

They stood together for a moment in companionable silence.

"Trouble's coming," she said at last.

Bulan nodded. "Dunno what it is, though," they said. "Can't be folk, or the pack would have taken up the cry."

Krushita had noted this as well. Usually, when a shvan smelled, heard, or sensed something unusual out in the desert and sent up a cry, the pack would instantly join in. With over fifty thousand of the creatures roving together, that made for a powerful clamor.

She stared out into the faint gloaming that heralded the coming dawn, her eyes losing focus as she allowed herself to slip into a half-awake, half-dreaming state. She knew that Bulan or anyone else watching her body would see her pupils shrink to pinpoints, while her mind traveled outward, seeking the minds of any sentient beings around.

After a moment's questing, she found a buzzard drifting on air currents high above, satiated from having fed only the night before. The buzzard was a carrion bird dedicated to only two things: flying and feeding. It was an easy one to ride, and she slipped into its head without any resistance, just a brief moment of adjustment and a lurch in her belly as she stared out of its eyes, looking down from a height of almost two thousand feet.

The desert sprang alive through the buzzard's dark-adapted vision, and she could see as clearly as in daylight.

The wagon train lay directly below her, a pattern of circles overlapping to form one large circle. She grew aware of hundreds of other buzzards riding the high currents around her, stacked at varying heights depending on who was hungriest. She had ridden buzzards before and knew that the birds, while loners, often flew in apparent flocks when following a sufficiently large food source. The wagon train was a rich one by desert standards; all the buzzards around were fat and lazy from feasting for the past five years.

She overrode the initial surprise and resistance from the buzzard, forcing it to flap its wings and fly northward, away from its bountiful traveling larder. The other buzzards paid it no heed; more feasting for them.

The wagon train fell behind almost instantly, lost in the vast, seemingly infinite expanse of red sand. Then there was nothing but emptiness for as far as she could see, even with razor-sharp buzzard eyes. But she could smell life everywhere: buzzards were among the only birds that had a highly developed sense of smell.

It always amazed her at such times how much life there was even out here, in this seemingly sterile wasteland. There were small and large creatures of numerous species living upon, above, and below the sand. There was even water to be found in the forbiddingly armored, fat fronds of the dull magenta sabbar plants that grew low and wide in patches. Almost invisible to most species, they were easily detectable to shvan and other desert fauna like the buzzards.

About thirty miles from the train camp, she glimpsed the shvan pack, a large furry mass that resembled a living, moving carpet. It undulated slowly, moving in a large circle centered around the train. Smaller splinter groups dotted the circumference of the circle, communicating through smell and occasional hoots and cries as they formed an irregular perimeter guarding over their owners and their belongings. She probed the mind of the shvan pack, a hive awareness that shared emotions in a manner not unlike a human crowd.

The pack was uneasy but unsure of the cause.

They sensed that something was out there, something threatening and imminent, but could not make sense of what it was exactly.

This in itself didn't mean much: shvan, for all their fierce loyalty and ability to ape human behavior, weren't particularly intelligent. They saw the world in fairly simplistic terms. Anything unknown was a potential threat and to be feared until it proved itself to be benign or friendly. They might be responding to almost anything. There was no real sense of alarm or emergency in their shared consciousness.

Krushita probed further outward, seeking the individual shvan who had raised the first alarm.

She was surprised to find it much farther away, almost a dozen miles from the pack or even the splinter groups. It was unusual for shvan to roam individually. Even shvan who had been exiled from the pack for one reason or another usually tagged behind the pack, hoping against all odds for forgiveness. Eventually these loners gave up, lay down, and waited to die.

This shvan was no outcast or exile.

If anything, she was a prima, one of the group of alphas that dominated and controlled the pack.

The prima was running a scouting mission, on the orders of the other primas. Krushita could feel her pride in being selected for such an important task, as well as her fear and unease at being on her own. She could still feel and sense the pack, and they her, but physically, she was on her own, cut off from immediate help, and she was terrified.

Krushita remained in the shvan's head, looking out through her feral eyes as she scoured the desert, seeking out a clue to the strange presence she had sensed only a short while earlier. It had been that presence that had prompted her to cry out the warning. The pack had not taken it up, only because they could make no sense of her call. She had not signaled any of the usual sounds that indicated a predator or even strangers. She had simply cried out once, saying roughly the equivalent of *I don't know what, and I'm not sure, but there may be something here that scares me!*

Krushita then tried something she had never attempted before: she remained in the mind of the shvan while also maintaining her hold on the mind of the buzzard high above. She always established this dual tether when switching minds, but that was only for the brief time it took to take hold of the new mind. This was the first time she was riding two hosts at the same time.

A sensation of nausea passed over her as the contrasting viewpoints and minds of human, bird, and beast collided, the shared views from three different sets of eyes disorienting enough to cause all three some discomfort.

She sensed Bulan putting out one hand to steady her human body as she swayed backward, keeping her from falling back against the master's wagon wheel, which was taller than her seven-year-old self. She made a note to sit down before attempting this again in future.

Then she exerted her will and took the shvan's and bird's minds, melding them together by sheer force.

One final moment of startlement, then she was viewing two points of view simultaneously, sharing sensations, sights, smells, knowledge, processing it all through two animal and one human consciousness.

Yes.

Something was out there.

It was close, and it was big and very strange.

And it was waiting.

Biding its time.

But what was it?

The shvan prima sensed a change in the air temperature, the fur on the right side of her haunches bristling instantly to point northeastward, the direction from which the temperature change had been detected.

Krushita turned the buzzard's bald head in that direction, gazing miles farther than the desert-bound shvan could see.

Dawn was creeping across the world, the eastern sky lightening faintly. Sunrise was only a short while away.

A speck caught the buzzard's keen sight.

She flew in that direction, beating the large wings slowly to move against the current, which was attempting to blow her sideways.

The speck vanished for a moment, then reappeared as she flew a mile, then two miles closer.

# 3

Almost fifteen miles away from the wagon camp, she finally glimpsed something.

An object was moving roughly southwestward.

Roughly, because the object wasn't making a beeline for the camp, but appeared to be undulating in a zigzag course that seemed insane in an environment where even a bit of wasted energy was precious. Whatever the thing was, it was not concerned with conserving energy like most desert denizens. It was more concerned about subterfuge.

The pattern of movement was one of the things that had confused the shvan prima. No predator she had ever encountered moved in such a pattern in the desert. The deadliest ones either lay in wait, then pounced on their prey, or ran hell for broke and chased them down.

What was this thing doing?

More importantly, what *was* this thing?

Krushita forced the buzzard to fly lower, dropping from current to current until she was just a few hundred feet high.

The thing had disappeared again.

She drifted over the place where she had last glimpsed it, feeling her own face frowning in irritation at losing sight of it.

The shvan prima shivered even as it bounded across the sand, drawn by Krushita's determination to identify the approaching thing. She had never been so far from the pack before: she felt isolated and afraid.

The buzzard hung in the still dawn air, scrawny neck craned as its eyes scanned the desert below.

The shvan slowed as she arrived only a hundred feet below, glancing up nervously.

Both bird and beast experienced a strange sensation as their eyes met briefly: they were linked by the powerful mind that shared their consciousness, and it was unsettling. Krushita comforted them with fuzzy thoughts of food, shelter, warmth, mating, and offspring.

Then all of a sudden, they forgot about each other, as new movement caught their attention.

## 4

Krushita flew further out, seeking the source of the disturbance.

A strange odor rose from somewhere below: to the buzzard it was the stench of carnage, of violent death, mayhem, the putrid odor of rotting flesh and offal. But she could see nothing in sight. For miles in every direction there was not a creature to be seen, apart from the lone shvan prima, who had finally stopped a few miles back, refusing to go any farther from her pack.

The buzzard's sharp eyes caught several smaller desert denizens — geckos, stone ants, even the leavings of a desert dragon several miles north, a withered koytee foraging for sand rats or snakes burrowed beneath the sand, of which there were several hundred all around if only one knew where to look — but nothing that accounted for the stench. This was not the stench from a single body. To the buzzard's mind, this much foul odor could only be from a battlefield littered with thousands of corpses, or perhaps a large wagon train after a mass slaughter.

But even through the bird's keen gaze, she could spy no sign of any such thing. Only miles upon endless miles of crimson dunes. The first rays of sunlight were sparking over the horizon now, and she could see even farther and clearer. There was nothing out there that didn't belong in the Red Desert.

The shrieking of the shvan prima startled Krushita. She flapped her wings, staying in place momentarily, then turning around and starting to fly back.

The shvan was going berserk with fear. Her panic and terror filled Krushita's mind and senses, flooding her own body. She felt herself cringe and sensed Bulan watching her. The master was squatting down near the wagon wheel against which they had propped her head, staring at her with frank curiosity.

Now the pack had picked up the prima's call and were echoing it. Their ululation of terror resounded across the desert all the way back to the campsite. Even miles away, she could hear it through the buzzard's ears.

She made the bird fly faster.

The prima was in sight now, galloping back toward the pack. A long trail of pinkish sand dust rose in her wake, leading back toward . . . toward . . .

What *was* that?

At first, she mistook it for a firestorm.

The crimson sand which earned the Red Desert its name was for the most part not very different from ordinary yellow or white sand. But in some parts, it contained fosfors, a brownish-blackish mineral that could conflagrate at the slightest provocation. In these regions, the very sand itself might catch fire, the resulting blaze often rising a hundred feet or higher, and traveling almost as fast as a racing dromad or horse. An uks team pulling a laden wagon stood no chance of outracing such a firestorm, which was why early warning from the shvan was vital when one was sighted.

But what she was looking at now was no firestorm. It was like nothing Krushita had seen in the five years on the trail, or heard of in the hundreds of tales recited by Bulan and other drivers around the nightly campfires.

She forced the buzzard to fly lower, trying to make sense of what she was seeing.

The sand itself seemed to be rippling.

It undulated in irregular bumps and dimples, like a carpet under which a nest of insects was swarming.

The writhing, shivering motion covered a very large area — miles and miles. At first sight, she thought it must be an earthquake. She had never actually experienced an earthquake but had learned enough to wonder if this might be one. Surely no earthquake could be happening in only one area — or could it? What else could be causing the sand to bulge and ripple like that?

She stared down at it, baffled.

One thing was certain: whatever this thing was, it was definitely the source of the stench. The odors she had sensed through the buzzard's keen sense of smell were emanating from those disturbances in the sand. Whatever was down there under the surface of the sand, it smelled awful. Ew!

The buzzard shivered and called out, responding to the unnatural phenomenon and the stench.

Miles away, still circling over the camp, its fellow buzzards heard the cry. Krushita sensed their awareness with the strange affinity that animals seemed to have, an almost preternatural link of consciousness. With that cry alone, the other buzzards could feel what this one was feeling: stark, raving terror.

The buzzard needed no further urging to fly faster. It was going as fast as its leathery wings and the air currents would carry them.

As the camp came into view in the distance, Krushita saw the shvan pack below.

The prima had caught up with them and was sharing her terror at what she had seen out there alone. They were echoing her sense of horror and passing on the warning to their masters, the drivers of the wagon train.

The buzzard passed over and overtook the pack, catching a hot current and zooming ahead toward its fellows. The other buzzards were scattering already, taking wing and flying away from the camp.

That was not normal buzzard behavior. The camp represented years of feeding, a veritable lifetime supply to the carrion birds. For them to abandon it and flee as fast as their wings would carry them was testament to their own fear.

After all, the possibility of death alone was something that drew buzzards, not scared them away. If danger was about to befall the wagon train, then they should be watching for it to strike. Death was their business. The more drivers and uks that were killed, the richer the pickings. Whatever that thing was beneath the sand, it had spooked even the death birds.

The buzzard cried out one final time as it chased after them, and Krushita could almost read its meaning in its own language.

*Fly, brethren, fly for your lives. This time death comes for us all.*

Krushita decided she had seen and heard enough.

It was time to pass on the warning to her own kind.

She had pulled out of the shvan prima some time earlier, focusing on the buzzard's point of view. The poor frightened shvan was too panicked to be of much further use as a scout. All she was thinking and feeling was pure, blind panic. Something bad was coming. Something that smelled bad and that no shvan had ever encountered before. Krushita knew all that already.

Now, with a disorienting wrench, she pulled herself out of the buzzard as well, falling back three hundred feet into her own body, still propped against Bulan's wagon wheel.

# 5

Krushita bent over and vomited out the contents of her stomach, which were only acid bile.

Bulan's huge hand supported her, two of their fingers holding her hair back, while the others cradled her skull.

She wiped her mouth with the back of her rough cloth sleeve.

"Move. We have to move now."

The master looked down at her. "The shvan are calling. What did they see?"

She shook her head, struggling to her feet with their help. Her head swam briefly, then the world settled. "Nothing that makes any sense."

The Vanjhani looked at her calmly. "Few things do. Try me."

She summarized what she had seen and heard — and smelled.

They frowned down at her. "Moving sand?"

"Not just moving, it was . . ." She tried to think of a suitable analogy. "Like the surface of a lake when things are swarming below the surface. You can see the ripples but not what's causing them."

Bulan still looked skeptical. "A lake, sure. The ocean, a river, a creek, sure. But the desert? Nothing lives below the sand except vermin and insects. Even the desert dragons live in the buttes and mesas and only fly out to hunt. And there isn't a dragon within flying range of this part of the trail."

"I don't know what it is, Bulan," she said urgently, placing her small hand on the wrist of one of their huge forearms. "But whatever it is, it's bad, and it's headed this way. I think we should get moving."

Bulan thought for a moment.

The early morning was filled with the screams of the shvan from all around and the cries of the buzzards up above. The camp was fully awake now, drivers and journeyfolk all standing around, looking mostly in Bulan's direction. A small crowd had gathered around Bulan and Krushita, listening to their conversation as they tried to understand what had excited the shvan. Everyone who had survived this long knew that whatever the crisis, the best person to go to for advice or leadership was the train master. Several of the circle masters were here too, with more joining them at every minute, wanting to be the first to know Bulan's orders so they could pass them on to their own circles and neighboring ones.

"No," they said.

"No?" Krushita heard her voice rise in panic. "But we have to!"

Bulan placed a hand gently on her shoulder. The palm alone spanned her back. "Krush," they said softly, using the nickname they had adopted almost from the first, "remember the Three Rules When Attacked on the Trail?"

She forced herself to swallow a deep breath, containing her impatience. "When chased, press on. When surrounded, stand and fight. When uncertain, circle the wagons and wait."

"Exactly. This is no firestorm, no dragon or bandit attack. We don't know what it is. Listen to those shvan; I've never heard of shvan acting like this in my life. Whatever's out there is coming for us, and until we know what it is, how fast or slow, and what kind of danger it's carrying, we stay put. We're already in the Perfect Circle, so here we stay until I say otherwise. Okay?"

Krushita released a long breath. "Okay, Bul."

They straightened up to their full height, raising both their voices to make themself heard as far as possible, which was several circles away. "Stand and defend!"

The gathered crowd and other circle masters all nodded, looking relieved at being given a clear command, and passed on the order. "Stand and defend. Train master's orders."

Since they were already in the Perfect Circle formation, that only left arming everyone and taking up defensive posts. The entire camp became a flurry of activity as masters shouted follow-up orders to their circles and uks bosses took charge of the herds, making sure they were all securely penned in the center of each wagon circle and had enough food and water. Each wagon's driver passed out weapons to their passengers, who took up their allotted positions.

Desert wagons were thrice the size of ordinary city or country wagons. Including the tongue, each ripcloth-covered wagon was fifty-four feet long, thirty-four feet high, and twelve feet in width, could carry up to thirty-four thousand pounds of cargo and passengers, and was drawn by a team of eight uks, with at least another eight for relief and rotation.

The uks themselves were massive beasts, around ten feet high at the withers and weighing some eighteen hundred pounds each. Four alone could draw a full wagon all the way across the Red Trail, but at their own leisurely pace. The excess numbers were to allow for the inevitable sicknesses, leg breaks, deaths by mishap, and speed. Horses or dromads could also be used and could run much faster, but they weren't half as strong or enduring as uks. The placid, sluggish beasts could trudge along at their leisurely pace for days without rest on little food and water, without complaining or collapsing. It was only when threatened by one of their natural predators that they became agitated and tried to stampede. Since firestorms, desert dragons, and of course, vicious mortals, were among that number, this was often an advantage. They didn't need to be prodded, poked, cajoled, or whipped to get them running from such dangers.

The bosses were expert veterans bonded with the uks teams, and their chief task was to care for them and protect them at times of danger. They were also responsible for providing, maintaining, and guarding the precious stores of water which the train depended upon to survive the seven-year journey. There were only a handful of fresh water sources on the Red Trail, and every drop was jealously guarded. Every wagon had a water filtration barrel, but after a year or so of drinking your own bodily fluids, reprocessed, fresh water was worth killing and dying for. The bosses were journey-hardened veterans who had the right to use violence against anyone who broke the water laws on the trail, and were often called upon to do so. There was a reason why they were mostly Urug, the only race on Arthaloka capable of dividing themselves into two or more parts, each capable of independent thought and action. As composite beings, they were formidable, even more so than Vanjhani like Bulan.

Krushita watched the boss of her own circle, an Urug named Shamsss (Urug names and speech used a lot of *s* sounds and were as sibilant as you might expect from a reptilian-derived race), secure the circular pen containing their uks, then check on the fresh water supply. This was stored in squat wooden barrels in the boss's own wagon.

Shamsss raised one hand to his shoulder and peeled off what seemed to be a section of his own arm, about a meter long. He placed the slim length of flesh onto the front of the wagon, and it instantly came alive, coiling sinuously and raising one end in a menacing hood. Two tiny black eyes appeared on the top of the hood, as did a slash-thin mouth. A triforked tongue slipped in and out of the mouth between sharp white fangs as the serpent hissed.

Anyone foolish enough to try to lay a hand on the freshwater now would receive a sharp jab and a drop of venom potent enough to kill within moments. Shamsss peeled off two more such snakes from his body to guard the wagon, then turned to arming himself for the coming conflict. He saw Krushita watching and raised a hand to wave at her, smiling and showing his own triforked tongue.

"Sssstay ssssafe, little one!" he hissed.

Krushita nodded and waved back.

She heard her name being called and went to her wagon.

Aqreen was armed and ready, a crossbow slung on one shoulder and a quiver bristling with arrows strapped to her back. She handed down a smaller crossbow to her daughter.

It had been built especially for her by old Fuashmat, their circle's bowyer, fletcher, and smith. The side of the barrel had her nickname, Krush, engraved into the wood. Aqreen's had Fauzi'al, her trail name. Krushita had been allowed to keep her name because any number of young girls born after her had been given the same name, a common practice in any kingdom. After five years on the trail, it attracted no attention at all.

Aqreen had also stopped wearing her veil and hibij. The rumors that Queen Aqreen and her daughter had been assassinated by agents of the Burnt Empire were accepted fact by almost everyone, especially since the burnt bodies of a mother and girl child around their ages had been found wearing Aqreen's jewelry, including the signet ring that marked her right to rule.

Krushita often felt a pang of deep sorrow for that poor nameless woman and girl; they'd had to be killed, by a White Marshal loyal to her late grandfather King Aqron, in order that she and her mother could live without fear of recognition and capture. But in the end, the one person who really threatened their existence had not been fooled by the deception, and even now, she knew that whatever that foul thing was out in the desert, it had been sent or summoned by her father. Jarsun was not susceptible to subterfuge.

But he — and the creatures that served him — *was* susceptible to the right weapon.

Which was why Krushita took the crossbow from her mother, reluctantly.

"I hate weapons," she said plaintively.

Aqreen handed down a quiver filled with arrows made to fit the smaller crossbow. "You don't have to love a crossbow, you just have to point it and shoot."

Krushita strapped the quiver to her back, the weight of the arrows feeling like a punishment. "I rode a buzzard and a shvan, that's how I spotted the danger."

Aqreen's brow creased.

Krushita still recalled a time when her mother's handsome face had been smooth and her hair pitch-black. Perhaps it was the relentless desert sun, the ravages of the trail, and the constant fear of Krushita's father's vengeance, but she looked like she had aged far more than five years. There were grey hairs sprinkled with the black now and creases that marked her frowns and squints more than smiles and laughter, both of which were increasingly infrequent.

Still, she was beautiful, and even in her trail garb, a shapeless sacklike thing that made it difficult at times to tell genders or even races apart, she carried herself with a certain bearing and grace.

She leaped down from the wagon and bowed from the waist, cupping Krushita's heart-shaped face in her palms.

"You should have waited for me to wake, Krush."

Krushita rolled her eyes, the movement limited by her mother's hands. "You hardly sleep at all most nights. For once, you were snoring away to your heart's content. I didn't want to spoil your sleep. Besides, it might have turned out to be nothing but a raggedy koytee or something, and I would have ruined your rest for nothing."

"But it wasn't nothing, was it?"

Krushita tried to shake her head.

She pulled her mother's hands away and repeated the action properly. "It's him. I can feel it. He's found us again at last, and this time he's sending something really bad."

Aqreen's face crumpled into that about-to-cry expression Krushita knew all too well. Her eyes turned inward. Krushita knew she was picking at the scabs of her old wounds or, rather, that one wound that had never truly healed, and perhaps never would. "Just when I had begun to hope that he had forgotten us, that he was going to leave us alone . . ."

Krushita put her hand up to her mother's sleeve, tugging to make her look down at her again. "I was able to ride the buzzard and the shvan both at once!"

Aqreen nodded, dabbing at the corner of her eyes. "That's good, sweetheart."

"Do you know what means?" Krushita asked, wanting something more than a perfunctory word of praise. "It means I can ride different kinds of animals at the same time. I was never able to do that before. Either a shvan or a buzzard or a sand rat or something or other, but never both together."

Aqreen attempted a weak smile. "That's wonderful. Your powers are growing. We knew that would happen."

"But, Ma!" Krushita persisted. "If I can do the same thing during an attack—"

"No!" Aqreen's voice was sharp and loud enough to distract the other people around from their own preparations. It was rare to hear Aqreen's voice raised in anger against her daughter, unlike most other parents in the circle.

Krushita glanced at their neighbors, showing them that it wasn't anything to worry about. They nodded and resumed arranging their arrows and crossbows and other gear for the coming attack.

Aqreen also shot them a quick, friendly glance, then lowered her voice, while keeping it firm and uncompromising. "No, Krushita. You will not ride any creature during an attack. We've discussed this before. It's too dangerous. Remember what happened the last time?"

Krushita pursed her lips and blew out an impatient breath. "Last time was a long time ago. I'm older now."

Aqreen's mouth twitched in a semblance of a grin. "Barely five months. You were six years old. Now you're seven."

"You said it yourself, I'm stronger now. My powers are stronger. I can do it. I did it already this morning. I controlled them both at the same time and could see and think through both bodies at once. It was amazing!"

Aqreen cocked a dark eyebrow. "And how did you feel when you broke the tether and returned to your own body?"

Krushita hesitated.

Aqreen pointed a finger. "See?"

"It wasn't that bad! It was like . . . well, like feeling dizzy for a second, that's all."

Aqreen looked unconvinced. "Bulan told me you puked your guts out. And for a moment there, he thought you might have passed out. That worries me, Krush."

Aqreen was striding over to the train master's wagon as she said this, Krushita hopping and jumping alongside her.

"It was just for a moment!" Krushita argued, determined to convince Aqreen. "I always feel tired after riding anything." She lowered her voice. "Or anyone."

While Krushita's powers were an open secret in the circle and across the train, they had been careful not to let anyone know she could actually ride *people*. Her mother had warned her that might not be well received. For all their camaraderie on the trail, many of these travelers had their own secrets and agendas, some very dark indeed. They wouldn't take kindly to a seven-year-old girl — or anyone, for that matter — being privy to their innermost thoughts and feelings.

There would be more than a few who might think it would be easier to simply kill Krushita and Aqreen rather than risk their secrets getting out. Aqreen had explained that they had challenges enough to face without having to worry about their fellow travelers turning against them.

Jarsun's reign of terror in Aqron was already legendary for its excesses. Some of the trail marshals and stray riders who had passed the train in the past five years had brought increasingly horrific tales of the things he had done or was rumored to be doing. And of course, Jarsun's power stemmed from his Krushan blood and the power of stonefire. Krushita shared the same blood and the same power, and if the full extent of her nascent talents and budding abilities were known, it would quickly become obvious that she had Krushan blood too.

Even if no one guessed that Aqreen and Krushita might be Jarsun's wife and daughter, just the stigma of being labeled Krushan would be enough to bring them instant ostracization. At the very least, they would be forced out of the train, left to fend for themselves on the Red Trail, which would be nothing less than a death sentence. At worst . . . there were some things even Aqreen did not say aloud to her child, but Krushita had seen enough bloodshed and mayhem in her short life to be able to hazard a guess.

Aqreen shot her a sharp sideways glance as they approached Bulan's wagon.

"Enough," she said quietly. "We will not discuss this in public."

Krushita subsided but felt her lips pout. She wasn't finished with the discussion, by any means. But she would revisit it at a better time, and she was confident she would convince her mother eventually.

They stood, waiting patiently for Bulan to finish what they were doing. The train master was giving a last set of orders in crisp, terse Vanjhani to their compatriots from the Fallen Kingdoms. They were a motley bunch: Vanjhani, Urugs, Pishaks, Ngyas, Vettels, and several other races whose names Krushita found unpronounceable or who used glottal or other impossible-to-imitate sounds and tonal combinations in place of names.

The Vanjhani and Urugs were the largest of them, but what the others lacked in size and bulk, they made up for in speed, ferocity, and organic defenses. The Vettels, for instance, could metamorphose into any creature they confronted, shocking the attacker while retaining the Vettel ability to inject a tiny bit of saliva through two curved fangs, which disabled their opponent while turning them into instant slaves compelled to do the Vettel's bidding. Each of the others had similarly exotic defenses, some quite hair-raising.

Their racial differences as well as physical appearances, eating habits, and other lifestyle differences made them not very well-liked by the other travelers in the train. But almost everyone accepted them because of their value in a fight.

This last, of course, was something that Krushita had deduced by reading between the lines of what people said — or, more often, didn't say — in the presence of her and the other children in the train, but also by occasionally peeking into the minds of some of the adult travelers. Just peeking, not actually riding; she didn't want them to know she could slip into their heads as easily as a boss rode an uks bareback. Some of those images had been quite gross, she thought.

Bulan finished and dismissed the group, all of whom hustled back to their respective positions around the circle, a few leaping over or wriggling under the interlocked swingletrees to their own circles.

"Me favorite matron and child," they said, turning to Aqreen and Krushita.

Bulan winked at Krushita.

She smiled back up at them. Bulan was as different on the outside as she was from everyone else on the inside. In that sense, they were both alike, and the shared knowledge of that made her feel more comfortable in their presence.

"What can I do you for?" they asked Aqreen.

"I want to fight," Krushita's mother replied.

"Everyone fight. Is trail law."

"I meant with the militia," Aqreen said. She held up her crossbow. "I've been practicing. You've seen me and praised me yourself. And on the last attack, I replaced our neighbor Liml when she fell in battle. I'm ready, Bulan."

Bulan glanced down at Krushita briefly before replying. "Militia fight offense, not just defense. Them that have to go outta the Perfect Circle, out there." They raised one of their fingers and pointed out at the desert. "Not the same as defend your circle from the inside. Is a . . . a whole other thing."

"Obviously," Aqreen snapped. "And I'm ready for it. I've been five years on the trail, Bulan. I've fought a dozen battles and more smaller attacks than I can count on both hands — or on all your hands! I've drilled and practiced and trained. Let me fight."

Bulan sighed with both mouths, then looked down at Aqreen. "Fauzi'al. What happen if you fight with militia and no survive? Who raise little Krush then, huh?"

Aqreen looked down at Krushita. Their eyes met. Krushita saw a flicker of uncertainty in her mother's eyes.

"Krushita was raised a warrior from birth. She comes from a line of warriors. She knows the price. Ordinary folk have a choice when faced with war: fight or die. They can choose one or the other. Leave the fighting to the army, the marshals, the militia. Born warriors have only one path: fight and die. To die fighting in battle is the best end any warrior can hope for. Krushita knows that."

Krushita felt a pain in her chest like when she had once been struck in the chest by a flung stone, a flaring heat behind her ribs. Yes, Krushita knew that her mother was a warrior and that warriors died fighting. But she didn't want that to happen. Not yet, anyway. Not ever.

Bulan didn't look down at Krushita.

They crossed all four of their massive arms across both their chests. They looked nowhere close to being convinced, but they also looked like they didn't want to have this argument continue a moment longer.

"Put you in de reserve," they said unhappily, then shot out an accusing finger at Aqreen. "Not pleased about it. Not one bit. But will put you in reserve. Ya won't see action outside the Perfect Circle, stone gods willing, but ya get a shot to prove ya's ready. Best I can do. Now, get the hell outta here and lemme do ma job."

And with those terse words, the master turned their backs on mother and daughter and leaped up to the platform of their wagon, craning their heads and peering out first in one direction, then another. Krushita knew they were checking to be sure the Perfect Circle was ready for whatever was about to come.

"Did you need to do that right now?" Krushita asked, not bothering to hide her irritation as Aqreen and she walked back to their wagon.

Aqreen smiled sweetly at her. "You stay by our wagon. I'm going to join the reserve. You're in the circle, you'll be safe here."

Krushita folded her own arms across her chest in imitation of Bulan and glared at her mother.

Aqreen glanced around to make sure no one else was within hearing distance.

Krushita knew they weren't.

Dor and Niede, the Gulsinda couple who owned the wagon to their right, were busy saying their prayers to their god, the Staffbearer, to keep their children safe. The children were inside the wagon, too young to fight or even to fetch ammunition, water, food, or the other necessities that children carried back and forth to the adults during a long, drawn-out battle.

"You know why I have to do this," Aqreen said softly.

Krushita continued to glare at her. She wasn't going to make this easy. Good if Aqreen felt guilty about leaving her daughter alone and risking her life fighting in the militia. She *should* feel guilty.

"This is all happening because of me," Aqreen went on. "Your da . . ."

She faltered. She hadn't used that word in years, and Krushita knew it had slipped out by mistake. "He is here because of me. All the other attacks until now have been the usual trail dangers. Bandits, the desert dragon, the wild shvan pack, even the firestorm we outran three years ago — those are all things that could happen to any train on the Red Trail. But what's coming today — right now — is because of me. If I weren't here, it wouldn't come. Our presence is putting all these people in grave danger. And it's no ordinary threat. It's going to be bad, as you said. Maybe too terrible to survive. A lot of people could die today — *will* die, most likely. And that'll be on me. I have to remember their screams and cries each night for the rest of my life. So the least I can do is fight with them, side by side, shoulder to shoulder. I owe them that much. That's why I have to do this, Krushita."

Krushita kept her arms folded and eyes glaring, but she felt her anger melt.

She did understand. She felt the guilt too, especially when a child died, like Dor and Niede's little daughter, Afrinu, who was killed by a stray arrow in the battle against the bandits last year. Even though she knew that bandits attacked trains all the time on the Red Trail, she still felt guilty.

It was the reason her mother didn't sleep well at night, knowing that Krushita's da would come, sooner or later, and when he did, it would be bad. Very, very bad.

Today was that day.

Now was that time.

But she still couldn't bring herself to say anything to her mother. She just glared and stood her ground.

Aqreen looked at her for a long minute. "I love you, little Krush."

Then she bent down, kissed her daughter on the cheek, and strode away, leaping over the gap between two wagons.

Krushita glared at her mother's back, almost wanting to slip into her mind and compel her to return. She *could* do it, she knew. Her mother was strong-willed, but she was an ordinary mortal, not Krushan.

Instead, Krushita sighed and opened her arms, shaking out her frustration. For all their complaining about children not behaving, grown-ups seemed to be just as impulsive and irresponsible at times. It was infuriating, but what was a girl to do?

She was still fuming and fretting—

When a shout rang out.

And when a sudden silence fell across the camp.

Krushita forgot her own troubles for the moment and turned her attention outward.

Trouble had finally found them.

# *Aqreen*

AQREEN HAD BARELY REPORTED to the sergeant in charge of the militia reserve when one of the scouts yelled out. The woman was on the Buzzard's Nest, a wooden bucket-shaped thing mounted on top of a tall pole.

"Dushmag!"

The woman was Reygistani, and the word was in her tongue. It meant "enemy."

The camp fell silent.

Aqreen could hear her own heart beating in her chest. *I'm ready for this. I am.* But her feet still trembled, and there was a queasy feeling low down in her belly.

She was not a short person. In fact, like most Aqronians, she was taller than the average Reygistani. But there were people from all over Arthaloka in the militia, and her view of the desert outside the camp was hindered by the larger militia ahead of her. As a rookie she had been put at the back of the line. She tried to peek between the muscled shoulders and waists of the taller ones blocking her view, but all she could glimpse was greenish blue sky and reddish black sand.

Wait. Was that—

She did see something now. Just movement, still distant. It was hard to tell distances without any topographical features.

Another glimpse, this time mostly of sky, but low enough to see the rising cloud of pink dust raised by the approaching enemy.

Soldiers all around this part of the circle were pointing and exclaiming softly. Their sergeants didn't order them to stay silent; they were too busy staring out themselves.

"Approaching fast!" the lookout shouted from the Buzzard's Nest.

The Perfect Circle was a complex pattern of interlocking circles. Of the seventy-one circles left in the train, only fourteen had a direct view of the desert, and only sections of these fourteen actually faced the desert. These sections were manned by militia, who were the first line of defense as well as offense if any outsiders tried to break in.

Aqreen was in Bulan's circle, but due to the pattern, the outward-facing sections of the other thirteen circles were adjoining each other. She could hear and glimpse the lookouts of the circles to her left and right also pointing out the approaching threat and their sergeants calling up questions. From the snatches she heard of these exchanges as well as the soldiers ahead of her — the very ones blocking her view — she gathered that the other militia circles had also spotted the enemy.

"Captain," the sergeant shouted to his commanding officer.

The Vanjhani in charge of the reserve turned a head to look at the sergeant, their other head still watching the approaching dust cloud.

"Sergeant?"

"Our lookout says the enemy is approaching on all fronts."

The Vanjhani froze for a moment.

Aqreen felt her thudding heart skip a beat.

The Vanjhani turned all four eyes and two heads toward the sergeant. "Say that again."

"Enemy has surrounded us, sir, and is approaching at speed on all sides at once."

There was a brief moment of stunned silence, then the militia began to mutter amongst themselves.

A reserve soldier near Aqreen cursed in Reygistani. "Stone Father. My aunt rolled the bones and warned me this trip would be a circle fuck! But I still had to come, I did!"

Another soldier near them, a Chingar, asked, "Why?"

The Reygistani. "Needed the coin, what else." He swore again, mentioning dromads and cursing the Red Trail in various creative combinations, then quietened.

The captain's loud voice cut through the chatter.

"Sergeant, any estimate on their numbers?"

The sergeant shouted out the query to the lookout.

Aqreen glanced up at the woman. She was clutching the sides of her bucket and staring bug-eyed at the desert. Sweat dripped down the side of the woman's face.

The lookout said something back in Reygistani that Aqreen didn't understand.

The sergeant said to the captain, "Sir, lookout says more than she can count."

The lookout continued in Reygistani.

The sergeant listened and added after a moment, "At least tens of thousands, and they still keep coming, sir. Carpeting the desert as far as she can see."

That news hit the squad like a falling uks. All chatter ceased as they took this in. At least *tens of thousands.*

"Stone Mother," someone said hollowly behind Aqreen, then turned and retched.

She smelled the stink of vomit but didn't turn to look. Even the smell alone was almost enough to set off her own nausea.

*You can do this. You're a born warrior. Raised in the tradition of warrior queens of Aqron. You can face it, whatever it is.*

She suddenly found her view much improved. The gaps between shoulders and waists had broadened suddenly. She was able to push forward through the gaps. The lineup had dissolved in the past several minutes since the lookout's first shout. The militia was not a typical army, obsessed with drilling and appearance; out here on the trail, the only thing that mattered was how they fought.

Aqreen found a broad back impeding her as she tried to go forward.

She realized with a start that the soldiers in front were retreating slowly.

A Gunjalan turned away, his face frozen in a stunned expression.

She found herself at the front of the line, leaning on the interlocked tongues of two wagons. She had a clear view of the desert now.

The dust cloud approaching the camp had resolved into a mass of bodies moving at great speed. As far as she could make out, they were all human-shaped and sized. If she had to guess, they were more or less the size of herself and other Aqronians. Not as huge as the Vanjhani, nor as tiny as the

Peniree, who were small enough that even her little Krushita towered over them. That was something of a relief. She had seen the Vanjhani fight in battle and wouldn't relish being confronted with enemy that size and strength.

But their numbers.

Dear Stone Mother.

The lookout had been quite right. Even the brief view Aqreen had seen between wagons showed a seemingly endless mass of moving bodies. It went on as far as her eye could make out.

"There's something unusual about those soldiers," the captain said, as if to himself. Aqreen realized she was standing right beside him.

"No reflections," she said, her throat feeling more parched than it had in the past five years on the trail.

She felt the captain turn his head to look at her.

"Yes," he said. "Any invading enemy would be brandishing their weapons by now. Those would catch the sun. I don't see anything shiny in that crowd, do you?"

"No," she said hoarsely. "No helmets or armor . . . or mounts either."

They watched the oncoming mass. Behind them, a nervous whispering had been growing. It swelled to a restless, murmuring unease. Aqreen could understand their fear. They were young people for the most part; most soldiers were, since war was a young person's work. They had expected bandits, the occasional desert dragon or two, that kind of thing. Not an all-out army charging at them in such numbers.

*Was* it an army, though?

Aqreen had seen a few battles in her young life. Aqron was largely a peaceful kingdom, but there were always a few pockets of unrest. And they were on the coast — the relatively tranquil east coast of the continent, true, but there were a lot of islands out there, and a lot of ships from distant ones coming and going.

Also, pirates.

Sometimes, those skirmishes and fights spilled over onto land and, on at least one occasion in her memory, to a tentative invasion. A number of island despots had decided that since landers — as all continental folk were to them — were such easy pickings out at sea, they were probably just as easy on land. They had made the mistake of testing their theory by attacking the outlying coastal towns of Aqron itself.

Her father, named after the kingdom of his ancestors, had responded with surprising speed and firmness. The resulting battle had been short but bloody, and he had insisted to Aqreen's mother that their daughter be allowed to attend. Not as an active participant — she was only eleven at the time — but to view the theater of war. That not been her first exposure to mass violence, but it had been her worst for a while. The coastal militia had burned the invaders' ships behind them, and the invaders, all hope of escape lost, had fought to the last man. The sights she had witnessed that day were seared into Aqreen's memory forever.

This was *some* kind of army.

Those shapes were resolving now into what was definitely a large number of very angry people. Judging by the speed at which they were approaching the camp, and their sheer numbers, they could hardly be some wild mob rioting from a nearby city. There was no human habitation for several thousand miles in every direction, only barren desert.

They couldn't be bandits, because bandits rode mounts. No one could traverse the Red Desert on foot alone. Wagon trains existed for a reason: it took a lot of supplies, planning, and organization to cross this killing wasteland even in seven years. And you were lucky if a third of your party reached their destination safely. No one could survive more than a few days out here on foot. And this many people? She couldn't begin to imagine how much it would require to feed them, shelter them, water them . . .

No, this was an army, all right.

She could even see the similarities in their garments now, as they came close enough to make out some details. They were all clad in what seemed to be identical uniforms of one kind or another, a light green kaftan of some sort. Except . . .

"Grungy looking bunch, aren't they?" the captain said. He sounded calm, as if they were simply two travelers out taking in a desert sunset.

He was right. Those kaftans looked almost . . . ragged.

She squinted, holding her palm over her eyes to shield them from the sun. They *were* ragged. She could just make out individual features now, and the uniforms on those soldiers were torn and tattered. All of them, she realized, scanning from left to right then back again. They looked like an army that had gone to the dogs and now resembled mendicants in the bazaars of some desert city, rather than soldiers in an active force.

The captain grunted as if he had been struck hard in the belly. "Stone Father," he said, showing the first emotion since Aqreen had met him.

"What?" she asked, feeling suddenly out of breath.

"They aren't —" he began.

He never finished.

The lookouts were yelling at the top of their voices. All of them. Their voices echoed one another's across the camp's outer circle, a multitude of ethnicities, genders, races, and accents.

She caught phrases and words she understood.

They chilled her to the bone, even in the searing afternoon sun.

"Ashabh!"

"Karafiyeh!"

"Marsabiyo!"

"Anakh!"

"Zano!"

They all meant more or less the same thing.

The dead.

# *Krushita*

KRUSHITA KNEW WHAT THE lookouts were seeing long before they began yelling.

She had sent her mind out to the buzzard almost immediately after her mother had gone to join the militia on the far side of the circle.

She would have preferred the shvan, but they were all several dozen miles away and still milling about in confusion and fear. They had managed to elude the invading army by slipping through the broad gaps in their ranks. The invaders now surrounded the entire camp in a gigantic circle that was converging at an alarming rate, but they had originated from that one broadly rectangular patch of desert that Krushita had seen earlier through the buzzard's and shvan's eyes.

It was only after they emerged from that one place that they had spread out, swarming to surround the camp before rushing at it in an enormous, coordinated charge.

Now she soared high above the camp, the buzzard unnerved by the sight as well as the stench of what lay below.

The same cremation-ground stench of rotted corpses, worm-ridden flesh, fly-infested carrion. No, not like a cremation ground. Like a battlefield. In the buzzard's mind, there was no word for such a place, of course. But it understood the concept. Death ground. A place where mortals fought and died in great numbers.

A feast for buzzards.

Except that these rotting corpses, wormy carrion, ripened bodies were moving.

Running.

Racing across the sand as fast as their rotting, mangled bodies could carry them. Which was pretty damn fast—faster than the buzzard had seen any humans move before.

Nothing moved really quickly in the desert. It cost too much energy, too much water. Least of all humans, who were so weak they could hardly survive a day or two without the liquid resource. Even buzzards were better than that, capable of going several days without drinking, and dromads were legendary for being able to endure weeks of hard trekking across the wasteland between drinks.

But not humans. Which was why their species moved like feeble lizards and needed dromads, horses, uks, or some other mount to carry their weak bodies across the red sands.

Yet these were sprinting across the hot sands now, all running toward the large camp filled with humans, uks, and all manner of strange things that made no sense to the buzzard's simple mind.

Why were they running?

That was obvious, even to a buzzard.

They wanted to feed.

To kill.

To rip.

To tear.

To bite.

Shred.

Gorge.

And the food they craved was only to be found here, in this vast wasteland of red sand.

Living mortal flesh and blood.

Food.

Food.

*Food,* their feverish brains yelled as their broken feet and cracked bones carried them at madcap speed over the burning sand.

Food.

That was why they were running.

They sensed food ahead, in plentiful supply.

And nothing would keep them from it.

*Nothing.*

The buzzard had never seen such insanity.

True, humans were insane as a species.

But even by their crazy standards, this was a new level.

Dead humans rushing to kill living ones, not to steal their things, their shiny metal, their mounts, water, or animal meat supplies — none of the usual things that humans seemed to fight over in the Red Desert.

They wanted to eat them.

Even the buzzard could sense their killing frenzy.

The noise from their feverish brains was audible to the buzzard's highly attuned senses.

Krushita didn't have to ride their minds to know what they were thinking, feeling, what they wanted.

They wanted to kill those living mortals and eat them while they were still alive.

The buzzard shivered, wings dipping and curling inward as it experienced a chill that was strange and alien to its buzzard mind. Almost as if some other being was within its head, sharing its thoughts and sensations, and, just for a brief instant, it had felt that other being's emotions too.

Terror.

# *Aqreen*

AQREEN SAW THE CAPTAIN of the militia's eyes when he heard the look-outs yelling and the same cry repeated across the width and length of the camp.

The dead.

He looked like a horse about to bolt.

"Captain!"

She clapped her palm onto his chest, hard enough to make him stumble back.

He stared at her, as if seeing her for the first time and wondering who she was.

"You have to give the order. Before it's too late."

His mouth fell open. He stared at her dumbly.

"Tell them to open fire!" she said sharply, ready to slap him if he didn't respond.

His mouth closed.

A look passed through his eyes.

He nodded once.

Then he turned back to the militia reserve.

They were all milling about in confusion and fear, wanting to do nothing more than to run, but not sure where to go. The sergeant, bless his brave soul, was doing his best to try to hold them together, shouting orders and threatening disciplinary action, but equally scared and confused himself.

The captain strode forward, clapping his hands together sharply.

It sounded like a whip being snapped across the haunches of a dromad.

"Sergeant, give the order to line up for defensive fire. Do it now!"

The sergeant stared at his caption wildly, then snapped to attention. "Sir!"

He turned to the soldiers. "You heard the captain, you sorry lot. Fall in!"

A brief moment of uncertainty.

"What are you waiting for," the sergeant barked, "your mothers to hold your hands? Get to it, militia!"

That got through. Falling back on habit and training in the face of madness, they regained their senses and surged forward, resuming the lines that they had stood in earlier.

Aqreen remained where she was, at the front of the line, letting the other soldiers take their positions to either side of her.

She had no intention of being pushed back to the rear again.

She wanted to see what was happening out there.

Stone Father.

She needed to see.

The sergeant continued to bark orders.

Aqreen had trained with the militia on several occasions. Every able person in the train had to do so. It was compulsory. On the trail, learning to fight and follow orders under battle conditions wasn't a choice, it was vital to survival. One's own as well as that of the entire train. *Everyone depended on everyone,* as Bulan liked to say. All matter, or none matter.

At the command, she raised her loaded crossbow.

She set it on the interlocked tongue of the two wagons, using the level surface to steady her weapon and aim through the two sights at the front and back.

The cloud dust resolved to a mass of rushing bodies.

Then to a smaller group of rushing bodies.

Then to an individual body, sprinting madly at her.

The enemy soldier, if he could be called that, was a nightmare made visible.

He had clearly died several days ago. The flesh on his face, arms, torso and legs was mottled blue, black, and purple. It was the swollen, bloated look of a body that had filled with gases and would burst at any moment. He might have looked like a man once, but right now, he looked like an overripe man-shaped fruit that had been badly handled by a vendor and left in a ditch for vermin to gnaw on.

There were chunks of flesh missing from here and there, strips of skin hanging and flapping.

His teeth were yellow, blackened lips parted in a rictus of insane hate.

His eyes were red with white speckles, open wide and pupils reduced to pinpoints. The only thing in them was stark, mindless insanity. Nothing rational resided behind them anymore.

He was approaching in a loping, jerking stride. Like someone who had been running for days and was far beyond exhaustion but could not bring himself to stop. His mouth hung open, a purple tongue hanging out to one side. It had been bitten more than once by his own jaws as they opened and closed from time to time, in a parody of what had once been the intake and outtake of breath. It hung ragged and blistered.

She heard the captain instruct the sergeant to fire at will.

The sergeant snapped out the order.

She aimed at the oncoming enemy soldier and squeezed the trigger of the crossbow.

The stock kicked back against her shoulder, a shockingly hard recoil, even though she had fired the weapon a thousand times before. The jolt brought her back even further into her own rational mind, back from the edge of the abyss she had almost peered over only moments earlier.

She saw her arrow strike the dead soldier's belly, though she had aimed higher, and watched in disgust as the swollen body exploded wetly, spilling a mass of putrefied, worm-riddled organs and flesh out onto the red sand.

The dead man's headlong rush carried him a yard or so further toward the camp and Aqreen, then his legs gave way and he collapsed face-first. A puff of sand rose, marking his fall.

Other deadwalkers — it was as good a term as any — were falling, shot by arrows from the company. The main militia companies were shooting too now, and she could hear the sharp crack of crossbows being fired and the whicker of arrows flying to their targets.

Aqreen had stepped away the instant she had fired, just as she had been trained. The second line stepped forward, aimed, and fired, then stepped back as well, letting the third line take their shots. She reloaded in the time it took two lines to fire their weapons, then had to wait as the fourth and final line fired.

In the brief moment of respite, she watched as the main militia forces fired. They lay flat on top of the wagons as well as under them. The top and bottom lines alternated fire, giving the other time to reload. Their aim was much sharper, bringing down an enemy, and even more than one, with every single shot.

Some of the deadwalkers were so badly decomposed that an arrow passed through two or even three of them in a row. Aqreen watched entire groups tumble backward, their soft parts exploding in little dark bursts.

It was her turn again, and she was steadying, sighting, aiming, and firing. Her target was struck in the face — she had overcompensated for the last shot — and flung back, disappearing in the melee.

Step back again, reload, then watch as the other lines fire.

Step forward, steady, sight, aim, fire. Another deadwalker down, this one spinning to knock two others off their scrawny feet as well. Nice!

She repeated this more times than she could count, falling into the rhythmic pattern of stepping forward, firing, then stepping back, reloading, until it became second nature, even though as a princess and a queen she had mostly trained with close weapons and was far better adapted to the sword and shield rather than distance weapons. Royalty fought only royalty or nobility in Aqron tradition, and archery was a legacy tradition in her homeland. But the weapon now felt as if she had always used it, a part of her own arm and body.

She was surprised when she reached for her quiver and found it was empty. She couldn't possibly have exhausted all one hundred arrows! Yet apparently she had. She had lost track of time and place, of everything but the simple, repetitive act of moving and firing.

"Arrows!" she called sharply. The shout was being repeated all around the circle and across the camp. How many arrows had been fired already? Tens of thousands? Hundreds of thousands? Possibly.

Yet the enemy kept on coming.

Even now, as she waited for resupply, she could see the mad hordes rushing pell-mell at the camp. For every frontline felled by a volley, a second replaced it in the time it took them to fire again. That was not good. Sooner or later, their strength would flag or — Stone Gods — run out of ammunition. When that happened, the deadwalkers would cover the gap and be on the camp. She tried to imagine what it would be like to fight soldiers as dead and putrid as those out there and couldn't quite picture it. She hoped it wouldn't come to that. Stone Father. There couldn't be many more of them left, could there?

The dust cloud from the enemy attack was high enough to be seen over the wagon tops now.

She couldn't see the back of it from down here and couldn't recall hearing the lookouts say anything about it either. That might not mean anything. The dust cloud itself would obscure vision beyond a few hundred yards.

But Stone Father, they had already shot one entire quiver load into the attackers, and they were still coming. If every arrow had taken down one deadwalker, then that was already a staggeringly high number. Would they never stop? Where were they coming from?

In the few minutes it took for the resupply to reach her, she found her head swimming with panic.

Then a fresh batch of arrows was deposited before her, and she snatched it up at once, cutting the thin band with her knife and dumping the arrows into her quiver. The shooting hadn't paused yet — the captains and sergeants had made sure resupplies were ready ahead of time, and the other lines had already begun firing their second batches.

She stepped forward at her turn, went through the whole ritual again, and had the minor satisfaction of seeing two go down with one well-placed shot.

Her shoulder and her trigger finger creaked after the brief respite, and she suspected they would be barking with pain for days afterward. That was no matter. All that counted now was stopping those disgusting things from reaching the camp.

The arrows burned through her crossbow.

Deadwalkers fell left, right, and center.

Step forward, step back.

Steady, sight, aim.

Fire, fire, fire.

Another quiver's worth depleted.

"Arrows!"

Resupply, then resupply once more.

Four times. Or was it five?

Finally, as she was taking aim wearily with an aching eye, bracing with a sore shoulder and firing with a numb trigger finger, she heard the sergeant call out, "Last arrows! Use them well!"

She loosed the arrow and watched yet another deadwalker pitch down, the one immediately behind him tripping over him and diving into the sand. She had long since lost count of how many she had shot down. If she was finishing her fourth quiver, it was at least four hundred. If it was her fifth . . .

Stone Father.

How many of those cursed things were there?

She heard other militia around her echoing the same question.

The captain called up to the lookout. "Report!"

The lookout replied shakily, "Still coming."

Still coming.

Mother of Gods.

She did a quick estimate in her tired brain, checking it twice to be sure she had her figures right.

As many as two million?

Maybe more?

No army in all Arthaloka had those kind of numbers.

Well, perhaps Hastinaga did. They certainly did, in fact. And if you counted the entire armed forces of the whole Burnt Empire, then it would be many, many times that number.

But these were not Burnt Empire forces!

They couldn't possibly be.

Besides, the Burnt Empire wouldn't waste an entire army on a mere wagon train out in the middle of the Red Desert.

And Hastinaga had no army composed entirely of deadwalkers.

Nobody did.

Not even Aqron.

She knew Jarsun was behind this attack. It bore his distinctive mark. The use of supernatural creatures out of myth and legend. The relentless attack. The sheer scale of the assault — not an attempt at conquering or subduing, but simply intended to wipe out. Eliminate. Slaughter. Yes, this was her husband's work for certain.

No other force in all Arthaloka hated her with so much passion. For that matter, no one else, politically motivated or otherwise, hated her at all. Her father had been well loved, not a feudal tyrant but a benign overseer of his kingdom's resources and a democratic dispenser of justice. Her family had ruled at the people's pleasure and with their full support for an eon. Aqron might not have been a utopia, but it was certainly not the dystopia that it was rumored to have become under Jarsun.

And Jarsun's vengeance was epic. Insatiable.

But where was he getting all these deadwalkers from, and how many more could there be?

And what would happen when they ran out of arrows in a few minutes?

Aqreen continued firing the last of her precious missiles as these queries swarmed through her mind.

# *Krushita*

KRUSHITA WATCHED THROUGH THE buzzard's eyes as the bodies piled up.

She couldn't begin to count how many must have fallen already.

And still the deadwalkers kept on coming. The mad rush at the camp from all sides continued unabated.

From up here, she could see that the attack was no longer as evenly dense all around the camp. There were many more deadwalkers coming from the northeast, the same direction she had traveled with the buzzard and shvan prima earlier. As they approached within a few miles of the camp, they spread out, flowing around the large circle of wagons like water around an island.

But as the arrow volleys took their toll, there were pauses. A few moments when the seemingly never-ending flow did slow to a trickle, then cease altogether. It resumed soon after with a fresh burst of deadwalkers, running faster as if to close the gap, and once the new wave reached the last of the earlier attackers, it was as if there had never been any pause at all.

But there were pauses.

She had an idea why that happened.

The deadwalkers were not coming from the desert.

At least not *this* desert.

They were coming from somewhere else.

Another world, another time, another dimension.

Her mother had explained to her about portals and her father's ability to use them to travel from world to world at will, though at some cost in strength and energy. She had understood the concept instinctively. After all, she had similar powers to her da, even if he chose to use them to do evil. She sensed that she could use portals like he did, but not just yet. Someday, she would be ready and would travel between worlds as he did.

Jarsun was bringing these deadwalkers through a portal.

That was what she had seen through the buzzard's and shvan's eyes earlier. The sand heaving and writhing. Her da had been forcing open a portal in that part of the Red Desert, using the passageway to push through hordes of the dead from some other place and time. Perhaps not even Arthaloka, but another world entirely. Or perhaps Arthaloka but another time.

Yes, that last bit was correct, she sensed.

He was bringing the deadwalkers from Arthaloka itself, but another era.

These were soldiers; she could see the similarity in their uniforms, ragged and threadbare though they were now.

They were soldiers in some army that had existed in another age, an eon earlier.

They had fought and died in this same Red Desert, on that same patch of sand. A battlefield carpeted with the rotting corpses of the dead.

Jarsun had opened a portal large enough to push them through to this moment.

He had somehow used his powers to infect them with the sickness that turned them into living corpses hell-bent on a single purpose: to feed on the living.

The army of deadwalkers scented the camp instantly on arrival. Once the first of them began running, the rest simply followed. That herd instinct coupled with the mindless, frenzied lust for living flesh and pulsing, warm blood had driven them to this headlong race.

They would not stop until they had their skeletal hands on the living bodies, their yellowed teeth sunk into live, juicy flesh. They could not stop.

Krushita felt the buzzard shiver and cry out in protest as she came too close to the hive mind of the deadwalker army.

*Live flesh. Hot blood. Food.*

*Flesh.*

*Blood.*

*Food!*

*Fleshbloodfoodfleshbloodfoodfleshbloodfood . . .*

It was a fevered, insane thing, like the buzzing of a swarm of hornets. It filled her entire consciousness, threatening to overwhelm her.

The buzzard's wings dipped, they lost height, plunging into a dive that turned into a free fall.

No.

Krushita gasped as she pulled herself back from the noise of the deadwalker army's consciousness. She had almost let herself fall into the vortex of their madness. The buzzard pushed down with its wings, breaking the fall and soaring over the heads of the racing hordes.

Some of them saw the buzzard and tried to leap up into the air.

*Live flesh.*

*Hot blood.*

*Food.*

She squawked in fright as the leaping bodies flew up several yards high, launching themselves off the backs and heads of those in front, desperate for the few morsels the carrion bird would bring them.

One, a horribly disfigured soldier with purple-black bruises all over his face and torso and a gaping hole where his stomach used to be, came within a yard of the buzzard's claws. He screamed in frustration as his outstretched fingers—denuded almost down to the bone—grabbed at empty air beneath her and fell back into the surging mass.

She flapped the buzzard's wings, rising as high as she could manage. It took her several tense moments to find an air current and ride it further up, and in that time, the deadwalkers had started to climb atop two, three, and even a half dozen of their comrades to gain more height before leaping through the air.

They all missed and fell to be smashed and pulped on the bones and skulls of those below, or crushed and dismembered under the pounding feet.

The Red Desert swallowed those that fell, the sands claiming the broken corpses. Around the camp, there was now a dirty red swath. Like a paintbrush had been drawn around it, marking the target. Their remains had been trampled, pounded, squashed, smeared, and spread like black currant jam, blending with the red sands.

Krushita reached for the minds of those in the camp, instinctively seeking normalcy after the horrific stomach-lurching nausea of her brush with that blood-crazed hive buzz.

She sensed the fear that pervaded.

The confusion.

The inability to comprehend what was happening.

Deadwalkers! Those things out of ghoulish children's tales and old dusty scrolls. And in such unthinkable numbers. It defied the laws of the universe, the reality of life and death. The dead were supposed to stay dead, not rise up and war against the living! It was obscene, a foul violation of the natural order. Their hearts were filled with dread that their weapons and training did nothing to dispel.

She sensed Bulan somewhere in there, a beacon of brave hope in the growing tide of unease. The train master was fierce and determined even now, all their four arms firing arrows from two crossbows at once, their powerful shoulder and back muscles working relentlessly, and even in the Vanjhani's dual brains, she read the bewilderment at the enemy's unstoppable assault.

She read terror as quiver after quiver emptied, even the train's vast ammunition supplies finally running out. Never before had any train encountered an attack on such a vast scale. The masters were not prepared for it; no one could be prepared for such an attack.

This had to be some kind of bizarre dream.

Except . . . they were all dreaming it at once.

And those arrows were real, the mothersucking orange sun overhead was very real, the Red Desert sand underfoot — and in everything, from collars to shoes to even food and water — was very bloody real, their exhaustion was real, the pain in their arms and shoulders was much too real.

How?

Why?

The questions multiplied.

The confusion grew.

The fear swelled.

As the quivers all emptied for the last time — most of that supply had been manufactured en route, meant for sale in Reygistan, not to be spent on ghoulish myths out in the middle of nowhere — throats ran parched, and endurance was tested to the limits, a common sense spread throughout the thirty-five thousand souls in the camp.

*Are we going to die out here?*

*We are, aren't we?*

*How else could this end?*

Krushita cried out. An angry, indignant scree from the throat of the buzzard. A muffled shriek from the seven-year-old's throat down by her wagon.

Her neighbors, Niede and Dor, turned to glance at her apprehensively: they were familiar with little Krush's "outbursts" and occasional fits of odd behavior, and more concerned with what was happening outside the camp. Their own limited supply of arrows had long since been depleted, and all they could do now was wait, watch, and pray. Their palms were joined in the palm-joining gesture that people of their religion used when praying to the stone gods. The resumed their litany, asking the blessings of Shaiva the Destroyer and pleading with him to spare their humble lives and those of their young ones.

Krushita had had enough.

She forced herself to look away from the attacking army of deadwalkers.

She flapped the wings of the buzzard, driving the poor bird harder than it had flown in its life, heading northward.

Away from the camp and those within its encircled wagons.

# *Bulan*

"ARROW!" BULAN SHOUTED.

But even as they yelled, they knew.

The arrows were all gone. They had used up their entire supply, including the twelve quivers they had bought to resell at Reygar, where white arrows made with Aqron elm timber sold for a pretty premium.

A deadly silence fell over the camp.

It wasn't a silence, strictly speaking.

The wordless roar of the attacking deadwalker hordes was still frighteningly loud, filling the desert and hanging over the camp like the billowing dust cloud, which now equaled any firestorm Bulan had seen.

But in the camp itself, there was silence.

The crossbows had fallen quiet.

The whickering arrows were all finished.

And none of the travelers had anything to say.

Bulan lowered their crossbows, feeling the leaden numbness seep through their arms and back and even their four legs.

They had put all their effort and concentration into firing without a minute's respite, doing the work of not just four militia at once, but four times four. The Vanjhani did not stop fighting until their enemy was down — or they themselves were down. That was the Vanjhani way.

The enemy was down and yet not down.

Bulan alone must have shot a few thousand deadwalkers. Their crossbows were twice as large as the crossbow most mortals could handle, and the arrows proportionally thicker and longer. Each arrow shot by their bows had downed four or a half dozen deadwalkers at a time, and they had tumbled like twelvepins when Bulan fired their two crossbows at once, aiming at a mass of oncoming deadwalkers a dozen yards wide or more. The enemy had fallen in greater numbers than Bulan had ever downed before, even in the worst bandit raids they had encountered some fifty odd years ago, back when they were just another Vanjhani mercenary for hire, traveling as bodyguard to a rich Janshswarthian merchant.

And still they were coming.

Charging at the camp like an unstoppable force.

"Seven hundred yards and closing!" the lookouts shouted.

Like a river of mad blood.

This was the stuff of myth and legend, come alive.

The only problem was, there were no stone gods in this one.

Just regular mortals.

Thirty-five thousand besieged souls, every one of them under Bulan's watch and care.

Only about four-thousand-odd were trained militia, including the reserves.

Perhaps fifteen thousand more could fight well enough to defend themselves and their families. Not soldier smart in battle, but enough to hold their own against evenly matched odds.

The rest, some fifteen thousand or so, were old, infirm, sick, injured, very young, or not reliable enough in a real fight. Sure, they could be pressed to fight in a pinch — when the chips were down, everybody had to fight — but they wouldn't survive against strong, determined, able fighters.

So Bulan had maybe twenty thousand halfway decent fighters, only a fraction of which they would want to watch their backs in a pitched battle.

And none of them were equipped, trained, or prepared mentally or physically to fight a thing out of myth and legend.

Definitely not deadwalkers.

*Why, Stone Father prove me wrong, I don't know if* I'm *prepared to fight deadwalkers.*

"Six hundred yards and closing!" cried the lookouts.

What the fuck were they to do?

"Master?" asked one of the Vanjhani near Bulan. Subed, the colonel of the militia. Both their narrow faces looked worn and harried — almost fearful, if Vanjhani could ever look fearful. They still held their empty crossbows, raised as if planning to throw them at the oncoming deadwalkers.

Fat lot of good that would do.

"Five hundred yards and closing!"

The deadwalkers' attack, finally allowed to roll on uninterrupted by arrow volleys, was surging across the red sand. The first deadwalkers were more clearly visible now, their crazed skeletal faces, bugged-out eyes, and spindly limbs rendering the nightmare all too real. As more and more emerged from the billowing clouds of sand dust, Bulan goggled. Their numbers were staggering, as was their frothing hunger-lust. It was as if all the million or two arrows fired by Bulan and his people made not the slightest bit of difference.

*Makes sense,* they thought. *If those are deadwalkers, as they appear to be, and if the myths and legends are right, then they don't have the capacity to think rationally anymore. All they can smell and see is live flesh and hot blood. A great fat supply of it. They're not living soldiers, who would have been daunted by the sheer scale of slaughter of their comrades, if not scared shitless. They're just corpses. Moving, hungry corpses, but corpses nevertheless. They can't feel fear, they can't feel emotions, they can't feel, period. They just want. Flesh. Blood. To feed.*

At least they could be downed. The arrow volleys had proven that. And they were fairly easy to kill — at least at a distance. The arrows had torn through their soft, putrid bodies like a sharp blade through fatty meat.

"Four hundred!"

A thought struck Bulan.

"Poles," they said, mostly to themself.

The thought took root.

"*Poles,*" they said aloud to the next in command.

Subed stared with four uncomprehending eyes. "Sir?"

"Poles," Bulan repeated, then turned and held up their hands to draw the attention of the dazed militia. "POLES! FETCH POLES!"

Their coordinated voices boomed across the circle, carrying to the neighboring circles as well.

The order was passed on like an echo down a subterranean cavern.

"Three hundred!" the lookouts shouted.

Every wagon had at least one pole. They were essential for correcting the course of the wagon when the uks team veered too far to one side or to help maneuver through the narrow canyons of Jardakh. Most wagons had two and some, like the Vanjhani, had four. What was the point of having four arms if you didn't use them when they were needed most?

Bulan pulled out their poles, passing them from hand to hand until they had one in each of their four fists. They held them high, over the heads of the other militia as well as the other Vanjhani — being tall for one's race had its advantages — and looked around the circle.

"Two hundred!" the lookouts called.

Several hundred sweat-limned, scared faces looked back at Bulan.

"Point, thrust, withdraw," they said, matching action to words with all four poles at once. "Point! Thrust! Withdraw!" they repeated loudly, repeating the actions as well to make sure everyone understood.

Eyes lit up with comprehension. Voices were already passing on the order.

"One hundred!" the lookouts called hoarsely, some sounding panicked, others simply despairing.

The sound of poles knocking against wagons resounded through the circle and the camp. Everyone was glad to be doing something other than simply gawking at the oncoming flood of certain death.

Bulan crouched, bunching their powerful legs and back, and leaped over the interlocked tongues of the wagons. They landed with a puff of sand outside the outermost circle.

"Fifty yards and closing fast!" the lookouts screeched, sounding nearly hysterical now.

The other Vanjhani immediately imitated his example. Other militia did the same, stepping out of the Perfect Circle, exposing themselves to the oncoming enemy without anything to protect them from the ravenous teeth and clawing fingers but the five-yard-long wooden poles they carried.

Forty yards.

"Vanjhani!" Bulan cried, using the deep sonorous tones that their people used at such times.

"VANJHANI!" came the answering response from three hundred and fifty pairs of throats around the Perfect Circle.

Thirty yards.

They were joined by other war cries and clan calls from the various races, castes, and denominations among the militia, as well as the journeymen travelers.

Most used the simple appeal to the oldest, greatest gods of all in the world.

"Stone Gods!"

Twenty.

Bulan could see the madness in those eye pits now, the bloodshot — or blood-filled — eyes gaping wider than any living person's because of the decayed muscles and depleted flesh. Many were little more than skeletons with rags of skin and flesh hanging from their legs and torsos, while a few were puffed-up bags of bloated skin, heaving and mottled with mortal injuries and missing chunks or limbs.

Ten.

The air to either side of Bulan bristled with poles now.

They could feel the pounding of hundreds of thousands of running feet even through the sand. They had thought the sand absorbed all impact and sound. Apparently, it wasn't true. Put enough bodies and weight and move them fast enough, and you could feel the sand shifting and trembling under your feet. Not the shivering, thudding impact that horses and dromads made on the packed sand of the cities, or the booming reverberation of a charging cavalry force on solid land. But still enough to be felt.

Bulan aimed each of their poles at four targets, crouching low and bending forward, bracing themself for the impact that would come. They hoped the non-Vanjhani would do the same. This was not a fighting technique or weapon they had trained for, but it was not all that different from fighting charging infantry with pikes, and they had done a couple of drills with poles during the militia training, even though they had no pikes, nor expected to ever need any. Who charged full tilt in the desert, under a brain-blasting sun? Not even the most desperate bandits were that insane.

Then the first of the raving hordes came within pole reach and Bulan had no time to think of anything but the task at hand.

# *Aqreen*

AQREEN FELT THE IMPACT of the strike shiver through the pole, all the way up her arms to her shoulders, neck, and back. Her legs were braced, stance wide and angled, torso bent low. She held the pole in both hands, careful to let the end hang free of her body. Had she been facing a cavalry charge, as they had been trained during the two drills, she would have pushed the end of the pole as deep into the sand as possible, bracing it with her foot. But for targets of mortal height, she had to angle it lower, to strike the softer stomach area.

The impact jerked her entire body sideways and backward, almost spinning her around. The side of the pole struck the corner of a wagon, and she used the wagon's weight to brace herself.

At the other end of the pole, a deadwalker had run headlong into the wooden shaft, impaling himself then pushing all the way to the middle of the smooth, well-weathered ash. His ripe belly burst, spilling gore and entrails as he screeched indignantly, limbs thrashing, lipless mouth frothing obscenely, like a bug on a dagger.

To her surprise, a second impact followed almost immediately. It was followed by a third, fourth and even a fifth impact.

The pole suddenly grew far too heavy for her to lift, but the impaled deadwalkers — five of them, Stone Father — couldn't do much more than wriggle and thrash and shriek impotently. She continued to brace the pole against the corner of the wagon, leaning against it hard to compensate for the drifting motion caused by the deadwalkers' thrashing.

All along the line, militia were impaling deadwalkers by fours and fives on their poles. She glanced at Bulan, only a half dozen wagons away, and saw them work those slablike arms, faces grimacing, as they shoved the poles forward again, and again, catching more and more of the charging deadwalkers.

She felt a shock of surprise pass through her.

Stone Mother. It worked.

As if reading her thoughts, the sergeant right behind her yelled at an ear-splitting volume, "It's working! Keep pushing those poles, you sand-diggers! Let's keep as many of them at bay as we can!"

She did as he ordered, putting all her strength behind the pole, shoving it forward, then using the edge of the wagon as a lever to turn it around.

The pole shuddered as more charging deadwalkers struck it. It probably couldn't skewer any more, but the bristling forest of poles with impaled bodies made for an effective barrier, preventing more from reaching the wagons. In a few moments, the perimeter of the circle was packed with tens of thousands of trapped deadwalkers, all howling and shrieking horribly.

"Deadwalker kebab!" said the militiaman to her left. He was a young Xorakiv named Kihrr, barely out of his teens, with a soft, downy mustache and barely discernible beard that matched his dark brown hair. He had the lean, muscled look of all travelers after five years on the trail. They had undergone basic training together, and he had been inducted into the reserve only a few days earlier.

He grinned at her as he said it, but there was a scared look in his eyes.

She grinned back, but knew she must look just as nervous as he did.

*What now?* she wondered.

There were a lot of deadwalkers still coming — Stone Mother only knew how many. She could hear them howling out there, and the dust cloud that had heralded their approach hung over the entire camp now, like a desert storm. They were barred from the wagons by the pikes and the crowds of their own, but they would get through somehow, and when they did —

Bulan bellowed orders.

The officers picked them up and passed them on at once. She heard the shouted commands ripple through the camp.

Pull. Release. Repeat.

The sergeant took up the task of implementing the order, bellowing into her ear at deafening volume.

She obeyed, but it was easier said than done.

Using both her hands and every ounce of her strength, she yanked hard on the end of the pole, pulling it into the circle. The deadwalkers impaled on it shrieked and foamed as they were brought closer to living flesh. The one closest to her flailed his scrawny arms, bony fingers clawing the air. His jaws opened and snapped shut as he sought to bite off a chunk of that meat he craved so desperately. He was still a good few yards away, but she had to force herself not to flinch.

Then, using the interlocked tongues of the wagons as the sergeant instructed, she used the far end to push the deadwalkers off her pole. The pole yanked free with surprising ease, the skewered bodies falling off and tumbling into a boneless heap on the sand. She let the end of the pole fall downward, hitting the sand. Its length was slick with sticky gore, and pieces of innards dropped with sickening, wet plops to the ground. The stench, already unbearable, worsened. She gagged at the sight, sound, and smell, turned away, and vomited. Hot bile and fluid fell out in a rush, lost instantly in the sand.

Other militia were retching or gagging as well. The captain upended the contents of his stomach. He had had a very hearty dinner or breakfast, apparently. He leaned against the side of a wagon, dark face wan. He was wiping his mouth with the back of his kaftan when his body jerked suddenly.

Aqreen and the captain both stared at each other. She saw a look of puzzlement on his face. Then, seemingly very slowly, he started to look down at his left foot.

Before his chin could drop all the way, the foot was yanked suddenly by an unseen force. Aqreen watched as his face changed with surprise and shock. Then crumpled as he felt what looked like excruciating pain.

"I —" he began.

He could not finish the sentence.

Once again, his foot was yanked hard. His whole body disappeared, falling with a bone-cracking thump, and was pulled under the interlocked tongues and out of the circle.

Aqreen and the young soldier beside her exchanged shocked glances, then bent together to look.

They saw the captain's body being pulled by reaching skeletal hands, then watched with horror as two deadwalkers fell on him. Those snapping jaws clamped down on his shoulder and belly, and tore pieces of kaftan and flesh free. The captain screamed and tried to drag himself back into the circle. A dozen other flailing arms grabbed him, and deadwalkers pounced from all sides.

Aqreen could see the gaping holes in their middles and their chests where they had been skewered by the poles. They ought not to have been able to move at all, yet they were still very much mobile, very agile, and very, very hungry.

A crowd of deadwalkers covered the captain's body, devouring him. His pitiful screams were drowned by the cacophony of deadwalkers shrieking, the sergeant shouting orders, and people shouting and yelling all around.

Only Aqreen and Kihrr had seen what had happened.

Aqreen turned to the sergeant, hitting him in the chest to attract his attention.

"The captain!" she shouted over the noise. "They took him!"

The sergeant stared at her, then looked where she was pointing. Only the mass of feeding deadwalkers were visible now, their mouths and hands red and dripping with fresh blood. He looked back at Aqreen with a frown, and for a second she thought he was going to reprimand her.

Then he slapped both her and Kihrr on their sides and yelled, "Poles! Use your poles, you sand rats!"

Aqreen picked up the end she had let fall into the sand and took a firm grip on it. The smeared gore was only a foot or two beyond her hands. She tried to ignore it, and lifted the ashwood. Aiming it into the middle of the feeding group, she jabbed it as hard as she could, once, then again and again.

The far end of the pole struck the head of a deadwalker stuffing a piece of wet meat into his gaping maw. His skull crunched, and he keeled over. The second and third jabs struck two other deadwalkers in the back and neck, knocking both off their prey. Beside her, Kihrr was working his pole as well, smashing skulls and crunching spines.

The sergeant was shouting furiously now, the turmoil so deafening that even his bellow was lost in the mass of sound.

Aqreen pulled and jabbed, pulled and jabbed, pulled and jabbed.

Over. And over. And over again.

Her arms, neck, and back ached, then went numb. Her legs felt like they'd turned to stone, then jelly. Her fingers and wrists cried out with pain.

Deadwalkers were coming through the gaps now, some crawling under the wagons and tongues. Others were clawing at the wagons, trying to climb sides, the ones behind them leaping onto their backs and reaching the top. Pyramids formed without forethought or planning. Apparently, they needed no master or officers to order and instruct them. They gained the tops of the wagons and scrambled over, leaping down heedlessly. Deadwalkers fell onto militia and travelers, burying teeth into their flesh instantly. Some fell on poles, or swords, or axes, and were impaled.

Aqreen saw one deadwalker falling onto a militia reserve who had the presence of mind to raise his pole end just in time. The deadwalker's teeth shattered as he bit with full strength at the ashwood. Two of his teeth snapped off, embedded in the wood. He tumbled to the sand, and the militia fighter stamped down hard on his face. The deadwalker's jaw — what was left of it — crunched and broke, but he still moved his mouth, trying to bite at the boot and getting only a mouthful of sand. The militia's foot stamped down again and broke the deadwalker's skull. He sprawled and lay still, face and head caved in, one eye staring up at the sky. He had a tattoo on his cheek that looked like a half moon.

All around her, deadwalkers were coming into the circle and militia were fighting them. She saw a deadwalker start to climb over the tongue, coming straight at her. She yanked her pole sideways, striking him in the ribs. They splintered, and the force drove him off the tongue. He fell back onto more deadwalkers who were following, and they roared with fury and tore at him before casting him aside. They weren't big on camaraderie either, it seemed.

Things were growing chaotic inside the circle. More and more deadwalkers were climbing and crawling in. Militia were fighting back, but for every deadwalker they felled, three more seemed to appear.

Aqreen's shoulders couldn't take the punishment anymore. Another deadwalker had impaled himself on the outer end, and there were others writhing under the tongue and scrambling over it to get at her. She dropped her end of the pole. It didn't fall far, impeded by the grisly kebab still skewered on the other end, and clanged down onto the metal tongue.

She unsheathed the two shortswords from the harness strapped to her back. The cloth-wrapped hilts felt like old friends. She had owned this pair since she was a young girl, training under Weapons Guru Shon'ayl, a withered old veteran whose face was so leathered with age it was difficult to tell her scars from the wrinkles. She had driven Aqreen brutally hard, bringing home the point that training wasn't merely a hobby to be indulged but a survival skill.

Aqreen kissed the flats of the blades, sending up a silent word of prayer to old Shon'ayl, gone to her grave some years ago.

Then she got to work.

Using the diagonal slashing technique she had mastered under Shon'ayl, she hacked into the skulls of two deadwalkers at once. The deadly sharp blades sliced into the bone with only the slightest resistance, and both creatures collapsed, spilling viscous brain matter that was nearly liquefied and stank to high heaven.

Kihrr saw them fall and dropped his pole too, drawing his sword. He wielded it two-handed, cutting the ankles of a deadwalker who had climbed onto the tongue and was about to launch himself at the rookie. The deadwalker fell face forward at Kihrr's feet, his head hitting the sand. But his arms and body still flailed, reaching sightlessly for the meat he knew was within reach.

"The skulls!" Aqreen shouted. "You have to smash their skulls!"

Kihrr hacked down at the deadwalker, who was rising, sand pouring out of his snarling jaws. The sword cleaved through the skull, splitting it open and spilling more of the same liquefied brain matter, releasing more of the noxious odor.

Aqreen was already fending off several more feeders coming at her. Her shortswords blurred through the air as she hacked through skulls. A deadwalker raised his hand, the ragged remains of his kaftan dangling from the still surprisingly fleshy arm, and one shortsword sliced through the forearm, severing bone and flesh as easily as cutting bread. It met the side of his head, cutting off the top of his skull at an angle. The severed top and the contents slid out, racing the rest of the corpse to the sand.

Blood and brains flew everywhere as she cut, hacked, jabbed, stabbed, and defended herself.

The circle had descended into a melee of madness. Deadwalkers were everywhere, leaping over the wagons and swarming through the gaps. The militia were fighting fiercely, each taking down dozens of the monstrous things, yet more kept coming. Was there no end to them? Where in the stone gods' green heaven were they coming from? How many were there in all?

Screams rang out all around her as militia were bitten by deadwalkers.

Their bites were infectious, poisoning the blood with whatever disease had caused their state, and the bitten turned feverish and died quickly, rising again as deadwalkers themselves. Everyone knew the myths. They were battling them now.

Through the storm of gore and horror that had descended over the camp, Aqreen's beleaguered senses found an instant to think of Krushita. Was she safe? She could see nothing in the boiling mass of bodies and sand dust and flailing limbs and weapons. The battle was raging thick and wild, and it could only end one way.

Tears spilled hotly from her eyes even as she whirled like a dervish, cutting down deadwalkers on all sides.

Stone Mother, keep my baby safe. I beg of you!

A shocked exclamation distracted her.

She glanced sideways and saw Kihrr hacking at a deadwalker who had latched onto his cheek. The new recruit reversed his sword and punched the point down into the deadwalker's skull. The creature fell, but he took a chunk of Kihrr's face with him. The young man's handsome features were destroyed, and the shocked disbelief on his face told Aqreen that he had realized that his time was ended now. The disease was already in his bloodstream and would turn him into one of them shortly. How long? Minutes? Hours? Aqreen didn't recall the myths and stories providing such helpful details. Myths never did.

Kihrr fought even more fiercely, and Aqreen turned away, too busy with her own defense. She didn't care to think about what would happen when Kihrr turned deadwalker. Or when the other living bodies around her also turned. The train was already on the verge of being lost. As if that wasn't enough, were they to also be punished with eternal damnation? The myths claimed that deadwalkers could never ascend to the Gardens of the Stone Gods. They were branded urrkh, the worst appellation possible. Urrkh could find a home only in hell.

Aqreen's arms worked, cutting skulls and spilling brains until she herself was covered with so much wetness, she no longer could tell if it was blood or gore or brain matter — or even her own blood. Had she been bitten? Could she already have been infected somehow and not know it? What if she turned too? What would happen to Krushita? Where was Krush now?

*Stone Mother,* she thought, barely able to complete the thought.

She punched the point of a shortsword through the eye of a deadwalker.

*Stone Mother.*

She hacked off the ear and side of the skull of a deadwalker.

*Stone Mother, keep her.*

She stabbed, sliced, chopped, swung, and cut down deadwalker after deadwalker. A nightmarish task that had no end.

*Safe.*

The din, the filth, the stench, the dust, the screams, the raw, searing desert heat, all enveloped her, wrapping her in a thick blanket of chaos and madness.

She fought on, barely more than a killing machine now, feeling her strength flagging, her arms losing their accuracy, her eyes dropping shut with exhaustion. Even the swords had lost their sharp edges, requiring more effort to cut through bone and flesh. Despite the muck-coated blades, she could see chips in the edges where they had caught on bone spurs or something harder.

She didn't know how much longer she could go on like this. Other militia were falling around her. The circle seemed to contain more deadwalkers than mortals. Stone Father alone knew what the state of the rest of the camp was right now. If militia were on the verge of utter defeat, what of the travelers? The old, the sick, the young, the infirm? It was a slaughter. A complete massacre.

The only thought that kept her alive was the question.

What about Krushita?

It was obvious Jarsun was responsible for this. Even if he'd chosen not to show himself thus far. He had somehow summoned up all these dead hordes from stone god knew where.

But if Krushita was infected too, if she was killed, then it would put paid to his plans to take the Burning Throne.

Urrkh could not be accepted in mortal society. Urrkh were unacceptable to every culture, including the morally questionable tyrants of the Krushan dynasty. Deadwalkers were urrkh. And if Krushita turned urrkh, she would have no claim to the Burning Throne, Hastinaga, the Burnt Empire. To anything, for that matter. She would become a monster, a creature of hell like all these filth.

Surely that wasn't what Jarsun wanted?

But imagining the destruction all around, the sheer scale of the slaughter, she couldn't see how it could end otherwise.

They were all going to die here, on the Red Trail, two years and two thousand miles short of Reygistan.

She cried out with frustration and rage, her emotion driving a last jolt of strength into her waning limbs, and swirled, hacking limbs, heads, bodies.

# *Bulan*

BULAN ROARED WITH FURY, hacking down deadwalkers by the dozens. All the Vanjhani had waded out into the thick of the enemy, outside the circle, and were making a stand. Bulan's four arms whirled constantly, keeping at bay the ones who tried to bite or grab at their feet. Not that any deadwalker would ever be able to pull Bulan off their feet; not even if a half dozen grabbed hold of one leg and pulled with all their might. Bulan was heavy even for Vanjhani, weighing in at almost seven hundred fifty pounds, most of it muscle and bone, and once they settled into a battle stance, it would take a gaja or a siege ram to knock them off their feet.

Their arms whirled constantly in curving arcs, each circumscribing a half circle, protecting their torso on all sides. They swung like threshers, lopping off skulls and liberating deadwalkers' brains as if they were ripe corn. Bulan knew that despite their valor and prowess, the odds were hardly being evened. The deadwalkers continued to appear from the desert in an endless river, seemingly as infinite as the great Jeel, Mother River of the world.

Few things could stand against a Vanjhani in full sword flow, and Bulan had battled against the best — and worst.

This present conflict definitely counted as one of the latter.

Still Bulan refused to accept or acknowledge the possibility of defeat.

That simply was not the Vanjhani way. Vanjhani fought to wipe out their enemy. Their goal was not to win, or conquer, or triumph, or any of those sentimental reasons that Krushan fought. The Burnt Empire? Paagh! Vanjhani spat on the Burnt Empire and their so-called undefeatable armies and champions. Vanjhani *fought*. Vanjhani did not cease fighting until the enemy was destroyed or had fled the field. And if the enemy was stronger, more wily, or more numerous — as was the case in this present instance — too numerous to finish off completely, and too stupid to flee? Well, rare as such a circumstance was, if such an event came to pass, then Vanjhani would fight. There was no other way. No retreat, no surrender, no parlay.

But Bulan had to acknowledge the fact that their own side was dying in exceptionally large numbers now. The militia were being wiped out. And if the militia were faring this poorly, then the other travelers in the camp were certainly worse off. True, every single traveler on the train knew how to fight and had done so since they could stand upright and hold a weapon, but this was no mortal enemy. This was urrkh. Only the stone gods could war against urrkh and hope to survive. For that matter, the stone gods had defeated the urrkh only through subterfuge and deception. And that was in the Age of Myth. If the oldest myths had no mention of urrkh ever being defeated in a standing battle, then how could any mortal, even Vanjhani, hope to accomplish such a task?

"Vanjhani!" Bulan roared the battle cry of their race, but heard the frustration in their voices now, felt their muscles creaking from overuse, their iron legs starting to melt with just a hint of fatigue. They had a great capacity and endurance, but even that had its limits. And these stonecursed deadwalkers seemed to have none.

"Vanjhani!" they bellowed again, chopping down a dozen deadwalkers with each swing. They had long since stopped giving orders or instructions. It was fight to the death, pure survival for everyone now. Bulan doubted there was any command structure left to pass orders on. Even the lookouts were probably all dead. They had seen the deadwalkers swarming up the lookout poles, snatching at the poor chaps, and pulling off their arms and legs. The lookouts had fought back as long as they could, but stood no real chance.

There was a worse problem brewing, if such a thing was possible. Something far worse than even these impossible odds.

Their own dead were starting to turn.

Out the corner of one eye, Bulan could see one of the captains pause in the midst of fighting and bend over, clutching her head in both hands, like someone in unbearable grief. Her fists opened, letting both her swords drop. She swayed briefly. No deadwalkers attacked her in this moment of weakness, Bulan noted, even though they could easily have taken her down.

Instead, they raised their rotting faces, sniffing through the stumps of noses and even, in one ugly face, just a single big hole where the nose once had been, then ignored the stricken captain and went on to seek other prey.

*The bastards know when one of us is infected. They can smell it on us.*

Suddenly, the captain dropped her hands. She opened her eyes, raising her head slowly, as if waking from a dream. They were red — not bloodshot, but filled with blood. Her lips parted, spittle dribbling from the corners, and she bared her teeth in an animal snarl. Any sound she made was lost in the deafening racket of the battle. Then she launched herself at Bulan, leaping through the air in an impossible arc. It was like watching a stone flung by a siege engine.

All of ten yards she leaped, coming down over Bulan.

One of Bulan's arms rose to meet her.

She was a deadwalker now, no longer human.

The captain's face landed on the point of Bulan's sword blade, a splash of gore bursting out the back of her head, and the maddened hunger in her blood-filled eyes was snuffed out like a blown candle.

Bulan shrugged and flicked the corpse off their sword like they were flicking a gibbet of flesh. The body flew into a mass of seething deadwalkers, taking several of them down. They were up again almost at once, surging toward Bulan with the same maddened hunger in their eyes.

Then the first Vanjhani fell.

Bulan did not see it but they heard the sound.

The unmistakable call of Vanjhani when downed in battle.

Not a cry of pain or plea for mercy.

Vanjhani did not acknowledge pain or beg for anything, whatever the circumstances.

This was a simple acknowledgment that they were going to meet their stone gods. That they were done with the business of living.

"Vanjhani arukku!"

It was a call to other Vanjhani.

A call to the stone gods they went to meet.

It was a promise and an elegy.

A goodbye and a challenge.

*Vanjhani arukku.*

*This Vanjhani is coming to their last fight. Be ready, whoever the fuck you are. Because this Vanjhani sure as fuck is ready.*

And then came the answering call, from a hundred Vanjhani throats as they responded to their downed fellow.

"Vanjhani arukku!"

The same words but with a different emphasis and tone.

*Go then, Vanjhani. Go to the last battle.*

Bulan felt something unexpected on their faces.

Not blood, or deadwalker brains, or gristle, or gore, or other bodily fluids, all of which they were liberally bathed with from heads to toes, as was every other person on this battlefield.

Tears.

Vanjhani tears.

As rare as a monsoon in the desert.

As unexpected as failure.

As shocking as loss.

"VANJHANI!" Bulan roared, leaping up into the air, swinging all four arms, then coming down on the heads and spines of a half dozen deadwalkers, crushing them with their feet to shards and pulp, hacking through the mass of writhing creatures like a sickle through wheat.

They would die, yes.

That was inevitable now.

But they would die Vanjhani.

They would fight until they were finally at the end of their tether. It would not be long. One misstep, one faltering arm, and the deadwalkers would move in to savage them. All it would take was one bite, even the smallest nibble.

That was when Bulan felt it.

# *Krushita*

~

## 1

KRUSHITA LOOKED DOWN AT the hordes of deadwalkers rushing away from her, back toward the camp. There were so many, and yet more kept coming. Miles and miles of nothing but deadwalkers swarming across the desert like an endless army of ants boiling up out of an anthill broken by a gaja's foot. She shuddered and issued a scree from the throat of the buzzard. The bird was scared of the stench that rose from below. Even its primitive brain sensed that although the smell was one of rank decay, it was *off*. Not even the odor of a million dead bodies ought to smell like this.

She flew through the dust cloud raised by the rushing of the deadwalkers across the sands, feeling sick to the stomach — both her own back at the camp and the buzzard's.

Finally, the end was in sight.

There, about a half mile ahead, she could glimpse bare red sand dunes again.

It was a relief. She had begun to fear that the entire Red Desert was swarming with urrkh. That was impossible of course: the Red Desert was more than twenty thousand miles from coast to coast, and none were quite sure how far it extended northward. No mortal soul had ever gone northward and lived to tell the tale: the Red Trail, which extended from the White Kingdom of Aqron, her mother's homeland, to the Desert Kingdoms of Reygistan, was treacherous enough to navigate. If there was an explorer or adventurer foolish enough to venture northward, their adventures and discoveries remained unknown and untold.

She dipped the buzzard's wings and flew lower, beating them to slow her forward progress, then tilting and turning to hold her position. She drifted on a hot current, neck bowed, gazing intently at the sand below.

Boiling was an accurate description.

The sand bubbled and erupted like thick hot broth in a cauldron over a campfire. One of Bulan's treacly Vanjhani concoctions perhaps.

But there was nothing appetizing about this phenomenon. The sand bubbled and boiled, pimpled and dimpled, breaking open to release the swarms of deadwalkers.

Krushita circled the spot, trying to see beneath the sand, but the dust, the heaving sand, and the hordes of deadwalkers made it difficult to see anything clearly.

She thought furiously, feeling frustrated. She couldn't ride the deadwalkers: they had no real thoughts to speak of, knew and cared nothing of what was happening or how it was happening. They were purely machines, their minds filled with a solitary thought: feed!

In truth, she was scared that if she slipped into one, she might . . . Well, she didn't care to think too much about what might happen. There were some things she simply couldn't do, whatever the circumstances or need.

But she had to do *something.*

People were dying. A great many people. The attack was very bad, too much for Bulan and the brave travelers to fight. Their only hope was Krushita. If she didn't do something, in a few more hours, the camp would be nothing but a great slaughterhouse filled with rotting corpses and lurching deadwalkers.

She'd had an idea. It was a good idea, she knew. She felt instinctively it would work. But to implement it — to even attempt it — she had to get below the sand. And how would she do that?

There were no shvan anywhere in sight. She had looked around, scanning the desert with the buzzard's sharp gaze.

The brave creatures, valiant and fearless as they were, had known that the deadwalker menace was something beyond their ability to cope with. They had fled the camp. She could sense the mind of the shvan prima she had inhabited earlier today, confused and frightened, sick with guilt at abandoning her human companions, but relieved to be with the pack again, to be alive, to be away from those awful urrkh. She knew there must be a history there: perhaps sometime in the distant past, maybe even as far back as the Age of Myth, shvan must have fought repeatedly with deadwalkers. Their fear now — the shvan female's fear — was primal, instinctive, deep-rooted, and unshakeable.

Krushita could have slipped into the pack's hive mind. Taken control of all the primas that controlled and led the pack. Forced them and the rest to return to the camp and engage the deadwalkers.

But what good would that do?

The shvan might bite or use their needle dart quills against the deadwalkers, but there were still many times more deadwalkers already than the total number of shvan and humans combined. All would be killed eventually. And all that would achieve was the extermination of the shvan along with their human masters.

Perhaps that was something a general or commander might do. Perhaps what one of the Krushan, those despotic tyrants of the Burnt Empire, might do.

Krushita knew her history, knew how her father's people would resort to any means necessary to win a battle, even expending all their mortal soldiers and animals.

Krushan themselves were empowered by the strange, deadly stonefire, and so long as there was some of that living black rock nearby, could be healed of almost any injury or wound. That might be why they could be so megalomaniacal in their campaigns of conquests, their dreaded legendary ashvamedhavaryas — the Ashcrit term for a military journey that involved capturing every foot of ground covered by the Krushan emperor. It was how they had expanded the Burnt Empire across most of the north and west of Arthaloka to create the largest united empire in the known world.

Yes, Krushan would force the shvan pack back into the fray, expending them all to bring down as many of the enemy as possible before their own forces were exterminated. That was the Krushan way. That was her father's way.

She was not her father.

Krushan blood flowed in her veins, but she did not share the cruelty of her lineage.

Aqronian blood also flowed through her. The blood of her mother and her grandfather, both kind, wise, fair, and just. Aqronian kings fought alongside their people, sharing their food, their facilities, and their fate. One law for all, one dream together.

That was the tradition she had been raised in. A tradition where social justice mattered more than conquest, wealth, and power.

She would not force the shvan.

She would find another way.

And she had to find it quickly.

She knew her mother was alive. She could feel Aqreen's brain still active, her heart still beating, but could sense that she was at the end of her strength. Even Bulan and their Vanjhani, those tall, proud, hulking two-bodied warriors, were beginning to feel fatigue, something she would not have dreamed was possible. The battle was lost. The camp, the train, everyone in it, was lost. Total massacre was only a short time away.

Krushita had to do something now.

She reached out into the desert, seeking something, anything that she could slip herself into, use its eyes and senses to see below that boiling sand. She needed to see the source of the deadwalkers.

No.

It was more than that now.

She needed to be at that source.

But how?

She could sense only the insects, worms, and other tiny denizens that lived inside the sand. Nothing with a brain intelligent enough for her to use. The snakes, vermin, sand hogs, and similar reptiles and mammals had been dislodged from their tunnels and burrows and fled the disruptive anomaly as fast as they could slither, crawl, or run.

There was no living creature that she could inhabit and use below the sand.

Far away, some thousand miles away, she sensed the reptilian brain of a sleeping dragon, burrowed deep below the surface where the sand was closer to the water table and cooler, away from the heat of the sun. It slept the days away and emerged by night to rove the desert, seeking hot-blooded mammalian prey.

She could slip into its mind if she tried hard, but the effort required to rouse it from its deep slumber, wrest control of its consciousness, then fly it all the way here only to burrow down in this spot would take precious time.

People could be dying every minute she hovered here indecisive. Her mother. Bulan. Dor and Niede and their little children, the eldest of whom, Afranus, was a year younger than Krushita herself. They depended on her. Even her own life depended on what she did next.

Her vulnerable body lay back in the camp, inside the wagon. She had no idea what would happen if she were to be killed back in the camp while still inhabiting the mind of the buzzard. Would she still be conscious, a disembodied soul like in a campfire ghost story? Would she remain part of the buzzard as long as the buzzard lived? She didn't know and didn't want to find out.

She came to a decision fatalistically.

There was simply no other way.

It had to be done, and it had to be done *now.*

With a final scree of protest, the buzzard flapped its wings, trying to fly upward, away from the horrific, unnatural stench, struggling against the mind that was forcing it to do something that no living animal would knowingly do.

Then she folded her wings, dipped her sharp beak, and dove.

She fell like a stone from the clear green sky.

Landed right in the midst of the turmoil.

In the heaving sand.

In the writhing masses of deadwalkers boiling up from below.

In the portal.

## 2

The buzzard screamed.

The poor bird was terrified of the foul stench of the deadwalkers. Bonded as she was with the bird's senses, the odor threatened to overwhelm Krushita too. Even her unconscious body back at the camp shifted uneasily, repelled.

Worse than the smell was the fear that came from being so close to the mindless insanity. Krushita could sense it seeping into her own mind, like the overflow from a cesspool. She knew if she didn't resist it with all her might, it would drown her. The long-dead brains of the deadwalkers functioned solely at the level of predators, like the sharks of the sea they told tales of in Aqron. All they knew was hunger, all they understood was feeding. Even the fact that they must kill in order to feed didn't quite penetrate their dehumanized consciousness. To them, the living were no different from a plant or a fruit. *Food.* The concept of life itself had no meaning for those who had already survived death. Hunger was all that mattered.

She was in the ground now, under the desert surface. The buzzard screeched pitifully, afraid of the darkness filled with unknown dangers. Sand flew everywhere, swirling, billowing, rising and falling in sheets and waves. It was something like being in a sandstorm, except there was no desert below. No ground. Only darkness, and a howling, deafening wind. Even the buzzard's primitive mind could sense that.

The wind terrified the creature too. This was not a wind that ruffled the bird's feathers or could carry it high above the desert, like the air currents it was accustomed to riding.

It was an absence of wind. A sucking, howling thing that had no actual body of its own, no substance, only absence.

It, too, was a kind of hunger. A bottomless, infinite craving.

From this pitch-black emptiness, the deadwalkers were being flung up onto the surface of the desert and deposited in the crimson dunes.

The buzzard could see them scrambling up, stumbling, lurching, then stepping out into the gaudy sunlit daylight.

From here, in the darkness, they were little more than silhouettes, like figures seen leaving a shadowy room as they stepped out into the afternoon sunlight.

Once in the open, they sensed the frenzy of those ahead and immediately began running, picking up speed, sensing live food ahead. Driven by the herd instinct, they poured out over the desert in the frenzied racing hordes that were headed for the wagon train's camp, only a few miles away. Food! So much food for the taking. *Run! Feed!* The hammering of their bony feet, thousands upon endless thousands, created a distant thunder that the buzzard sensed in the fine, sensitive tips of its wings. It shrieked again, protesting at being in such an unnatural place, under the surface of the world, in a place that was somehow not of this world.

Krushita turned the buzzard's attention away from the sight of the deadwalkers and forced it to look down into the abyss, keeping its wings moving constantly to stay afloat. The buzzard fell silent, its sense of terror shocked out of it as it viewed the madness that lay below its belly. Above was death and madness; below was so far beyond its comprehension that it could form no response to it at all.

As Krushita and the buzzard descended lower and still lower, plunging impossibly through what seemed like hundreds of yards of emptiness, they approached a vista both familiar and unbelievable.

They were above a battlefield. High up, above the clouds, above a vast, infinite plain that stretched in every direction as far as the buzzard's sharp eyes could see — which was quite a distance.

And far below them, glimpsed as a scattering of ants upon a great panoply, were the remains of what must have been a terrible battle.

*We're in the sky again,* Krushita thought, trying to make sense of the view through the buzzard's eyes. *We went down below the desert's surface and somehow emerged* above *another place.*

How was that possible?

It didn't matter now. What mattered was that she was here in this *other* place and the source of the deadwalkers was in sight.

She forced the confused buzzard to fly lower, dropping down several hundred yards. The battlefield came sharply into focus. She could now make out individual details. A great battle had been fought here some time ago. Days, perhaps even weeks ago. She could tell that from the buzzard's senses as it responded to the scents and sights of decaying corpses.

Bodies lay strewn in the grass like sand grains on a beach. Millions, perhaps tens of millions. She had never heard of such a battle.

Except perhaps in the Age of Myth. Everything back then had been in the millions or billions, be it the number of kine owned by a lord, or soldiers in their armies. Even urrkh, who the myths claimed were infinite in number.

Her mother had cautioned her that the ancient sages who had recorded the myths — verbally at first, using the time-honored tradition of Ashcrit rote recitation, then on bits of bark and leaves, and finally on the scroll-books that were used in this modern era — had a tendency to exaggerate. All it took was the addition of a shunya, the ever so-useful-zero digit, or even more than one shunya.

But this was no exaggeration. What she was witnessing here was the detritus of a battle so enormous, she couldn't begin to comprehend its vastness. Without physically counting the numbers of dead, she suspected it ran into the hundred millions.

But that would mean almost every living soul in Arthaloka.

No such battle had been fought in known history.

Unless . . .

The thought came to her with the same instinctive insight that had helped her adapt so quickly to being here in this *other* place.

*Unless this is a battle that has yet to happen.*

In the future.

Incredible as that might seem, it somehow made more sense than what she was seeing. Yes, she felt, *that* must be the explanation.

This was a time yet to come, the future. And this was a great battle that would be fought someday, involving all the nations and tribes of the world. The Mother of All Wars. Such a war had been foretold in the legends, and all the sages insisted solemnly that it would come to pass. But none were clear about the when or where or why and how of it.

She didn't dwell on it.

All that mattered now was that she was here, and that this was the source of the deadwalkers.

She could see the place where the portal extended down to the ground below. It was shaped like an enormous funnel, one of those spinning clouds that touched the ground and caused great devastation in some parts of the world that she had heard of in Bulan's campfire tales.

What did the Vanjhani call them? Tornadoes?

The portal had assumed the shape of a tornado, extending down from the sky to touch down on the battlefield below. There it sucked up the corpses of the dead soldiers from both sides, drawing them up through the funnel, up to the sky and beyond the dark, brooding mass that hung high above. From there, up through the surface of the Red Desert. Somehow, during that journey, the corpses were reanimated, brought back to a grotesque parody of life. The dreaded urrkh creatures of myth that rose from their graves and fed on living flesh and blood.

She could see the tornado moving steadily across the great plain, sucking up hundreds and thousands of corpses everywhere it touched ground. It had denuded a sizable patch of the vast battlefield, but there was still a plentiful supply to draw on.

*If it continues this way, the camp will be overrun, everyone wiped out, before I can even return to my body.*

If *I can return to my body.*

She forced the buzzard to fly closer to the tornado, close enough that the bird could feel the power of the spinning dervish in its wingtips. She felt its heart flutter with fear and forced her will over it. She dropped down until she was close enough to view the spot where the funnel touched ground, sucking up the corpses. She didn't know what, if anything, she was looking for, but she had a feeling she would know it when she saw it.

The sound of the tornado grew louder, enveloping her. It was like nothing she — or the bird — had ever heard before. The growling, grinding roar of a mindless giant. It filled her senses and made rational thought seem impossible. This was like a force of nature, something beyond mortal understanding.

Yet she knew it was not so. No. This was her father's doing, the work of his powerful Krushan sorcery. She had to figure out how it worked before she could try to stop it.

She flew around the howling funnel, careful to keep a distance — in the buzzard's judgment, that was about a half mile, to be on the safe side. Any closer, and she risked being drawn into its maw.

She completed a full circuit, returning to the place where she had started with no new knowledge or insight. It was a tornado, that was all she could make out. Grey-black as a monsoon cloud, spinning at impossible speed, drawing up everything from the ground, and hurling it miles above into the dark brooding mass which masked the way to the other world, her world.

After two more such circuits, she was none the wiser.

She screeched a cry of frustration through the buzzard's beak. It was lost in the howl of the tornado.

She flew faster, venting her frustration by doing another full circuit of the tornado. She had to adjust her flight trajectory because the tornado was constantly shifting, and at one point, the bird squawked in dismay as it felt the vicious tug of the storm.

She flapped its wings fiercely, driven by the anger she now felt, breaking free with an effort. The buzzard emitted a sound more like a mewling complaint than a bird's cry. Its simple animal brain could no longer make sense of its own actions: they went against the very grain of its survival instincts.

She ignored it, her temper rising as she completed yet another circuit and started round again. She must find a way; she simply *must.* If she'd been on solid ground and had use of her feet, she would have stamped them and tossed her head.

She remembered her mother admonishing her. *Krush, getting mad never made anything better.*

But she was mad now.

She was mad as hell.

She was mad at her father for doing this. For being such an awful man. Did he think that by massacring the entire train, he would win Krushita back? All he had done was make her even more determined to fight him. She would *not* let him win. Even if it killed her to resist. She would fight him till her last breath.

She was screeching with rage now, driving the buzzard faster and faster, beyond all physical limits, powering its flight with her own power.

The bird felt the raw power rushing through its body, felt the energy flowing all around it.

In its own way, it understood this.

This was a river of energy, not very different from the river of wind that flowed through the skies of Arthaloka.

The buzzard knew that such rivers, and their currents, could be used to hitch a ride for vast distances. This was part of its skill set.

It rode the Flow, letting the raw current carry it even faster, and faster still, until it was able to fold its wings back, lower its beak, and dive headfirst into the wildest spin of its entire existence.

It spun round the tornado shape of the portal, zooming round and round at a speed so great, there was no way to even estimate it.

Krushita sensed a change.

She expanded her senses beyond the consciousness of the buzzard, sending tendrils of perception out into the flow.

In the visionless dimension of the Flow, the tornado was a dark void, spinning in one direction at a tremendous speed.

She and the buzzard were spinning in the same direction.

And they were matching the speed of the tornado.

As their speeds equaled, the tornado seemed to disappear.

In its place was only a black funnel. Not the color black. A void. An emptiness, an absence of light, a negation of vision.

At this incredible speed, the portal seemed curiously still, silent, passive.

A sentient nothingness.

It hung in the Flow, an absence of energy, of power.

Just . . . there.

Krushita reached out to touch its periphery, throwing caution aside.

She had come this far, this close, she could not go back having failed.

She *must* succeed.

She felt an electric sensation as her expanded consciousness made contact with the portal itself.

Then a numbness that seeped into her mind, her heart, her entire being.

She floated in the void, blackness overwhelming her, filling the world, blocking out all thoughts of the living, of life itself, of the physical normal world she knew. The world of laughter and living, love and family, childhood and death, hunger and sleep, everything disappeared. All that remained was the void.

It was like being in the space between worlds, far outside of Arthaloka, the great sun that warmed and lit the planet, like being in that infinite blackness that was simply *beyond*.

And somewhere in that vast space, somewhere far away in its vast, infinite emptiness, was another consciousness. Very, very faint, like the tiniest pinprick of light from a star whose presence was sensed rather than seen. The only star in an otherwise pitch-black space.

She went toward it.

The star was countless miles away. Not even miles, for the concept of distance itself did not exist here. It was simply *away.*

Krushita frowned to herself, thinking. She knew that the usual laws of nature did not apply inside the portal.

This was a place beyond space and time, beyond the rules and laws of the natural world.

There was no such thing as distance here. No such thing as past and present and future. There simply was, or was not.

And that light, that other consciousness, *was.*

And so was she.

It was like, she thought, grasping at an insight, like the way she had reached out to Ma when she was a baby. When she had been too young to use language. When her world had been only emotion and Flow. Pure, raw energy.

She had only to reach out, and Ma was right there. It didn't matter if they were in the same room or a mile apart. And she had sensed that it wouldn't have mattered if they had been a thousand miles apart, or even a million times a million miles. In that Flow, she had only to seek Ma, and Ma was right there with her. Close enough to touch with her mind.

She let herself slip back into that mode of connection, letting her subconscious take over, reaching out through the Flow.

With a shock, she saw the tiny pinprick of light expand almost instantly.

It grew into a blinding halo. A bright white light tinged with dark blue at the edges.

She had made contact with the other consciousness.

With the other being inside the portal.

She sensed the Other grow aware of her, turning its attention to Krushita.

*His* attention.

For it was a masculine presence, this Other.

She sensed that clearly.

A very powerful, old, wise Other.

The Other turned toward her, bathing her in the wash of blinding white-blue light, studying her closely.

All this happened in the fraction of a fraction of an instant.

Then the Other spoke.

**Child?**

Krushita didn't respond. She didn't know if she should respond.

She couldn't tell if this Other was a friend or a foe. There was something . . . intimidating . . . about him. She sensed that he could be either, depending on what served his need. It was this realization that made her stay silent.

**Yes, child.** He seemed certain of it now. **A mere child. But one powerful in the Flow. A Krushan, certainly. But something more than just Krushan.**

More than Krushan? What did he mean? Krushita knew her father was Krushan, which was why she had his blood, his powers, in herself. And the

Krushan were the most powerful race in the world. What could be *more* than that?

He chuckled. It was a startling sound in the emptiness of the portal.

**There are more things in the universe than you know, little one.**

She frowned. She already knew that. Her mother never stopped reminding her of this fact, especially when she made some mistake because she assumed — incorrectly — that she knew the right way to do something.

She didn't need some strange man reminding her as well.

Now he smiled.

She sensed the amusement, rather than saw it.

The white-blue light pulsed yellow briefly.

**You are far more than just your father's daughter, little Krush,** he said. **More than your mother's as well. Even I am not entirely sure of what you are. But this much I do know. You have a great destiny ahead.**

She rolled her eyes. Big help that was at a time like this, rambling on like one of the cheap fortunetellers on the wagon train. She needed to know how to close this portal, not what a bright and shining future lay ahead for her. Because unless she stopped the attack of the deadwalkers, her future would die up there in the Red Desert, along with her mother. And that was the only future that mattered to her right now.

**I see. Yes, yes, of course. I am being pompous. That is one of my many faults. But I do not exaggerate the importance of what you are, of who you are. In the great god-game played out on the chaupat board of Arthaloka, you are no pawn, or even a rook. You are a queen. *The* Queen. The Dark Queen of whom the prophecies foretold in the Age of Legend.**

Krushita was silent. Was this man mocking her? No. She sensed that mockery and humor were not part of his repertoire. He meant every word.

**I do. You have existed in one form or another ever since the beginning of time. Perhaps once you *were* Time itself. You are immortal, you are infinite, you are the all-knowing and everlasting. In every age, you take new avatars, each appropriate to the purpose at hand. For this age, this is one of your avatars: Krushita, daughter of Jarsun Krushan and Aqreen Aqron, niece of Sha'ant and Jeel. But this is not your only avatar in this era. There will be more. Indeed, I sense you will have another birth within the next several years, perhaps in a short decade or two.**

She let the words wash through her, simply taking it all in, not fully processing it or even attempting to do so. There was a sense of inevitability about his pronouncements. She felt as if he was merely putting words to things she had already known, had been born knowing.

**Yes, you know this already. It is part of your journey, the knowledge of things yet to come. Yet remember one thing, little Krush. Even the gods have free will. As do all living things. Even though destiny be carved in stone, fate decreed, fortunes set, yet then too the living can shift mountains if enough force is applied. How? Because of the Flow. The great river of energy that is perceived on Arthaloka as Jeel is in fact the Mother Goddess of All. The source and end of all life, all energy, all matter. It has no beginning, middle, or end. It is simply . . . the Flow. An endless cycle of energy creating and uncreating. It has had many names in many cultures, many worlds. Ouroboros. Kala. Omega. Chukwa. Ganga.**

He fell silent then. In the absence of his words, she waited.

**In this age, you shall be known as Krushni. But that is only one of your names and forms.**

She thought then that she knew what he would say next. That she would also be known as Krushita, since she already was. But instead, he said:

**Krushni. The life that comes after this one, little Krush. You know as well as I do that Krushita will never live to see a full life, middle age, old age. That is not your destiny. Your fate lies elsewhere.**

An image coalesced through the light.

It formed out of the light itself, the color turning from white-blue to yellow, then deeper, darker, fiercer shades, until it pulsed yellow, red, scarlet, saffron, a cycling range of hues. She sensed within that fiery kaleidoscope an object, something large and ominous.

A great black throne in a vast chamber.

The black stone of which it was made pulsed and throbbed with raw power, a living awareness.

It glowed, then burst into flame.

*Come,* it said, *come unto me, you are mine.*

She felt its pull like a nail drawn toward a lump of magnetic ore.

**Upon the Burning Throne,** said the voice again, tinged with sadness now. The weary acceptance of a mind that had seen much pain and suffering and would see much more yet. **That is where you belong. It will call you, and you will go. You cannot resist its summons. That is what is meant to be.**

*Come,* said the Burning Throne, its call louder and more urgent as the flames roared around her, inside her, through her. *We belong together, you and I. We are one and the same.*

**And when that comes to pass, great things will follow.**

Another pause, this one briefer than the one before.

**Great, terrible things.**

She knew then with a flash of insight: This battlefield. The corpses. The Mother of All Wars. She would be a part of it somehow. She would be one of the combatants. No, not just one of them. She would be the main initiator. It would be on her command that this war would occur, that this enormous conflict unfold, that this unimaginable price be paid. She did not yet know why, or how, or when, but she knew this much for certain. This would be a war of her own making.

**Free will,** he said, reminding her gently. **It is what differentiates us from stones and sticks. What fuels our lives. Even the stone gods were overthrown once, not by other gods, or even the urrkh, their eternal enemies. But by mere mortals. That is the power of free will. You have it, little one. Use it when the time comes. Remember, you are no pawn in the God Game. You are a queen. The most powerful queen of all. You are the Dark Queen herself. When the time comes, you must rise. You alone can do it, and when you do, then destiny itself will alter to match your path.**

His voice was fading now, the large halo of light retreating rapidly into the black void. Now it was barely a hand's width; now it was the size of a thumbnail.

**Remember, Krush. You are only one half of a great and powerful equation. Find your other half. Unite. And discover what you are meant to become.**

Now he was only a pinprick again, the tiniest star in an infinite cosmos.

The star winked out.

## 3

Krushita drifted in the void for an unknown time.

She sent her consciousness out in all directions, but it was no use.

The old wise one was gone. She sensed that she would find him again someday, that she even knew who he was, where he was. A name floated up from the pool of her memories. *Vessa.* A name spoken by her mother, and by Bulan in the campfire tales. A name linked with many tales, many other great names, great doings. But it mattered not now.

All that mattered now was that she knew.

She knew what she must do to save her mother.

She could not stop the portal.

It was eternal and infinite. Like a door that had always hung on unseen hinges. Simply *there.*

She could not stop it any more than she could stop light or time.

But she could *mold* it.

As her father had molded it into the shape of a tornado to funnel up the corpses and transform them into deadwalkers.

As he had moved the portal, placing it between this future time and her present back in the Red Desert.

She could do the same.

He had already done the hardest part.

He had set it up, leaving it to run on its own.

Then he had gone on some other errand or mission. Something more important and urgent than the killing of her mother and the slaughter of all those innocents. Something that required his physical presence in the natural world.

With him gone, she had no opposition.

He had not expected that she would find a way to come through the portal and beyond it, into the Flow, into the void itself, the place from which the portal itself came.

He had not even conceived of such a possibility.

That was his mistake.

She worked her will, reaching out to the void, connecting with the cold, mindless power of the portal.

Talking to the tornado.

She told it what she wanted it to do.

And miracle of miracles, the tornado listened.

Then obeyed.

# *Aqreen*

AQREEN WAS AT THE end of her strength. She had backed herself against a wagon wheel, holding the swords by her sides. Deadwalkers threw themselves on the blades to get to her. She barely had to move the tips to catch their throats, the softest, most yielding point at which to enter the brain. The swords passed up and through their skulls and out the tops of their heads. All she had to do was aim and brace her elbows against the spokes of the wheel to take the impact, then turn the blades to let the corpses slip off before angling the swords up again to meet the next attackers.

Even in this position, she could not last long. She was beyond exhaustion, her body and mind functioning purely on survival instinct, and even this was giving out. After all, even the most determined creature eventually decided that survival was simply too hard to struggle for anymore, then lay down and surrendered to the inevitable, craving the blissful numbness of eternal rest.

Then, all of a sudden, everything stopped.

The rushing deadwalkers slowed their forward momentum and came to a halt. They raised their heads as if listening to unheard music from some distant source.

Aqreen felt her weary face muscles attempt a frown. A nerve jumped in her cheek, misfiring from fatigue. She could hear nothing at all. Except . . . well, except *silence.* There were no wounded crying out as would be usual at any ordinary battle. Those who were wounded had succumbed to the deadwalkers, who tore their vocal cords from their throats in a flash, while those that had been bitten turned into deadwalkers themselves and no longer felt the pain and agony that mortals were subject to.

Then she heard it.

Faint, distant, but growing closer rapidly.

A deep, rumbling vibration so low that she felt it in the bones of her chest rather than heard it.

She thought that Bulan must have heard it first, along with the other Vanjhani. Their own voices and guttural sounds were so low-pitched, they could hear things that other humans never caught.

Earthquake?

That was the only natural event she could think of.

What else could make such a sound, on such a scale?

It was not just in her chest now. It was in all her bones, even her skull.

Everything vibrated.

Thrummed.

Like the lowest string on a bass sitraal. She had heard an orchestra from the Mountain Kingdoms play once, on her travels with her father. At a crucial point in the symphony, the rest of the orchestra had been silenced by the conductor and only the bass sitraals played on. They had begun with a single string on a single instrument. Then, still vibrating, it was joined by a second, then a third, and so on until a score were playing their lowest strings. The resulting wave of bass sound had reverberated so deep, Aqreen's teeth had ached for an hour after the performance — she had been an adolescent girl, and her wisdom teeth had been cutting through — but the sheer wonder and epic beauty of the effect had been like nothing else she had heard before or since. It was a profound experience.

This sound was deeper, and louder.

Much, much louder.

It carried with it a sense of immense power, a vast untameable force of nature. An avalanche. A volcanic eruption. An earthquake. A tsunami. Or all of the above.

Even the deadwalkers had stopped attacking.

They stood, heads raised and tilted, as if listening to the sky.

She saw ravaged faces with flesh hanging in rags look upward, the harsh sunlight doing them no favors.

She relaxed her arms slowly, not because she no longer feared attack, but because her muscles were simply exhausted. They screamed with relief as she lowered them to her sides, the swords hanging limply from her fingers.

She was tempted to let the weapons drop to the sand, to let herself tumble and fall face-down, letting whatever was to happen happen. But she resisted the urge, forcing herself to stay awake and alert, ready to fight again. She was a mother. She had Krushita to think of. Her life was not just her own to do with as she pleased.

She glanced around, using the reprieve to look properly at the circle, at what remained of the militia. She was not surprised to see familiar faces lying dead or turned into deadwalkers themselves, but she was shocked all the same.

Nothing could have prepared her for the sight of a friendly face, now with blood-filled eyes and mouth snarling open, dribbling saliva, turning and moving like a badly strung marionette. Those were people she had known, traveled with, laughed with, sung with, drunk with, eaten with, shared personal stories and insights with, made emotional connections with, for five hard years on the trail. They were the closest thing to real friends and family she had now. It was heart-rending to see them lying savaged on the sand, or staring with that maddened hunger, no longer mortal.

She avoided looking at them, trying to take in the scale of the slaughter, the sheer quantum of loss.

How many in the camp had died already? The ones who had turned were as good as dead, if not worse. How many had fallen this terrible, unspeakable day? And it was not even noon yet. Only high morning. Had it really only been a few hours? During the last attack—bandits—the train had held its own in the Perfect Circle for nearly two weeks, ultimately costing the bandits more lives than they were able to claim. That process of steady attrition and their excellent defenses had finally dissuaded the band. On the twelfth day, the survivors had ridden their dromads away into the desert, cutting their losses.

Bulan ran the train like a military operation, and in full strength, it was a formidable force. She had heard stories of epic battles in the distant past, not led by Bulan themself, who was barely five hundred years old, but other Vanjhani train masters. Back in the olden days when trains had numbered as many as a hundred thousand wagons. A train was nothing less than an armed force in its own right. A traveling fortress of sorts.

The fortress had fallen.

The army was against the wall.

The battle, if it could be called that, was lost.

But now something was happening.

Something that thrummed and vibrated with the ominous warning tones of a major natural event.

And it seemed to be originating from the sky.

Was it thunder?

Aqreen squinted up, using the overhang of the wagon roof to shield her eyes from the morning sun, already high in the east.

The sky above the Red Desert was as spotless green as always.

Green, not blue like the sky above Aqron and the White Desert, because the Red Desert was so vast, its hue was reflected in the blue expanse above, resulting in a color that varied from aqua to turquoise through the course of the long desert day.

She had grown accustomed to the shade, even though she had spent all her earlier life under cerulean skies.

There was not a cloud in sight.

Yet there was something.

It began more as a shimmering, a kind of wavy disturbance in the light above the camp.

It resembled a heat mirage, the flowing waves of heat over the desert on a hot day, often tricking the ignorant into thinking it was water.

The Reygistani word expressed it best: *galtanazarun*. False sight.

It was their term for an optical illusion or mirage. But it also meant a delusion, hallucination, trick of the light, and a number of similar illusions caused by the shifting heat waves, air currents, and strange reflections of the red sands.

But how could a galtanazarun appear in the sky?

She had never heard of such a thing before.

Yet whatever she was seeing now, it was up there.

The sky seemed to tremble, shivering like the placid surface of a pond into which a stone had been dropped slowly.

The deadwalkers were all staring up now, transfixed.

She looked down at the ones nearest to her.

They were close enough to reach out and grab hold of her limbs. Her swords were dangling by her sides. If they came at her with their frenzied suddenness, she didn't know if she would be able to bring the blades up in time. She was just too damn tired. But they weren't interested in her any longer. They were hypnotized by that phenomenon in the sky.

The deep bass sound changed.

Now it was almost like an avalanche coupled with thunder at the same time.

She looked around wildly, convinced she would see a mountain somewhere nearby, with snow and boulders rolling down its side. Or a volcano sprouting lava.

But there was only the camp and the Red Desert.

She was forced to raise her hands as the rumbling grew louder, deeper, more ominous.

It was like the baying of war horns now, those enormous yellow ones used by the Mountain Kingdoms to announce the declaration and cessation of wars, the sound designed to carry across vast distances, penetrating into valleys and caves and city fortresses within the mountains themselves.

Out here in the wide open wasteland, the sound was terrible, inescapable.

She felt the sand beneath her feet shivering.

The wagon she was leaning against shuddering.

Her teeth chattering in her mouth.

She tried to hold her jaws shut. The pressure was so intense, she was afraid her teeth would shatter. She opened her mouth again, keeping her teeth far enough apart that they would not clatter.

Her head began to fill with the sound now.

She was forced to block her ears to shield them from the sound. The sword hilts came in the way and she sheathed them quickly so she could press her palms to her ears. Even with her hands against her ears, her mouth wide open, she could still feel the rumbling shaking her.

Everything was shaking now.

The wagons.

The sand.

The deadwalkers.

The corpses.

The world was shuddering.

The deadwalkers began to moan, still staring up at the sky.

Their open maws released a disturbingly mortal sound, a kind of groaning complaint, like a sick man might make when in too much pain.

She looked up again at the sky.

The shimmering had darkened.

Now she could see that it wasn't the sky itself that was shimmering.

It was the air above the camp.

Some hundreds of yards above her head, a strange disturbance had formed, a roughly drawn circle almost as large as the Perfect Circle formation of the train itself.

This patch of air was sparking and flashing, not with lightning, but with a blackish light like nothing she had ever seen.

Black lightning? There's no such thing!

Yet she could see it up there, jagged black slashes across the aquamarine sky.

One, two, three, four of them.

They spread from north to south, as if the cloth of a green tent were being rent by the claws of a jaegura, the pitch-black feline beasts that roamed the hills and forests of her motherland.

A wind rose from nowhere, blowing sand up into the air. She blinked, then quickly clawed at her throat, pulling at the musl scarf she wore around her neck. She tugged it up to cover her mouth and nostrils. After five years on the trail, she was accustomed to sudden sand flurries, even sand dervishes spinning like pirouetting Regyari dancers. She debated whether to pull it all the way up to cover her face, but decided to wait a moment to see if it continued.

It did.

Growing steadily, the wind rose in moments to a howling banshee frenzy. Sand rose everywhere, seeming to drift upward rather than sideways. She had never seen that before. How could a wind come from the ground and rise up?

As she pulled the musl scarf over her face, protecting her eyes from the grit, she saw four black slashes joined by four more, these going across the length of the anomaly from east to west. It made a crisscross pattern. More slashes now appeared at a faster rate, at random, ripping at the still visible sky. Had this actually been a tent and the cause a jaegura, the creature could easily have stepped through the rent canvas, to feast on the sleeping campers.

Instead, the sky burst open.

*No,* she corrected herself, squinting against the storm of sand that was rising up now, *not the sky, just that big patch overhead. The anomaly.*

The black slashes became an enormous black hole. Not a storm cloud, but a void. An absence of light.

The sand was rushing upward in a torrent now, the wind a deafening roar.

And with the sand, the deadwalkers were rising too.

She saw the ones closest to her shriek as they were lifted off their feet, their ragged flesh and even more ragged garments flapping furiously, and rose up through the air at an increasing speed.

All around the camp, or at least as far as she could see, the deadwalkers were being dragged upward.

The ear-shattering shriek that rose with them could have been the wind and the sand, or a million deadwalkers screaming.

Aqreen couldn't tell which.

She shut her eyes, holding on to the side of the wagon with all her strength. She wondered if she would feel her feet leave the ground too at any moment. The wagons? The entire camp? Everyone in it?

But for some reason, the wind and whatever force was pulling the deadwalkers upward asked nothing of her. Nor did the wagon she was clinging to budge even an inch.

How was that possible?

How was any of this possible?

She didn't know and didn't care.

All she could think about was Krushita. Her baby. *Is she safe? Is she well? Is she . . . alive?*

It came to her then.

A touch out of nowhere.

*Ma.*

She started. "Krush?"

She looked around.

But there was nothing there except the wagons and the billowing sand.

The voice was in her mind.

Krushita had been inside her, just for an instant, touching her mind to let her know she was well, she was safe.

"You're doing this, aren't you, Krushita?" she said in wonder.

She tried to look up. Even with her scarf over her eyes, the sand stung, blasting her eyeballs through the thin cloth. She was forced to shut her eyes to protect them, but in the brief instant she had looked up, she had seen something.

It looked like two gigantic hands holding open the ends of the rent in the sky.

Two hands that were enormous in scale but were very much like her seven-year-old daughter's tiny little hands.

Krushita was doing this.

"A portal," Aqreen whispered in amazement.

Krushita had opened a portal to another place, or time, or wherever it was that black hole led to.

And she was forcing all the deadwalkers through to that other place.

Far, far away from the train, and Aqreen, and Krushita's physical body.

Her little baby had saved them.

# *Bulan*

BULAN OPENED THEIR EYES slowly.

The air was clear.

A few sand particles were drifting down, pattering like raindrops on the wagon tops, but the wind had died out completely.

The desert was as bare as it had been before this morning.

Not a deadwalker was in sight.

They looked around, blinking rapidly to make they weren't imagining it. It had been a long time since Bulan had chewed gajjna; they had been in Vanjhani military school, much younger, much more foolish, and much more willing to experiment. They wanted to be sure this wasn't some kind of drug effect. Or hallucination. Or dream.

But they were alive, awake, alert. Or as alert as they could be after that grueling battle. Tired, exhausted to the point of wanting to drop right to sleep here on the sand, but in their senses.

They turned a full circle, their heavy feet sinking in the soft sand.

The only people left in Bulan's view were the living.

They saw the other Vanjhani staring back at them, as dazed as Bulan, also trying to make sense of what had happened.

Bulan looked up at the sky.

It was a clean, unbroken slate of aqua again.

Gone was the gaping black hole, or tunnel or funnel or whatever the fuck it had been.

And the deadwalkers had gone with it.

Bulan began to laugh softly.

It started as an involuntary chuckle deep in one of their chests.

Then it built to a laugh.

A choking, gasping laugh that grew louder and louder till it burst from both Bulan's throats and into the startled air.

People turned to stare at him. Some with hands raising swords and axes and other weapons, their faces still stunned and confused, prepared for anything.

Bulan laughed until the entire circle filled with their booming laughter.

Another Vanjhani joined in, giving in to the manic release.

Then another.

In moments, everyone was laughing along with Bulan, Vanjhani or not.

The encircled wagons echoed with the laughter of the survivors.

Vanjhani clapped hands together, locked embraces, and slapped one another on their backs, laughing merrily.

People hugged and laughed and kissed one another on the cheeks, some directly on the lips.

A few began to dance, hopping and skipping and singing happily.

"We live!" Bulan said to themself, scarcely able to believe it.

Then, as the realization became acceptance, they said it louder:

"WE LIVE!"

Others took up the cry, repeating it, passing it on, in the instant way all messages were passed on in the train, over wagons, from circle to circle, all around the entire Perfect Circle, until it came back again to Bulan moments later, like a delayed echo.

"WE LIVE!"

They celebrated being alive.

# *Aqreen*

AQREEN CRADLED KRUSHITA IN her lap, kissing her daughter's head.

"How?" she asked softly.

Krushita opened her eyes, looking up at her mother tiredly. "I just *did.*"

She shifted in her mother's embrace, trying to find a more comfortable position. That wasn't likely, since she had outgrown Aqreen's lap some years ago. But Aqreen didn't care. Right now she was happy to hold her precious child close to her body, as she had held her that first time after she had emerged from Aqreen's womb, gurgling quietly in contentment as her mother gazed down in wonderment. *This? I made this? Beautiful!*

"I'm tired, Ma. Really tired."

Of course she was.

She had just saved the train. Thousands of people. Including herself and her own mother. Aqreen couldn't begin to imagine the power and energy it must have taken to accomplish a feat of that scale. *Could even Jarsun had done something like this?* she wondered.

She knew Jarsun's powers were formidable, but she had never actually seen him at war, though she had heard tales of the Krushan in battle, and of course, the legends of the Burnt Empire were told throughout the world.

But a mere child of seven?

That was unheard of.

Only the myths of the stone gods told of such feats. And even they were taken with a heavy dose of salt and skepticism these days, except by the fanatically devoted.

Aqreen passed her palm gently over the dozing girl's brow, humming a soft lullaby, one that had always comforted Krushita and helped her fall asleep during those first troubled months after they had fled Aqron, when every sound in the night, every voice had seemed hostile and strange and frightening. She rocked her daughter gently from side to side, ignoring the protests of her aching muscles and joints. She would ease her own pain later. Right now she was a mother first, a woman second.

Krushita's thumb had found its way into her mouth, and she sucked at it unselfconsciously, something she hadn't done since she was newly weaned. Aqreen made no attempt to dislodge it or admonish Krushita. If her daughter wanted to suck her thumb, she could damn well suck her thumb.

She had just saved the world, or at least the world as they had known it for the past five years.

Krushita could do anything she damn well pleased.

# Part Three

## *Rise of a Demon Prince*

# *Vasurava*

~

## 1

IN THE ARRGODI PAVILION, a great host of richly garbed and bejeweled royalty joined their few hundred voices to the roar of the hundreds of thousands thronging the avenues and streets and by-lanes. The gathering in the pavilion itself was such as few had seen before in their lifetimes.

Karna Sura and Padmeen, Vasurava's parents, were present, joyfully radiant. His sister, Karni, and her adoptive father were there. All Vasurava's family was present. As was Kewri's family. Only Tyrak was missing. Not that anyone seemed to miss him. *Certainly not me,* thought Vasurava. With each passing year, Arrgodi and Mraashk missed Tyrak less and less — which really meant that their first relief at his departure had turned into full-blown joy over time. All that was known of Tyrak was that he had gone north to Morgolia; nobody was clear about the why of it or had any details of his ventures there. Not that anyone cared.

In the years since the extraordinary incident at the army camp and Tyrak's subsequent disappearance, the air of Mraashk had changed from the fetid stench of the dungeons into the floral freshness of a garden in full bloom. The Mraashk wedding invitees who had arrived with Vasurava in his procession had grown so accustomed to Harvanya honey wine, it was all they drank night and day. In his quarters, the revelry had raged morn to night, then all night long. The wedding unleashed a great many pent-up emotions, all positive, that had been building since Tyrak's departure. Today they were all set free to roam the length and breadth of the capitol city. Both nations united in celebration of the wedding of Kewri and Vasurava, a literal and symbolic joining of the two sister nations in holy ceremony.

*And we actually love each other,* Vasurava thought, smiling to himself. Unlike so many matches fixed for political reasons.

It was with a great effort that Vasurava had succeeded in remaining relatively sober during this festive period. He alone could not easily forget how precious this occasion was, how hard-won this joy, and how each peal of laughter or whistle and cheer had been paid for by innocent blood. He was also concerned by the incessant flow of news from distant regions, news of a great war campaign being waged by the demoniac Jarsun of Morgolia and his many allies. Accurate news was hard to come by, for few survived or were able to flee this far to tell their tale, but from the fragments that had drifted this way, he had formed a rough outline of a terrible invasion in progress. Even the most tenuous accounts and rumors all agreed on one thing: the scale of bloodshed was epic, the slaughter massive. His brothers, his allies, the Council, all shook their heads and stroked their beards sadly and commiserated with the plight of the people in those distant lands. But they also thanked the stone gods that their own misery had ended so fortuitously with the departure of Tyrak and the success of the peace treaty enforced by Vasurava.

It did no good for Vasurava to remind them that the storm that raged in their neighbor's yard could easily turn and ravage their own tomorrow, or that Tyrak had only gone away, not died a mortal death. Arrgodi were positive thinking in outlook and did not care to dwell on the worst. People of the moment, they seized the day and every little pleasure that it brought. It was the only way to gain some satisfaction and joy from an uncertain life.

But now Vasurava himself succumbed to the enormous swell of sheer delight sweeping him along. How could he resist? What pomp, what splendor, what majesty! It was a wedding that would have honored a stone god! His head swam to even count the many rich treasures he had been gifted, and his heart filled with pride that he had been able to afford to gift the queen's ransom he had given the Mraashk in return. To quote Kewri's favorite phrase, truly today, they were both rich. Rich in pleasure, love, and goodwill, as well as in coin and kine!

He savored the warmth of the sun on his face, the fragrance of blossoms, the color and pageantry of the pavilion, the taste of the delectable soma distilled from the same Harvanya vineyards Kewri and he had walked amongst so many evenings, and the uplifting roar of the crowd. Ahead was the uks cart, the uks painted gaily as was the Mraashk custom, the drover seated and waiting to carry them away. It was time to go home and unlock the door to the future.

Vasurava turned to his bride to assist her up to the cart. Her face peeped out of the deep red-ochre wedding garments, bashful and demure as if she had only just picked him out of a swayamvara lineup and was suddenly contemplating the implications of going home with an absolute stranger for her husband.

He winked at her, and she blushed even redder but winked back with a coyness that thrilled him. Ah, he would have great children with this woman, a prodigious flock that they would raise together to be the joy of all the Arrgodi world. Five, ten, a dozen bonny children! And that number was the one she had spoken of, shyly, with eyes averted but with a mischievous twinkle in them.

His bride safely ensconced upon the uks cart, Vasurava leaped up beside her. The crowd achieved a new level of ecstasy, as dhol drums, kettle drums, conch shell trumpet and every manner of musical instrument, vocal performance, and accompaniment including the joyful baying of hounds, neighing of horses, lowing of kine, and trumpeting and foot-stamping of elephants all combined to create a deafening wave of sound that threatened to raise the cart itself up and carry it all the way to his doorstep. He laughed till tears poured from his eyes in joy, and put a hand gently on the shoulder of the drover of the cart, speaking into the man's ear to tell him he could start the long, slow procession. It was customary for one of the bride's brothers to drive his sister and her groom home in order to extend the filial connection as long as possible. Since Kewri had no brothers present, he assumed that the man was one of her many cousins filling in.

The man turned his face to Vasurava, and suddenly it mattered a great deal.

The man driving the uks cart was none other than Kewri's own brother: Tyrak.

## 2

Vasurava's brothers, each seated with his bride in an identical uks cart drawn by painted uks and driven by one of Kewri's cousins, shouted to him to get a move on. Vasurava heard their voices as if from a great distance. His entire attention was focused on Tyrak's face.

The prince of Arrgodi looked so different, Vasurava even tried to convince himself at first it was one of Kewri's other cousins. But there was no mistaking that heavy brow, those almost colorless grey eyes, the jutting jaw, and general mien of menace. The face was sun-darkened, as were the burly arms gripping the uks reins, and the body had filled out, grown more muscular, bulging powerfully beneath the incongruous gaily colored wedding garb. There was something different about the man that went beyond just the physical muscularity; it was as if Tyrak had grown into a new person during the years he had been absent. Not that he had aged, if anything, he seemed more vital and vigorous. It was an overall drawing in of energies, a focusing of psychological and physiological strengths, a sharpening and a tightening. It was, it was . . . Vasurava groped to understand what he saw, even as his mind raced wildly through the myriad implications and likely possibilities that Tyrak's reappearance entailed . . . It was, he realized at last, as if Tyrak had voyaged into the northern wilderness alone and had undergone some rite of passage that had made him a man.

Yes. For the face that turned to look back at Vasurava was not Tyrak the spoiled brat of a prince accustomed to having his own way in everything. Or even Tyrak the brutal bully who viewed the entire Arrgodi world as his playground. It was the face of a man who had grown into the full possession of his adult faculties.

Vasurava had no idea what this man might do or what he intended. He could not read his eyes, his face, or his inner spirit.

And now the question was, would the man act exactly as the boy had done? Or . . . ?

And in that "or . . ." lay an infinity of possibilities.

Vasurava felt a hand on his back, prodding him gently, insistently.

It was his bride, one hand holding her coverlet in place to maintain the custom of modesty, while urging him eagerly onward.

He swallowed and looked at Tyrak.

To his surprise, his brother-in-law merely smiled slyly and began driving the uks forward. The crowd roared with delight, their excitement reaching a peak as their princesses and their new husbands clattered away on the uks carts. Children ran alongside the carts, yelling, smiling. Those too old to be out on the streets watched, beaming, from their houses. All the onlookers cheered uproariously. The sound of drums and music could be heard all across the city. Beside him, Vasurava's new bride laughed with pleasure, an open-throated sound that should have made him smile and laugh as well.

But all Vasurava could think was *Tyrak is back!*

What did he mean to do? Surely he wasn't going to just drive them home like a good brother?

Vasurava looked at the broad back and tried to guess what was going through that man's mind. Tyrak had changed so much that even the crowds they were passing did not recognize the crown prince at first glance. Those who noticed him at all probably assumed he was one of his brothers — after all, there was a striking resemblance. Did that external change reflect an inward one as well, or was the change only physical? What were Tyrak's intentions?

Vasurava did not have to wait long to learn the answer.

Suddenly, a sound broke the din of cheering and celebration, a sound that almost seemed a part of the overall cacophony at first.

It was the sound of a woman screaming.

It was joined by other screams, both male and female.

Slowly, the jubilation in the great square began to die out as people realized that something was amiss.

As the cheering and yelling and whistling dwindled, the screaming grew more clearly audible.

Then even the music stopped.

And the terror began.

# *Tyrak*

~

TYRAK HAD NOT RIDDEN directly home to Arrgodi.

Jarsun had promised him an army of his own when he returned, the better to help him take charge of his homeland and weed out the rebellious elements among his own forces. It was to collect this fighting unit that he had first gone after leaving Jarsun.

During the years they had fought together, Jarsun had taught Tyrak a great deal about the waging of warfare, battle strategy, governance, dominion, and related matters. He had mentored Tyrak more effectively than any tutor ever had. Unlike the gurus Tyrak had had as a boy, Jarsun taught more than calmly analytical philosophical theory; his were hard-won ground truths, ripped raw and bleeding from the reality of Jarsun's own life and adventures. Tyrak's enthusiasm also enabled him to learn more effectively; instead of the sullen resentment or sneering indifference he had shown to earlier gurus, he received every mote of wisdom from Jarsun with admiration and respect.

True education came about through insightful learning, not from simply being taught; the greatest lessons were those gained through self-awareness and realization, not merely rote repetition, especially for a warrior whose most valuable knowledge was practical and often made the difference between life and death. Tyrak had learned his lessons well with the king of Morgolia, and among them was the crucial insight that while any good leader could rule a kingdom, it took an extraordinary one to continue to rule it.

His encounters with Vasurava and the shocking failure he had experienced on both occasions had shown him the importance of relying on more than brute force to defeat his enemies. The news of his own army's disbandment and the subsequent dissolution of the Marauders made him realize the necessity for an elite unit that would serve him with absolute loyalty. His own countrymen and clansmen, while great fighters, were too independent minded. He needed a group of prime soldiers who would obey and serve him unquestioningly unto death.

Jarsun had given him the Eoch Assassins.

An army of eochs.

A motley collection of soldiers taken as slave children from enemy camps and kingdoms during Jarsun's many raids and invasions, clinically indoctrinated, then trained into superb fighting units, the eochs had no nationality, no family, tribe, clan, faith, or affiliation. They lived and fought purely for the honor of the warrior code. Their only means of proving self-worth was through fulfilling the wishes of their commander.

In this case, Jarsun had raised a particular unit to obey Tyrak as their leader. To them, Tyrak was stone god incarnate, the ultimate being, and could do no wrong. By implication, all those who opposed him were evil incarnate and must be destroyed. Their world was neatly divided into these two convenient compartments. Tyrak = good. Tyrak's enemies = evil. Indoctrinated so deeply into this conviction, they could not comprehend any worldview that challenged it. In short, it was simpler to kill them than to attempt to argue them out of the conviction that Tyrak was stone god.

And killing them was not simple at all.

The dregs of their communities, witness to the most horrific war crimes, abuse, atrocities, brutalities, and every other variation of human cruelty, they had had every drop of humanity drained from them through a training program designed by Jarsun himself, a regime of such sustained and vicious indoctrination that only the hardiest, most indestructible specimens could survive it at all.

Those that did survive were deemed to have excelled, because survival against such odds as Jarsun stacked against those pathetic eoch orphans was excellence in itself. They came out as lethal killing machines, superbly conditioned and honed to fighting prime, obeying only Tyrak, committed to destroying all others, regardless of the risk to their own lives or well-being.

His Eoch Assassins could be ordered to maim themselves, commit suicidal actions, or even endanger the lives and limbs of their fellows, at a single command.

Jarsun had squandered several Eoch Assassins just to demonstrate this fact: those that survived with mutilated bodies or severed limbs had to be executed because an Eoch Assassin had to be self-sufficient and ruthless to a fault. Even Tyrak was not privy to the training regime nor to the process of indoctrination, as these were personally supervised by Jarsun himself, and none but he possessed full knowledge of all the details and methods employed.

It did not matter. He had created such a formidable fighting unit that no other force comparable in number could survive an encounter with Tyrak's Eoch Assassins. If anything, they could be put up against a force far superior in numbers, position, or means, and while they might not triumph against impossible odds, they would cause such damage and cost to the enemy as to render that enemy's victory hollow.

It was this band of fighters that Tyrak had gone to collect from the remote wilderness camp where they were billeted, spending their days in endless training and preparation. Jarsun had not permitted the Eoch Assassins to be used in his own army, or to serve anyone but Tyrak himself. At one point, Tyrak had wondered aloud, if the Eoch Assassins were that effective and loyal, then what would happen if he were to command them to go to battle against Jarsun?

"You would cause me great losses," Jarsun replied, answering the question quite seriously and without taking offense. "But eventually your Eoch Assassins would be wiped out to the last individual."

Tyrak had chuckled and said that if the Eoch Assassins were able to get to Jarsun himself before being cut down by superior numbers, it wouldn't matter if they were all wiped out. After all, the ultimate goal was to kill the enemy's leader, was it not?

Jarsun had smiled and said that Tyrak had a great deal left to learn about warfare. (This was in the first days after Tyrak had joined him.) "The purpose of war is not merely to kill one's opposing king or commander; it is to render that kingdom or force incapable of attacking you again. It's not enough just to cut off the head; it's more important to sever the limbs and puncture the vital organs."

Tyrak had frowned, not able to grasp the application of this anatomical metaphor to actual warfare. Jarsun had shrugged, saying he would understand in time. "But to answer your question about the Eoch Assassins," the Krushan said, "they might succeed in causing me great losses before being cut down to the last man, but they would never succeed in harming me personally."

Tyrak had again laughed and suggested that Jarsun was only saying that because he could not accept the idea of defeat.

"No, my friend," Jarsun had said good-naturedly. "I say that because, while my Eoch Assassins will indeed obey you unto death, they do so not because they are loyal to you but because they are loyal to *me*. You see, they obey you because I tell them to obey you. They obey me because they are trained to obey me. That is a crucial difference. If, by some unhappy mischance, you were to order them to attack my army, they would do so, but they would stop short of causing me any personal harm."

Tyrak frowned and asked how that was possible, if the Eoch Assassins thought of him, Tyrak, as stone god incarnate.

Jarsun smiled his calm smile and said, "They think of you as stone god incarnate, but of me as the stone god himself."

And so, Jarsun had explained, he could name any man or woman as his avatar and the Eoch Assassins would worship that person as their master thereafter. But Jarsun himself always remained their true stone god and commander.

After that, Tyrak never asked any theoretical questions regarding the loyalty of the Eoch Assassins. He simply accepted the gift and used it as best he could.

And when he returned to Arrgodi, he took the Eoch Assassins with him.

Now he raised his whip and spun the lash out at thin air, once, twice, then a third time, giving his aides the predetermined signal to start their "festivities." It was time to let Arrgodi know their crown prince was home again.

# *Kewri*

AT FIRST, KEWRI COULD not comprehend what she saw.

The procession had only just begun moving. She had even prodded Vasurava insistently to be on their way. After all the ritual ceremonies and feasting and celebration, days and nights spent with more people than she had ever had around her in her whole life, she wanted nothing more than to be alone with Vasurava. *My husband.* The words created a warm glow in her heart.

She was happier than she had ever been, looking forward to spending the rest of their lives together. As the uks cart trundled forward, she laughed, raising her hands to wave gaily at the crowds, at the children running alongside, at her sisters in the carts following them —

That was when she saw the eochs attack the soldiers.

Soldiers of both Ugraksh's and Vasurava's armies were lined up along the avenues, ostensibly to keep the crowd back and clear a path for the wedding procession, but also to keep the peace. Little chance of that happening with the populace wild with joy and venting years of pent-up energy on this tumultuous event.

Most of the soldiers had a festive look — the citizens had smeared colored powder on their faces as well as one another's — and made no attempt to curb their smiles. Both armies intermingled freely, chatting, exchanging views on the wedding, the food, the festivities, boasting of which wedding party had celebrated the most, consumed the most honey wine, eaten the most sweetmeats, and otherwise behaving like brides' and grooms' relatives at a wedding feast.

Kewri's gaze happened to fall upon an eoch approaching two soldiers from behind. The eoch in question was dressed in similarly gaily colored garb as the rest of the crowd, but it was the way she moved that caught Kewri's attention. She had a litheness about her that was almost like a dancer about to perform an acrobatic step.

As Kewri watched, grinning and laughing, her hand flailing to acknowledge and return the cheers of the ecstatic crowd, she saw the eoch raise her hands. In each hand, she held something that flashed brightly in the morning sunlight. The eoch moved her arms with great grace and speed, and abruptly the two smiling soldiers lost their smiles and collapsed where they stood.

The next moment, the eoch was lost in the crowd.

But not before Kewri saw the objects in her hands rise again to catch the sunlight: this time they did not flash as brightly, for they were covered with something dark and reddish. She knew at once what they were. Blades. The woman had just killed those two soldiers, cutting them down from behind like sheaves of wheat.

Kewri caught another glimpse of flashing steel elsewhere and turned her head.

She saw another eoch hacking down another soldier, then a second, then a third, and yet another. The eoch moved with a fluid, effortless grace that was no less than any classical dancer, swirling, flowing, slashing . . . She moved and swung the blades, and soldiers died.

Suddenly, there were flashes of steel everywhere as far as she could see, winking in the sunlight, visible even through the dense colorful crowd.

Flashes of steel.

And splatters of red.

Then the screams began. First from someone who stumbled over a freshly slain corpse.

Then several more as they found other dead soldiers.

Then the puzzled shouts as people found corpses too, or glimpsed other soldiers being killed.

Slowly, the din and cacophony of celebration died down, even the music faltering, then halting altogether.

A terrible moment of silence fell.

And in that moment of silence, Kewri heard the sounds of slaughter: The liquid thuds of knives hacking through flesh and bone. The choked death grunts of dying soldiers. The swishing and tinkling of garments as the killers went about their deadly work, incongruously clad in festive garb.

Then a new cry rose from the crowd.

"Assassins!"

At once, a new mood swept the enormous collective. The same crowd that was ecstatic with joy only moments ago was now terrorized.

Soldiers were dying across the city by the hundreds. Arrgodi soldiers as well as Mraashk. The soldiers killed were only a fraction of the whole force, but the vast number of soldiers untouched by the violence could barely comprehend what was happening, let alone identify the ones responsible.

For one thing, the killers were eochs clad in wedding garb like a hundred thousand Arrgodi and Mraashk women. Dressed in this manner, and of more or less average height rather than the giant specimens he had encountered abroad, they were therefore virtually undiscernible from the rest of the crowd.

They killed, then hid their weapons beneath their voluminous garments and moved to their next target, working with chilling efficacy and ruthlessness. Nothing the soldiers had experienced had prepared them for such attackers. How could they fight the enemy when they could barely tell them apart from the hundreds of thousands of ordinary female citizens?

For another thing, the crowd was drunk on celebration and joy; emotions ran sky high, and the moment the killing began, people overreacted mightily. Some began attempting to flee, causing stampedes. Others began trying to apprehend the killers, either getting themselves killed, or grabbing the wrong people in their haste. Chaos broke out. And the only ones who benefited from the chaos were the killers themselves. Moving through the crowds, killing at will, they reaped a terrible harvest.

Safe on the uks cart, Kewri saw blood and slaughter and stampedes all around. She saw children run down by panicked crowds. She saw soldiers draw their weapons and hack blindly at the crowds around them, confused and angry at the deaths of their comrades. She saw citizens take hold of the assassins — only to be cut down brutally in a moment.

The celebration had turned into a slaughter. The wedding procession into a charnel procession. The cheers and whistles and cries of joy turned to screams of terror and howls of agony.

Kewri clutched hold of Vasurava's robe and yelled to make herself heard over the din. "Do something, my lord! Stop this madness!"

But Vasurava did nothing. He only sat there and watched the terror spread like wildfire around them.

She stared at his face, unable to understand why he did not act, or at least stand up and shout to control the crowd. She could see the look of horror on his face, the wide, shocked gaze, which meant he was aware of everything that was going on. Why did he not act or speak?

"Vasurava!" she cried.

Slowly, he turned to her. She was moved by the infinite sadness in his gaze. As always, his face made her feel she was looking upon some exalted force.

He stared at her silently for a moment, then lowered his eyes in sadness.

"My lord," she sobbed. "Your people are dying!"

She realized her mistake and corrected herself: "*Our* people are dying!"

He did not respond in words. Only raised his eyes sadly again, looking over his shoulder at her brother at the head of the cart.

Frowning, she looked in the same direction, unable to comprehend his meaning at first.

Then she saw who was driving the cart.

That familiar face, only somewhat darker and more leathery, the body more muscled and manly.

And suddenly, she knew why Vasurava did not respond. Why he could not respond. And why her wedding day had turned into a nightmare.

"Greetings, sister dearest," said Tyrak, grinning amiably. "Allow me to offer my heartiest congratulations on your nuptials, and commiseration, for you will not live to enjoy a long and happily married life."

# *Tyrak*

TYRAK WAS THRILLED AT how easily his plan was accomplished.

Working with Bane and Uaraj, he had hatched the idea of infiltrating the city and striking when Arrgodi was most vulnerable: during the royal wedding. With the kingdom in the grip of wedding festivities and visitors arriving by the tens of thousands from all corners, it had been a simple matter to enter the city.

Procuring suitable garb had posed no great challenge either, with the markets filled with tradesmen and craftsmen from all across the Arrgodi and Mraashk nations offering wares and services for sale. Not that he had needed to purchase anything; they had simply taken what they wished but been cautious enough not to do anything that would arouse too much attention.

Once they had secured the appropriate garb from a number of houses lying empty as their denizens caroused at the wedding feasts, his Eoch Assassins had mingled with the crowds and awaited the start of the procession.

As for his taking his place on the uks cart, he had simply kept enough of his face concealed by his head cloth to confuse the guards into assuming he was one of his many brothers and clambered aboard. His brothers never suspected because once they saw him seated on the leading cart, they automatically assumed he was this or the other; they were merry in their cups as well by then, after all.

Most of all, his greatest advantage lay in the fact that he was not expected by anyone. Not to appear at such a time, least of all to make his presence felt in such a surreptitious manner. It had never been his way. The Tyrak of yore, the younger, brasher Tyrak, would have charged in galloping, roaring with fury and hacking at or riding down anyone who obstructed his path. These devious subtleties were all Jarsun's teachings bearing fruit.

Once the procession began to move, he had given Bane and Uaraj the predetermined signal for the Eoch Assassins to go to work. And they did so with the same ruthless ease with which he had watched them hack down enemy warriors during the training skirmishes Jarsun had enacted for his viewing pleasure.

The sheer tumultuous chaos of the wedding, the enormous crowds, the emotional fever pitch, and the silent, deadly smoothness with which his Eoch Assassins moved through the city, killing Mraashk and Arrgodi soldiers alike, made him thrill with excitement. It was almost artistic in its speed, precision, and acrobatic beauty.

There, an Eoch Assassin slashed her blade under the guard of an Arrgodi soldier, pirouetted, then pierced the abdomen of a Mraashk soldier who was rushing at her in a blind rage, then swished around in a third spin, her swords disappearing into the folds of her garment, and the next instant she was lost in the crowd, head lowered, working her way discreetly to her next target as the horde of horrified witnesses around her tried to make sense of what had happened.

Here, a small band of soldiers formed a protective cordon around his cart, putting their bodies and their lives in front of the royal couple they sought to protect, as an Eoch Assassin came sprinting from their flank, ducked under their slow defensively raised lances, and slashed briefly but with killing perfection at each of them in turn, not killing at once, but mortally wounding. The cordon collapsed as one man, bleeding to death in agony as the uks, unable to stop in time, stomped over their prone bodies, and the wheels of the cart lurched and heaved as they crushed the dying men.

Everywhere, the same dance of death was being performed.

Tyrak glanced back at his sister, gratified at the expression on her face and that of Vasurava's as well.

"Well, sister, how do you like my wedding gift?"

Kewri stared back at him. "Wedding . . . gift?" she repeated, uncomprehending.

Tyrak gestured broadly, indicating the city, the crowds, the screams of chaos, the dancing Eoch Assassins slaughtering Arrgodi soldiers by the dozens, the hundreds, the stampedes, the terror, the madness and beauty of the whole scene. "A great performance, is it not? Have you seen such artistry from our classical danseuses? I think not. I trust you are pleased with this great demonstration."

"Abomination!" she spat, recovering her senses. "How could you do such a thing? During your own family's celebrations?"

Tyrak laughed. "My *family's* celebrations?" He clucked his tongue at the uks, guiding them past a pile of writhing bodies left in the wake of a stampeding horde; most of them were very young children. He ignored their pitiful cries. "No, sister. You confuse politics with family. This is merely a part of my plan to take control of Mraashk. You are merely a bonus!"

Kewri made a sound of despair. "Stop it at once, Tyrak. Call off your mad dogs! Stop this mindless killing." Tears spilled from her eyes, causing her kohl to streak. "I beg of you, brother. Lay down your arms. This is an occasion of peace and brotherhood!"

Tyrak grinned at her. "You have been thoroughly brainwashed, sister. I am merely doing now what our enemies would have done very soon to us anyway."

Vasurava spoke up, cautious but unafraid. "You are killing your own warriors as well as mine, Tyrak. Are they your enemies as well?"

Tyrak shrugged, avoiding looking directly at Vasurava just yet. "They are either with us or against us. By standing with your men, they show themselves to be your men. Therefore they must be put down. I intend to clean out the rot from Arrgodi completely this time. And oftentimes, to save a healthy body one must sever an infected limb. I fear that my kingdom's military is badly in need of overhauling." He lashed the whip at some fool woman joining her hands together and begging the lords on the cart to help save her dying sons. "It is time we brought some fresh blood into Arrgodi. And now is as good a time as any."

Everywhere he looked, he was pleased to see the plan was proceeding perfectly. Arrgodi soldiers were no match for the ruthless efficiency of his Eoch Assassins and were falling like flies. In moments, he would be clear of this crowded avenue and would proceed to the next part of his plan, which was to—

**Tyrak!**

He dropped the whip. His head screamed with excruciating agony. "Guru!" he cried involuntarily, calling out for Jarsun as he often had during the preceding years when in positions of extreme risk or pain, appealing to the only man who had ever treated him as a father ought to treat a son, the only real teacher, master, preceptor he had ever acknowledged as worthy of commanding his attention.

**Jarsun cannot help you. This is your bane to break. And break it you must. Or it will break you!**

"What are you babbling about?" he cried, not caring that he was shrieking the words aloud, or that both Kewri and Vasurava were exchanging glances and staring at him, as were several of those in the crowd who were not too preoccupied to recognize the altered but still recognizable face of their crown prince.

**Kewri, your sister, will bear the male child that will be your undoing. Kill her now, or she will grow the seed of your destruction within her womb.**

Tyrak writhed in agony. The previous times that Vessa had spoken to him, in his mind as well as in spectral form in the forest, there had been only a gnashing sensation, like a deep rumbling of thunder too close to his head for comfort. But this time, it was as if the thunder was inside his head, crashing and resounding across the battered walls of his brain.

"I . . . am taking control . . . of my destiny . . ." he said, panting when he finished the brief statement. It was a statement he had learned from Jarsun. This part of his plan was taking control of his own destiny, instead of waiting for it to be handed to him as he had waited all his life. He had a plan, a beautiful, perfect plan. And the first part of the plan was going masterfully. "My Eoch Assassins —"

**Your Eoch Assassins will not save you from the One who approaches. Once he sets foot upon this mortal plane, none will succeed in opposing him. Not even your great guru, Jarsun. Though he may try mightily. The only way to protect yourself is to kill the woman who will bear his mortal avatar in this lifetime. Kill Kewri.**

"But . . ." he said, unaware that he was lurching from side to side like a drunkard in the seat of the uks cart, or that even his Eoch Assassins had stopped their slaughter to stare at him in consternation. Bane and Uaraj were watching him as well, open-mouthed with astonishment.

With a mighty effort, he raised himself up and roared to the skies. "What can a single mortal child do to me? Who is he? I fear no man!"

Silence fell across the avenue then as all stopped to listen and stare. Into that silence, Tyrak heard the voice of the bodiless one speak like thunder out of a clear sky, and this time, not just he but everyone around him heard the words as well.

**He is Vish incarnate. A stone god reborn.**

# *Vasurava*

## 1

KEWRI CRIED OUT AS Tyrak grabbed her by her hair and dragged her to her feet.

Vasurava stood as well. The uks cart shuddered under the shifting weight of the three of them, but he was careful not to make any sudden or threatening movements. It was obvious that Tyrak was already far beyond the verge of madness.

Tyrak held Kewri up by her hair like a rag doll, as she screamed and wept copiously—not in fear, but in shame at being treated thus. Kewri was a strong woman, brought up in the Arrgodi matriarchal tradition to regard women as the true leaders of their clans. To be treated in this fashion by any person was unconscionable, let alone one's own brother on the day of one's espousal. Tyrak seemed to care nothing for the humiliation or pain he was causing his sister. His eyes were wide, the whites showing all around, the pupils mere pinpricks, face engorged and red with blood, a vein pulsing in his temple, the muscles and tendons of his powerfully muscled neck, shoulders, arms, and chest bulging and straining as he held his sister up high, as if displaying her to the whole world.

Everywhere, across the great square and the avenues approaching it, on rooftops and windows, casements and verandahs, from the palace and from the streets, horrified eyes watched the drama unfold. Even Tyrak's own Eoch Assassins, swords dripping blood, had paused in their slaughter to wonder at what was about to happen. The dying and the wounded groaned and cried out, unattended, as every citizen, shaken to the core by the brutal shock of the unexpected assaults, and now by the bestial behavior of the resurfaced crown prince, stood in a tableau depicting shock and disbelief as all eyes looked toward the foremost uks cart in the procession.

"This woman?" Tyrak bellowed, his voice carrying like a lion's throaty roar across the square. "This woman would be the cause of my destruction? My own sister?"

His voice revealed his outrage and hurt. It was difficult to believe that a man like Tyrak could be hurt emotionally, but of course, he was no less vulnerable to the arrows and barbs of human pain than any person. If anything, Tyrak was more sensitive than most, imagining slights where none had been intended, humiliation where none existed.

As a boy he had spent many hours and days brooding over things his companions or playmates had mentioned casually in passing or in play, refusing to rejoin their games or pastimes, often venting his anger on his pets, horses, kine, servants until he was old enough to enact his rages upon those who caused him these hurts, gradually working his way up the social scale until the day he threw his old tutor out a palace window to his death. There was a self-righteous sense of outrage about his temper fugues, an air of being treated unfairly by an unjust and biased world.

And never was it so evident as now. Even after all his many atrocities and brutalities, after he had crept deviously into his own kingdom's capital on the very day of his sister's nuptials, wreaking havoc and mayhem all around, yet here he was, eyes brimming with tears of outrage, holding up his own blood kin like something less than human, heartbroken at her betrayal! Thus are the wicked utterly convinced of their own righteousness, and thus are those who pose as the most upright often the least capable of upholding their own lofty principles.

"Tyrak," Vasurava said gently, careful not to provoke Tyrak further by action or vocal inflection. "Kewri means you no harm. She loves you, as you are her brother. Look at her. See for yourself. She is unarmed and intending no violence."

Tyrak turned his mask of fury upon Vasurava, and it took all the Mraashk king's self-control to keep from flinching. It was indeed like looking upon a mask rather than a man's face, so distorted and engorged and fattened by fear and hate was Tyrak's visage. "Are you feeble, Mraashk? Did you not hear the great sage's words? She will bear the child that will destroy me! Her womb will carry my slayer into this mortal realm."

Vasurava kept his head lowered, deliberately crouching a little to keep his considerable height below Tyrak's eye level, his own eyes cast downward. He was keenly aware of how tightly Tyrak's hand was wound around Kewri's hair, and of the drawn sword in Tyrak's other hand. "But she is newly wedded to me, barely a wife, let alone a mother. How can there be any child in her womb? Do you think she and I would violate the sanctity of our customs and traditions thus? Never! Whatever the great sage may say, Kewri does not mean you any harm, nor does she bear any child that could possibly harm you!"

Tyrak was in no mood to listen. He turned his flashing eyes to Kewri again, the poor woman squirming and writhing with pain, for Tyrak's grip twisted her neck and torso agonizingly. Vasurava saw that were Tyrak simply to wrench his hand in a certain action, he would break Kewri's spine and neck as easily as one might snap a dried twig. Given his musculature and strength, the sword was redundant; Tyrak was capable of killing Kewri with barely a flick of his wrist.

The crown prince of Mraashk heaved and said in a tone of infinite suffering, "What you say matters not, Vasurava. She is the one who will someday bear the instrument of my death. The only way to protect myself is to kill her now before she slips out of my grasp and fulfills her destiny. The great sage warned me to do this now. There must be good reason why he chose to instruct me of this now and not tomorrow or ten years from the morrow. I must obey."

Tyrak hefted the sword with the ease of an accomplished warrior, tossing it up in the air and catching it easily, now gripping it with the point poised directly above the weeping Kewri's breast.

She stared in misery at the weapon of her destruction, crying out for mercy. Vasurava felt his whole world tremble on the brink of an abyss. It was impossible to believe that only a short while ago, his new bride and he had been about to embark on the first journey of their newlywed lives. What evil twist of karma had turned their joy into terror so abruptly?

He knew that being subservient and obsequious would not serve any longer. He must penetrate the veil of conviction that Tyrak had wrapped around himself. And he must do it at once. In a moment, his world would lie bleeding upon this uks cart.

Vasurava raised his head, rising to his full stature, speaking in his normal voice. Despite his gentle nature and love of all living beings, he was nevertheless a chieftain, a general, a king among men. His voice rang out clearly across the sea of stunned faces filling the square.

"So you serve a voice, then? That is Tyrak's lord and master? A disembodied voice that only you can hear and which speaks inside your head?"

He did not curb the scorn in his tone, the natural cynicism in the phrasing. He sought now not to appease but to provoke, to draw ire upon himself. Words were his only arrows, his voice his only bow.

Tyrak's back tensed, his arms clenched. Slowly, almost without realizing it, the fist holding the twisted mass of Kewri's hair loosened just enough to give her a moment's relief.

She gasped, hitching in breath and hope.

Tyrak turned again to look at Vasurava, head lowered on his powerful neck, eyes glowering like those of a wound-maddened boar deep in the Harvanya forest.

Vasurava still bore the scar of that boar's left tusk on his calf where the beast had cut him open a gash in passing. He had never forgotten the malevolence with which the boar had watched him from the leafy depths of the undergrowth, challenging the two-legged intruder to face him in his domain. Vasurava had been seven years of age. He had killed the boar, not because it had wounded him but because it had killed three other children and two grown men and had become a menace to their village.

Tyrak's eyes glowered in the darkness of his face. He raised the sword, fingers deftly maneuvering the blade till it was once again held in a forward grip. Now the point was aimed directly at Vasurava's right eye.

"I serve no master. I have no lord. I am Tyrak," he said, the words bursting from his mouth with frothy spittle. "You dare call me a slave?"

Vasurava had done no such thing, but that was Tyrak's way, to exaggerate everything in order to emphasize how unjust and unfair the other person, or the world, or the universe at large was to him, Tyrak.

Vasurava met Tyrak's fevered eyes without blinking. He used Tyrak's own paranoia against him. "A voice speaks, you obey. If you are not its slave, why do you obey? How do you even know what the voice tells you is true?"

"Because it has spoken before, and what it said came to pass!" Tyrak said, still holding the sword pointed at Vasurava. "I have no time to bandy words with you, Mraashk. The great sage has told me this woman will be the cause of my destruction. I believe it. I do not care if you believe or not. I will kill her to protect myself."

"And be known as a craven forevermore!" Vasurava's voice rang out loud and clear.

Tyrak stared at him.

"You command an army of eoch warriors," Vasurava gestured at the Eoch Assassins, "you raise your sword against an unarmed woman, your own sister, no less. What will history say about you in times to come? It will say that Tyrak was an urrkh among mortals, a monster who recruited others of his kind, who did not dare to face warriors with weapons, he chose only to kill by stealth and deception, and attack defenseless women of his own house!" Vasurava raised his hand now. The tip of the finger was barely inches from the tip of the sword. "You will be known as a craven without *Auma.*"

Tyrak roared with fury, bristling with such rage that he was momentarily speechless.

Vasurava moved closer, into the arc of the upraised sword, close enough that the edge of the blade was now almost touching his own neck. He looked directly into Tyrak's eyes, challenging him openly. "Too craven to fight me as a man."

## 2

All Mraashk held its breath as Vasurava stood before Tyrak, his neck bared to the edge of Tyrak's sword. One sideways cut of that muscular arm, and the blade would sever his most vital bloodline. The Mraashk king had no defense nor a weapon of his own to counter Tyrak's.

Yet Vasurava stood ramrod straight, eyes unblinking, face fearless and set in the equanimous manner of a warrior who faced death daily and accepted its inevitability. For Vasurava was a true warrior. Not a mercenary thug like Tyrak who fought for personal gain and selfish motives, but a warrior of the highest order, serving only the cause of *Auma.* Not just a soldier of *Auma,* a *sword* of *Auma.* And what does one sword have to fear from another?

It was Tyrak's hand that shook. It began as a small tremulous quiver, just a single ripple of his etched-out muscles, as if the sword had grown too heavy for him to hold straight. Then the entire arm began to shudder and shake, and then the elbow bent and the sword descended, falling out of Tyrak's numb grip to clatter on the wooden planks of the uks cart.

He shuddered as well, a quaking of his entire body that bent him over double, bringing him to his knees in a posture curiously like supplication. His other hand, grown as numb as the first, released his sister involuntarily, and she fell, gasping with relief, to lie on the cart. Tyrak shuddered and shook and shivered like a man in the grip of a malarial fever, and from his mouth came a trickle of drool . . . and a single word . . .

None but Vasurava heard that word.

Then Tyrak buried his head in his lap, his arms held out by his sides, twitching of their own accord. To all those watching, it seemed as if he had surrendered to Vasurava and was now repentant. It was a profound moment for all those who witnessed it. A moment of great clarity. For in that moment, every Arrgodi knew the truth: whether by divine miracle or by dint of superhuman power, Vasurava could not be defeated by Tyrak in single combat. This was the third and final encounter between the two men, and even the most skeptical supporter of Tyrak or hater of the Suras and Mraashk could no longer deny the stark evidence of their senses. Tyrak could not kill or harm Vasurava. "Not so much as a hair on his head," people would say with pride and wonder afterward.

Vasurava looked to his bride. Kewri lay crumpled in a heap, crying a little but mostly just in shock. Vasurava cradled her in his arms gently. She looked up at him, and while she said nothing, her light brown eyes, the color of freshly threshed wheat from a good harvest, spoke eloquently. His own eyes read them easily. He knew she was telling him that he should have killed Tyrak long before this day, that her brother was a monster, a demon, an urrkh among men, and deserved no more than to be put down like one. She was pleading with him to do it even now. Her eyes cut away from him, seeking out, then finding the sword that Tyrak had dropped and which now lay only a foot or two from Vasurava.

Vasurava's heart filled with a great sorrow. He knew that Kewri was right. Pacifist though he was, he was no fool. Had Tyrak never returned to Mraashk, there would have been no need for Vasurava to go after him.

But now that he had come back, celebrating with a showering of blood and death, then laying violent hands upon his own sister, Vasurava's wife, he was a tangible enemy.

And the voice. It had said that Kewri would bear the child that would kill Tyrak. Vasurava had heard it, even if Kewri had not. He had also heard Tyrak's conviction that everything the voice said to him was the truth. He had called it a "great sage," and who was to say that it was not a great sage speaking to him from some ethereal plane?

Kewri looked up at Vasurava, waiting.

When Vasurava made no move, she took the initiative. Reaching out, she took hold of the sword and picked it up. She turned it around, inverting it so the hilt faced Vasurava and offered it to him.

As soon as she did this, the watching crowds broke out of their stupor.

First one citizen shouted hoarsely, "Aye!"

Just that single word, so clear yet terrible in its surety.

Then: "Kill him!" This from the woman who had begged Tyrak for mercy and aid before he stopped the uks cart.

"Kill the prince!" cried another. A chorus of ayes followed this one.

Then a young boy's voice called out, "Lord Vasurava, save us!"

And the dam broke.

With one voice, the entire populace shouted for Vasurava to kill Tyrak, to slay their own crown prince, to destroy the monster, to put down the urrkh, to kill, to slaughter, to slay, to finish it.

Vasurava looked around, not sure whether to be pleased or saddened. Pleased, for it was evident how dearly the people loved him. Sad, because it was their own crown prince they wanted killed. He gazed at the sea of upturned faces, shouting mouths, and pumping fists.

Amongst the crowd, he could see Tyrak's mercenaries, confounded by the developments of the past several minutes and unable to decide what to do next. At least the killing had stopped for the time being. He also noticed the soldiers of both Arrgodi and Mraashk colors moving in discreetly to ring Tyrak's warriors. He saw Tyrak's allies and aides, Bane and Uaraj, both looking around in disconcertment as they saw the obvious fury of the crowd. It was one thing to infiltrate a happy and celebratory crowd of wedding voyeurs and take them by surprise and quite another to stand in the thick of a raging mob who knew exactly who you were and wanted you dead. Right now, the people's attention was on Tyrak. The moment Tyrak was slain, they would look around to seek out his soldiers, and judging by the intensity of their anger, they would flay them alive for the deaths they had caused today.

Vasurava raised a hand, requesting silence. Reluctantly but respectfully, the people quietened and he was able to speak.

"I know you desire this, and I do not say it would be wrong. What Tyrak has done today is itself sufficient to condemn him forever. But even so, I cannot take his life summarily."

Querulous cries of outrage rose from all around. Vasurava raised a hand again.

"I signed a pact of peace with your king Ugraksh not long ago. Regardless of how many times and in how many ways your own prince and your own soldiers — his erstwhile Marauders — may have broken that pact, I myself cannot do so. I *will not* do so. I have upheld the sacred accord signed and sealed between myself and King Ugraksh all these many years, and I shall do so even today. Tyrak shall be taken before your king to be judged by him and done with as he sees fit. It is King Ugraksh's place, not mine, to judge him and grant him whatever danda he sees fit."

Out the corner of his eye, he glimpsed Bane and Uaraj sidling away, seeking to make good their escape.

Raising a hand, Vasurava pointed directly at them, drawing the attention of everyone around them at once. Both men froze, aware of the dozens of pairs of angry, vengeful eyes upon them.

"However, the men he brought with him today who caused this terrible chaos, resulting in the deaths of so many innocent bystanders, as well as the many honorable soldiers who were slain in such cowardly fashion from behind as they stood at their posts, these men are neither Arrgodi nor Mraashk." He paused, raising the sword to point directly at Bane and Uaraj. "Upon these men I pronounce judgment by the power vested in me as king of the Mraashk nation as well as the co-protector of the Arrgodi nation. Apprehend them at once, dead or alive."

With a terrible roar, the crowd moved to do his bidding. The Eoch Assassins, unable to understand the dialect of Mraashk or the Arrgodi tongue fluently, were unaware of exactly what Vasurava had said. They sensed something was amiss, and several were ready to act. But this time, they were hemmed in tightly, and it was difficult to pirouette and spin and dance acrobatically with flailing swords when they had barely a foot of clearance in any direction. The crowd converged on them like a pond swallowing pebbles, and while several succeeded in causing more deaths and wounds before succumbing, the sheer force of numbers brought down the rest.

Vasurava watched grimly as the crowd meted out the punishment they felt Tyrak deserved upon the mercenaries who had done his bidding.

"Is it just?" Kewri asked him. "To condemn ordinary soldiers, even mercenaries, to death thus, while sparing my brother simply because he is a prince? Is this not unfair and unequal treatment? Are not all people to be treated equally under *Auma* in Arrgodi law, by your own words?"

Vasurava nodded. "I do not spare Tyrak because he is a prince. I spare him because he is an Arrgodi, and I have signed a pact to kill no Arrgodi." He pointed at the crowd slaughtering the assassins. "Those assassins may be equal under *Auma.* But they are not Arrgodi."

Kewri caught his arm, pressing herself against his side so she might whisper into his ear. "If you will not do it, let me," she said. "Give me the sword, and I shall kill him. We cannot let him live."

Vasurava caught her hand gently before she could take hold of the sword. "We must let him live and let your father judge him under law. Or we would become as demoniacal as he."

She looked up at him, and in her eyes he saw her acceptance but also her suppressed rage.

# *Ugraksh*

THE COURT OF KING Ugraksh was filled to bursting. Nobody sat, and even so, there was barely room to stand. Outside the sabha hall, hundreds more waited, and the grounds of the palace and the streets were packed with people as well. The entire kingdom waited to hear the outcome of the trial of Tyrak.

A flurry of excitement rippled through the crowd as King Ugraksh emerged from a private entrance and took his place upon the royal dais. Queen Kensura was by his side. Vasurava and Kewri were present, as well as the ministers of the court, the preceptors, the purohits, the brahmins. In many ways, it was a curious echo of the same collective that had gathered in this same venue for the sealing of the peace accord.

Ugraksh waited for the court crier to reel off his long list of antecedents and titles before taking his seat. Everyone else remained standing, but he knew he could not get through this procedure on his feet. He could barely get through it at all. He glanced at Vasurava, wondering what alien mettle the man was made of. Had he been Vasurava's age and in his place, he would have struck down Tyrak where he stood without a second's hesitation. There was no law, no *Auma,* no Arrgodi court that could condone all the evil that Tyrak had visited upon his own people as well as their neighbors.

The years of his absence had been among the most blissful of Ugraksh's latter life; he had even begun to hope that his son was dead, lying slain on a foreign battlefield or murdered in the dark filth of some alley behind a drinking house or place of ill repute. The difference in his queen had been palpable as well. The shock of learning what Tyrak had been up to had turned her into a pale shadow of her former self. Now, though she was no longer quite the stunning beauty he had married more than three decades ago, she carried her age gracefully, which was more than could be said about himself.

Now, he decided, it was time to end this travesty once and for all.

"The facts of the matter are unquestionable," he said. "This morning, we have heard them all, reported by the most reliable witnesses possible." He glanced warmly in Vasurava's direction. "I shall not dither or delay justice any further. *Auma* dictates that Crown Prince Tyrak be given the sharp edge of the fullest extent of the law for his many crimes against humanity."

A murmur of approval passed through the gathering.

Ugraksh went on grimly, ticking off the points of his judgment one by one as the court clerks raced to keep pace with his recitation. Later, the pundits and scholars would rephrase and clean up any of his statements to ensure that the official record was properly pompous and officious for posterity. Right now, he used brevity and incisiveness to convey his points, concerned more with getting it done than with beauty of phrase.

"First, I strip Tyrak of his crown. No longer is he crown prince." That was crucial under law, for a crown prince was by the title itself not subject to any judgment of any court of the land. In fact, since the king was himself the chief dispenser of justice in an Arrgodi republican court, the crown prince was the chief justice in waiting, so to speak. A court could hardly rule against one of its senior-most officials. By stripping Tyrak of his crown, he had removed that legal hurdle.

"Secondly, I divest Tyrak of all his royal titles, possessions, lands, properties, and anything else of value that he may currently own, may have previously owned, or may claim to own in the future, under my authority as the king of the Arrgodi nation. As all possessions of the royal family are merely community property given to them for their use, all that belonged to Tyrak in truth belonged to the Arrgodi nation as a whole, and the Arrgodi nation hereby takes them back." With his wealth, inheritance, property, laborers, servants, soldiers — in short, with everything gone, Tyrak no longer possessed anything of value with which to buy support or raise military opposition, and neither would any heirs he might have appointed or produced biologically of which Ugraksh was not currently aware. Again, a point of law, but a crucial one to avoid future complications.

"Now Tyrak is an ordinary citizen, subject to ordinary laws. As such, I find him guilty of multiple counts of abuse of the peace accord between our nation and the Mraashk nation. I also find him guilty of numerous instances of assault, murder, conspiracy, rioting, and other crimes."

Ugraksh paused, eyes sweeping the rapt faces of the gathering. After a long time, he felt strong, in command, as if he was truly king again. *Tyrak unmanned me,* he thought bitterly. *Unable to accept the truth of his misdeeds or punish him myself, I lost all confidence in myself as a ruler.* That was another debt he owed Vasurava. By his honorable actions and decisions, exemplified by the brilliant manner in which he had apprehended Tyrak rather than simply executing him, he had reasserted *Auma* in Arrgodi once again. It was a powerful message and one that Ugraksh intended to underline now.

"For all these crimes, I, Ugraksh, king of the Arrgodi tribes collected into one nation on the banks of Jeel the Mother River, Vish the Preserver, and Brak the Stone Father, condemn Tyrak to execution in the public square before the palace."

He raised his rajtaru, pleased to note the steadiness of his grip and the firmness of his voice. "Such sentence to be carried out at once." The rapping of the scepter on the floor of the dais boomed and echoed throughout the sabha hall.

# *Kensura*

~

KENSURA SIGHED AS UGRAKSH pronounced judgment. As a mother, her heart broke to hear such a sentence. Not because she disagreed. But because she lamented that her son, her flesh and blood, should have brought himself to such a pass. What had she done wrong? Should she have nursed him longer as an infant? Cared for him personally rather than have the daiimaas govern him? Been stricter in her punishments? She was racked with self-doubt, questions, anxieties, guilt . . .

The people suffered from no such dilemma. The roar of approval that greeted Ugraksh's sentencing made that clear. The enthusiastic cheers and shouts that echoed through the sabha hall, the palace, and the streets below could not be called jubilant — for which kingdom enjoys the execution of its own crown prince? — but it was certainly fraught with relief. Nobody had doubted that justice would be done, but after long years of Tyrak's atrocities and the ugly disputes, feuds, and other conflicts, the people's faith in the king had slipped somewhat.

Today, that faith was renewed with vigor.

Shortly after, Kensura stood at the balcony overlooking the courtyard of the palace. As with the sabha hall, every inch of space was packed with eager nobles and citizens wishing to witness the execution of the prince with their own eyes. Never before had such an event occurred. She prayed it never would again.

Beside her stood Ugraksh, discreetly leaning on a royal crook that was not visible to the crowds below: a king had to keep up the appearance of strength, even if he was in truth ailing and frail. Vasurava and Kewri stood with them. Tyrak's other brothers and sisters and their spouses stood nearby.

The atmosphere was grim and heavy, and fraught with a certain tension that she understood: not tension for the event itself but a kind of taut anticipation, awaiting the end of the event, so they could breathe freely again. Even Tyrak's brothers, blood kin though they were, displayed the same impassive expressions, waiting for the danda to be carried out and the black sheep of the family to be eliminated. Growing up, Tyrak had made enemies of them one and all, and the chief reason Ugraksh had sent them all to govern other regions of the kingdom was to avoid their coming into mortal conflict with Tyrak. Kensura could see no vestige of love or regret on any of their faces, and this made her sad as well.

For the people there was a far larger implication to today's event. This execution would change the history of the Arrgodi and Mraashk nations forever. It proved that no one was above *Auma*. It reaffirmed faith in a republic that had been faltering for years.

Kensura forced herself to look down at Tyrak. He had been pressed into a kneeling posture on the execution platform below, his head resting upon a wooden block. The executioner, a giant of a man who was in reality a shepherd of the mountain tribes — the only community that undertook to perform such executions — stood patiently beside him, the large mace leaning against his thigh.

Oddly enough, Tyrak himself had done nothing, said nothing throughout the brief trial and sentencing. He had simply knelt thus, as he knelt now, head bowed, long hair unfettered and falling across his face, concealing any expression or trace of emotion.

She supposed he was filled with remorse for his actions and misdeeds and overcome by guilt and shame. She hoped that was the case. It would have been too terrible to bear had he ranted and raved and called out for mercy or abused his accusers. True, he had the right to do so, but it would only have made people pity him. Weakness among Arrgodi warriors was unforgiveable. They would have mocked him, hated him, scorned him for being unable to accept his death like an Arrgodi. At least this way, he would die honorably, executed by royal danda, punished under *Auma*. He could even be cremated officially, his ashes scattered into the Jeel as were those of his ancestors. *And soon, my ashes will fall into the river as well,* she thought, sadness pressing against her heart like a cold fist, *for how will I live with the shame of this knowledge?*

The magistrate presiding over the execution looked up at the balcony. Ugraksh raised the rajtaru, the signal to begin. The executioner took up his mace, his powerful hands hefting the massive length of iron, dimples appearing in his shoulders and back as he raised it above his head. Unlike the maces carried into battle, this weapon was not plated with steel, silver, gold, or even copper or brass. No filigree work adorned it, no shaping altered its menacing bulk. It was simply a black pillar of iron with a bulbous head thrice as large as any grown man's, pitted and scored and dented in several places from previous use. She wondered how many condemned men the mace had crushed to death, whose blood would mingle with her own, for the blood that ran through Tyrak's veins was her blood.

The head of the mace lifted as high as the shepherd's muscled arms could raise it, the man steadied himself to take careful aim. He was known to accomplish his job in a single blow, and Kensura prayed that he would do so today as well. *Make it merciful, make it quick,* she prayed. *That is my son after all.* In the end, whatever he had done, whatever had gone wrong, it all came down to that: Tyrak was her son. And she could not find it in her heart to wish him cruelty even now.

The mace hovered in the air for a moment, then began its terrible descent. A sound rose from the crowd, an instinctive natural sound, a wordless growl, that originated deep in their breasts. As the mace descended, the growl rose to a roar and exploded.

The mace crashed down, hard enough to smash a skull to pulp, to end life instantly, to shatter bone and mash flesh and splatter blood.

The executioner grunted with the effort.

But instead of meeting skull and flesh, the bald-headed mace struck an upraised hand and—

Stalled in midair, an inch above Tyrak's face.

A gasp rose from the watching crowd. Incredulity. Shock. The executioner himself stared down, baffled. Then he tried to wrench the mace up, intending to smash it down again, this time to do the job properly. Somehow he had not wielded it correctly the first time; it was the only explanation that made sense.

But though the executioner struggled fiercely, his corded arms, shoulders, back, and neck muscles straining until they stood out in etched relief, the mace did not budge.

Then Kensura saw Tyrak's fingers begin to close upon the head of the mace.

And the iron yielded.

His fingers pressed into the metal like a child's fingers molding a ball of mud. The executioner lost his grip on the mace and backed away. Nothing in his life experience had prepared him for such an occurrence. People across the courtyard gasped and cried out in shock, pointing.

Tyrak rose to his feet. In his right hand, he held the mace by the head. He looked down at it and slowly closed his fist, crushing the solid iron bulb as easily as the mace itself ought to have crushed his head moments earlier. Then he tossed the mace aside — directly at the executioner. A killing weight of iron struck the man in the chest, shattering him. He fell off the execution platform, landing on his back on the stone courtyard, broken beyond repair. People screamed now, unable to comprehend what was happening. Perhaps the oddest thing of all was the way Tyrak looked at his own hand, flexing the fingers, then looked at the dying executioner with the mace embedded in his chest, as if he were . . . as if he were as shocked at his own feat of strength as everyone else.

Tyrak seemed to accept his newfound strength at last and raised his head, looking around at the watching crowd. His hair fell into his face, concealing most of his features. Only one eye glared out, bulging, red-veined, the pupil reduced to a pinpoint. And brilliant white teeth, flashing in the dark shade of his hair-curtained face. He lifted his squared jaw, looking to the balcony above, and Kensura flinched as his eyes sought out and found her. She thought she saw him grin by way of greeting, then that terrible wild-eyed gaze passed on to find his father, Ugraksh. There it stayed. She sensed Ugraksh standing his ground, neither flinching nor showing any reaction that might give Tyrak satisfaction, but from the trembling of his hand upon the crook that helped support him, she knew that effort cost him dearly.

Tyrak chuckled.

Suddenly, Kensura realized, he had expanded in size. Instead of his normal two yards' height, Tyrak was a good yard taller now, and growing. She had barely taken her eyes off him for an instant, to glance at her husband, and when she looked down again, he was a head taller. Now he was twice his original height, his width expanding proportionately. Now thrice . . . She heard the platform creak as his weight increased as well. Now four times, then five times — then suddenly he was growing exponentially, rising like a coiled cobra expanding to its full length. The crowd in the courtyard screamed and shouted with terror.

And still Tyrak continued to grow.

# *Ugraksh*

"PEOPLE OF ARRGODI!"

The voice boomed like a peal of thunder mingled with a grinding metallic sound. Ugraksh's ears throbbed painfully at the sonic assault. Beside him, Kensura clapped her hands over her ears. Kewri did likewise. In the courtyard below, people reeled and fell back, stampeding to get away from this monstrosity that stood before the palace. Elsewhere, horses reared and whinnied in panic, elephants trumpeted in anger, kine lowed in protest, babies howled in dismay.

The being that had been Tyrak only a few moments ago now towered above the palace itself, its head a hundred yards high. It was the width and thickness of a mansion. Dust clouds, raised by its movement, boiled and seethed around it, lending it an air of sorcery, as if some conjuror had tossed down a crystal ball of magic powder and this impossible thing had emerged. The old puranas told of such things, creatures that altered shape at will, grew in size or diminished in stature as they pleased. But this was no creature out of a puranic tale. This was Tyrak. His son!

"By condemning my mortal body to death, you have released my true form. Until today, even I had only premonitions and glimpses of my true identity. But by putting me to the point of death, you have unlocked the secret of my true nature. This is who I am. Not a mere mortal like yourselves. Look upon me and weep, for I am your destiny."

Ugraksh sucked in his breath, struggling to support his weight on the crook. He realized he was inadvertently stepping back, causing his balance to fail. He reached out and grasped hold of the balustrade, using it to prop himself up. It no longer mattered if anyone saw; no one had eyes for him or for anything except the giant urrkh that loomed in the palace courtyard. Yes, urrkh, for what else would you call that being? His mind shuddered to accept that which he was witnessing with his own senses. It was something out of scrolls recording ancient tales and forgotten legends.

Grotesque, malformed, hideously shaped, and barbed at unexpected places, it appeared to be more a war machine than a living creature. Its size was the least unusual thing about it. Its massive muscles were an epic parody of Tyrak's own physique; its feet were ringed with a woollen down more goat- or sheeplike than human. It took a step forward, crushing the remnants of the execution platform to splinters, and the earth reverberated with the thud of the impact. When it spoke, its tongue protruded, a violent, swollen purple thing crawling with life: were those serpents weaving in and out of the flesh of its tongue? And the eyes, those terrible bulging eyes with the pinpoint pupils — there were living things squirming in its eyeballs as well, wriggling to and fro, falling off to land with a sickening plop on the courtyard far below. Each was the size of a finger and trailed a blood-red mucoid residue.

Yet despite this macabre transmogrification, there was no question that the being was still Tyrak. That face, swollen and fat with hatred and rage, those eyes glittering through the curtain of filthy ropes of hair, the overall shape of those features, that body, the way it moved and walked and turned its head . . . even the voice, thunderous and with its undertone of gnashing metal, was still recognizably Tyrak's voice. As the creature turned, speaking almost to itself at times, with curious lapses into a kind of self-questioning tone, Ugraksh realized that the being was discovering its true self even as the rest of them viewed its transformation.

"Too long have I endured in this frail mortal form. Too long have I stayed imprisoned in that putrid cage of mortal flesh and bone. This is the day of my resurrection. By condemning my mortal body, you have set my true form free. Yet I do not thank you, for this too was ordained, as were all things that have passed and those that have yet to come to pass."

The giant Tyrak took another step, this time stepping directly onto a section of the crowd of watchers who had come to witness the execution. Ugraksh saw a dozen innocents crushed like ants beneath the giant woollen foot. Tyrak did not even realize he had ended their lives; all he had done was shift his weight from one foot to the other. Ugraksh realized he must take charge of the situation somehow, or at least attempt to do so. At least the being was still trading words. Perhaps if he kept it talking for a while longer, he could delay any greater violence.

"Who are you?" he cried, his voice cracking with age and emotion. "You are not my son Tyrak. What are you? Identify thyself, creature!"

Tyrak turned and looked down at him. The yard-thick black lips curled to reveal ivory white fangs. "Who am I? Why, I am the one your wife named Tyrak. Do you not know why she named me so? Ask her, then. Ask her why she thus named your firstborn son."

Ugraksh frowned. What was the creature talking about? Surely it was raving. Then he glanced at Kensura and saw the way she stared up at the urrkh, her face drained of all color, and suddenly a realization came upon him.

"My queen?" he asked. "What does this monster mean? Can you explain?"

She looked at him. In her eyes, he saw a terrible truth: *She knows what the urrkh means. She* knows!

"My lord," she said. "It is a creature from the netherworld. A being out of myth. It seeks only to delude and confound you. Do not believe anything it says."

But her voice rang false, and her face betrayed the truth.

Ugraksh hobbled over to where she stood, the crook striking the marbled floor of the balcony with a sharp crack. "Speak the truth," he commanded her. "I demand it."

She blanched and turned away. But he caught her arm and pressed upon it.

Slowly, with her head lowered and tears starting to drip, she said, "He was named after Tyrak the Urrkhlord."

"Indeed," said the giant towering above the city, its voice carrying to the farthest corner of Arrgodi, its terrible form visible everywhere across the city. There was a tone of glee in its voice now, as if it had finally unlocked a key secret, something it had long sought. "The Tyrant of Keravalune. For that is who I was in my past life until the stone god Vish defeated me and the Stone Sages condemned me to generations of imprisonment."

Stone god Vish had defeated this being? Yes, Ugraksh recalled hearing some tale of this derring-do from his preceptor as a boy. Never had he expected to see the stuff of those fireside tales and bedtime stories come to life in this manner.

He raised his crook, pointing it angrily at the giant.

"What is it you seek here now? Why have you returned to Arthaloka? And why did you choose the body and form of my son as your receptacle?"

The bulging face stared down at him. Ugraksh saw now that there were things moving beneath the surface of the urrkh's skin as well, all over his body. Tiny writhing forms in a variety of shapes — centipedes, millipedes, roaches, bugs, and other crawling creatures — traveling to and fro, causing the beast's skin to ripple and bulge at unexpected places and in unsettling ways. He swallowed nervously, not letting himself think of the impossibility of fighting such a being. What weapon could he use against it? How many warriors would it take to lead an assault? Where and how would they strike at it? Could it be wounded? Killed?

"Your son?" The being that had once been their son issued a sound that made even Ugraksh cringe with pain. It was like a horse coughing right into one's ear. Its spittle was alive; several writhing forms spattered onto the balcony coated in slimy white fluid. Ugraksh saw one crawling at his foot and brought the crook down upon it, impaling it. A tiny scream of agony reached his ears. He resisted the urge to void his guts over the balcony railing.

"I am not your son, Ugraksh. I have never been your son. I am not born of mortal man. Again, ask your queen if you do not believe me. Ask her with whom she lay in order to conceive me. It was no mortal man, lord of Arrgodi."

As the being laughed, spewing living saliva, Ugraksh glanced at Kensura. She had fallen to the ground, her face buried in her hands, weeping bitterly. He felt sadness for her, but also anger and disgust. Could it be true, then? Her reaction suggested it was. What did it matter now anyway? The crisis that faced him, that faced them all, was far greater than a mere question of paternity. The future of their entire race was under threat. He could be an angry husband later, in the privacy of his bedchamber; right now, he was still king of Arrgodi. And as king, he needed to know the enemy's intentions.

"Tell me, then," Ugraksh said. "What is it you desire now from us?"

Tyrak looked down at him, then up at the sky, then around. From that height, Ugraksh guessed the giant could surely see all Mraashk, as well as much of the surrounding countryside. *He could probably cover the entire kingdom in a few hours if he leaps and runs. And he could destroy it in days if he wished.*

Finally, the giant completed his examination and looked down again. Ugraksh glimpsed that same hideous smile again and shuddered. "Only what I deserve," Tyrak said with unexpected simplicity, then added, "To rule the Arrgodi and Mraashk nations from now until the end of time. For I am immortal, and this boon is given unto me as my just reward."

He seemed to pause and think for a moment, then all at once his face brightened grotesquely. He beamed with insane delight. "I am your new king, and as of this moment, I crown myself King Eternal. Bow to me, Arrgodi. Bow . . . or die!"

# *Tyrak*

~

## 1

IT WAS SEVERAL MONTHS into Kewri's pregnancy. A pall of dread hung over Arrgodi. As people of the land, the Arrgodi put great store in signs and omens.

All the signs were ominous.

Calves had been delivered stillborn or deformed. Milk had curdled everywhere in the kingdom; even freshly drawn milk lay in frothy lumps in the pail.

A mysterious illness had swept the kine population; many believed it was engendered by the vile effusions the giant Tyrak exuded. Hundreds of thousands of heads of cattle died, and more continued to die in the weeks that followed.

Sown fields were picked clean of seeds by birds. Crops ready for harvesting were suddenly devastated by rodents, vermin, or fungi.

Yokes cracked, uks broke legs and had to be put down, horses went mad and attacked their minders, elephants went into heat outside of season, rampaging through the villages, causing havoc.

One moment the sky was densely overcast; the next moment it was bright and cloudless.

A river broke its banks and washed away a village — even though it was late summer, almost autumn, and there was no logical explanation for the deluge. Other rivers dried up overnight, leaving fish gasping and dolphins flailing pitifully on the riverbeds, the villages they served reaching drought-like conditions despite a record monsoon.

Strange phenomena appeared in the western and eastern skies, as if the sun was about to rise at midnight, or had just set at midday. Priest acolytes who had been able to recite thousands of Ashcrit verses perfectly found themselves blank-headed, barely able to stammer a few lines.

Water drawn from the sweetest wells came up foul and rancid.

Newborn babes found no milk in their mothers' breasts; others choked in their cribs and died of unknown ailments.

People saw their dead ancestors move amongst them, warning of impending doom, urging their descendants to migrate to distant lands.

Soothsayers, astrologers, priests, madmen, philosophers, poets, cowherds . . . all agreed that a great and terrible disaster was imminent.

Many predicted the extinction of the Arrgodi race was nigh. Nobody laughed or disagreed.

The reign of Tyrak had begun.

## 2

Tyrak smiled as the masons worked. He had reduced himself to his normal size again, but he still seemed somewhat larger than before. Vasurava had observed that each time he expanded into his giant form and then regained his original human body, he appeared a little changed. Once, he had seen something creeping beneath the skin of Tyrak's arm, sluggishly, as if unable to move as energetically in human flesh as it had in the urrkh body. Slowly, as Vasurava had watched discreetly, it seemed to be absorbed back into the arm. Another time, Tyrak's eyes reduced to normal human size along with his body, but remained urrkh eyes, the contrast between the human face and urrkh orbs horrific to behold.

Vasurava wondered if each transformation changed something in his substance. If, perhaps, eventually, Tyrak would become all urrkh, with no trace of the human left.

It was a chilling thought. Already, Tyrak was the terror of the land. After the day of his execution — "the day of my rebirth!" he called it, demanding that it be made a public holiday to be celebrated by all the Arrgodi people henceforth, on pain of death — he had initiated a pogrom of terrible efficiency. His aides-de-camp, Bane and Uaraj, had miraculously survived the battering by the crowd on Vasurava's wedding day and had been scheduled for execution following Tyrak; they were freed and reinstated; he had proclaimed them generals. He had executed all of Ugraksh's ministers, leaving Bane and Uaraj to manage the kingdom's day-to-day affairs. He had also slaughtered the rest of the court's officials, nobles, and other Arrgodi who had either opposed him in the past, disagreed with him privately or publicly, or otherwise looked cross-eyed at him. Each one was brought before him for "trial and sentencing" under his new expedited "justice system." He seemed unable to recognize several, but simply shrugged and gave the command for execution anyway.

The new execution platform, constructed overnight to replace the one Tyrak had shattered as a giant, soon turned red with the blood shed over its planks. Nobody came to witness executions anymore, for often Tyrak would point randomly at the crowd and say he recognized a woman who had once giggled when he was passing through the streets, or a boy who reminded him of a long-ago playmate who had won a race against him, or some such whim, and the person would be dragged up to the platform and executed there and then. All grist for the mill.

Now he was overseeing what he termed the "restriction of facilities" for the "former" king and queen Ugraksh and Kensura. Since he had declared himself King Eternal, Ugraksh and Kensura were redundant, their very presence an offense to the current sovereign. Arrgodi tradition required raj-warriors to retire to spend the third autumnal season "in the shelter of the forest." In point of law, he was correct. By tradition, Ugraksh ought to have retired to a simple hermitage in the forest by now, Kensura accompanying him voluntarily, available to his children and former citizens as a mentor and advisor, the physical remove from active politics and prohibition against owning property or accumulation of wealth ensuring that the retired king could never become a political rival to his heirs. He was well past the age; in fact, he was on the verge of the age of complete renunciation, when the raj-warrior devoted his entire living energies and remaining lifetime to the contemplation of godhead, preparing himself for union with the infinite power of *Auma,* the all-pervasive. The only reason Ugraksh had remained on the throne until now was because he had known Tyrak was ill prepared to take on the task of running the kingdom. That, and the enduring strife between the Arrgodi had kept him on the throne, draining his dwindling strength in statecraft when he ought to have been enjoying the fruits of his long life and considerable accomplishments.

Tyrak reasoned, in the roundabout manner he had developed since his "rebirth," that since Ugraksh had failed to retire himself at the prescribed time, regardless of his reason for flaunting tradition, he had thereby consumed part of Tyrak's birthright. At this point, Tyrak reminded those listening sullenly that he was of course not Ugraksh's son, but Kensura's. Since Arrgodi dynasties and society were matriarchal, he was nevertheless the heir to the throne and, as Kensura's eldest son, entitled to his reign. Because Ugraksh had deprived him of his entitlement, he had committed treason against Tyrak, the rightful king. And as such, Tyrak was justified in doing with him whatever he pleased.

Tyrak had chosen instead the sentence he was now overseeing.

Vasurava watched with great sadness as a hundred masons, bricklayers, stone workers, and other artisans and craftsmen worked feverishly to complete their given tasks. They were building a wall around the private chambers of Ugraksh and Kensura — not the entire palatial mansion, a veritable palace in itself, which they had formerly occupied, but a tiny section of the same, barely more than an apartment. It was in fact the apartment that had housed Kensura's maids and, as such, was grossly unfit for a queen, let alone both king and queen. It had been stripped of any "luxuries" and filled instead with dirt, assorted plants, and even insects and rodents especially brought from the woods and set loose inside the rooms. The roof had been painted half blue and half black. A hole had been made high upon one wall, and a pipe trickled water from this hole into one chamber, where it spattered on the muddy floor beneath, turning it to mush. It was apparently up to the occupants to provide a pathway so that this "river" would flow neatly through their "domain." There were no facilities for the two occupants to use as a toilet, merely the two medium-sized chambers filled with this assortment of filth and vermin. Two tiny windows set high near the ceiling provided whatever little and air could find its way into that claustrophobic space.

This, Tyrak said proudly, was to be their idyllic forest world!

And to ensure that they remained within this space as surely as they would have remained in the actual forest, he was having it walled in. An elephant would have had a hard time breaking through the two-foot-thick stone barrier rising from floor to ceiling. No door remained to enter or exit the "forest world." From time to time some raw vegetables, mainly herbs and roots and tree bark, and the occasional fruit, would be pushed in through the high windows or the water pipe to perhaps be found and eaten by the residents — or if they were not quick enough, their fellow inhabitants.

Now Tyrak turned to Vasurava and said cheerfully, "There, it is done. Isn't it marvelous? They shall be so happy in their forest world. So restful. I think they shall become true yogis in no time at all."

Vasurava had already tried his best to plead on behalf of the imprisoned king and queen, begging with Tyrak to give them even just a clean apartment with daily meals and facilities for their toilet. But Tyrak had simply acted as if he did not hear him and had extolled the virtues of his own "brilliant" plan in a succession of self-aggrandizing compliments. Vasurava had known that were he to press the point, it would only turn Tyrak's anger upon himself, yet he had tried and tried again, risking his own life and not caring. Tyrak was executing a death sentence upon his parents, a slow, agonizing death through starvation, disease, pestilence, deprivation, or all of the above.

Tyrak had neither budged an inch from his plans nor lost his temper at Vasurava. If anything, he seemed to have grown remarkably fond of Vasurava, treating him like his own family, displaying a disturbing warmth and affection that was a stark contrast to his earlier hostility. This itself was enough to make Vasurava's stomach churn with disgust. He hated to have to stand by and watch Tyrak commit these atrocities, let alone be treated as if he were complicit in them. But for Kewri's sake, he held his peace.

Now Tyrak clapped a hand on Vasurava's shoulder. "Come now, brother-in-law, let us retire in private. I wish to have words with you. It is time for us to resolve our situation."

# *Kewri*

KEWRI PACED THE HALLS of her chamber, waiting anxiously for Vasurava to return. Under the new martial law imposed on Arrgodi, women were not permitted to travel unaccompanied by a man outside their homes. Even when they did travel with their menfolk, they were compelled to be clothed from head to toe in garb that must not be found provocative in any way, and their faces veiled. A woman found violating any of these conditions would be regarded as chattel and thrown into one of the many detention centers that had been built for this purpose, there to be suitably punished by Tyrak's soldiers for as long as they saw fit.

There were stories, fearfully whispered, of Generals Bane and Uaraj deliberately lifting the veils of women they passed by, and, if the faces they saw pleased them, accusing the women in question of violating the law by having "enticed" them through provocative gestures, words, or simply the way they walked; it was straight to the detention centers for those poor unfortunates. The lucky ones were too ugly, too old, disease-stricken, or otherwise unappealing. Naturally, to avoid falling prey to this gross injustice and misogyny, virtually all women had stopped traveling outside at all, and even Kewri had no choice but to stay indoors.

She heaved a sigh of relief as she saw Vasurava's familiar neatly combed hair as he passed across the courtyard of their house, disappearing below the balcony on which she stood. She spun around as his footsteps sounded on the stairway, and the instant he appeared at the top of the stairs, she went to him eagerly. The sight of his face, pale and drained of all strength, shocked her. She glanced behind him, then over her shoulder at the courtyard once more, fully expecting to see Tyrak's soldiers — the New Army, they called themselves — come with him to bear them both away for immediate execution. Every day since their ill-fated wedding had been spent in expectation of that moment. Seeing Vasurava's face, she feared it had arrived at last.

But there were no soldiers, only Vasurava sinking down into a seat, holding his head in one hand, eyes wet with emotion.

"What is it, my lord?" she asked, "Pray, tell me. Is it execution for both of us? Has he condemned us at last? He has condemned and executed almost everyone else by now. Why not us as well? Tell me, Vasurava, is it execution?"

He looked at her at last, his hand finding her hand and stroking it passionately. "No, my beloved. It is worse. Far worse."

She stared at him, wondering what he meant. What could be worse than execution?

He told her.

And it was so. There were things far worse than merely having one's head crushed to death or being put to death in any fashion, however slow or quick. Her young life and limited experiences had never allowed for such possibilities, but that did not mean they did not exist.

By the time he finished explaining the terms of Tyrak's "solution," she was shaking. Her head turned from side to side, trying to deny it all, to pretend she had never heard it. But the tears that fell from her eyes to splash hotly upon her own hands contradicted that gesture. Finally, she broke down, sobbing bitterly, chest heaving, as he put his arm around her, comforting her; even in her deep distress, she could feel his own pain, as his eyes shed tears too. Together, they held one another and wept.

"It is a nightmare," he said at last, "and like all nightmares, it will end. But for now, we must live through it. Do you understand, my love? We must live through it."

She nodded, then shook her head stubbornly. "Why? Why not just —" She could not complete the thought.

He shook his head firmly. "Someday, his time will come to an end. And if we end our lives, then how can we stand up to him when that time comes?"

"What if his time never ends? What if he really does rule forever as he says he will? King Eternal!" She spoke the phrase scornfully, directing her emotion at the cause of her misery.

"No living thing is forever. Anything that is born must die. Tyrak was born of mortal woman. He is half urrkh and possessed of great power. But someday, he too will end. Or be ended. And we shall be the instruments of that ending."

She looked up at him, wondering at his conviction. "We shall kill him? Is that your plan?"

He nodded. "Perhaps. I shall certainly try. Although I fear he may be grown too strong for any mortal man to kill. Still, I intend to make an attempt."

Her heart clenched at the thought of losing him. "When?"

"When I go to him with our first . . ." He swallowed, looking down, unable to say the word. "Until that time, I shall do exactly as he says, hoping that perhaps, against all odds, he shall relent, perhaps even set us free to go home to my people. If he will not, if he dares to try to harm our first . . ." Again he seemed unable to say the word. "Then I shall kill him."

She was silent. She recalled their conversation in Harvanya when she had urged him to kill Tyrak and he had refused. She did not begrudge him that refusal, nor his refusal to see that Tyrak was no mortal man but urrkh. She respected the fact that Vasurava was his own man, made his own judgment and choices. But she feared that the time had passed for that mode of action. She feared that things would be different this time. Quite different. She was not sure how, or even how she knew they would be, but she felt they would.

But she said nothing. Perhaps she was wrong. Perhaps Vasurava would succeed. Perhaps he would not need to try that last, desperate step. Perhaps . . .

She shook her head, trying to clear it. As she did so, she felt her belly stir. She put a hand to her stomach instinctively.

Vasurava looked at her, concerned. "Are you well? Do you require anything?"

She shook her head. "No. We are quite well. Healthy. All is as it should be."

He was silent for a moment, contemplating the irony of that. "How long?"

She had made the mental calculations already and was prepared with the answer. "Late summer, no later, probably during the month of Bhaadra."

Less than six months from now.

They were silent then, contemplating the future, the possibilities, the ifs and the buts, and everything in between.

Darkness fell as they sat there. Tyrak had denied them servants or aides, allowing them only this one house, guarded by his sentries day and night. Nobody else could enter or leave apart from Tyrak or his emissaries, and they themselves could leave only when summoned by Tyrak. It was home imprisonment, no doubt about it, but it was a far cry from the miserable incarceration to which he had condemned Ugraksh and Kensura. Vasurava kissed his wife's forehead and thanked the stone gods that Tyrak had not treated them as he had his own parents. The thought of Kewri suffering thus through the term of her pregnancy was unbearable. This way, at least she could bring the child to term safely and hygienically.

And then?

Vasurava had said he would kill Tyrak if he attempted to harm their firstborn. He had meant it. But he did not think that this Tyrak was subject to the same limitations as the Tyrak who had faced him on those three previous occasions. Besides which, Tyrak had been unable to harm or kill Vasurava those three times, but Vasurava had never attacked him yet. What would happen when he tried? There was only one way to find out.

Six months. He would find out in six months.

They sat together in the gathering gloom of dusk and waited.

# *Tyrak*

~

THE EOCH STOOD BEFORE Tyrak's throne.

This was a very different sabha hall from the one Ugraksh had presided over. A very different throne as well. This was part of the New Palace that Tyrak had redesigned to suit his purpose, part of the New Arrgodi. It was a new world after all, reborn in his image to serve his needs and intents, and altering its appearance was important to him. He had never liked the gaily colored pageantry of the Arrgodi, the attempt to mirror all the emotions and shades of life in garments, accoutrements, art, décor, architecture, and everything else that was manmade. What about death? Was not death a part of life? Was it not out of his own death that Tyrak had been reborn? One age must die in order for the next to begin, as the day died every sunset to give way to the night, as one lifetime ended in order for the soul to transmigrate to the next. Death was an essential part of the cycle of existence. And what was the color of death? White, of course. The absence of color. Not black, or even grey, for somber though they were, they were nevertheless part of the color palette. White was what you got when you did not have color at all. Utter blankness. Emptiness. Void. A blank scroll upon which one could write anything one desired, remake the world in one's own image if one wished, create new worlds, erase old ones.

And so he had had everything painted white. The walls, floor, ceiling, even the tapestries on the wall had been painted over with lime; the statuary, the houses of the city, and everything else that had been colored was made white. He introduced a compulsory dress code for all citizens, and of course, that was white as well. Nobody was permitted to sport so much as a dot of color anywhere upon their person. Tyrak himself permitted only fair-skinned beautiful people within the royal precincts, which was also the only part of the city where women were permitted — encouraged, even — to move freely, dressed as they pleased, even underdressed if they so desired or, rather, if he so desired. White was right. White was might. White was wonderful. This was Tyrak's world. A white world.

The eoch was dressed in black.

It offended Tyrak.

He thought of having the eoch stripped, then flayed, then fed to his pets. He had a courtyard filled with wild beasts at the back of his palace. Anyone who displeased him he had thrown off a balcony into that courtyard, to be eaten by the beasts. They rarely went hungry. Only this morning he had been compelled to have a serving boy thrown into the courtyard for . . . for? Well, he couldn't recall exactly why he had had the boy thrown down, but it must have been for good reason. And even if he hadn't had a reason, he was King Eternal; he could do as he pleased.

He had had men and women thrown down for far lesser reasons than not wearing white.

Like this eoch.

The fellow was tall, strongly built, like all Jarsun's Eoch Assassins. That was the result of the special diet and exercise regime that Jarsun kept them on, apart from the fact that he recruited only the tallest, biggest specimens. He was dusty from the long journey, and clearly exhausted. But he stood straight, eyes steady and unwavering, waiting for Tyrak's answer to his message.

Tyrak had forgotten what the message had been.

"What was it that Jarsun said?" he asked, irritated that he should have to ask again. Clearly, the courier had not delivered his message with sufficient clarity the first time, or Tyrak would not have forgotten it so easily. Incompetence was such a disease these days.

"My lord," the eoch said, bowing his head again as he repeated his missive. "My lord Jarsun inquires after your well-being and asks if you require his assistance in governing your kingdom."

Tyrak frowned. "Assistance?"

The courier dipped his bald head again. A shiny spot beamed through the layer of road dust; that must have been where the man touched his head with his folded hands while bowing in the Krushan fashion. "Military aid, financial aid, or anything your lordship desires, my master will provide."

Tyrak waved away the offer with a sneer of contempt. "I require no aid or assistance. This is my kingdom; I am quite capable of ruling it myself. Besides, your lord might not have heard, but of late, I have discovered my true nature. I am reborn."

The eoch bowed again before speaking. "My lord is aware of this. He says to congratulate you upon your rebirth and to wish you much success in fulfilling all your ambitions."

Tyrak nodded. "Good, good. Now, is that all Jarsun sent you to say? Because if it is, I have other matters to attend—"

"There is one last thing, my lord Tyrak." The eoch sounded almost apologetic.

Tyrak looked imperiously down his nose at the man. Something wormlike and slimy emerged from his right nostril, coming in his field of vision. He ignored it. After a moment, it dropped off and fell with a small plop to the floor, where it began squirming its way across the polished floor, leaving a trail of slime. "Well?"

"My lord says to take the prophecy seriously."

Tyrak raised his eyebrows. "Prophecy?"

"The prophecy of the eighth child."

"Ah. My sister's eighth child. Yes I am aware of that prophecy. After all, it was delivered to me by the great sage Vessa. I would hardly forget it." But inwardly he was thinking, *The eighth child? Vessa mentioned only the seed of her womb, a male child. Did he mention if it would be the first, second, or another number? I don't think so. How does Jarsun know more than I do?*

"Of course, my lord. Emperor Jarsun merely wishes to ensure that you realize the—"

"Did you say emperor?"

The eoch bowed. "Aye, your majesty. My master is now the declared God-Emperor of Arthaloka, with his capital at Morgolia. The New Morgolia, that is."

"Yes, I know about the New Morgolia. I saw the city while it was being built. But God-Emperor of Arthaloka?"

The eoch simply bowed in response.

Tyrak thought about that for a moment. God-Emperor of Arthaloka. What did that make *him?* A mere king? Why couldn't he be an emperor of Arthaloka too? All he had to do was go forth and conquer the rest of the world. It would not be difficult at all, not now with his New Army and his newfound powers. But that would mean leaving Arrgodi, leaving the Mraashk too. And the Mraashk were itching to rise up against him, the fools. He could not afford to leave Arrgodi just yet. Also, Jarsun had now declared himself God-Emperor. He would not like it if Tyrak did so as well. There could hardly be two emperors! Tyrak would have to fight Jarsun in order to claim sole emperorship. He did not wish to do that. Jarsun was like a father to him. Also, he was the only person Tyrak considered more fearsome than himself.

"What were you saying?" Again he had lost the thread of the courier's missive.

"The eighth child, my lord. It will be your undoing. You must ensure that it is never permitted to be born."

Tyrak nodded, distracted by thoughts of empire and emperorship. "Yes, yes. I have already seen to that."

The eoch persisted: "My lord Jarsun urges you to slay both the woman and her husband immediately. It is the only way to be sure."

Tyrak looked at the eoch coldly. He felt more wormlike things wriggling down his nose. He felt other things squirming and crawling and creeping about his body as well. Getting upset did that to him, it fed his parasites, making them increase in number. The eoch had finally succeeded in upsetting him by daring to tell him what to do, rather than simply delivering his message and keeping quiet as he ought to have done.

He started to give the order for the eoch to be thrown to the beasts, then paused. This was not one of his lackeys or servants, or even a citizen of Arrgodi. This was one of Jarsun's personal guard. The elite of the elite within the Eoch Assassins. Jarsun's most trusted inner circle. He might not look kindly upon Tyrak having the man fed to wild pets.

Then again, Jarsun had declared himself God-Emperor of Arthaloka. While Tyrak was still just king of Arrgodi, at best king of the Arrgodi and Mraashk nations.

He gave the order for the eoch to be fed to his pets. He ignored the man's shocked admonitions as he was dragged away, as well as his threat that Jarsun would not be pleased. So what? If Jarsun did not like Tyrak's treatment of his courier, he could come himself and sort it out. He might be God-Emperor of Arthaloka, but here in Arrgodi, Tyrak was King Eternal!

He plucked a particularly troublesome parasite from his nostril, stared it in honest curiosity, then crushed it between his thumb and sixth finger — the new finger which he had recently grown between his thumb and forefinger. White slime dripped from his hand. He wiped it off on the armrest of his throne just as a soldier came in to inform him that Chief Vasurava was here to see him, at Tyrak's own request.

# *Vasurava*

## 1

VASURAVA CRADLED HIS NEWBORN son in his arms. Precious, precious child. Fruit of his and Kewri's love, most beautiful creature upon Arthaloka. He wanted only to cradle and love and cherish the boy until he grew into manhood. This child was the fulfillment of his life, the symbol of his love and happiness. He ought to walk through perfumed gardens, bathe in cool rivers, frolic with kine and dogs and playmates, be schooled in the vidya, sit wide-eyed while listening to tales of great legends and mighty epics. He should be nursed, fed, clothed, educated, bred, and groomed to be a lover, a brother, a husband, a mate, a friend, a citizen, a chief, a king. He deserved all the wonders of the earth and everything upon it. His name was Kirtiman.

Vasurava held out his hands, cradling the newborn carefully in both hands, and offered him to Tyrak for viewing.

"My lord," he said, fighting to keep his voice level and all emotion at bay. "As you commanded, I have brought to you my firstborn son. This is your nephew. A beautiful, perfectly formed boy. Look upon his beauty with your own eyes. We have named him Kirtiman."

Tyrak had moved from the throne as Vasurava spoke to lie upon a cushioned bed. Female attendants had begun removing his garments and pouring scented oil onto his back. Now, as Vasurava raised the infant up for viewing, he grunted and turned his head a fraction, glancing carelessly down. The attendants began massaging him, kneading the muscles expertly, rubbing the oils into his skin. Vasurava tried not to look too closely at the places where unspeakable things bulged and protruded and writhed beneath the skin, or peeped out from Tyrak's nostrils, ears, or even his eyes, but the female attendants seemed unperturbed by these parasitical abominations. They even seemed to be finding them out and pressing down harder on those spots, as if trying to crush the moving parasites beneath the skin. The sight filled Vasurava with disgust. He fought to retain his composure.

"Why does it not cry?" Tyrak asked.

Vasurava was at a loss for words. "My lord?"

"Babes cry. They bawl. Why does this one stay so silent? Is it without tongue?"

Vasurava swallowed. A trickle of sweat escaped his hairline and ran down his temple to his ear. "My lord, babes only cry when they are in need or when something troubles them. Our little one is a peaceful, contented child. He does not cry because nothing troubles him yet."

Tyrak grunted, turning his head away, shifting slightly to allow the masseuses better access. They continued their kneading and pressing, and — Vasurava was certain of it now — sought out parasites to kill all over Tyrak's body, not just on his back. Apparently, this was a daily ritual. Vasurava waited for several moments. When nothing further was forthcoming, he began to think that perhaps Tyrak had fallen asleep. He dared not speak again. Better to wait in silence. If he fell asleep, then Vasurava might be able to slip away quietly. Kirtiman would be hungry soon, and Kewri was waiting eagerly back home, on pins and needles. Every moment Vasurava was away must have been agony for her.

Just when he was certain Tyrak had fallen asleep, the urrkh said, "Make it."

Vasurava had no idea what Tyrak was talking about. "My lord?"

Tyrak turned his head again, his eyes staring down at the infant in Vasurava's arms. "Make it cry."

Vasurava swallowed. Two more beads of sweat burst free from his scalp and trickled down. He was sweating profusely now, even though it was relatively cool and quite breezy in the palace. "Make him, my lord?"

"Yes. Make the little creature cry. Make it bawl. Make it howl with terror. That way, I will know that it fears and respects me. Right now, I take this calm silence to mean that it is content unto itself, that it neither acknowledges nor fears me. That is gross disrespect. I will not tolerate such behavior from one of my citizens, let alone my own nephew. It must be taught manners."

It. It. It. As if he spoke of a thing, an inanimate object. Even though he had heard Vasurava speak his name clearly. Kirtiman. My son. Not an it.

"My lord." Vasurava felt a tear brimming in the corner of his left eye. He fought to blink it away, to prevent it from spilling forth. "This is your nephew, my firstborn son. As promised, I brought him to you. As you can see, he is a harmless babe."

"The prophecy says otherwise."

Vasurava struggled to find words that would be brilliant and incisive in their logic, glittering diamonds of intellectual rigor, perfect gems of eloquence. Words were all he had to convince Tyrak, to plead with the urrkh for his son's life. "The prophecy . . . if it was a prophecy . . . spoke of the eighth child of your sister, you said. The eighth. Not the first. This is her firstborn."

Tyrak sat up. He gestured. The masseuses moved back at once, heads lowered, eyes averted. Another gesture, and they stepped away, as he leveraged himself off the cushioned couch and stood. His body gleamed with oils, red splotches marking where the parasites had been squashed beneath the skin in various spots. Already the first ones were turning pink, lightening in color as his body absorbed them.

*He is growing less and less human each passing day. More and more urrkh.*

"I received another message today," Tyrak said. "It warned me to take the prophecy seriously. It advised me to kill my sister as well as you. That way, there is no way the prophecy can ever come true."

Vasurava felt the bundle in his hands grow lighter with each passing moment, as if Kirtiman were turning to air, to dust, to ash . . .

"But the sender of the message did not know that I have already tried to do that, in my attempts to kill you earlier. And we both know how that went."

Tyrak grinned unexpectedly, like a man sharing a guilty secret with an old friend. Vasurava, taken by surprise, tried to summon up a smile in response. But from Tyrak's expression, he knew he had not been very successful. Sweat and tears mingled on his face, streaming down freely now.

"I am unable to kill you, Vasurava," Tyrak said casually, stepping down from the royal dais, taking each step very slowly, every corded muscle in his lower body working like an anatomy lesson. "I do not know why. It does not matter why. I cannot do it. That is a fact. So the only way is to kill Kewri. And end the prophecy."

"No!" Vasurava blurted out. "You cannot! You must not! She is your sister."

"She is the bearer of my doom," Tyrak said calmly, now standing on the same level as Vasurava, only yards away. He moved toward Vasurava, his eyes on the babe in his brother-in-law's arms.

"I beg you!" Vasurava cried. "Spare Kewri. Please. Spare her life. I will do anything you say!"

Tyrak stopped before him. He was within reach of the babe now, only a yard from Vasurava himself. He looked down at the infant, then at Vasurava's face. "She means a great deal to you, does she not?" He sounded almost kindly, gentle even.

"She is my world," Vasurava wept. "She is my life."

Tyrak considered this for a moment. Then said quietly, "Give me the child."

Vasurava raised his eyes. He looked into the eyes of Tyrak, urrkh eyes, no longer human—perhaps they never had been human. He searched for words. There were no words left to be said.

Vasurava reached out. He handed the bundle to Tyrak. The child. Kirtiman. A peaceful, gurgling, uncomplaining boy. Beautiful boy. Boy of a thousand dreams, a brilliant future. Some woman's lover, husband, brother, some man's friend, brother, companion. He handed over his own life to Tyrak, and he felt his heart diminish. A part of it was gone forever, never to return.

Tyrak grasped the child by the leg. He held it up to look at it.

"Slayer of Tyrak?" he said scornfully. "This?"

He turned his head this way, then that way, examining the babe intently.

"So," he said. "It does know how to cry after all!"

He laughed.

And then he swung the child around, over his head. With great force and speed.

Once.

Twice.

Thrice.

And then he released it.

## 2

With a great roar, Vasurava rushed at Tyrak.

The urrkh was taken by surprise. Since his rebirth, not many had dared oppose him. Even fewer had dared attack him. His demonstration of his powers on the day of his execution and rebirth had ensured that. Who would dare to go up against an urrkh capable of expanding his size a thousandfold, until he was large enough to crush entire hills, uproot whole forests, toss herds of elephants like pebbles? Only the doomed or utterly desperate. Both had tried. And failed. The swift ease with which Tyrak had dispatched those first few comers had cemented his reputation. He was unbeatable, unkillable. Better to try running away from him than attacking him.

But none of them had been a king. A commander of armies. A warrior by caste and parentage.

Vasurava was all these things.

Like all true pacifists, he was a great warrior. A master of weaponry and tactics, attack and defense, combat and strategy.

He had hoped, prayed, and begged for his newborn son's life.

But he had failed to save Kirtiman.

Now he had no choice but to attempt a violent assault.

He came at Tyrak as his back was turned and he was poised at an angle that made it hardest for him to respond quickly. He deliberately roared to attract the urrkh's attention toward himself, even as he then changed his approach and attacked from the other side. He raised his right hand at first, showing a bare fist ready to pound Tyrak, but in in his other hand, he held a rod of wood with a sharpened metal point. Denied all weapons, he had used his cowherd's crook and part of a cooking vessel to fashion a makeshift one. A two-yard-long rod with a tapering metal point, not unlike a spear, but with the triangular edges sharpened to a fine keenness. He had concealed the weaponized crook down the leg of his lower garment.

He held it low and out of Tyrak's field of vision. By roaring and waving his right fist as he rushed at him, he compelled the urrkh to swing in that direction, anticipating a blow from a fist.

Then Vasurava came from the left, wielding the spear aimed upward in a trajectory that, if completed, would pierce Tyrak's torso just below his ribs and enter his vital organs, either injuring him grievously or killing him outright. It was intended to be a killing blow. Vasurava's only hope was to attack and kill the urrkh before he could expand his size. If he failed, then not even a hundred Vasuravas could face him, at least not without weaponry and assistance, whether human or divine.

His feint worked perfectly at first. Still laughing at the ease with which the brother of the prophesied slayer had been dispatched, Tyrak was not expecting an attack. When he heard Vasurava's roar, he assumed the Mraashk king had finally lost his wits and was foolishly attempting an assault. He swung around, intending to easily block the fist and hammer a blow at the side of Vasurava's head.

But then Vasurava changed tack. And did it so quickly that Tyrak had no time to react. He was still turning to block the fist when Vasurava suddenly seemed to slide a whole yard to Tyrak's right. The next instant, he was right there beside Tyrak, driving what appeared to be some kind of spear into Tyrak's body.

Under ordinary circumstances, this audacious move would have succeeded. Tyrak would have been mortally wounded, unable to fight effectively, perhaps even killed. And everything would have changed right there and then.

But instead, Tyrak discovered something incredible.

The spear came straight at him, broke through his skin, and entered his body. He felt the sharp jag of pain as it pierced skin and penetrated flesh, scraping against his lowest right rib, then skewering his liver like a piece of meat to be roasted, before punching through his back and emerging again, with a small explosion of blood and gristle.

Vasurava stepped back, already preparing his next assault. Mortal blow or no, a warrior was always prepared to counter. Too many fights were lost because one assumed an enemy was downed when in fact they were not.

Tyrak looked at the spear sticking out of his body. He realized it wasn't a spear at all. It was Vasurava's crook. The same crook that had shattered his sword, a mace, several arrows, and sundry other weapons at the war camp.

He reached down and snapped it off. It broke quite easily, given his new urrkh strength.

Then he reached behind with both hands, groped once or twice, found the spear point, grasped hold of it, and pulled the weapon out of his back.

It came free with a further burst of bodily fluids and a sucking, crackling sound. He brought it around and looked at it. The metal spearhead had bent and twisted during its progress through his body.

He tossed it aside. It clattered on the polished floor, sliding a good many yards before it came to rest beneath a wall still splattered with the remains of his nephew.

He looked at Vasurava.

Then he put his hands on his hips.

And he laughed.

Vasurava stared at him in astonishment.

Tyrak pointed down at his own chest, still laughing.

Vasurava looked. And saw the open wound closing of its own accord, the organ regenerating instantly to regain its normal form.

Tyrak turned, showing his back to Vasurava, showing how the exit hole in his back was closing too — now it was closed already — and the wound had healed itself.

Then he turned back and spread his arms wide. His laughter reverberated through the large white sabha hall.

"I thought you understood," he said to Vasurava. "When I said I was immortal, that meant I cannot be killed. Not by any mortal at least. That is why I am King Eternal. I will live forever and rule forever."

In two swift strides he was at Vasurava's throat, grasping it in a single hand. The hand expanded several times in size, while the rest of Tyrak's body remained human size. Vasurava coughed and struggled as the hand lifted him off the ground to hover a yard in midair, feet kicking and flailing uselessly.

"That one I grant you as a learning experiment, brother-in-law," he snarled. "The next time I will break our pact and kill Kewri. Do you understand? Answer me. DO YOU UNDERSTAND?"

With a supreme effort, Vasurava managed to croak out a mangled "Yes!"

Tyrak released his grip and let Vasurava drop to the ground. Immediately, his hand began to return to its normal size.

"So long as you uphold our pact and bring each of Kewri's newborn children to me upon their births, I shall let you both live. Those are the terms of my pact. Uphold them. Or face the consequences."

# *Kewri*

THROUGH THE TERRIBLE YEARS that followed, Kewri was kept alive by only two thoughts:

One was Vasurava's admonition to her at the outset, that evening when he came home and told her of the awful pact he had been forced to make with Tyrak. *Live through this,* he had said. And the simple power of that command struck a deep chord within her. For it was true: If they did not live, they would have failed without Tyrak needing to lift a finger against them. And if they failed by giving up, by letting themselves die, or by killing themselves, then Tyrak would surely have succeeded. And then what chance did Arrgodi have? Or the Mraashk nation? Or Harvanya as a whole? For what Tyrak was doing to Arrgodi, Jarsun and his allies were doing to the entire civilized world. No, whatever else happened, they must endure, they must outlast, they must survive. After Vasurava's failed attempt on Tyrak's life, they realized that their best interest lay in upholding the pact.

The second thought, and most powerful of all, was the knowledge of that eighth child. The one yet to come. The one who was prophesied. Slayer of Tyrak. She mouthed the words silently to herself each time she felt her womb quicken and through the subsequent months of pregnancy. *You will come and save us, Slayer of Tyrak.* She called him by that title, for it was the only name she knew to call him. Or her. All she knew was that the eighth child she would bear would bring about Tyrak's doom. And if Tyrak could be defeated, then surely Mraashk could be saved . . . the Arrgodi race freed of its yoke of oppression . . . and in time, Arthaloka rid of the evil of Jarsun and his allies. The eighth child spelled hope. The future. Infinity.

And how could she birth the eighth child if she did not survive?

But of course she had to do more than just survive.

For a mother could not simply pretend. She must care. Thrive. Prosper. For what she felt, thought, experienced, her unborn children would feel, think, experience as well. So she must be strong and resilient and happy and healthy in order to produce children that were all those things, and more. She must *live.*

*I am rich today,* she had said once to her father, the father she had not seen in over six years now. And she was rich even now. Rich in the love of her husband and companion. Rich in hope. Rich in promise. Rich in prayer and faith and conviction.

For six years, Vasurava took her newborn children to Tyrak.

And six times in as many years, Tyrak destroyed the babes.

Took them by their feet, swung them overhead, and smashed out their tiny brains on the walls of his palace.

Six times. Six years. Six lives.

Innocent, beautiful, perfect, wonderful lives. Snuffed out. Destroyed.

Of all the crimes he committed, all the injustices, all the atrocities and brutalities, surely that was Tyrak's worst offense?

To kill innocent babes the very day of their birth? For no good reason at all.

And now she was about to bear a seventh. Where had the years gone? They had gone to the same place that her dead babes had gone. Into the mouth of Sesh, the serpent of infinity, its coils winding around the Samay Chakra itself, the great Wheel of Time, upon which all creation revolved. And once Sesh took hold of anything, it never returned. What was gone was gone, dead was dead, past was past. *Think only of today and of tomorrow, Kewri. The eighth child comes. Slayer of Tyrak.*

But this was the seventh. The seventh, not the eighth.

Even if somehow the eighth was born and survived the wrath of Tyrak and lived to grow to manhood and fulfill the prophecy, that would come later. The prophecy said nothing about the seventh killing anyone. So it would go the way of the first six.

Somehow, that broke her heart more than the grief she had lived through each year for the past six years.

*Not another one, Goddess Artha. Not this one.*

She prayed to the goddess, her patron deity, with fervent ardor. Before her mind's eye flashed the incandescent image of the Mother Goddess, creator of the universe and progenitor of the stone gods, together with her sister Jeel. Resplendent, omnipotent, magnificent in feminine power, the many forms of the goddess appeared before her one by one and seemed to meld into her own essence, like layers upon layers of thinly beaten metal joining together to form a single blade.

*Let me be the mother of the Deliverer, Goddess, let mine be the womb that brings into this world the Slayer of Tyrak.*

# *Tyrak*

TYRAK PROWLED THE CORRIDORS of his palace. He now commanded the largest Arrgodi standing army ever maintained, a force great enough to challenge most other kings, perhaps even great enough to challenge Jarsun himself. The past seven years had seen him grow from strength to strength. Today, even Jarsun's emissaries dared not raise their eyes to look directly at him, and spoke only soft sweet assurances and words of agreement. He still fed the occasional messenger to the beasts in the back courtyard, just to make sure they stayed humble and polite. In his own kingdom, none dared even speak to him unless spoken to. He ruled with an iron hand. Absolute power. He had it, he enjoyed its fruits and spoils, and he would rule forever.

Perhaps the only thing that troubled him was the change in his physical form. Whereas at first the urrkh elements had showed themselves only in small ways or at certain times, with the human form dominating, now it was the other way around. He was almost all urrkh now, and only occasionally did he lapse back into human form. And even those times were not by choice; they happened involuntarily, and he was never quite sure what triggered or sustained them.

The only thing he could sometimes control was his size.

He had settled on a more or less permanent size of around one and a half times the size of a big human warrior, which made him about ten feet in height and as thick around the chest as a bull's torso. From time to time, he would expand further, often without meaning to, but becoming smaller than this was nigh impossible. He tried at times, if only because a large size often made it awkward to move through doorways and ride elephants. Even though he had had the palace redesigned to accommodate his new size, if he grew several more yards in height as he often did, a twenty-foot-high doorway could still be too low to get through comfortably. And even elephants had a limit to how much they could carry.

It was as if, the more he used his urrkh abilities, the less human he became.

But this was not what troubled him now.

Kewri and Vasurava had succeeded in saving their seventh child.

He knew this with perfect certainty. He had just returned from visiting his brother-in-law and sister and he had heard their account of the unfortunate mishap. They had both been visibly distraught, and their performance was credible but he had smelled through it at once. There was an odor of truth about their claims, but underlying that was a whiff of something else, not quite a lie, but not the whole truth either. They had held something back.

He had demanded to see the remains and had been shown a mangled mess that was convincing enough. But he knew he had been deceived. The question was how. Nobody had entered or left their house. He had had the house watch tripled the past month itself, anticipating treachery as the crucial time approached. He had employed spies to infiltrate the community of daiimaas who assisted Kewri during pregnancy and deliveries.

The verdict was unanimous: somehow the child had been miscarried. He had even bitten off the head of one spy — a habit he had acquired over the past year or so and resorted to when one of his own people was being inefficient or obtuse. It always produced excellent results, though not from the person whose head he had bitten off, of course. The heads made for satisfying snacks as well; he enjoyed the crunch of the skulls and the tasty sweetmeats inside. But while that had elicited the proper reactions from the other spies, it hadn't brought forth any further intelligence.

He could find no way to prove that the child had been born in Arrgodi, or any trace of it anywhere.

Yet he knew that somehow he had been deceived.

**It is so, Prince Tyrak. You have indeed been deceived.**

He turned to see the great sage Vessa standing in the corridor. The sage's image looked solid and real enough, but when Tyrak tried passing a hand through it — he swung a fist with enough force to fell a horse — the hand passed through empty air, the image undisturbed.

"*You,*" he said. "It's been a long time since you showed your bearded face. And I'm King Eternal now, not Prince."

**It was never my intention to become your friend or lifelong companion. And as for the title you bestow upon yourself, I may call a house built with uks dung a palace, as many do, but that would not make it so. So long as King Ugraksh lives, you shall always be Prince Tyrak. Or simply the Usurper, as you are better known amongst the people.**

Tyrak snarled, expanding himself till his head touched the vaulted ceiling, his arms the walls of the four-yard-wide corridor. "Why don't you appear before me in your flesh form, priest? Let us then see if you dare insult me."

Vessa laughed shortly. **I do not come here to bandy insults or threats with you, merely to warn you. The seventh child of Vasurava and Kewri has slipped through your grasp.**

Tyrak swore and thumped the walls to either side with his fist. Plaster crumbled, and great cracks appeared in the walls, running up to the curved ceiling.

Vessa flinched, looking up as pieces of the ceiling clattered and fell around him in a shower of dust and debris, then seemed to recall he was in no danger.

Tyrak said, "I knew it! They deceived me somehow. But how?"

**They have powerful allies. The stone gods themselves assist them. Stone Father Brak instructed Mother Goddess Jeel to spirit the child from Kewri's womb to another location.**

"*Where?*" Tyrak pounded the floor, sending a giant crack running all the way up the length of the corridor—between the great sage's feet. Again, Vessa almost jumped but controlled himself. "Tell me where, and I will go and crush it like a grape in my fist."

**That was not made known to me.**

"What do you mean, not made known? Who makes these things known to you?"

Vessa hesitated, glancing over his shoulder as if concerned that someone might overhear him. Tyrak frowned. There was nobody in sight the entire length of the corridor at this time of night. No matter what Tyrak did or what sounds came from his chambers, none of his people would dare intrude upon his privacy until called for, unless they wanted their heads bitten off.

He realized that Vessa was not looking back at this corridor in Tyrak's palace. He was looking back at the place where his physical body was right now, in some distant location.

**I do not have much time, son of Kensura. I urge you, listen to my words and heed them well. This may be your only chance of ensuring that the eighth child is never born in this lifetime.**

Tyrak frowned. Did that mean the child could be born in some *other* lifetime? There was more to the matter than Vessa was saying to him; he had always sensed this. Now he knew it was so. "First tell me this — why do you help me?"

Vessa looked at him. **What do you mean, Tyrak?**

"It is a simple enough question. Why help me? I am . . ." He gestured at himself, not needing to describe his own appearance or nature. "I am what I am. Usually stone priests like yourself, especially great sages, would be training warriors to kill persons like me. Instead, you appear mysteriously from time to time and offer me advice and warnings that have helped me prosper and gain power. Why are you so benevolent to me? Have I done something to merit your protection and blessing?"

Vessa looked away, avoiding Tyrak's eyes. **What difference does it make? I am helping you, as you yourself admit, so take my advice and use it well. There is an old saying among cattle farmers, perhaps it even originated from the Mraashk: Do not look a gifted uks in the mouth to check its health, for that might insult the one who gifts it to you! It is advice you would do well to heed.**

Tyrak nodded. "In that case, begone."

Vessa blinked. **What did you say?**

Tyrak waved a hand dismissively. "Begone. Away. Leave us be." He looked at the great sage insolently, grinning wide enough to display his inner set of teeth, the ones that clamped down to break down particularly hard items, such as skulls or human thighbones. "I do not trust intelligence provided for unknown motives by one who openly says he is not my friend." He smiled slyly. "And who is a known associate of the stone gods, sworn enemies of all urrkh, of which race, in case you were not aware, I am a member."

Vessa glared, angry now. Great sages were not accustomed to being told to get lost.

Tyrak turned his back on his visitor, stretched his arms, and yawned languorously. "Now, either tell me what I wish to know or turn into a cartwheel and roll away."

Vessa sulked for a long moment. Tyrak finished stretching and yawning and started to walk away. He was amused when the sage called him back. Good. Now, he would get some real answers, and then he could figure out how to make sure that little slayer was never born.

# *Vasurava*

## 1

VASURAVA AND KEWRI WERE asleep when Tyrak's men arrived. Vasurava leaped out of bed, heart thudding, and thought, *This is it, he has finally broken our pact and has come to have Kewri killed.* He told his frightened wife to stay inside and went out, barring the door and standing before it. He would kill anyone who tried to harm her. He was not immune to the attacks of others — he had been manhandled enough times by Tyrak's men to know this to be so — and he did not care. He would rather die than stand by and watch his beloved Kewri be killed. If this was to be his last stand, so be it.

The men were led by Bane himself, clad in resplendent robes and richly ornate armor proclaiming his status as Saprem Senapati. It offended Vasurava's very core to see a man like Bane given charge of Mraashk's armies, not merely a man without any sense of *Auma* or morality, but a known slave trader even before he had allied with Tyrak. Vasurava himself had once delegated a force to stop Bane's thriving trade in child slaves. They had crippled his operation considerably, if not ended it altogether. He knew that Bane had always borne him a grudge for it. That showed now as the thin, tall man stood before him, slapping a free glove into the gloved palm of the other hand as he grinned.

"Vasu," he said, then added with heavy irony, "Stone Father!" He looked around. "I thought stone gods resided in Stone Heaven, yet here you are, amongst us humble mortals. What have we done to deserve your presence, lord?"

He laughed. His soldiers laughed as well. There were over a dozen, Vasurava noted, all armored and armed. Clearly, they had not just come to deliver a message. He heard the sound of heavy clinking and glimpsed a length of chain in one man's hands. What was that for? Were they to be shifted to a dungeon now?

"What are your orders this time, Bane?" Vasurava said calmly. "Did he toss a stick and tell you to go fetch it?"

Bane's smile vanished at once. "You would be well advised to watch your tongue, Mraashk."

Vasurava didn't retort. His first barb had struck home; that was enough.

"Move aside," Bane said.

Vasurava folded his arms comfortably. "These are our private quarters. None may pass."

Bane grinned. "Why, Mraashk? Do you fear we might molest your wife?" Several of the thug's men chuckled at that.

Vasurava would not let himself be provoked by such puerile taunts. He remained standing in their way.

Bane sighed irritably. "We are here on the king's orders. It is best if you let us do what we have to and leave."

Vasurava shook his head. "Not until you tell me what you are here to do."

Bane gestured to the man at the back. He came forward, the chains dragging on the ground with a nerve-rasping sound. "You are to be chained and manacled henceforth." He pointed to one side of the house. "And restricted to one half of the house."

Bane beckoned again and a pair of stonemasons approached, their implements in hand. "They are to raise a wall dividing the house into two halves. You will reside in one half, and your wife in the other half." He added with evident pleasure, "She is to be chained and manacled as well."

Understanding swept through Vasurava at once. His heart shrank with dismay. Whatever he had expected, this was not it. Violence, a direct assault, an attempt on his or Kewri's life, these things he was prepared for . . . But to chain Kewri and he and keep them in separate halves of the house? And why raise a brick wall between them? Only a demon like Tyrak could conceive of such a move.

Bane grinned, seeing Vasurava's expression. "When one wishes to rest the bull, one puts the uks in another pasture and raises a fence between them." He took hold of the chain in his soldier's hand and shook it, making it jangle loudly. "And to keep the bull from jumping the fence, we chain its leg."

He grasped Vasurava's hand roughly and clapped the manacle on it. "And that is how you make sure there are no calves born."

The sound of his soldiers laughing filled Vasurava's ears.

## 2

Now he sat on one side of the wall. Kewri was on the other side. He could hear her, but it was not possible to see her from any angle. The chains and manacles made sure of that. Everything they did, they were compelled to do within reach of the chains, each barely a few yards long. His heart wept at the thought of Kewri chained like a common criminal in a dungeon. *What crimes have we committed, Lord? Why do you make us suffer thus?*

They talked through the wall, Kewri and he. They talked more than ever. The separation was agonizing. Only a few yards away, and yet so far.

But as the days passed, he realized how devilishly simple Tyrak's plan had been. Without harming Vasurava or Kewri, without breaking the pact between them, without killing his sister or brother-in-law, he had made it impossible for the eighth child to be conceived.

The one thing that had succored them both, had kept them moving forward purposefully through the terrible years and days and nights, was the knowledge that someday the eighth child would come. The Slayer of Tyrak. Now there would be no slayer, no end to this perpetual nightmare. And what of the future? Were they to live like this till the end of their lives? Perhaps from time to time, Tyrak would degrade their lives further in some new way, finding new methods of harassing them, torturing them indirectly. Perhaps someday he would wall them in completely as he had done his own father and mother, neither of whom had been seen since that day seven years ago, though they were believed to be alive inside that hell-ish prison. A life lived thus, Vasurava mused bleakly, was worse than a good clean death.

He turned and looked at the newly built wall. It loomed five feet thick and reinforced with rods of iron. It was as solid as a fortress wall. Even if he attempted to dig through somehow, he would be found out within a day by the guards who patrolled the house constantly. And the attempt itself might worsen their plight.

He sat back, shoulders slumped despondently, and slept.

## 3

When Vasurava awoke, the first thing he noticed was the light.

Night had fallen. The house was dark. The patch of sky visible through the open window was black as pitch. If there was a moon, he could not see it through that narrow portal, nor any stars.

But the wall glowed with light.

He blinked and looked up, certain he was dreaming.

A shape very much like a large oblong had appeared on the wall at eye level. It seemed to be formed entirely of some kind of brilliant bluish light. He had never seen the likes of it before. It glowed rhythmically, pulsing and throbbing slowly, like . . . like . . . a heartbeat? Yes. That was exactly what that pulsing rhythm resembled, a heartbeat.

Slowly, he came to see that the shape of the light was the shape of an egg. A very large egg, perhaps the size of a man's belly.

Or a woman's womb.

Yes. That was precisely it. It was not an egg but an embryo. An unborn infant, nestled within the safety of its mother's womb, pulsating with life. And the light, this wondrous bluish glow he was seeing, perhaps this was how the world appeared to an embryo within the womb.

Even as he thought this, the light began to take clearer shape and form. Now he could see the shape of the womb, the fluid sac that acted as a vital protective shield cushioning the unborn life, and within it, the unmistakable shape of the infant child itself, curled in that primordial fetal pose.

He slid backward on the ground, suddenly afraid. The chain clanked in protest. He was at its farthest limit. The manacle dug into his shin and calf, cutting open the scabs of crusted blood and making his wounds bleed again.

*Do not fear me, Father.*

He exclaimed.

*I will never harm you.*

Vasurava felt himself shudder, then fought to regain control of his senses. "Who . . . who are you?"

*I am your son.*

He did not know what to say to that. His son? *Which son?* he was about to ask. For he had had several, all dashed to death by their brute of an uncle. Surely this was the restless aatma of one of those poor unfortunate dead. But the voice sensed his confusion and clarified it:

*Your unborn son. Your eighth child.*

Vasurava resisted the urge to gasp aloud. With an effort, he said, "But you have not yet been conceived!"

*That momentous event shall take place tonight, in a few moments.*

"But . . . how?"

*Through the power of* Auma, *guided by your will, I shall be transported into my mother's womb. All you have to do is will me there, and thy will will be done.*

Vasurava was silent. He knew what the child was saying was true. He accepted it as he had accepted all the miracles of *Auma.* He felt his mind grow calmer, his pulse steady, his heartbeat return to its usual pace.

"But after that, what next? The moment Tyrak hears that his sister . . . your mother . . . is carrying the eighth child, he will not sit idly by."

*I shall tell you what you have to do. All will be well. Just do as I say, Father, and I shall take care of the rest.*

Vasurava thought a moment longer, then nodded slowly. "Yes. I shall."

*Then let us begin. Focus your mind on me, become one with me, and the rest shall come to pass.*

Vasurava looked deep into the blue egg of light, at the being that floated there, suspended in that ethereal sac of sacred illumination. And slowly, by degrees, he felt his consciousness rise up out of his body. He felt his spirit soar up, up, up, high above the ether, and down, down into the blue light . . . the blue light of *Auma* that the sacred Ashcrit verses of the great texts referred to . . . and a great sense of peace and fulfillment swept through him. Every anxiety wiped clean. Every worry washed away. Every pore of his body alive with energy, with shakti.

He felt that energy pass from him through the wall to the other side . . .

To his beloved, Kewri.

# Tyrak

A GENTLE BREEZE ROSE from the Jeel and blew through the city. It stirred the senses of even the most miserable souls in Arrgodi, awakening them to a tingling sense of expectation, of something about to happen. Rivers that had grown murky, sluggish, or parched began to flow with their full strength, their waters clear as crystal, sweet and fresh as if drawn directly from a glacier. Ponds that had dried up or turned to scum-covered mosquito breeding nests became clear and were filled with lotuses. Trees whose branches had withered straightened their bent boughs, turned slowly green again from the roots up to the highest leaf. Bees began to buzz and make honey, sweeter and thicker than ever before. Sacred fires burned on, even without fuel, as astonished brahmins exclaimed, each wanting to take credit for the miracle. The minds of penitents were at ease; hermits felt they had achieved the goal for which they had spent decades meditating. Chanteuses found themselves singing songs they had never heard before, and never knew they knew. Every sign, every omen, every portent, was auspicious.

In his palace, Tyrak had been gnawing on the thighbone of an uks while he listened to the tally of a new land tax he had imposed upon the Arrgodi and Mraashk nations. He was already enraged by the low count and the excuse given, that more and more Arrgodi were choosing to migrate to other lands rather than continue to live under his reign. He ordered all those found leaving their homes to be killed on the spot. But it occurred to him that if he killed everyone who could afford to pay the tax, then who would be left? Only those who could not afford it.

That was when he smelled the breeze blowing into the chamber, and smelled as well the secret message it carried. He rose from his throne and threw it across the sabha hall, breaking the great door of the assembly chamber. He threw back his head and bellowed in rage.

Somehow, despite all his efforts, the day he had feared had come to pass. The eighth child had been born. It was impossible — Vasurava and Kewri had been apart all this while, and Kewri had displayed no signs of pregnancy — but somehow the impossible had been accomplished.

He strode from the assembly hall, bellowing orders as he went. Bane and Uaraj scurried after him, trying to keep pace. Tyrak had expanded to thrice his normal size, and as he went, he banged his fists against walls, knocking out chunks of stone and brickwork, and slammed his shoulders into pillars, cracking them in two and endangering the ceilings they held up, shattering statuary, and generally demolishing his own palace without knowing or caring.

He emerged from the palace and bellowed for his mount. A very frightened mahout bowed low and tried to find a way to tell him that he had killed his war elephant during his last ride by losing his temper and expanding himself so suddenly that the beast was pressed to pulp beneath him. No mount, elephant or steed, could bear him.

Bane and Uaraj stood at a safe distance and attempted to pass on or execute Tyrak's orders. From what they could follow, he wished to mobilize the entire army!

At that moment, the breeze changed.

Tyrak froze.

Suddenly, he went limp, his urrkh features settling, blazing red eyes rolling up in his head, and he fell to the ground like a sack of potatoes. Or a small mountain of bricks, because his body crushed the poor mahout, who was still bowing before him, as well as several other soldiers who were nearby.

Bane and Uaraj stared at this extraordinary sight.

"The king has fainted?" Uaraj said, barely able to believe the words himself, although he could clearly see Tyrak lying prone, arms flung out, drool dribbling from his parted lips. Something insectile with a thousand tiny hairy legs emerged from Tyrak's mouth.

Bane was about to respond to Uaraj when suddenly his eyes rolled up and he collapsed as well. Uaraj followed. So did the soldiers standing or running around the courtyard of the palace. Within the palace, every single person did the same.

Across the city, everyone fell unconscious where they stood, or sat, or rode. People, animals, birds, insects, every living creature.

Because of the curfew, most citizens were safe in their homes at the time, and fell asleep in their chairs or beds. Tyrak's soldiers, enforcing the curfew, patrolling, or engaged in other soldierly duties, were less fortunate. Some fell into horse troughs, others into cesspits; hundreds fell off their horses or elephants and broke their arms or legs or necks. Many died in bizarre accidents, like the captain of a company of soldiers who was about to set fire to a farmhouse because the owner had refused to supply free milk and butter to his soldiers. The captain had taken a burning brand from one of his soldiers, wanting to set fire to the house himself as the farmer and his distraught family watched and wept. The wind changed, and he fell off his horse, onto the burning brand. As he slept, the flames consumed his unconscious body, immolating him on the spot.

But most of the population was merely lulled into a sweet loss of consciousness.

Arrgodi slept.

# *Vasurava*

## 1

VASURAVA HELD THE BUNDLE in his arms carefully and rose to his feet. As he did so, a great wind raged through the house, as if cheering his accomplishment, then passed as suddenly as it had risen. He smiled at Kewri, who beamed up at him happily, then he turned and left.

As he reached the first of several doors, a loud clanging sound echoed, and the bolt broke off the door and fell to the ground with a soft thud. The door flew open and stayed open as he passed through. The same thing happened with each door. Outside each door he found guards fallen unconscious at their posts, some in ludicrous postures, at least one with a severe fracture or worse.

The city was quiet as he walked through the streets. Not a soul stirred. Not so much as a bird flew across the night sky. Not a single insect chirred or cricketed. Not a dog or cat or even a mouse scurried in the shadows. Everywhere he passed soldiers fallen off horses, elephants, the towers that stood at every junction . . . Glancing into a few houses whose doors or windows lay open, he saw the people inside sleeping as well. The entire city was asleep. Tyrak too, for nothing else would have prevented him from being there otherwise.

As he walked, he recalled the events of the night.

Kewri and he had both been awakened by the reappearance of the same blue light. She had seen exactly the same thing that he saw, but from her side of the wall.

No longer was the child a fetus. It had appeared within the egg of blue *Auma* shakti as a newborn come to full term.

The child was a boy with four arms.

In his four hands he clutched a horn, a mace, a flower, and a disc.

He had a radiant jewel at his throat. He had marks upon his chest. He was swaddled in a yellow garment which contrasted pleasantly with his clear blue skin.

He smiled down at his father and mother, and the beauty of that smile filled them both with a deep glowing warmth and inner radiance. For the rest of their days, they had only to think of that smile, and they would be filled with complete peace, tranquility, and joy.

Vasurava joined his palms in greeting and bowed. "My son. Who are you? What are you? Pray, enlighten us. We are but simple mortals, we know nothing."

The boy smiled. "You are Vasurava and Kewri, my parents. Everything I know comes from you and through you. Without you, I would not be able to set foot upon this world."

"Yes," Kewri said, "but it is you who make this possible, Lord. We are only the instruments of your miracle. Looking at your radiance, feeling your *Auma,* I am convinced that surely you are Stone Creator Thyself, the Supreme Being."

The boy smiled enigmatically.

He looked to one side and then looked back. His gaze brought with it a flowing river of images, sounds, sensations. With a flick of his fingers, he diverted the flow to Kewri and Vasurava, both of whom reeled back in amazement. Their minds were filled with perceptions like memories of experiences actually seen, heard, and felt.

Vasurava gasped. "You are Vish incarnate."

Kewri said, "You took incarnation as Venen the dwarf once. As Axor. As Sia Kandra. As Swan God. As Boar God. As Gryffon. As Chukva. As Haranviyan. And as Mashandor. In different ages of the world, you assume different forms for different purposes. But this alone is your incarnate form."

The boy smiled. "Not only I — you two were born before and lived other lives before these ones. Do you not recall them?"

Kewri and Vasurava shook their heads.

"You, Vasurava, were a stone priest named Tapseu. And you, my mother, were Progyor. This was during the Age of Myth. And I was born to you in that life as well, where I was named Preshnor. Would you like to know more?"

Both nodded eagerly.

"Then listen. I shall show to you the entire history of our past lives together as well as those yet to come."

Both Vasurava and Kewri closed their eyes as a fresh flood of visions swept through them, carrying them upon the tide of time, across the oceans of eternity.

Finally, after communing with his parents-to-be for an undetermined time, he stopped and sighed. "It is now time. The hour of my birth is at hand."

Kewri reacted. The child saw her react.

"You fear your brother's wrath?"

"Yes, my son."

"Have no fear. He shall not harm you tonight. Now I shall take my place within your womb, my mother. And you shall birth me as any human child. Once in human form, I shall be subject to human qualities and failings as well. For even though I am incarnate in this amsa and not merely a partial avatar, there are inherent limitations of the human form that cannot be overcome completely. I shall seem to be a normal newborn human baby. But do not be deceived. I am here to set things right once and for all. However long it takes, no matter what I have to do, I shall see this through. You shall be freed of the yoke of the oppressor. So shall all the Arrgodi. The race of Arrgodi shall enjoy a time of such prosperity and satisfaction as they have never seen since the beginning of their line. This I promise you."

"Wait," Vasurava said, palms still pressed together. "What shall we name you, Lord? You are no ordinary child. Surely we must grant you some special name as well?"

He smiled. "Drishya."

## 2

Now Vasurava stood before the Jeel, carrying his newborn son in his arms. As he recalled the wonders that he had been shown and the knowledge and memories he had been given, he wept, and had to pause to wipe the tears of joy from his eyes.

A new challenge awaited him.

The river was in spate, flowing with a roaring rush. At this time of year, even elephants could not be bathed in this stretch of the river, nor bridges spanned, nor boats travel safely. The only way across was to go downstream several tens of miles where the river split into its tributaries, then cross using a raft anchored by an overhanging rope system.

But Vasurava had been told by his son that he had only until dawn to deliver him to his destination and return home. The place he was to go was a fair distance away, no easy walk, even without having a newborn child in his arms. The detour downstream would make it impossible: he would not reach his destination before daybreak, let alone return. And his son's instructions had been clear. The sleeping would last only until dawn, at which point, Tyrak would rouse and send every soldier in Arrgodi in pursuit of him.

He looked around, feeling the frustration born of years of imprisonment and abuse swell inside him. Then he realized how foolish he was being and smiled. "Lord," he said quietly, "you must surely have provided for all contingencies. Pray, allow me to cross the river."

*Certainly, Father.*

The response winked in his mind like a flash of light. He thought he heard a tiny baby gurgle as well.

Thunder rumbled above. Vasurava glanced up nervously but saw only a clear night sky. Not a cloud in sight.

A single bolt of lightning cracked down and struck the center of the river.

Water rose in a geyser spout, rising up hundreds of yards into the air. Slowly, it fell back. When it had settled, Vasurava saw that a crack had appeared in the river. A thin line drawn straight from bank to bank. As he watched with incredulous eyes, the line widened until it was several yards across, revealing the bottom of the river.

The river began to slow. Downstream, it remained the same, gushing along at breakneck speed. But upstream, it slowed steadily by degrees, until finally, after several moments, it ceased flowing altogether. He looked at the downstream flow — it continued unabated.

Thunder growled and grumbled overhead.

*Ours not to understand everything that happens. Ours merely to do our given task.*

He stepped down the side of the riverbank, careful not to slip, and descended.

Just as he reached the bottom of the river, the sky cracked open and a torrential rain poured down. It was the heaviest rainfall that Vasurava had ever seen. Fat, heavy drops struck the ground, splashing mud. In moments, the world was blanketed by rain.

Yet not a single drop fell on Vasurava or his newborn son.

He looked around in wonderment, raising one arm and stretching it out. At its farthest extent, he could just feel the rain. He brought back his fingers, dripping wet, and looked at them. They smelled of fresh earth and rain. He looked up and saw that the invisible protective canopy that shielded him from the rain took a curious shape, like a tapering . . . hood? Then he remembered his son's words from earlier, explaining this very thing:

*The hood of Sesh, the eternal serpent. Sesh shall travel with you, protecting you from all dangers, big and small.*

Vasurava nodded and started off across the bed of the river. Perfectly natural for the eternal serpent to appear out of mythology and protect him as he carried his newborn son, stone god incarnate, across a divided river. Quite natural.

He reached the far side a while later, and trekked up to the other bank. He started off in the direction of Harvanya. From there, he would make his way deeper into one of the oldest of Arrgodi territories, Arghbhoomi, the heart of the Arrgodi nation. It was a long walk. And he must complete it and return home before dawn. Or else even his infinitely powerful son would not be able to save him from Tyrak's wrath.

He reached the tiny hamlet some hours later, bone weary yet filled with joy and anticipation. As he had been told, a light was burning in one of the modest huts. As he came to its doorway, he had a moment of anxiety. What if . . .

But everything was exactly as promised. Every single person he had passed between Arrgodi and this remote rural hamlet had been fast asleep. He had even seen a cowherd resting on his crook and snoring as his cows lay asleep around him.

Inside the hut, he found a woman on a cot, with an infant lying beside her, suckling. It was evident that she had only just given birth before falling asleep as everyone else had.

A man lay prone on the floor beside the cot, as if he had been taken by the sleep as he sat or stood beside his wife. As Vasurava entered, the infant stopped suckling and turned its head to look at him. Its arms and legs began to move in the manner of all babies, kicking out excitedly. He saw that it was a girl, as he had been told it would be.

He put his son down on the cot beside the woman and picked up the infant girl. She squealed with delight as he took her in his arms, and he felt a rush of love and tenderness. It helped make it easier for him to turn his back on his own son.

He returned to Arrgodi just as the first flush of dawn was creeping across the eastern sky. He put the baby down beside Kewri, who took her in her arms and cradled her with as much welcoming love as if she were greeting her own child. He looked at Kewri for a long moment, brushed the tears from her cheeks, then kissed the baby on her head — she kicked and gurgled happily — kissed his wife on her forehead as well, then returned to his side of the wall.

He put the manacle back on his foot and waited.

Only moments later, as the sky reddened and the wind changed, shouts and cries of alarm and indignation began to ring out across Arrgodi.

The city was awake again.

# *Tyrak*

TYRAK WAS SILENT.

All in his presence exchanged glances, their faces showing their fear.

Never before had he been so quiet for so long. Tantrums, rantings, rages, furies — they were accustomed to all these. They did not relish them, but they expected them. They were like earthquakes and hurricanes, floods and famines: inevitable.

But they had not expected this silence.

He sat there on the royal dais, head resting on one fist, the other fist resting on his thigh. The throne lay in smithereens around him. He had smashed it to bits when he found he could no longer fit upon it. The rumor among the men was that he could no longer control his size changes and other bodily processes. Nobody had any idea what that meant or portended. But absurd and amusing though it was, nobody dared laugh or speak of it anywhere within hearing distance of him. They remained as silent as he was even now, waiting with dread in their hearts.

The eighth child had been born, as prophesied.

It had been a girl.

Those who had been with Tyrak, Bane, and Uaraj when they went to Vasurava's house said that they saw the newborn girl themselves. It was evident that she had been born that very night, no more than a few hours earlier.

How a woman could deliver a perfectly healthy baby when she had not exhibited a single sign of pregnancy just the day before, nobody dared to ask.

How the bolts of all the doors had been broken, the chains shattered, the manacles unclasped, the wall brought down, nobody could explain either.

Tyrak had roared with rage when he saw the newborn child.

Snatching it out of Kewri's arms — she had cried out as he did so, raising her hands in a gesture of pleading — Tyrak took the girl infant by the leg, swung her around once, twice, and then a third time, as he always did when killing infants. He had been seen doing the same thing hundreds of times before, with nary a variation. He had even mused to himself that it was the most efficient way to do the job.

But this time, as he swung the child around the third and final time, she flew out of his hands — not across the house, but up into the air, above Tyrak's head.

Where she floated, gurgling happily.

Tyrak turned and stared at his empty hand, then up at the floating child. Everybody stared as well.

The baby laughed and clapped her tiny hands. They didn't meet perfectly, because babies did not have very good coordination. But the action was unmistakable.

And then the baby transformed into a goddess.

Resplendent, with beautiful blue skin, decorated with garlands, rich robes, jewelry, and accoutrements, she floated in midair.

"I am Jeel, sister of Vish. My brother bid me come here to give you this message."

And then she said it, the thing that nobody dared speak aloud in Tyrak's presence. Even though every soldier here knew that across Mraashk, across the Arrgodi nations, the same words were being repeated with laughter, with tears of joy, with cheers and applause and celebration, with festive glee.

"The Slayer of Tyrak has been born. And he is safely out of your reach."

Then the devi had vanished, leaving only flower petals that fell in a shower to the ground. Her laughter echoed in the air, more like a baby's gurgle than a woman's laugh.

Tyrak had returned to his palace and now sat still, silent. He had seemed bewildered ever since the appearance of the goddess.

Finally, plucking up their courage, Bane and Uaraj spoke up, both taking turns, as if they had decided that they should share the risk of bringing the king's wrath down on themselves.

"My lord," Bane said, "there is unrest in the city. The events of last night have thrown the people into a frenzy. Every hour soldiers bring word that Arrgodi are challenging our soldiers, defying them in small ways."

Bane glanced at Uaraj, who swallowed and took up the cudgels. "We must act now to suppress them, while they are still disorganized. If we allow time to pass, there could be an uprising. What happened this morning . . ."

He trailed off, looking at his associate. Bane flinched and spoke up: "Word will surely spread soon. Once everyone knows, they may feel emboldened to rebel openly. We recommend you act before it is too late."

"If you wish, we could send word to Lord Jarsun to ask for a few contingents to back us up. His men will kill Arrgodi more readily than our soldiers," Uaraj said in a nervous rush.

Bane added hastily, "Not that our men would not do as ordered. We only point out all the possible courses of action for you to decide in your great wisdom."

Tyrak raised his head slowly. "There will be no need to send for Jarsun's army. We will act ourselves, and now, before the people have a chance to gather their wits and rise up."

He stood, towering over everyone else in the large hall. His head bumped the ceiling, twenty feet above the floor. He seemed not to notice.

"You are right," he said with surprising mildness. "We must quell this petty defiance before it blossoms into outright rebellion. We must also quell this rumor that is bound to spread after this morning's events."

"Rumor, sir?" Uaraj asked hesitantly.

Tyrak looked at them. His eyes were pointing in separate directions, they noticed, and he seemed to have difficulty focusing them. But finally he managed to settle at least one eye on them, while the other roved the far wall, making the soldiers on that side grow nervous for their own lives.

"This stupid rumor of a slayer being born," he said.

He laughed. A small burst of insectile forms landed at the feet of several men, writhing and crawling.

"Slayer of Tyrak!" He shook with silent amusement. "How absurd. How impossible. I cannot be slain. I am immortal."

Then he was silent for another half hour. Just standing there, brooding, eyes rolling in separate directions, wildly.

Finally Bane dared to speak up again. "What shall we do, sire? Shall we do a purge, round up the most obvious troublemakers and make examples of them as usual?"

Tyrak started as if disturbed out of deep thought. "What? Oh yes. Of course. No, we shall dispense with the usual methods this time. This calls for something more drastic."

"Yes, sire?"

Tyrak toyed with something growing out of the underside of his ear. Uaraj looked away, unable to watch.

"The people believe that my slayer has been born today. So we shall rid them of this notion. We shall kill the slayer wherever he might be."

"But, my lord, we do not know where he is."

"Exactly." Tyrak smiled cheerfully. "Therefore we shall kill them all."

"All, sire?"

"All the newborns. Male and female. Across all the Arrgodi nations."

Bane and Uaraj stared at him, speechless.

Tyrak's left eye peered at them. "Assemble every soldier. Every last one. We shall need them all."

"Even the reserves, sire?"

"Even the reserves."

They flinched. Tyrak was regaining his normal tone and volume now. He stalked the hall, looking like a man who had reached a decision at last after long pondering.

"They believe a slayer has been born to save them. We shall see to it that this slayer, whoever he may be, wherever he may be, will not live to see another day, let alone live long enough to slay me. We shall do this today and quell all rebellion, all challengers. We shall slay every newborn child in the Arrgodi nations. Assemble all the army, divide them and send them out to start work at once. Tell them to kill every newborn child . . ." He paused. "No, make that every child born in the past ten days, just to be sure they don't trick us by pretending he was born last week or the week before. When in doubt, kill all the infants." He thought for a moment. "No, make that all the toddlers, even those who seem a few years old. If in doubt, kill every child. Cut off their heads and bring them to me. I want a full tally by tomorrow morning."

He looked around the hall at the stunned faces staring up at him. "What are you all looking at, you fools?"

Bane looked at Uaraj, then back at Tyrak. "Sire, you don't mean . . . *all* of them?"

Uaraj spoke up. "What Bane means, sir, is that he and his wife have just had twins, only three days ago." He gestured around the hall. "There must be thousands of our own soldiers whose wives have delivered babes in the past few days as well."

Tyrak shrugged, already distracted by other, more important considerations. "Then we must start with them first. Lead by example." He placed a hand on his man's shoulder, in a mock-friendly gesture, and said in a cheerful tone. "Set an example to your men by showing your loyalty to your King Eternal." He clapped Bane on his back. "Start with those bonny twins of yours."

# Part Four

## *The Stone in Your Fist, The Fire in Your Heart*

# *Vessa*

A PORTAL OPENED ABOVE the Sea of Grass.

It was roughly the size and shape of a doorway, though it shimmered and blurred at its edges, appearing to any casual observer, had there been one, as some curious trick of the light rather than a gateway to another time and place. In any case, there was nobody to observe the opening: it was high noon in the heartland of the Sea of Grass, and even the local fauna were taking a siesta under the harsh sun.

Vessa stepped through.

He stood on nothing but air for a moment, then descended slowly to the ground. The grass bowed and bent beneath his bare feet, depressed by some unseen force. Even though he appeared to be standing on solid earth, he was in fact a few inches above it.

He began walking slowly southward. Caked with reddish soil, pressed leaves, and crushed flowers, his feet resembled the roots of an ancient tree more than mortal limbs. His toes were calloused and gnarled from a lifetime of shoeless travel, matching his wild hair and features that seemed to contain as much animal as human in their detail. The wildwood staff in his gnarled fist, the red-ochre robe with its legacy of stains, the piercing black eyes, all added to the impression of a force of nature rather than a mammalian being.

Indeed, after centuries spent meditating in the wild, eternal jungle in the heart of which he resided, Vessa was more animal or tree than a member of the civilized world. He felt more at home in that primordial forest than in the great cities of Arthaloka. This was the reason he preferred to arrive in private chambers, behind closed doors, or in uninhabited places such as this grassy plain, where he would not have to endure the shocked reactions and staring gazes of curious people.

The Sea of Grass was aptly named.

A vast ocean of rolling grasslands that carpeted the eastern corner of the great continent, it appeared mostly uninhabited at first glance. But like its nominal counterpart, the salt-laden sea that lay beyond its easternmost boundaries, an entire ecosystem of animal and insect life lived within its body, like the symbiotic parasites within any biological creature.

The creatures that roamed the great grassy plains, such as the enormous herds of wild uks, were mostly hidden by the waving grass itself. The grass grew as high as five yards or taller and concealed a flourishing population of predators, herbivores, and every manner of creature between the two kinds. The uks herds were rivaled by the even more numerous flocks of birds that ruled the skies above. And a whole other population of creatures resided beneath the springy roots of the grass itself, burrowing, tunneling, and traveling underground across the length and breadth of the sea.

It was these denizens that Vessa had come to seek out, not his own kind. That was why he had arrived at a place hundreds of miles from the cities and settlements of Mraashk, Arrgodi, and Gwannland. Far to the southeast lay the White Desert and the port cities and coastal villages of the White Kingdom, with its capital, Aqron, marking the southeasternmost point of the continent. To the south and west, covering an area almost as vast as the Burnt Empire itself, was the Red Desert, where Vessa's cousin and nemesis sought to build his Reygistan Empire.

Vessa now walked in a large, roughly circular pattern, leaving behind him a trail of bowed grass. Unlike the trail of an ordinary mortal, the grass stalks in his wake were not broken under his weight; they were simply bowed down flat by the same mystic force that enabled Vessa to inhabit this space without being physically present. Every stalk pointed in the same direction: the direction Vessa was walking.

After a period of time, a bird flying overhead might have looked down and seen a perfectly geometrical pattern that followed a mostly unbroken spiral with brief gaps left at precise intervals. In this spiraling maze were smaller patterns, precisely and artistically made. The whole was the exact replica of a complex and powerful mandala. A visual pattern that was the silent equivalent of a potent Ashcrit mantra. Not merely a mantra of prayer or supplication, though there were marks and intervals that offered praise to the appropriate stone gods, but one of secret intent. The mandala was designed not to be understood or even seen by mortals — it would have seemed like nothing but the random flattening of grass by a mating uks or some such natural cause — but by the very soil of Arthaloka.

Or, to be precise, Artha herself. The mythical stone goddess whose body was the very continent named after her; Artha being her name, *loka* meaning "place."

The sage reached the center of the mandala and stood motionless.

A soft breeze, indolent and heavy with the heat of the overhead sun, stirred the grass. A susurration rose and fell as waves rippled gently across the endless expanse.

The legend went that once the winds of Gwannland — which was the ancient Ashcrit name for the Sea of Grass — blew so fiercely that mortals built skiffs made of the mythical timber airwood and mounted them with musl sails that caught the legendary winds and carried mortals and their cargo hundreds of miles across the Sea of Grass, very much the way sailing ships rode the winds and currents of the oceans beyond Gwannland port.

This wind was nothing like those fabled currents; it barely stirred the fur on the rumps of an uks herd dozing on their feet some fifty miles away. But it blew across the mandala pattern drawn by the sage Vessa — and there, something remarkable happened.

The mandala glowed.

A deep bluish light marked the pattern, growing in intensity and brightness.

The sage remained standing in the center of the mandala, eyes shut as he chanted Ashcrit mantras that none but the most accomplished of his order would dare utter. The light increased steadily as he continued chanting, and the wind rose, growing more frenetic until it howled and swirled like a gale — but only above the mandala. Outside the pattern, a grass dog popped its furry head up, ears twitching curiously; its fur was not so much as ruffled by the howling wind mere inches away. But the alien light startled it, and it squeaked an indignant protest before burrowing back down into its underground residence.

The wind and light increased their frenzy until there was a blue tornado swirling above the mandala pattern. It whirled at impossible speed, producing a high-pitched whine that set animals to howling fifty miles away. It seemed improbable that the sage was able to stand at its center, his beard, hair, and robe barely touched. His face was calm, his eyes shut, his voice unchanged in tone or volume.

He finished reciting the mantras.

He opened his eyes and raised both arms, pointing the staff up at the peak of the blue tornado.

A blinding flash, obliterating the world from vision.

Then it was all gone.

The blue tornado, the howling gale, and the venerable sage himself.

Only the mandala pattern remained, burned into the grass, into the very earth. A permanent mark. Nothing would ever grow over this spot, nor any animal, insect, or person broach the space. Even birds would instinctively alter their flights subtly to avoid flying directly overhead.

The grass dog popped its head up again, prepared to duck down instantly if the strange two-legged being and the bizarre phenomenon was still visible. It saw nothing notable. The Sea of Grass stretched far and wide in every direction. To its eyes — and the senses of every other living creature — even the mandala pattern itself did not exist; it was invisible. Yet as it hopped forward, it instinctively went around the circular rim of the scorched earth, its paws never once touching that dead space.

The day wound on, sultry and lazy as any afternoon in the Sea of Grass.

# *Aqreen*

## 1

"REYGAR!"

Afranus jumped up and down on the back of the uks drawing his family's wagon. He turned, still jumping on the animal's broad back, and waved to Krushita, who was at the reins of her own wagon. "Didja seeit, Krush? It's Reygar!"

His parents, Niede and Dor, waved him down with admonishing but indulgent gestures. The uks whose back he was standing on was the prima, and if he grew irritated, it would upset the entire team — and perhaps even other uks teams nearby.

Afranus stopped jumping and settled for waving his hands over his head instead, but on the bed of his wagon, his half dozen siblings danced and shouted as they matched his excitement. At least three of them had been born on the Red Trail during the eleven-year-long journey — four years more than the usual seven, due to the unprecedented challenges faced by the train — and to these three as well as their slightly older siblings, Reygar was akin to the mythic cities of the stone gods that the Vanjhani spoke of during the nightly campfire tales.

"DidjaseeitKrush?" Afranus repeated, running his words together as he always did when he was excited, which was more often than not.

"I seen it, Af," Krushita replied, managing a grin which turned into an eye roll the minute Afranus turned his back to get another look at the barely visible dot on the horizon.

Aqreen gave her daughter a look.

"What?" Krushita said.

"*Seen it?*" her mother asked.

Krushita shrugged. "That's how Afranus talks. You don't correct him."

"That's because he's not my kid. What is the point of all our lessons if you're not going to speak grammatically?"

That earned Aqreen an eye roll. "I know the difference, Mother." To prove her point, Krushita promptly recited "saw it" in Agrish, Vanjhani, Krushan, Aqronian, and then in High Ashcrit.

"Now you're just showing off," Aqreen said, secretly pleased. One of her constant worries — she seemed to have no shortage of them these days — was that her daughter lacked the proper formal education that she herself had enjoyed. She mourned the lack of the fine tutors she had had growing up in Aqron. Some of the circles had their own classes — Sixth Circle had a fairly decent one called Comparative Languages and Cultures of Our Arthaloka — but most were well below the level and standard that Krushita would have had easy access to as a princess of the White Kingdom. As it was, Aqreen was her primary tutor, and being a single mother *and* private tutor was not an easy task. It was so hard to draw a line between being too hard on her sole pupil and being a good mother.

The fact that Krushita was a brilliant pupil was no consolation: the child had had to see, experience, and survive things that most people might not in an entire lifetime. At least not in the peaceable White Kingdom of Aqreen's youth, during the long and prosperous reign of King Aqron, one in a long line of familial rulers who had kept his realm free from the vicious territorialism, opportunistic wars, and feuds that ravaged their two nearest regalities, the numerous conflicted realms of the Red Desert to their west, and the fewer, but no less contentious grassland kingdoms to their north.

As it was, the seemingly endless eleven-year journey had taken its toll on both of them. The frequent attacks and constant stress of awaiting the next one had been hard enough, but the actual battles, skirmishes, and other acts of violence that Krushita had been exposed to in her most tender years were heartbreaking to a pacifist like Aqreen. Never would she have dreamed that she would have to bring up her daughter under such circumstances.

Krushita had grown up on the road, as it were. Even though only thirteen, she had come of age on the Red Trail. She had weathered all storms and survived. Thrived, even. But that was no cause for celebration. Even as her role as the resident protector and in-house wizard of the train — neither phrases Krushita's words — had been accepted, then become cemented in the minds of all the travelers, so had her responsibility increased. It was one thing to raise a young girl on the Red Trail, surviving the usual hazards and deprivations of the Red Desert, but to expect her to watch over and protect thousands of lives that effectively depended on her for their very survival was a burden nobody should have to bear, let alone a thirteen-year-old girl.

*And almost all the dangers that threatened us on this trip were her own father's doing,* Aqreen thought. Even a decade after she had left Jarsun's house — really her ancestral home that he had usurped — she still felt the anger like a hot blade in her heart. *Why won't he leave us alone?*

In a sense, Jarsun had done just that. It had been over a year since the last attack. After the worst of them all, the Battle Against the Deadwalkers, as it was now known in campfire tales, there had been only two sporadic attacks: by bandits and a band of eoch fanatics. Neither had required any supernatural agency to overcome: the Vanjhani alone were able to hold off the bandits, and the train's fighters had dispatched the eochs with only minimal losses. Neither Aqreen nor Krushita was naive enough to think that Jarsun had given up his quest for vengeance — and the retrieval of his chief political asset, Krushita herself — but at least it had given them a season of respite.

Which was a mercy, because Krushita had been in no shape to do anything on the two most recent occasions.

After the Battle Against the Deadwalkers, Krushita had been ill for a very long time. Not in body and health, although her already thin frame had seemed skeletal to a concerned mother's eyes, but in mind and spirit. Whatever she had done to save the train from the deadwalkers had taken a heavy toll on her inwardly. Even now, more than six years later, she had never really opened up about what had happened once she went through the portal. Aqreen had tried any number of ways, but finally she had given up, knowing the danger of pushing too hard. Krushita had inherited her mother's obduracy, and when pressed too much too often, she dug in. To be fair, it was the only way one could survive out there.

But finally they were within sight of Reygar. And soon they would have a roof over their heads and a real bed to sleep in, not the hard bed of a wagon rolling and heaving constantly. *And real food,* she thought, *without the damn incessant wind-driven sand that gets into everything.* Yes, soon they would have something akin to permanence and could start building a new life for themselves.

"We're not that close, you know," Krushita said.

Aqreen looked at her daughter. Krushita's pretty, heart-shaped face was still woefully thin, her cheekbones more prominent than her sunken eyes, and her heart went out to the child. She put her arm around her daughter, squeezing her gently. Krushita permitted it, but didn't turn to her or bury her face in her mother's side as she had once done instinctively. She was already at that age when a maternal hug was barely tolerable. Aqreen hoped she would outgrow that, but she worried that she might not.

"We're within sight at least," she said in response.

"Distances are deceptive in the desert," Krushita said. "Reygar is built on a mountain that's almost four thousand yards high. Its peak is visible from almost one hundred fifty miles away. And that's if what we're seeing is actually Reygar."

Aqreen frowned at that. "What else would it be?"

"A mirage? Bulan says that the heat haze can mirror objects that are twice as far away."

Aqreen thought about that. "So Reygar could actually be as much as three hundred miles away?"

Krushita nodded.

Aqreen smiled, brushing back a lock of hair that had fallen over Krushita's brow. "When did you get so smart?"

"It's nothing, Ma," Krushita said, waving away Aqreen's hand, which was now cradling her head.

"Not for Afranus," Aqreen said, gesturing in the direction of their neighbor's cart, where the boy in question was still jumping up and down in excitement with his siblings, some of whom were squealing.

That earned another eye roll. "Afranus is a *kid*," she said matter-of-factly. "He thinks Reygar is a magical city, with the most wonderful things to see and do, and nothing bad ever happens there."

*There was a time you thought that too,* Aqreen thought, feeling a pang of regret for the Krushita she had brought out of Aqron. That girl hadn't shown herself for a long time, but Aqreen hoped she was still in there somewhere. "Well, do me a favor, my love. Don't tell Afranus that he's wrong. Or that what he's seeing might not be Reygar. Look at him. He's so happy now."

She gestured around. "The whole train is happy, can't you feel it? They've waited a very long time and traveled a long way to get here. Let them enjoy their relief at finally reaching their destination. Besides," she added after a brief pause, "even three hundred miles is a whole lot closer than twenty thousand, don't you think? Let Afranus have this moment."

"Of course I won't say anything," Krushita said with a long-suffering air. "I know how to speak to children."

Aqreen cocked an eyebrow at that. "You know, there's some who might say you're pretty much a child yourself."

Krushita looked at her.

Aqreen was always surprised by her daughter's clear-eyed look: it was the look of a much older, much more mature woman.

"Chronological age isn't an accurate measure," Krushita replied. "Look at the Vanjhani. Bulan is barely five hundred years old, but to us they don't look that different from Agolon, who's more than sixteen hundred. It's how you've lived, and how much you've experienced, that matters, not just the number."

Aqreen had no answer to that.

Sadly, almost tragically, her daughter was right.

Krushita was a young woman wise beyond her years.

*And it's all the fault of that vile Krushan.*

Jarsun.

## 2

That evening by the campfire, Aqreen found her way to Bulan. The train master was sitting by themself for once, a rare occurrence in general but a common one when they were indulging in their favorite hobby.

*Their* only *hobby,* she thought as she approached. The Vanjhani was holding a block of wood in each pair of hands, turning it by minute degrees as they worked. They appeared to be whittling the wood with special knives meant for working sala wood. Sala was among the hardest woods, one of the heavier kinds of timber. It took a lot of strength to whittle it away in tiny chips and flakes as Bulan was doing right now. Too much strength for most mortals: most Aqronians, for instance, worked with the much softer soapwood or bulsewood.

They carved and whittled at astonishing speed, singing absently to themself all the while. Their voices were pitched low, in perfect harmony, but she could make out the tune as she came within a few yards. It was a very old tune, one even she recognized. Aqronians knew it as "The Ballad of the Lost Wanderer." She stopped and listened. Even though she didn't understand the Vanjhani lyrics, she knew the song well enough to feel the heart tug of its lament. It brought a lump to her throat and a dampness to her eyes.

Without pausing an instant in their whittling, Bulan said casually, "You mays be coming forward, missun. Never good idea standing for behind Vanjhani. Makes our skin creep, it is."

She approached and bent low, kissing them on each of their four cheeks by way of greeting. "That was beautiful."

One of their heads — the one she thought of as the masculine one because it had more facial hair than its companion — arched an eyebrow. "Aqronians is knowing old Vanjhani traveler's song? How is such?"

She adjusted her garment and sat on one of the stumps nearby. "We have our own version. We call it 'The Ballad of the Lost Wanderer.' The melody is almost exactly the same, except we sing it in a higher pitch, and the chorus line goes . . . *Laith harran akleef fown shaar* instead."

Now they paused in their whittling, both faces looking at her. "You singing? Why none singing at firetimes, lady? Youse having good fine voice."

She smiled. "Thank you. I'm no singer. The only things I sang were lullabies to put my Krush to sleep, and those aren't much in demand of late."

They rested their elbows on their hairy thighs. "You are worried about Krush. Don't be, lady. She will be fine."

Aqreen laughed. "First of all, tell me how you do that? Switch to perfectly grammatical sentences at times but seem unable to fit grammar, gender, and idiom together correctly at other times. Or should I ask, *why* do you that?"

Bulan shrugged, setting the block of sala wood and the knives aside. They dusted the wood dust off themself and rubbed their palms together briskly over the fire. The flames sparked and glowed a little brighter, happy to be fed. The sweet fragrance of sala wood drifted to Aqreen, mingling with the usual odors of roast meat, uks, horses, shvan, and people of multiple races.

"You know what Vanjhani are called by some people, lady?"

"What else would they be called but Vanjhani?" she replied. "And don't call me lady. I thought we were past that years ago. We've been through far too much together for formalities, don't you think?"

Bulan smiled with both their faces, a friendly but sad smile. "Vanjhani do not call high people by their first name. It is most rude. I am not calling you queen, am I? Merely lady."

At her startled reaction, they raised all four arms in a placating gesture. "You have no need to fear my telling anyone, my lady. Your secret is safe with us. Bulan knows what lies at stake for you and little Krush. It is only between you and us and the fire. Bulan is like this fire. Once we eat a secret, it is part of us forever."

She had risen to her feet and remained standing, her heart racing. Her first instinct was to deny it hotly, to argue and stamp out angrily. But this was Bulan. What they said was true: Vanjhani were legendary secret keepers. Because of their long life spans, they were often relied on to settle old feuds, disputes, resolve debatable wills, or even settle arguments over some minor detail of an incident or event that had occurred decades or even centuries ago. Even her court used Vanjhani scribes because of their prodigious memories and ability to recall even the most insignificant-seeming minutiae of old pacts and deeds.

The train master lowered their four hands, gesturing for her to sit again.

Slowly, her heart still thudding in her chest, she forced herself to sit. Whatever Bulan knew, they knew already. Making a scene over it would only attract unwanted attention — and risk alienating the best friend she had gained on this otherwise accursed journey.

"How?" she asked.

Bulan picked up a water flagon and handed it to her. She took it gratefully and helped herself to a deep draw. Water was carefully rationed for obvious reasons, but they had hit a well only a few months ago, and the water in the flagon still tasted wonderfully fresh and sweet, compared to the years-old supply they had had to make do with for most of the journey.

She corked the flagon carefully and set it down, safely distant from the fire, then swiped her mouth with the back of her sleeve.

Bulan jerked one head back in the direction of her wagon. Krushita was visible to her, sitting with Afranus and his siblings and playing some kind of game of wits. Krushita could have easily won every single time if she wanted, but she was gracious enough to let Afranus win just often enough to make him believe he was getting better and would soon beat her.

"Krush," Bulan said simply. They offered no further explanation.

Aqreen sighed and let her face drop into her palms. They still smelled of the wool she had been shearing from her uks team. Winter was coming soon, or so she assumed because all the uks in the train had begun growing thicker coats for the last few weeks. Winters in the Red Desert were much the same as other seasons, except that in winter it grew even colder by night, and it rained for a few minutes precisely at midday, every day. The first rain, when it came, would be a day of celebration for the train, as it was across the Red Desert.

Why had Krushita betrayed their secret?

She must not have considered it a betrayal. Bulan was as good as family now. Aqreen had seen the bond between them growing steadily over the years, particularly the last six years.

Since the Battle Against the Deadwalkers.

But she herself still wasn't ready to trust anyone, no matter how trustworthy, so she had naturally assumed that Krushita wouldn't do so either.

This was a reminder that, mother and daughter though they were, Krushita was her own person.

"She knew she could trust Bulan," the Vanjhani said now, quietly. Nobody else was within hearing distance — the travelers respected the master's privacy, especially during these precious post-campfire hours. Bulan spent every minute of every waking day seeing to their needs and their security; they deserved this little time to themself. Still, Aqreen couldn't help glancing around. It was sheer instinct by now.

They tapped their heads. "She sees inside us. Inside everyone. She knows we can be trusted. She would like you to trust us too, but she knows you still have much fear in your heart. Perhaps too much to ever trust anyone again fully. This is a sad thing, but she understands this and accepts it. To protect you, she did not tell you. But she and I have talked of many things privately. As we said before, your secrets are safe inside us."

Aqreen released a held breath. It blew away an errant spark drifting from the fire. The spark danced away upward like a firefly, then was lost in the night. There was no point critiquing Krushita's decision: she knew what was at stake just as well as Aqreen did. All Aqreen could do was trust her judgment and accept that Bulan knew.

"You were saying," she prompted, diverting them back to the earlier topic.

Bulan nodded one head. "*I was saying* people, some people, call Vanjhani two-faced."

"I would never—" she began, but they raised a hand to forestall her explanation.

"Only *some* people," they repeated. "And they are right. Vanjhani are two people in one body." They indicated themself. "But of course, they mean something else entirely. In that, they are wrong. Even though Vanjhani have two heads and two faces, we are in perfect synchrony. There is a word for it in Vanjhani—"

"Avishki," Aqreen said. "It means two heads, one mind. Or two hearts, one love. Depending on the context. It refers to the inherent biological synchronicity in the duality of Vanjhani physiology. It also has deeper spiritual implications, since *avishki* was a word first used to describe the seemingly contradictory singularity within the duality of the stone god twins."

Both their faces raised a brow apiece. "Precisely. You are knowing Vanjhani, lady?"

"We always have—" She corrected her error. "We always *had* Vanjhani working with me in the royal palace. My head of palace security was Vanjhani, and I considered them my good friend."

Bulan nodded both heads. "Yes, we have heard this of your family. You were not among those who discriminate against us." They indicated the train. "Here in this train, there are many merchants who employ Vanjhani for security. But they would never think of permitting us to eat with them at their table or contemplate having any other relationship with our kind."

"The world is full of bigots, but bigots are not the world."

"Truly spoken. The House of Aqron has long been renowned as an enlightened, progressive one. We of the Vanjhani know full well how rare this is in our present time. Once, of course, Vanjhani were accepted in high society and treated as equals. But that was long ago, back in the time when we had a homeland, before the Krushan invaded and annexed our realm, then drove us out of our own homes." They paused, gazing across the fire into the darkness of the desert night. "Those of us that survived the genocide."

"I have read the histories," Aqron said, sipping the drink Bulan had passed her. It was a mild mulled wine spiced with distinctive Vanjhani flavors. "It was in Ashalon's time, Year 817 of Chakra 55."

"The invasion, it was. But the genocide continued for much longer. Even to this day, Vanjhani are forbidden to enter Burnt Empire territory. It is reason why we fear stonefire even now."

Aqreen sighed. "It senses when Vanjhani are near and tries to consume you if you come within range."

"Us, and anyone else unfortunate enough to be between us and stonefire, or close enough to be harmed. Stonefire is not particular. It only seeks to feed."

Aqreen shivered, despite the warmth of the fire and the wine. "It's vile."

"Vile is what a villain is, who commits crime for a purpose. Stonefire is pure evil. It destroys for love of destruction. Vanjhani believe that if stonefire were not controlled by the will of the emperor or empress, it would consume all living beings. As it once did in the Time of the Burning."

At the end of the Age of Myth, said the histories, stonefire had arrived on Arthaloka from an unknown place of origin. Its first act was to wipe out all life on Arthaloka. That couldn't literally be true, since most species had survived. But it was what the histories all claimed. They also claimed that stonefire had then spawned Kr'ush, and if they were to be believed, Kr'ush was nothing less than a god in mortal form. Some histories differed on this point, claiming that stonefire had wiped out even the stone gods, forcing most of their number to retreat to their celestial abodes, where they remained to this day. The few that remained, such as the Mother Goddess Jeel, hesitated to take mortal form again for fear of the dreaded living rock. But one stone god, the wily and avaricious Lankeshva, had made a bargain with stonefire. The alien substance had consumed his body and used the mortal form to create the being known as Kr'ush, the first Krushan. Kr'ush had then repopulated Arthaloka in his image. And thereafter, stonefire had been symbiotically linked to the Krushan, serving them as well as giving them powers and abilities. So long as a Krushan ruled on Arthaloka, stonefire would remain contained. But if the Krushan were ever to be wiped out, then stonefire would once again burn all living beings and end life on Arthaloka permanently. Or so the histories claimed.

"I'm aware of the myth," Aqreen said, "But with the Burnt Empire dominant, there's little danger of that happening."

Bulan was silent for a spell. The train master seemed to be absorbed in their own thoughts, staring into the fire. The train quieted around them as travelers took to their beds and campfires dimmed. Shvan called out from far away, performing their nightly circuit of the camp. Somewhere, a baby cried briefly, then fell silent. The silence deepened. Aqreen felt the spiced wine pleasantly warming her blood and calming her nerves. It would not dispel the omnipresent sword of anxiety that hung over her, but it would help dull its edge.

"It has been long since the last assault," Bulan said at last. "Krushita says it is because he has been busy battling the Burnt Empire."

Aqreen stared at the head that had spoken. The other was looking over at the sentry patrolling the perimeter of the Perfect Circle. The sentry, an elderly but fit Aranyan, raised her spear in greeting to Bulan. The head nodded back, raising a hand.

"She knows this?" Aqreen said doubtfully. This was the first she had heard of Krushita being aware of Jarsun's activities during the intervals between attacks.

"She watches him from a distance, through a secret window he does not know of," Bulan said.

Aqreen frowned. "A secret window?"

"She says it is of the same kind that enabled him to bring the deadwalkers from the other world, or time, or wherever it is." Bulan made a Vanjhani gesture that she recognized as one of surrender. "I do not wholly understand it, but I believe she may perhaps be speaking of what we Vanjhani know as a gufaondo, a tunnel between realms. Though Bulan has only heard it spoken of in campfire tales and old legends. No Vanjhani I know of has actually seen or been through such a one."

That was close enough. "He calls it a portal. It is a tunnel of sorts between realms, or places, or times. It is real enough. I have traveled through portals on more than one occasion."

Both heads looked at her as all four hands made a peculiar sign that she also recognized as the Vanjhani equivalent of the sign of the Staff in her culture. A religious warding sign, asking protection from the Savior — or, in the case of Vanjhani, their stone gods.

"Stone Father," they both said. "You did not lose your souls?" They paused and considered briefly. "Soul." They were referring, presumably, to the superstitious belief that anyone who dabbled with powerful magic sacrificed their soul.

She resisted the urge to laugh: Bulan looked too spooked and might feel offended. "As far as I know, my soul, and every other part of me, is still very much intact. It's just a means of going from one place to another very quickly, almost instantly. For instance, when he took us from Aqron to Hastinaga for the Burning, nine years ago, we went through a portal. A journey that would have taken us at least a decade by land and would have involved many hazards. Instead, we arrived there only moments after we left Aqron. Of course, we exited the portal several miles outside the city, to avoid causing a panic, but that was only a few hours' ride."

Bulan made the sign again and shook both their heads. "It sounds like another of stonefire's evil workings. Bulan would rather die fighting than go through one."

She nodded. "I felt much the same. Such power is dangerous, even if used for seemingly good purpose. But to be honest, after the first several months on the Red Trail, I found myself secretly wishing I could have spirited Krush out through one. It would have gotten us to Reygar within days, instead of years. And after these past eleven years . . ." She shook her head, feeling her eyes prickle. "I never thought I would raise my daughter in this manner."

She felt one of Bulan's hands patting her shoulder gently. Like all Vanjhani she had known, they could be surprisingly gentle, despite their enormous size and strength — or perhaps because of it. "Is not your doing. 'tis his. Had he been a good father and husband, you would not have been forced to such actions."

"Yes, but sometimes I think about what could have been . . . had I stayed, and I wonder if I made the right decision."

They looked at her steadily until she felt their gaze and looked up.

"You did," they said without an iota of doubt. "You did the only thing possible. And you saved her life and her soul."

"You really think so?"

"I know so. Krush is wonderful girl, a beautiful person. You are the reason. You are great mother. Someday, your name will be written in tales of legends."

She laughed at that unexpected compliment. "I hardly think so! But it's kind of you to say it. Thank you, Bulan. For everything you've done for us. And most of all, for being you."

She looked from one pair of eyes to the other, and both smiled back with warmth and respect.

"Now," she said, getting up from the stump reluctantly, "I shall take myself to bed before I lapse into maudlin sentimentality."

One of Bulan's faces made a curious expression. "Vanjhani love sentimentality. Our drinking songs are all suchlike. I would be happy to wallow with you sometime. But perhaps not tonight. We are close to our destination and must be on the trail again early tomorrow. Be of good heart and mind tonight, my lady, and Bulan will see you on the morrow."

She paused to kiss the master on each of their foreheads, then made her way back to her wagon. Krushita lay in her bed already, the covers half thrown off as usual. Aqreen pulled them over her daughter's slight frame, bending to kiss Krushita on her head very gently to avoid waking her.

"Sleep well, my love," she whispered.

Then she fell into her own pallet and descended into the first deep, dreamless sleep she had had in years.

# *Krushita*

~

## 1

KRUSHITA LOOKED DOWN AT the mandala pattern on the vast, grassy plain.

She had felt it and followed it through the portal, like a sound heard in a dark house.

She sensed the power in the pattern. It throbbed and hummed, reverberating somewhere deeper than hearing, vibrating beyond the limits of vision. This pattern had great potency. But it was not a disruptive, chaotic one, like those made by her father when he opened a portal. This had a different signature, one she recognized. It was the work of the same being she had first encountered within the portal through which the deadwalkers had been summoned. She knew the being's name now, from their previous encounters over the past six years.

Vessa.

He was kin to her, in a manner of speaking. The relationship was a complex one, like most in the Krushan dynasty. But they were linked to each other, as well as to Jarsun himself, and to the Burning Throne.

More important than this familial kinship was the relationship they shared to power. The kind of power that enabled them both to travel these spirit paths, open and pass through portals, and perform other feats that would be considered magic, or urrkh maya, by most people. His was earned through meditation, accrued over centuries, developed and mastered into a fine art through his inventive, creative use of Ashcrit mantras. She had sensed this on their previous encounters, and he had shown her some of his past, permitting her to look beyond the shield that guarded most of his private thoughts and feelings.

She knew that if she had used her powers aggressively, she could have exploited that point of entry to probe far beyond the permissible, but she had never done that. She would not abuse the trust he had shown her. She sensed that he had no animosity toward her; if anything, he sought her friendship and had earned it fairly, by showing her ways to enhance and wield her power more skillfully.

"You have raw power," he had said. "The inborn power of your Krushan father, which is to be expected. But you also have something more, something . . ." He paused, and she imagined him looking contemplatively into the distance, even though she couldn't actually see or actually hear anything in the portal — whatever happened there was far beyond the realm of the senses — before looking at her again, so to speak. "I am not sure how you have it or where it comes from in your genealogy, but you have been touched by the grace of Jeel and Artha, both." He seemed to think about that for a while, then, just as she began to wonder if he was still there, he continued, "Perhaps other stone gods too? I am not sure. I have never encountered anyone with powers of this level. You are certainly blessed by the stone gods. It is almost as if . . ." Now, a longer pause. "No, it cannot be."

"What?" she asked, curious now. The natural curiosity of any child when an adult was praising her qualities.

He hesitated again. "I am wrong, of course. It rarely happens. But it must be so."

"Tell me." She added after a second, with an unconsciously plaintive tone, "Please. I want to know. I need to understand."

"Let me just say this," he said, choosing his words carefully, as if afraid to say too much, "I have only felt such power in the stone gods themselves."

She was stunned by his response.

Whatever she had expected him to say, it was not this. Praise, yes, that was wonderful to hear. Especially since even her mother had to still be a mother, which naturally meant scolding her at times, correcting her constantly, teaching her, guiding her — and inevitably left little opportunity for unguarded praise. This was like bathing under a waterfall of compliments after eleven years in the Red Desert.

But . . . stone gods?

"Are you saying—" she began.

He cut her off quickly. "Of course not. You are very much mortal. The stone gods are . . . well, they are the stone gods."

"Then they really do exist?"

He laughed. Or whatever was the equivalent of laughter in a place where there was no physical matter, no physical senses, no mass or time or geography or biological entities. "Of course. Did you think the stone gods were merely campfire tales told by your Vanjhani friend—what is his name?"

"*Their* name is Bulan," she said. "I don't know. I just thought . . . Well, grown-ups tell children all kinds of things. Go to sleep, or the sand dragon will come and take you away. Eat your food so you can grow up big and strong and fight urrkh. Don't eat sand, or you'll become a deadwalker. I thought maybe the stone gods were like that. Stories to frighten little children."

He stopped laughing. "People have reason to fear the stone gods. They are not all benevolent and all-caring. People who worship them all blindly often fail to realize that the only difference between the stone gods and urrkh is the fact that we worship one and dread the other. There was a time when they were one and the same. Indeed, some urrkh are better than some stone gods. While some stone gods can be more devilish than any urrkh."

She listened with interest. These were definitely not things they talked of at worship or in the campfire tales. They sounded almost blasphemous. She could imagine Niede and Dor making warding signs and muttering incantations if they heard Vessa saying such things. To them, the stone gods were the be all and end all, and no one dared say otherwise. Even Afranus and his siblings were dogmatic about their faith and prayed the requisite three times daily, raising and lowering their little shaggy heads and hands as they offered obeisance and unwavering fealty to each of the stone gods in turn. Shajarus, the youngest, could already recite the entire catechism in Ashcrit without a single error.

Vessa and she talked a great deal. Mostly at nights, when Aqreen thought she was fast asleep, Krushita was actually training and learning from the sage. There were long periods when she could not find Vessa in the portals, when his mind was closed off to her and she sensed great turmoil and conflict or other incomprehensible adult emotions as he fought battles, or gave chase, or did other things that he never spoke of to her in their sessions. She sensed that much happened that he did not speak of, or could not speak of, and that much of it, if not all of it, had to do with her father and his enmity with the Burnt Empire. She knew that Vessa's loyalty lay with his mother, Dowager Empress Jilana and her extended family, but she also knew he had a special fondness for his son Shvate and watched over him as often as he could. These were things she picked up without him telling her, just as she picked up numerous other little details by inference or extrapolation.

Yes, she learned a lot in those sessions with Vessa. Perhaps much more than she did in the lessons she learned by day from her mother and in that tiresome school where all the other train children seemed so backward and clueless to her increasingly mature mind. But she was also sensible enough to know that her impatience with them was because of her unusual parentage and the intense pressures of her and her mother's situation. Another part of her, the thirteen-year-old-girl part, envied them and their innocence. That was her. The Krushita that she could have been, would have been, had her life been normal like theirs. But it wasn't. So she was Krush instead. A young woman, as her mother often reminded her. A young lady, as Bulan addressed her. And her job was not just to cope, but to watch, protect, defend, and fight when necessary.

After the Battle Against the Deadwalkers, she had taken a long time to recover. But eventually, when her strength returned, she was determined that in the future, she would be better prepared. She would learn how to confront and deal with such threats more effectively. Though she had saved the train, thousands had been lost. Even now, the population of the train was barely a seventh of what it had originally been, and not a day went by when she did not wish she had been stronger, smarter, better trained in her powers. *I could have saved more lives* was a recurring thought, so much a part of her that it was like one of Bulan's tattoos, carved permanently into her brain. She *would* save more lives the next time. She was not just older, stronger, more powerful; she also knew many tricks and tactics that would enable her to fight more offensively, rather than simply reacting and defending.

Vessa was the reason for all that, of course. He had made her promise not to tell her mother. Not only because Aqreen might forbid it, but also because it would add to her mother's burden of anxieties.

"She carries a load heavier than herself. As do you. Yet there is no alternative. We do what we must do in order to survive. It is the way of the world."

Now she looked down at the mandala pattern Vessa had left in the grass and wondered if he would be angry at her.

This was the first time she had followed his trail through the portals. Previously, she had stopped short of actually going through into any physical realm. She knew the risks involved. Whatever happened to her in the physical plane would affect her body back in the wagon, asleep on its pallet beside her mother. Vessa had dinned this into her more times than she could count. It was one of his favorite litanies: "There are still places you must never go, and things you must never do, even though you can, child. Never cross those boundaries."

"Why not?" she had asked, perhaps a little more aggressively than she had intended. She was so keen to explore the limits of her powers, and he always made her stop far short of what she knew, simply *knew,* she could do easily. "When the deadwalkers came, I probably shouldn't have gone into the portal and done what I did either, but it saved my mother and Bulan and so many other people, didn't it?"

"Yes," he admitted reluctantly, "but there was a cost. You were weakened considerably and took a great deal of time to recover your strength and health. Using the portals takes a great toll. And you are too young to fully understand the costs. Once you are of age, you can do as you please. But until then, I must endeavor to preserve your innocence."

She wanted to yell at him, to say that she had lost her innocence the day of the Battle Against the Deadwalkers, but she restrained herself. She cherished Vessa's lessons. She needed them. She did not want to offend him, and she knew that if she pushed him on this point, he would not let her make contact for a long time. Months, maybe years this time. Until she was "of age," as he put it? Possibly. She didn't want that. She couldn't wait that long. But now was not the time to argue. So she backed off. "Very well, Guruji." She had taken to using the term out of respect, for in every sense of the term, he was her guru, and she his pupil, even if they only met on the spirit roads and not in person.

And now she had crossed one boundary. A soft one, but still a boundary. She had come looking for him in the portals and sensed a faint trail, like a fragrance in an empty room that one might follow to the person who wore that scent. She had decided to follow the scent, and it had brought her to this vast, seemingly endless grassy plain with the mandala pattern burned into this one spot.

She could still go back, back to her body, which lay sleeping beside her mother, and go to sleep. For real. Though the spirit travels were not physical, they could be more exhausting than actual physical work. Vessa did something with his mantras and exercises that refreshed her and made sure that when she awoke the next day, she felt rested. But she knew that the energy and time spent roaming the portals at night cost her body and mind, and made her mother worry about her health. Still, she could not help it. It was more than an addiction now: it was a necessity. Their survival depended on it. Sooner or later, Jarsun would come again. Stone Father alone knew what he might unleash upon them the next time, and she wanted to be prepared for it.

"Knowledge is a weapon," Vessa often said. And she very much wanted to know why he had come here, why he had made this pattern in the grass, and what would happen if she followed him further.

She hesitated a long moment.

The wind blew over the grass, making a sound that reminded her of the one Niede made when her little ones weren't able to urinate at night. *Shhhhhhh,* she would go, and sleepy little Maranus or Tomanus, or sometimes both together, would finally start releasing their pungent streams at the sand-caked spokes of the wagon wheel as they swayed, eyes still shut, and their mother kept her hand lightly on their backs to make sure they didn't fall over on their little tushes.

*Shhhhhhhhhh,* went the wind, and she wanted to tell it to shut up, it was making her feel sleepy too. This was such a lazy, indolent place, so green and lush and . . .

Later, she would think it was the wind sound. The hypnotic shushing. But perhaps it was her own subconscious desire to follow Vessa further, all the way, to see what actually lay beyond one of his forbidden boundaries. The desire to know.

Either way, she fell through the pattern.

She toppled forward, into the mandala symbols, and through them, passing not into the ground, but somewhere beyond.

It was as easy as letting herself fall forward into soft, yielding sand.

## 2

She was in pitch-darkness. That made her panicky at first, because she had been through a portal once and found herself in darkness just as dense but filled with strange malevolent spirits. A Darkness, Vessa called such a place. He said there were such spots scattered in the endless labyrinth of time-space tunnels that they called portals, like pits in the ground under a garden maze. Sometimes weaker spirits who ventured too far or whose physical bodies had been injured or killed while they were in the portals fell into those pits and were trapped forever. Over time, a number of spirits could collect there, and if you were unfortunate enough to fall into a Darkness, you could lose your mind and be trapped there as well. That, he had told her with the grim satisfaction of an adult explaining the ways of the world to a child, was why she must never go roaming the portals without his supervision.

She flailed around in the darkness for one heart-stopping moment, expecting at any time to feel the creepy, damp presence of some vicious spirit — or several. Then she regained control of herself and breathed calmly, knowing that her physical body back in the wagon would draw and exhale a deeper breath as well. Her heartbeat slowed again, and she took a step forward, then another, then walked slowly but cautiously ahead. She expected to see something — a light in the distance maybe? That was often how Vessa appeared to her in the portals, as a distant glow, like a firefly, that drew closer and grew in intensity and brightness until she almost had to shield her vision to avoid being blinded.

But no light appeared. She sensed no other presence here, neither malevolent nor benign.

Wherever she was, she was all alone.

In pitch-darkness.

But not a Darkness.

That was a relief in itself, but it also confused her.

What was this place? Where was she?

She had never followed Vessa this far before. She always turned back when she sensed his scent ending in some physical realm or other. It had been enough just to know that she could follow if she wanted.

But now she had followed him, and she had come to a place that wasn't like anything she knew or understood.

She continued walking for what seemed like hours — or days, or weeks — time was strange in the portals. Vessa said there was no time here, no space. All the normal rules of the physical world didn't apply. It was beyond the material and physical plane.

Finally, she began to hear a sound.

It was very faint, barely the possibility of a sound.

She wondered if she was hearing her own mind speaking. Or the mind of someone else she was close to: Aqreen and Bulan would be the most obvious. Her bonds with them made their minds easily accessible to her. She had learned how to disguise her intrusions expertly enough by now that any mind she slipped into, unless it was a highly trained mind like Vessa's, wasn't even aware of her presence. She could go into someone's head and make them do anything she willed.

She had never had reason to use it to manipulate her mother or the train master — and never would have done that to anyone she loved — but she could if she wanted, and neither would be the wiser.

The outcome was that she listened so often to their inner thoughts that it was like an automatic habit. Like the conversation Bulan and her mother had had by Bulan's fire tonight when they thought Krushita was off playing with Afranus and his siblings. She had heard every word and was relieved that her mother had so easily accepted Bulan sharing their most important secret. Bulan was family, after all. She couldn't imagine life without the Vanjhani now. It was one of the things that made her worry about how her life might change once they actually reached Reygar, which, it seemed, would be soon enough.

She listened as she walked, changing direction several times to see which one brought her closer to the source of the sound.

In time, she began to make out the voices. That was what she was hearing. Voices of people speaking from a very long distance away. It was like walking through a dark mansion with thousands of rooms and being able to hear a conversation somewhere in the vast house, but not knowing who was speaking, where they were, how to get there, or even what they were saying.

But as she grew closer, she began to make out individual words.

One voice was definitely Vessa's. She had sensed that from the first.

The other was Jarsun's.

At the sound of her father's voice, she stopped.

Her first instinct was to turn and run. To fly. There was no up or down, forward or backward in the portals, Vessa had taught her; it was the realm of spirit and thought. You could move as quickly and easily as you desired, just by willing it. But it was important to be ready for what you would find at your destination. There were many things and places that could drive you insane at first glance, or cause you great harm, or be undesirable in one way or another, and that was the only reason the mind emulated the physical acts of walking or running or flying: in order to give you time to adjust to what you would experience once you arrived.

She could be back in the grass in the space of a thought.

And from there, she could travel back to her body in the wagon in another flash of a fraction.

But she stayed where she was. Barely daring to breathe.

## 3

"— obstruct me at every turn, it will not stop me, old man! The Burnt Empire is mine by right, and I will claim it. I will sit upon the Burning Throne, whether you like it or not, and neither you nor all the sages in Arthaloka can stop me from achieving my goal."

"You will try. You will not succeed." Vessa's voice was calmer than Jarsun's, cool water to the Krushan's steaming fury, but there was a vein of steel running through it. His conviction was absolute.

Jarsun laughed. The laughter rang out eerily in the spaceless void. It drove a splinter of anger through Krushita's heart. "You think either of your two ill-gotten offspring will take the seat? You are a fool if you think so. Neither the blind one nor the albino is capable of standing in my way. They may be Krushan by law but not by blood. That fact is evident in that they have no power. In battle, they are forced to rely on mere mortal skills, the archery, charioteering, and field tactics that any mortal warrior can match. And they are both weak of body and spirit, each in his own fashion. The only reason they even survived the battle was because the son of Jeel took the field."

"And beat you roundly," Vessa countered. Krushita could almost imagine his eyes twinkling with amusement. "In fact, the battle was a complete failure for your side. All the rebels you recruited in that uprising have returned to the Burnt Empire, each having learned their lesson so well, they will not so much as lift their eyes to look at Vrath or Jilana directly again in future. The whole world knows of your failure, Jarsun. And you know the way the world works. You gave it your best effort, investing years of planning and scheming and preparation, bullying those allies of Hastinaga into turning against them. Instead of succeeding, you showed the world that, once again, to oppose the Burnt Empire is fruitless. Your very name is no longer feared as it once was across the realm. Children laugh and mock your failure."

Jarsun issued a roar that was more bestial than human. Krushita wondered why he did not simply lash out at Vessa in rage. *He never hesitated when he attacked my mother and me,* she thought bitterly. *Perhaps he fears facing a man with as much power as himself.* But she knew it was more than that: this was some kind of prescheduled meeting. A parley perhaps? No, not quite. Jarsun didn't believe in parleys or truces; that was not the Krushan way. Total conquest, complete subjugation, nothing less would do for him. This was something else, then. She tried to move closer, till the voices were louder in her head. They hadn't sensed her presence yet, so she assumed she was safe.

"I will return," Jarsun said in a threatening tone. "And I will not fail this time. Or the next. Nothing you say or threaten will sway me from my goal, old man. I will have what I desire, what I deserve. The Burning Throne will be mine."

Vessa replied, "At best, you can seek to seat your daughter upon the throne. You yourself have no claim. Your own brother saw to that. Stonefire will never accept you again."

Jarsun laughed, but his laughter was hollow, undercut by a lack of conviction. "We will see about that."

"No, we will not. Even you are not desperate enough to test stonefire. The rock is unforgiving and merciless. If you attempt to sit upon the throne and it rejects you, your end will be swift and very painful. Indeed, I wish you *would* attempt it. Then the world would be rid of your menace forever."

"You wish it were that easy, sage. I will not give you that satisfaction. I have no need to fulfill your whims. My daughter has the claim, and it has been tested. If Jilana were truly Krushan, she would never have denied Krushita her birthright."

"It is true Jilana is not Krushan herself, but Vrath has stonefire running through his veins. He is the son of Sha'ant. He did not uphold your claim either. Because, like Jilana, he saw through your wily stratagem. Your goal was not to give your daughter her birthright; it was to use her as a puppet liege while you ran the Burnt Empire. Just as you have done with Belgarion of the Mountain Kingdoms, Prince Tyrak of Arrgodi and Mraashk, Dirrdha of Reygar, and your other lesser puppets scattered across the world, and as you are now preparing to do with Dronas of Gwannland. Across the length and breadth of Arthaloka, you are raising your own proxy lords to slowly dominate the entire continent. Only the great forestlands of Aranya are beyond your reach, because of your urrkh ancestor Ravenous's history with the realm. But all your politicking and maneuvering will get you nowhere, because in the end, you will fail. The Burning Throne itself will deny you, and the day that happens will also be your last upon this earth.

"You admit, then, that only stonefire can best me," Jarsun said, the sneer audible in his tone, "because you know that you and your puny offspring don't stand a chance against me."

"You mistake my prediction for weakness, Jarsun. Just as you mistake the inability of the heirs Shvate and Adri to defeat you in battle for weakness. They were mere boys, children not old enough to grow hair on their lips. Challenge them again when they are older and see if you have such an easy time of it. As I recall, even in that battle, even at their tender age, they still put up a valiant fight. Once they come of age, you will be the one tested to your limits."

"*If* they ever come of age," Jarsun said. "And if they still oppose me when they are grown. Who's to say they will still be loyal to the old dowager and the prince regent? Much can change in the span of a few years."

"You would be well advised to remember that yourself."

They seemed to reach an impasse then, both exchanging further words in a similar vein. As far as Krushita could tell, neither was able to say anything new or gain an advantage over the other. They seemed to realize it as well, for soon after, their exchange reached a conclusion.

"Why wait till then?" Jarsun retorted after Vessa had again extolled the virtues of his sons once they were fully grown. "Why not face me now?"

"We are already at war. And I have already told you that I will not battle you directly because I fear the damage it will inflict upon Arthaloka. When demigods, gurus, and gods do battle, it is the mortals who suffer. I still hope we can find a way to settle this without taking such a heavy toll on mortal life. That is why I requested this dialogue."

"That's all you have, old man. Dialogue. Talk. Words and more words."

"Then consider this. I offer a bargain."

"Finally you speak words of interest. What kind of bargain?"

"Your champion against mine."

Jarsun laughed. "Which one do you propose to send, the blind boy or the albino? Both together could not harm a nail on my smallest digit."

"You have no toenails, Jarsun, nor fingernails, nor hair or bones. You are more serpent than man. At best, you are a convincing imitation of a mortal man. I have seen your true form, and I know you for what you really are."

"Are you going to continue bandying insults or will you explain yourself?"

"My champion will come forward when the time and place are right. All I ask is that you be there and you face them in open combat."

There was a moment of silence as Jarsun considered this. Krushita wanted very much to probe his mind, to probe both their minds, but she held back, knowing that any further intrusion would alert them to her presence. As it was, she was using every cloaking trick she had learned from Vessa to conceal herself in this unspace.

"This is no bargain, old man. Whoever your champion, whenever and wherever they appear, I will crush them. You have none who can challenge me in open combat. Your fate is to fail. Unless . . ." Jarsun's voice turned cautious and crafty. "Unless it is Vrath himself you intend to pit against me."

"Vrath does not do as I command. He fights only to defend the Burnt Empire, and I know you will never make the mistake of challenging him again. You learned your lesson well the last time," Vessa replied. "Nay, Jarsun. I do not speak of Vrath but of another. This person, my chosen champion, will arrive in good time. All I seek from you is your oath that you will face them openly and battle unto the finish, not flee as you did after the Battle of the Rebels."

Jarsun snorted evasively. "The Krushan do not flee, old man. I made a strategic retreat, as was my right in battle. And that was only because Vrath, being a demigod as well as a Krushan, proved a worthy opponent. Let us not banter words over that. Say that I accept your challenge and face your champion. I will certainly crush them, no matter who or what they are. So where is the bargain in this? What do you offer me when I am already assured victory?"

"An opportunity to stake your claim to the Burning Throne legitimately, with a fair chance of achieving your goal."

The silence was absolute.

Even Krushita was shocked.

Vessa was offering her father the whole Burnt Empire. Which, in Jarsun's megalomaniacal plan, would encompass the entire world in time. Why was the sage doing this? Even without probing his mind, she could feel her father's shock as well. Whatever he had expected from this talk, it was not an offer to grant him the very thing he desired.

## 4

"Is this a trick, sage?" Jarsun asked suspiciously. "Another of your ploys?"

"You are the one who resorts to tricks and ploys. I offer you an honest exchange. Give me your oath that you will face my champion to the death, and if you best them, then I will personally escort you to Hastinaga and grant you your opportunity to present yourself to the court and legitimately stake your claim to the Burnt Empire."

"They say the mind grows porous with age. It must be true. You forget that I have already tried that," Jarsun said contemptuously. "The dowager empress will never permit me an audience. She will set her watchdog Vrath upon me the very instant I enter her presence. It was she who humiliated me and my family when we staked our legitimate claim — and proved my daughter worthy of sitting upon the Burning Throne. You expect me to subject myself to another round of humiliation and verbal assault from that old shrew?"

"Speak of her with respect," Vessa cautioned, his tone sharp. "She is my mother. And as my mother, she values my opinion greatly. I have the power to convince her to give your daughter Krushita a second chance, and I will even argue Krushita's case to Jilana with every intention of achieving success. You will find that my influence over my mother is considerable. You will not be humiliated.

"It has been my experience in the bazaars of the world that when a bargain seems too good to be true, it means there is something amiss. Are you attempting to sell me a bill of goods, old sage? Trickery of words, perhaps?"

"Phrase it any way you wish. I am offering you my solemn oath as an ordained priest of Vish, and a high sage. I will even swear on Vish himself if that pleases you. It is a fair bargain and an honest one."

"So all you seek is that I fight your champion? That is it?"

"That is all I seek."

"And if I defeat this champion, you will accompany me to Hastinaga and argue my daughter's case in open court?"

"Yes. And when I argue, I win. I will accompany you to Hastinaga and insist upon your daughter's right to rule the Burnt Empire. The Burning Throne has already acknowledged her as a legitimate heir. The only hurdle in your path is Dowager Empress Jilana. My mother. If I convince her, which I am confident of doing, Krushita will take her place upon the stonefire seat and rule."

"And as her father and guardian, I will be prince regent until she comes of age," Jarsun added quickly.

"Indeed you will. She will be empress, and you prince regent, and the two of you will replace Prince Regent Vrath and Dowager Empress Jilana in those roles. They will remain respected elders and advisors of the court, of course."

"Of course," Jarsun said snidely, but there was something in his tone that suggested he did not agree wholeheartedly with that point.

"And you will rule the Burnt Empire on your daughter's behalf until she comes of age and takes the power into her own hands."

"Of course," Jarsun agreed again, and once again he sounded less than sincere.

"Do you accept this bargain?" Vessa asked — almost casually, as if he didn't care a whit whether Jarsun agreed or refused.

"I do," Jarsun replied. "I am surprised, old man. I thought you would waste my time with more posturing and bickering. But I am impressed. At last you speak my language. I accept your bargain and your terms."

*You hear that, little one? You are witness to our bargain now.* Vessa's voice sounded faintly amused and genial as it echoed in Krushita's mind.

All at once, Krushita knew why she was here. Why she had overheard this exchange.

*Vessa led me here!*

*He deliberately left a scent trail for me to follow.*

*He knows I am here even now, that I have heard every word. He wanted me to hear this. To know about this bargain. This was all part of his plan. I thought I was being so clever by tiptoeing through the portal and cloaking myself to eavesdrop on them, but he was the one making sure I remained concealed. That's why my father hasn't become aware of my presence yet: Vessa is using his power in addition to mine to cloak me from Jarsun's view.*

Suddenly, Krushita was overcome by an emotional rush too powerful to bear. She knew that if she allowed herself to succumb to it, she wouldn't be able to remain concealed. She retreated through the portal quickly, not bothering to cloak herself now that she knew that it was really Vessa concealing her, and once on the grassy plain, she opened a portal to return to the wagon train, and to her own bed.

Back in her own body, she gasped and thrust a clenched fist into her mouth. She wanted to shout out to the world what she had heard. But she didn't want to startle Aqreen, lying beside her, and everyone else. Let them sleep. This was her secret to keep. Hers alone.

It took her a long while to fall asleep.

# *Bulan*

BULAN WATCHED THE LONE rider approaching.

*That spells trouble,* their instinct told them.

Nobody crossed the Red Desert alone. Not under any circumstances. Reygistani were more likely to cut their own throats than attempt such a journey. Yet here was a Reygistani coming from the largest populated city in the Red Desert, heading out into the sands.

In all their years on the Red Trail, they had never seen such a thing.

They did not flatter themself that the rider was merely coming to meet them. Wagon trains arrived every few months from one Reygistani city or other. Even wagon trains from as far as Aqron, as this one was, were not infrequent enough for Queen Drina to send a welcoming committee. Besides, what kind of welcoming committee consisted of only one person? No, there was something strange here, and in their experience, strange or different or unusual almost always spelled trouble.

"Orange Alert," Bulan said to their second in command, a young Vanjhani named Muskaan, who had stepped into the position after Bulan's previous number two had been eaten alive by deadwalkers during the battle six years ago. Young, in Vanjhani terms, meant only a couple hundred years of age, but despite their tender years, Muskaan was proving quite competent. If they lived long enough, they might even make a damn good train master someday. For now, though, they had an irritating habit of questioning some orders instead of simply doing as instructed.

"Is that necessary? It's just one rider," Muskaan said, as if on cue.

Bulan glanced at them with one face, eyes cutting sideways with an expression of displeasure. "I didn't ask for your opinion," they responded curtly. "I said Orange Alert."

Muskaan did as they were told, calling out the alert to the watchers in the towers, who passed it on across the train.

They watched as the rider approached, passing the first several circles without stopping the dromad. That suggested familiarity with train organizational structure, the knowledge that the train master's circle would be in the middle of the caravan. In itself, it didn't mean anything. Hundreds of thousands traveled with the trains. It didn't take special knowledge to know where to find the train master. Still, it did suggest the rider had business with Bulan.

As the dromad came closer, Bulan's keen vision judged that its rider was female. And not any female. This one had the look of a Maatri or even a Maha-Maatri. It was in the way she held herself on the dromad, sitting hard and proud, not hunched over or draped over the humps as some commonfolk might do.

That suggested trouble.

As she brought her dromad within reach of Bulan's wagon and was intercepted by the militia, Bulan's feeling grew steadily. By the time the rider had been checked for concealed weapons and permitted access to the master, they were certain that this wasn't any ordinary visit.

The rider was a tall, statuesque woman of indeterminate age, with the attitude and stance of an experienced warrior. Definitely a Maatri at least, Bulan judged. And one who had seen a fair bit of combat and some hairy battles.

"Maha-Maatri Ladislew," she said, raising her open hands to touch her cheeks in the Reygistani greeting. "Whom do I have the pleasure of greeting?"

"Vanjhani Train Master Bulan," they replied. "Forgive our manners, Maha-Maatri," Bulan added. "We had not expected such an illustrious guest. We are honored by your presence. Pray allow us to offer you the humble courtesies owed to a fellow traveler. Will you do us the honor of joining us in a breaking of bread and taking of nectar in our wagon?"

Ladislew made the Reygistani gesture of acknowledgment. "I regretfully decline. My mission is urgent, and time is precious. I must be on my way."

Bulan nodded. "Then, if I may be so impudent as to ask a question?"

"You may ask."

"Are the streets of Reygar grown too crowded for you, Maha-Maatri? Why does a Mother of the Great City venture out into the Red Desert on her own?"

A muscle jumped in Ladislew's cheek as acknowledgment of Bulan's humor. "Not the streets, not yet, but the environs of Reygar, yes. I take it from your query that your scouts have not yet spotted the army of the traitor?"

Bulan frowned. "Not as yet. Which traitor would we be speaking of here? It has been a few seasons since we visited Reygar—please excuse our not being current with the state of politics."

"There is only one traitor worth speaking of. The wretch named Dirrdha."

"Brother to Queen Drina herself? We have heard tell of him. Last we knew, he was sent into exile by his sister some twelve years ago."

"He was, and he has now returned, at the head of an army. It is of that force I speak. They are stationed some two hundred miles north and east of Reygar."

Bulan hated it when their instincts proved right. "Where would the traitor Dirrdha have got himself an army? No Reygistani force of any size would dare challenge Drina and the might of the Maatri or dare to act against the Holy City."

"Dirrdha has found a sponsor. A Krushan named Jarsun."

Bulan sighed with one mouth and swore with the other. "We know of him. He has plagued our train all the way from Aqron. We had hoped we were well rid of him, as he has not made a move against us for some time now."

This earned a look of sharp interest from the woman. "Jarsun has attacked your train? Personally?"

"We have been spared that honor. Nay, only his minions. And by minions, I refer to a wide and varied number of devices, most of them not of this mortal realm."

Bulan quickly summarized the attacks by the deadwalkers and desert dragons and other calamities that had befallen the train on the Red Trail. Ladislew listened with keen interest, asking pointed questions. From her interest and the questions, Bulan guessed she didn't simply happen to be here to bring them up to date on the latest occurrences in the city.

She was on a mission. And they would wager that her mission was to seek little Krush's accursed father himself. That would explain her being alone on the road. The Maha-Maatri were renowned as the world's most skilled assassins. Unlike the Maatri, they engaged in battle only if it was absolutely essential. Instead, they focused their energies on singling out and quietly eliminating high-ranking individuals among the enemy.

"You seek the Krushan. To eliminate him." Bulan's tone was neutral, casual. They had no desire to provoke or offend a Maha-Maatri. Not only because such a lapse might prove fatal, but also because they respected the Maatri more than the usual Reygistani rabble. This was a great, ancient race of matriarchal assassins and warriors who had more knowledge and experience of warcraft than most entire civilizations on Arthaloka. They had even heard of Maha-Maatri Ladislew herself. In a sense, they were in the presence of a celebrity, a legendary assassin. And as chance would have it, they were in a unique position.

Ladislew's eyes swept the circle. "Your numbers are sorely depleted by your hardships on the trail. You must be low on resources as well. It would be difficult for you to withstand another sustained assault."

She had sidestepped the question as well as put the master on warning. Bulan saw their second in command reacting belatedly as understanding spread across both their faces: they shot Bulan an alarmed glance as if to say, *So this is why you issued the Orange Alert.* Bulan ignored the novice, keeping their attention focused on the visitor.

"We have a common enemy, my lady," Bulan said, choosing their words carefully. "And by the stone gods' graces, Bulan is in a unique position to assist you in your goal."

Ladislew's eyes flickered with interest. "Go on."

"You seek the Krushan, no doubt because he is the force behind the traitor Dirrdha's return, and the army that he now commands. You are probably one of several Maha-Maatri dispatched to multiple locations, each tasked with the mission of seeking out and eliminating the Krushan. Your destination is probably Aqron, since you have been told that is the seat from which he operates as ruler of the White Kingdom and self-styled God-Emperor of Arthaloka."

She looked at him for a long moment. "You are wise even among Vanjhani," she said. "Continue."

"Jarsun is not in Aqron. You would waste the better part of a decade traveling there only to find him absent. I seek to save you that effort."

A tiny muscle twitched in her forehead, not even the full wrinkle of a frown. "My mission is eternal. A Maha-Maatri does not count years or decades. All that matters is the fulfillment of a given task."

"Indeed. And we seek to assist you in that fulfillment. By sending you to Arrgodi rather than Aqron. Arrgodi is where Jarsun now spends his time. He has installed a puppet there named Tyrak and married his daughters to this tyrant."

"Jarsun has more than one daughter? I have heard only of the one named Krushita, who is reputed to be dead, slain by his own hand."

Bulan made a brushing-aside gesture. "He has as many wives and children across the land as a Maatri has lovers."

That earned a smile. "Careful, Train Master. I might be offended if I thought you were comparing us to that cursed oppressor."

"Not at all, my lady. He is not worthy of comparison to your boot heels. I point out only that Jarsun has many alternate identities and spouses and offspring. None, however, have inherited his powers, tending, for the most part, to take after their mothers. So you are right, only the one named Krushita remains his true child and heir, a Krushan by blood and ability."

A raised eyebrow. "Interesting choice of words. So you believe she lives yet?"

"We will come to that presently. What do you say to our offer? Will you accept our aid?"

"In directing me to Arrgodi? You have done that already. If your information is true and up to date . . ."

"It is. As of this very day. Jarsun is in Arrgodi. He travels around the East extensively, but spends most of his time in Arrgodi city itself, with his son-in-law and puppet liege Tyrak."

"You seem very confident of your sources, especially for one who has been traveling from Aqron to Reygar and is a long way from Arrgodi."

"My source is accurate. My information is current. And I offer you the means to confirm it for yourself before the sun sets on this day."

For the first time since they had begun speaking, Ladislew looked startled. She regained her composure at once, but the widening of her pupils told Bulan that their arrows had struck home.

"You speak a big game, Train Master Bulan of the Vanjhani. But now you exceed your abilities, I fear. Not even a Maha-Maatri can cross the Red Desert and half the Sea of Grass in less than a single day. Ten, fifteen years, possibly. Those are the realities of space and time."

"Not to me," said a voice from behind her.

Ladislew spun around, blades flashing in both hands.

She stared at Krushita who stood only a few feet away.

"How did you approach me from behind?" asked the Maha-Maatrika. "No one has ever done that to me, or to any Maha-Maatrika. It is impossible."

Krushita smiled. "The same way I will take you to Arrgodi. Silently and instantly."

# *Krushita*

IT WAS SEVERAL DAYS before Vessa finally reached out to Krushita.

She was upset with him. She had spent the last many days seeking him out in the portals. She had found not so much as a scent trail. She was certain now that he had deliberately lured her to that unspace within the maze of portals to witness the meeting with Jarsun. She burned with eagerness to know why but also resented being made to wait.

**Little one,** he said with his customary calmness, **we must have words. It is important.**

*What if I don't want to talk?* she asked irritably.

**Very well, then,** he replied, **I will leave you alone.**

*Wait,* she cried as he began to retreat from her presence. She should have known better than to show pique to the sage. He took things too literally. *I didn't mean it. Please stay. I do wish to talk.*

He returned, moving closer in her mind. **Are you unwell? You sound . . . strained.**

She laughed a little. *You sound like my mother!*

**I apologize if I seem overprotective. I am an old man who spends most of his time listening and talking to the wind, water, trees, and animals. My people skills, as you may say, are less than desirable.**

*You talk to wind and trees and water? I can communicate with animals, but to talk to things? Is that even possible?*

**It is not difficult. It requires only that you learn to listen. It is less a matter of skill than patience.**

*Will you teach me?*

He paused. She sensed a distance in him, not a physical distance, but within his mind. As if he was shielding thoughts that he didn't want her to access. She knew she could access them if she really tried, but she didn't do it. There were too many questions she wanted the answers to, and he was the only one who could answer them.

**We need to talk about what you heard that day.**

She knew he had done what grown-ups often did: avoided her question entirely and begun talking about something he wanted. She hated it when they did that, but she had learned to accept it — at least with Vessa. With her mother, she would have persisted, even argued. She knew that approach would never work with the sage.

*You meant for me to follow you through the portals, to eavesdrop on your conversation.*

**Did you understand what it meant?**

Did he mean the conversation itself or the fact that he had lured her there? She thought he must mean the former. *You cut a deal. That's the way my mother says it. She learned that from Bulan. When people negotiate or bargain, they cut a deal that neither person really wants, but both accept it as the best one they can get.*

**Yes, yes. But the larger implications?**

She frowned. *Larger implications?* She knew what the words meant; she didn't know what he meant by them. *About him facing your champion. Not running away as he always does when he's losing. Standing and finishing it. To the death.* She wanted to add what her mother used to say: *like a man.* But Aqreen had taught her that was inaccurate. Everyone was the same. The male gender wasn't more brave or "man-like" simply because they only had a penis and none of the other parts. If anything, they were the lesser because they *only* had a penis. So it was wrong to say "like a man" for any situation. That made sense, even though some people (Aqreen had been one of them) still used the phrase: people did that all the time, said stuff even if it wasn't true. That didn't make it true. She settled for *like an honorable Krushan.*

**Yes. That is very significant. Do you understand why?**

*Because if he stands and fights your champion, instead of running away, then he will have to either kill your champion or be killed himself?*

**He will die. By agreeing to that pact, Jarsun has signed his own death warrant. He is too arrogant to ever realize it, but it is the truth.**

Krushita mulled on that for a moment. *This champion of yours must really be something. Are you really sure he can kill the Krushan?* She no longer thought of Jarsun as her father. She saw him as what he really was — a mendacious, cruel monster who wanted to kill her mother and use her as a pawn in his game of power. If she had ever felt any trace of filial affection for him, he himself had quelled it before it could take root, through his actions.

**Perhaps. Perhaps not. My champion is no mere warrior. He is an avatar.**

*A real avatar? You mean, he is one of the stone gods?*

**Slow down, little one. He is not a stone god. Just an avatar, and a limited one at that. For one thing, he was sent to Arthaloka to fulfill only one purpose.**

*To kill the Krushan?*

**No. And therein lies the problem. His purpose is solely to slay the tyrant usurper named Tyrak.**

*Who's that? I've never heard of him.*

**He is the prince of Arrgodi, a great city in the East, one of three principal kingdoms in the region known as the Sea of Grass.**

She remembered the vast plain of grass and the mandala pattern burned into it.

**Yes, that is only a few thousand miles from Mraashk, where the Deliverer lives, awaiting the day of the prophecy. When the time comes, he will face Tyrak and slay him. Once that is done, his task as an avatar will be done, and he will seek sameduan.**

*What is . . . sammydon?*

**Sameduan is a ritual immersion in the sacred waters of Jeel, to seek transcendence.**

*You mean . . . suicide? By drowning?*

**It is more than that. I cannot explain further, but someday you will understand it. It is not pertinent to us today. The main thing is, Drishya the Deliverer was sent to Arthaloka only to slay Tyrak. Once that is done, he will depart this mortal coil, and his essence will return once more to the realm of the stone gods.**

She had so many new questions, her mind was bursting. But she understood that now was not the time. *Then how will he fight and kill the Krushan?*

**That is where you come in.**

*Me?*

**You have mastered the ability to possess almost any form you choose. Your skills are quite impressive for one so young, although I have learned over the ages that physical age is far less important than one's talents. Your talents are prodigious, far greater than your father's.**

*I . . . thank you, guruji.*

**Live long, my child. The instant Drishya slays the tyrant Tyrak, I wish you to possess his physical form. With your Krushan powers and his martial mastery, you will be able to confront and kill Jarsun. That is my plan.**

She could hardly believe her ears — or, her mind, actually, since physical senses had no relevance in the unspace. *You want me to kill him?*

**With your powers and Drishya's body, yes. You will perfectly complement each other. Jarsun will see only the Deliverer and knowing, as I do, that he has served his purpose once Tyrak is dead, he will assume an easy victory. He has long been a hated enemy of the stone god whose avatar is Drishya, and I am counting on that emotional factor to motivate him further, in case the pact he made with me is not sufficient. Jarsun fights only when he is confident of winning, as most bullies and cowards do. He will face Drishya, and with your help, Drishya will kill him. The world will be rid of a great and malevolent villain, one who threatens the stability and peace of all Arthaloka and will otherwise cause the deaths of untold millions. You and your mother will be safe forever after, and can live your lives in peace wherever you please.**

Krushita's mind raced as she tried to embrace all the implications and possibilities.

She pictured her mother and herself living in a house high on Reygar Mountain, with a grand view of the Red Desert, shvan puppies frolicking at their feet, going shopping in the bazaars, traveling in caravans to exotic, faraway places, eating the spiciest savories and sampling the sweetest treats. She imagined her mother happy again, laughing, her forehead free of the worry wrinkles that seemed to deepen with each passing year, dancing and singing and practicing the flute and the sarodi — both instruments bought with money Krushita herself earned from working in the bazaar or for some merchant. Bulan and their Vanjhani friends coming to visit, all of them feasting and singing and dancing to Vanjhani songs, and having a gala time.

Could it really happen? Was all that truly possible? She had stopped hoping, stopped believing. But Vessa was a wise sage, a guru, a greatly knowledgeable priest and master of lore. He must have planned this scheme for years, decades maybe, laid all the parts down so carefully, preparing it piece by piece. He had even gotten Jarsun to agree to the confrontation. She had witnessed that herself. And by playing her part in this, she would be rid of the monster who had plagued and harried them these past so many years.

Ever since her birth, it seemed, Krushita had seen her father as nothing but a monster. A terrible bully, a demoniac tyrant who would do anything, kill anyone, to get what he wanted. She knew he would never back off. The only way to stop him was to kill him.

She didn't want to be the one to do it. She knew how terrible it was for a child to kill their own parent, no matter the justification. But who else was there? Jarsun was powerful, too powerful to be defeated by any mortal. Only a demigod, another Krushan, or a stone god could end his tyranny.

From where she stood, she couldn't see any other demigods, Krushan, or stone gods lining up to take a stab at Jarsun.

She was the only one.

In a sense, it was her task and hers alone.

She had too many questions to ask. She settled for just one.

*Do you think I can do it?*

The guru contemplated her question seriously. That made her respect him all the more. He didn't reply offhandedly, the way most grown-ups did to children, taking it for granted they knew everything simply because they were adults. He considered the query carefully, thoughtfully, even though she knew he must have spent a great deal of time and effort considering it before he even embarked on this plan. That was Vessa's way. He was not the rooster who thought the sun had risen because he crowed. He had lived far too long and seen far too much to take anything, including himself, for granted.

**I believe there is a chance.**

She exhaled in frustration. *But you aren't sure.*

**There is only one way to be absolutely sure of the consequences of any action.**

*To do it.*

**Yes.**

She considered the question as well. She might not be Vessa, hundreds (or was it thousands?) of years old, knowledgeable in all the Ashcrit lore since the age of the stone gods, capable of things most mortals could not even imagine, but she had lived a lifetime in her handful of years, and she had been forced to learn more than most children could ever imagine. She knew what was what and that some things had to be done, whether one wanted to do them or not.

She had not wanted to go into the portal from which the deadwalkers were coming, but if she hadn't, the entire train would have died that day, and their corpses would be rotting in the Red Desert — or worse, tottering around as deadwalkers themselves. She had done what was needed when it was needed, and people were alive now because of it. Her mother was alive. Bulan was alive. Niede and Dor, Afranus and his siblings, so many others in their circle and across the train, people she considered friends and who liked, respected, and admired her for her abilities and what she had done that day. She had a place in the world. She was loved. She loved her family and friends, even the shvan pack who recognized that she was special and treated her specially. She wanted to go to Reygar, to live the life she and her mother had talked about so many times on the seemingly endless journey. She wanted happiness for Aqreen, for Bulan, for all of them.

And the only way to get that happiness, that freedom, was to rid themselves of the menace of Jarsun.

And now she had a chance.

Not a guarantee — there were no guarantees, as Bulan often said — but a chance.

In a way, the decision was already made for her.

It was made the day she walked out into the desert in the night and witnessed her father about to kill her mother, and had used her powers to stop him, to summon the shvan pack and use them as weapons.

She had sacrificed their lives to protect her mother's.

She had wanted to kill him that day, but hadn't known how, hadn't possessed sufficient power, maturity, or skill.

Now she had all those things, and much more.

She had a reason to kill him.

An imperative.

And a chance.

*Yes,* she said to Vessa firmly, feeling her mind and heart as clear as they could ever be, *I will do this. I will kill my father.*

# Alinora

~

FROM FAR AND WIDE they came. From every corner of Goluka the Mraashk arrived by uks cart, riding astride bullocks, or traveling on foot. Clad in their gaily colored rustic apparel, driving their favorite kine along, talking and singing and chanting aloud as was their custom. It had taken them several months to converge, many emerging from deep hiding, and required much coordination to ensure that they would not be waylaid by Arrgodi troops en route. But they were here at last. Ironically, they were gathering to celebrate a birth, but the infant had already begun taking his first steps, several months ahead of schedule. Some even claimed that he was gifted with extraordinary powers, but this was whispered only in secret. For someone might overhear and send word to Arrgodi. The baby killers were always listening.

The prophecy had come true: the Deliverer had been born. The family graced by this blessed event was that of Eshnor and Alinora, two of the most beloved in Goluka. All knew the danger of speaking aloud such words as *Deliverer* or *Slayer*, or even hinting at such, for the spies of Tyrak were everywhere, and even the wind was not to be trusted. But they could celebrate the birth of a long-awaited child to a popular couple, surely, without raising any suspicion: Eshnor and Alinora had been childless for over a decade, and had long since given up hope of bearing any progeny.

And now they had a beautiful, bonny boy.

That called for a grand celebration!

"This is the blessing of stone god Vish," said Alinora's father to his daughter and son-in-law. "He is pleased with you for resisting the tyranny of the

Usurper." Like many Mraashk, Alinora's father preferred to refer to the king of Arrgodi by that derogatory term rather than speak his vile name.

Alinora and Eshnor exchanged a meaningful glance. She raised her eyebrows questioningly. Barely perceptibly, he shook his head to answer in the negative. They had debated whether or not to reveal their infant son's extraordinary nature to their family and friends. In the end, they had decided against it. Whatever he did openly, they could not cover up. But there was no need to: people invariably attributed every miraculous action to the blessings of some deity or other.

Once they said aloud that they believed their son was something more than human, perhaps even touched with a trace of divinity, surely that would change people's perception completely. Word would spread like wildfire, and soon enough everyone across the kingdom would know about it. Including the Usurper. And while they already knew their little tyke was possessed of great power, they had no wish to test the limits of his abilities and invite the terror of Arrgodi to come and attempt to slay him. Whatever he might be, he was but a boy. And he was *their* boy. It was through his power the entire village had been spared the massacre of the infants. Empowered or no, there would be time enough for him to reveal the full extent of his abilities to the world, or not, as he pleased. It was not wise for them to boast about it here and now, not when Arrgodi's spies were everywhere, watching, listening, still seeking the prophesied Slayer.

"This child is a form of Vish himself reborn!" said one of the village elders, and she was echoed in turn by a hundred others. Everyone repeated the same thought. It was a customary ritual to exclaim that a newborn was this or that stone god reborn. Husband and wife exchanged a conspiratorial smile.

Then followed the inevitable rituals of the Mraashk after such an event. First all the cowherds of Goluka formed a protective circle around little Drishya. He giggled and turned around to look at the cowherds, regarding it as some kind of game. Still unsteady on his chubby feet, he swayed constantly, and Alinora kept wanting to dart out her hands to grab him before he fell, but somehow he always managed to retain his balance. He danced around, stuffing the back of his fist into his mouth and sucking on it noisily. His antics amused all present, and all were entranced by the way he moved and danced.

"Govala! Govala! Govala!" chanted the crowd. The word simply meant "cowherd," but it was also a title of sorts, accorded to a boy when he proved himself able enough to herd the cows of his family or clan, protect them from inclement weather or wild beasts, and bring them home safe. Govala was also the universal term for the Celestial Govala who herded all cattle everywhere, and therefore was a deity to cowherds everywhere. The term also had a playful connotation, for among the Mraashk, cowherds played as they worked, flirting, making music, dancing, feasting, and doing as they willed. To apply the title to an infant who had barely learned to walk was high praise indeed. Alinora felt herself flush with pride at the sight of her son being called by the title of govala, as the whole community watched and sang along.

"Govala! Govala! Govala!" sang the crowd, and little Drishya laughed and danced round and round, clapping his hands unsteadily, sometimes missing and almost losing his balance—but quickly regaining it and resuming his lurching dance.

One of the cowherds, an attractive woman named Shyamolie, came forward holding a cow's tail. She waved it around Drishya as he danced, encircling him. The tip of the cow tail tickled Drishya's ears and neck, and he giggled and reacted, squirming. Looking up at the object that had stimulated him, he tried to grasp it, but Shyamolie kept it out of his reach. He laughed, trying to spin faster to grab it. Alinora saw that he could spin as rapidly as a top if he desired—as rapidly as the wind itself—and she caught her breath, afraid that the cowherds would witness the superhuman side of her little tyke. But Shyamolie finished the cow tail waving and retired, and Drishya slowed. Alinora heaved a small sigh, smiling with relief.

Then came the bathing of the child in cow's urine. This part Drishya ought not to have enjoyed as much as the chanting and dancing, but he even slapped himself and splashed the urine on the faces of the cowherds who were bathing him. They laughed, undeterred. All products of Mother Cow were sacred and to be revered; there was no shame in being splashed with cow urine.

Next came the sprinkling of cow dust, literally the dust from the dried cow dung. This left Drishya's bluish-black skin powdery brown. He beamed brightly at his mother as if to say, *Not to worry. I'm fine, Mother.* She was glad he did not speak to her mind just then; she might not have been able to avoid reacting in front of so many people.

Then came the writing of the names of the stone god under whose protection he was believed to be born. Using fingertips dipped in wet cow dung, twelve different names of Vish were written on twelve different parts of Drishya's body — the forehead, throat, chest, belly, left and right sides, left and right shoulders, left and right biceps, top of the back and bottom of the back.

As Alinora watched from behind the circle of busy cowherds, she saw each name glow from within as it was written, as if her Drishya's skin reacted to the shape of the letters. The glow was very faint and only visible if you were staring directly at that spot at that instant: the cowherds were too busy writing the next name to notice. So only she saw this subtle effect. But it was unmistakable in its power and meaning. Each name glowed a distinct deep blue, then dissipated inward. It was as if the names were being absorbed into the bloodstream of her son, leaving only the shapeless crusted cow dung on the skin. She swallowed and looked around, wishing she could share this new evidence of her son's extraordinary nature with someone, then subsided and reminded herself it was for the best that this be kept a secret.

It was ironic, though, she mused silently, that the cowherds were invoking the protection of Vish upon one who was empowered as Vish himself!

The cowherds then sprinkled sacred water — brought from the river — over their bodies, then applied the bija seed mantra to themselves, invoking the first syllable of the deity's name followed by the nasal *Auma* sound. Then they applied the same bija seed mantra to Drishya, who gurgled happily and raised his arms in the air.

In conclusion they chanted verses designed to chase away the evil urrkh known for abducting or harming infants.

By the time the cowherds were done, even Drishya had tired. Sucking the back of his fist, he curled up and slept, and had to be carried by his mother indoors. She fed him from her breast till he was sated enough that he fell asleep with the teat still in his puckered wet lips.

*Perhaps,* Alinora thought, *even a mortal imbued with divinity is still subject to weaknesses and limitations of mortal flesh. He may be empowered beyond imagining, but he is still a human babe. He still tires, needs sleep, nourishment, and rest, and he performs all the bodily functions of the mortal beings whose form he has chosen to adopt. If a stone god resides in a tree, he must grow roots and leaves and needs sunlight and water. If a stone god resides in a babe, he needs milk and sleep and laughter and love!*

She cradled him in the warmth of her embrace. Mother and son slept soundly and peacefully through the night and well into the next morning. Eshnor came often to check on them, and a constant guard was maintained around the clock to ensure nobody came within harming distance of the mother and infant.

# *Eshnor*

ESHNOR TOO WAS ANXIOUS. If he failed to express his anxieties to his wife, it was because he did not want to alarm Alinora any further. But he had received word from Rurka to beware of assassins from Arrgodi.

How to protect Drishya? That was the most daunting question of all. He could hardly surround Alinora and their son with armed guards all night and day. It would look preposterous and would invade her privacy. She would never have a moment alone, and the presence of the guards themselves would make her anxious and nervous. He knew his beloved wife well. She believed that carrying a sword was itself an invitation to violence. The presence of armed warriors would rob her of all peace of mind.

So he set several of his most trusted govalas to watch discreetly from a distance. There were family among this number: he recruited her brothers and sisters as well as his own. This way, she would see familiar beloved faces around her and take comfort in their presence, while their mission would be to watch over her and send for the real guards the instant they sensed danger. The armed guards would be kept out of Alinora's sight but within quick hailing distance. They would operate in shifts and be on alert at every moment of the day or night. Eshnor received more volunteers for this duty than he required. Then again, how many were too many? Who knew what powers the assassins might possess? Who knew how they would attack?

Still, all he could do was prepare and anticipate, and he did so.

He offered to pay the volunteers for the time spent away from their herds, but they would not hear of it. They readily agreed to drink his famous Goluka milk and consume its products, though! That was payment enough, they said, brushing milk off their upper lips with the backs of their hands, grinning.

So began a routine of Alinora and Eshnor pretending that all was normal, smiling, laughing, talking, going about their daily chores, meeting and receiving people, doing everything they had done before. But with a pall of anticipation hanging over them that dampened everything they did. Eshnor would see it clearly: Alinora would be talking with her sisters and friends and notice some stranger approach Drishya. Her smile would vanish, and she would start moving toward him with a lurching gait that betrayed her alarm, only to stop short abruptly when the man turned and she saw he was her friend Tarangaksi's fiancé, coming to greet the little hero for the first time. Her face would relax again, but the creases remained, and Eshnor knew exactly how she felt because he felt the same way.

He prayed daily that this anxiety would be removed from their lives. In a way, the warrior spirit within him wished that the assassins would show themselves sooner rather than later, so that this ordeal could end once and for all. It was the waiting and anticipation that caused the greatest distress.

# *Alinora*

## 1

AS DAYS WENT BY, Alinora saw that Drishya was indeed very much like all the other infants his age, sons and daughters of her sisters and friends who came daily to play with him. These were the children who had survived the massacre along with Drishya, each one a precious child that represented hope for the future, and it warmed her heart to see them frolic together. But there were times when she noticed him looking into the distance with contemplative eyes, almost as if he were thinking through some complex problem. When he saw her watching, he always smiled and gurgled reassuringly. She began to wonder if he was concealing his true intelligence for her sake.

She could not fault him; a part of her wanted him to be the child she had always desired, her own son. Even though she knew quite well he was no more her son than he was an ordinary babe, she liked the pretend play. She accepted his subterfuge. After all, he must appear completely normal and ordinary to anyone watching. If there were ears everywhere, those ears also had eyes connected to them. Unusual behavior could be more easily observed, without a word needing to be spoken aloud.

Eshnor seemed preoccupied and distracted as well. There was talk of rebellion and of an alliance against Arrgodi. Eshnor had always been clear on the matter of politics: whatever the problem, war and violence were part of it, they could never be solutions to anything. His staunch insistence on pacificism was both a necessary counterpoint to the constant heated tempers and enraged debates as well as a frustration to those who felt the time for talk and peaceful methods was long past.

Perhaps the best news that came out of Arrgodi was the rumor that Vasurava and Kewri had escaped into exile, and nobody knew exactly where they were even now, only that they were safe and well. She was relieved at that news. She was less relieved to hear that Rurka and the Mraashk rebels were seeking support from the distant realm of Stonecastle, ruled by their eponymous king who was, of course, the adoptive father of Karni, sister of Vasurava and therefore naturally sympathetic to anyone suffering under Tyrak's tyranny. But Eshnor felt that Stonecastle was an ambitious and grasping king, a warmonger who would rouse his army and ride on Arrgodi without much provocation. He thought that Rurka had erred in bringing Stonecastle into this fray — but it was the only nation willing to risk Tyrak's wrath by sheltering Mraashk refugees seeking to escape the Usurper's yoke, and such support came at a heavy price.

If Rurka reached an agreement with Stonecastle, then Stonecastle might someday march on Arrgodi. And if Stonecastle attacked Arrgodi, Hastinaga could not stay neutral. Vasurava's brother-in-law Shvate was too young and lacking sufficient power as yet to commit Hastinaga's considerable might, but Shvate's uncle, Prince Regent Vrath, certainly could. And if Vrath aligned with the forces against Arrgodi, then it was almost certain that Jarsun Krushan the Morgol would join in the melee. It would be a war on every front, and it could be decades, or even centuries, before peace descended on the Mraashk again. Eshnor knew and feared this more than the actual threat of violence. It was one thing to suffer the yoke of Tyrak. But was it worth risking war against the Burnt Empire in an attempt to throw off that yoke? And who was to say what the eventual outcome might be? After all, the Krushan dynasty, from which Hastinaga's rulers were descended, specifically the Krushan line, were the forebears of the Mraashk. And Arrgo, founder of the Arrgodi and Mraashk nations, had been cast out by his own father, Ragan Krushan, and banished to these regions. There were still tribes who recalled that ancient humiliation and resented it, believing that Mraashk and Arrgodi had equal claim to the throne of the City of Elephants and Snakes, Hastinaga. What might begin as a sincere attempt to support an oppressed people and overthrow a tyrant might well end up as a war engulfing the entire continent.

So Alinora kept silent about her concerns, thinking she would give it another day or two, then another week, then another fortnight. For now,

Drishya was her beloved son. He was healthy, happy, playful . . . Most of all, he was alive! The first child she'd had who had not been stillborn. Although she knew that was not true, the reality of his presence enabled her to pretend it was so. She was grateful for that.

## 2

Now that Drishya was walking, it was harder to keep track of him. Most infants took a few steps one day, then stumbled and fell, then gradually progressed over the next few weeks. Not Drishya. One day he was sitting and creeping and crawling, the next day he was standing up, and from that day onward, he walked like any toddler. He lurched, he stumbled, he almost fell — and sometimes actually fell — but mostly he regained his balance and continued on his merry way. He had some trouble going downhill. On one occasion, Drishya was sitting beside Alinora and playing with a wooden wagon cart. Alinora heard her name called by Aindavi and Kirtida, her best friends, and turned her head for a moment. As they approached, Aindavi put her hand to her mouth and screamed. She pointed over Alinora's shoulder, and Alinora spun, her heart leaping with panic, to see Drishya trundling down the grassy slope. The cart had gotten away from him and was rolling downhill, and he had decided to follow it. As the cart picked up speed, so did Drishya, his chubby arms raised and waving as he sought to maintain his balance. The pull of Mother Artha, the earth goddess, drew him, and he ran faster after the rolling toy.

Alinora called his name and ran after him, followed closely by her friends. She could hear Drishya laughing in his baby gurgle as he went, and it was evident that he was neither afraid nor aware of the possibility of coming to harm.

About halfway downhill, he lost his balance, went head over heels on the grass — and kept on going. Alinora gasped, running faster. Drishya tumbled a few times, then came to a rest sitting up. His heavy head jerked forward on his slight neck, and he released a choked burst of laughter. Alinora came running up beside him and crouched down, cradling him to her chest, swaying from side to side, tears of relief pouring down her face. Her friends knelt beside her, reassuring her, touching her arms, touching Drishya, and she realized in that moment that, divine or mortal, it didn't matter to a mother's heart. To a mother, even a god infant was still her son, and even if he was invulnerable to every conceivable danger, she would still worry her heart out over him.

When she finally released Drishya from her smothering embrace, he smiled at her proudly and held up his fist.

"Ma!" he cried, the only word he could speak aloud. The wooden cart was clutched in his chubby fist.

"Ma!" he cried again, waving the cart at her until she nodded and acknowledged his triumph.

He had chased down the cart and caught it. To him, it had been a little adventure, nothing more. Soon after, he had his milk, burped happily, then fell asleep with arms and legs sprawled as usual, still clutching the wooden cart. She tried to pry it loose, but when the wood creaked as if it was about to crack, she let go at once. He wasn't about to give up his prize that easily.

After that first little triumph, the adventures increased in number.

One day she was feeding one of the cows, Drishya beside her. He loved being around the cows. He had a way of putting his hand on their bellies, palm pressed upward so he could reach their bulging stomachs, and making a resonant nasal sound in his sinus before saying, "Ma!" It was possible he meant to say something completely different, but as it happened, it was an appropriate term to use. Cows were quite literally go-maata. Cow-mothers. She couldn't help feeling that even his little ritual of placing his palm on their bellies and making that odd sound was a kind of blessing.

She wasn't in the least surprised when some cows began yielding richer, sweeter milk than ever before. She was certain they were the very cows her little Drishya had touched.

One day she came out her front door to find every untethered cow gathered outside, waiting patiently. She stopped short, taken aback. The cows stood silently, as if waiting for something or someone. Moments later, the pitter-patter of little bare feet sounded and her dark rascal came to the threshold. At once, the cows sent up such a lowing and mooing that people came rushing from around the house to see what was going on.

Drishya clapped his hands gleefully, smacking the palms together in that uncoordinated way infants have, sometimes missing and slapping empty air, giggling open-mouthed. Then he raised his palms and showed them to the gathering of cows.

At once, they subsided. One solitary calf right at the back, probably unable to see from behind the big cows, lowed once, plaintively. Drishya put his finger to his lips and made a shushing sound. The calf subsided as well.

Then, as Alinora and the other family members watched in amazement, he began making that nasal sound again. Except that this time it was almost recognizable, despite his inability to pronounce words clearly just yet. Alinora felt certain it was the sacred syllable *Auma.* The way Drishya made the sound, it was deeper, more primal somehow, like something that transcended language and words and meaning. Something that went back to the beginning of time and the human race. It was a sound filled with great power and history, made by the nasal septum of a two-year-old infant standing naked on his doorstep!

Then he raised his palm again and held it out to the gathered cows. Alinora blinked as something passed from that open palm to the cows. She could not say what it was exactly. It was not light, not quite a glow. It was wholly invisible — yet perceptible. Something that she could only describe as . . . a force. An energy. A blessing.

The cows lowed loudly again, this time with a tone of satisfaction, the sad-sack tone of cows since time immemorial, then turned ponderously and clumped their way back to their foraging grounds. They didn't need to be herded; they found their way quite well by themselves.

Only the little calf remained. She started to follow her mother, then hesitated and turned her head back, looking mournfully at Drishya.

Drishya smiled. Alinora saw him beaming brightly as if he knew exactly what ailed the little calf. And he stepped off the threshold, almost losing his balance as he reached the soft grassy ground of the courtyard. She felt her arms reach out instinctively to grab him, but saw that he needed no help. He padded across the courtyard to where the calf stood waiting uncertainly.

He laughed and threw his little arms up to the calf's neck, and to everyone's surprise, he gave the calf a big wet kiss on her lips. The calf lowed softly, then was quiet. Drishya laughed and swung onto the calf's back, sitting astride it as he must have seen some of the young govalas do.

The calf seemed pleased and lurched forward, running after her mother, following the herd. Drishya held on easily, laughing his gurgling laugh, absolutely fearless. Seeing him heading downhill, the cowherds closest to him began to shout out warnings and run after him. Drishya continued undaunted, squealing with joy. The calf mirrored his childish enthusiasm, galloping like a horse.

"Ma!" Drishya cried happily as he passed over the hilltop and out of sight. "Ma!"

It was still the only word he could speak aloud.

Shaking her head in amused despair, Alinora ran after him. Even though she knew no harm would come to him, she could not simply stand there as her son rode recklessly down the hillside.

From that day onward, until the end of her days, that little calf never once fell ill or had any complaints or problems. Eventually, she would become the oldest living cow. It was only much, much later that people realized the connection and harked back to the day Drishya had blessed the cow with his own life essence, shared through a kiss.

# *Drishya*

~

DRISHYA HAD A LOT on his mind. He knew there was a great deal of time left before he would face the urrkh who masqueraded as a prince of the Arrgodi. He knew this as surely as he knew the urrkh's name was in fact a title, Tyrak of Keravalune, shortened to Tyrak in the urrkh tongue. Tyrak the Urrkhlord as he had been known once, in a forgotten age.

Drishya knew this just as he knew that he himself was born of the essence of Vish that had been left in the *Auma* surrounding Arthaloka, awaiting just such a contingency. Stone god Vish had defeated Tyrak in that Age of Myth, and the Stone Sages had imprisoned him in a secure place with countless other urrkh — not their physical forms, for those had been destroyed when the stone gods unleashed the dreaded celestial weapon that erased all physical life on Arthaloka. Their essences were held captive; call them souls, if you wished — it was as good a term as any.

Somehow Tyrak had escaped and assumed a temporary physical manifestation which he used to impregnate a mortal woman, Queen Kensura of Arrgodi, before his urrkh essence was forced back into that prison by the power of *Auma*. Queen Kensura then gave birth to the mortal Tyrak, passing him off as the son of King Ugraksh instead of the urrkh-human halfbreed he was. The same force of *Auma*, to maintain the Eternal Balance, had released a portion of Vish's essence and allowed it to take physical form as well, to counter that of Tyrak. Thus was Drishya created, with Vasurava and Kewri's eighth child acting as his physical vessel. All this he knew already. There was something else that troubled him.

*How* had Tyrak escaped his eternal prison? Only a Stone Sage or a stone god had the power to release him, even for an instant. Yet there were no

Stone Sages or stone gods in this era upon Arthaloka. On distant planets and far-flung worlds, yes, but that was of little relevance to this matter. Whoever or whatever had enabled Tyrak's escape had to possess great power, perhaps even urrkh maya, and that troubled Drishya. Even as he spent his days playing at games and sports and herding the cows, his mind continued to seek an answer to this riddle.

The answer came to him one fall day, from an unexpected source.

He was sitting beneath a shady tree on a hillock with a clear view of his family's herd. The rolling green hills of Harvanya, long said to be the richest and most nourishing grazing in all the Sea of Grass — which they truly were now, simply because Drishya enriched the soil he walked upon, and he had walked every mile of these hills of his homeland — lay lazily in the genial sunshine of an autumn afternoon. A flute rested silent in his lap; he had set it down a moment ago to muse upon the same old quandary that had preoccupied him almost since the day of his birth.

After several minutes of fruitless musing, added to the tally of tens of thousands such minutes he had expended in the pursuit of this same question, he raised the flute to his lips again.

# *Gaurika*

AT THE SOUND OF the flute's sweet song, the cows raised their heads from feeding and stared appreciatively up at the boy on the hill. Gaurika, the cow who had once been the calf he had blessed, mooed softly with pleasure and swished her tail. She loved Drishya's flute songs; every cow in Harvanya did. At the close of each day, all he had to do was play a certain tune, and they would return obediently to their pens.

The cow dogs, who had once grumbled at the loss of their livelihood, now wagged their tails in delight too when they heard his flute; they loved his songs as much as Gaurika and responded just as readily. Birds came from near and far to listen as well, cocking their heads and paying close attention. Later, they would try to imitate some of his notes, but that was all they could manage; Drishya, on the other hand, could imitate the sound of every bird in the sky, every creature in the wild, and speak to them as eloquently as they did to one another.

When the flute broke off in midsong, sounding one startled misblown note, Gaurika looked up curiously. She lowed in complaint, urging Drishya to play on. She was surprised to see the boy engaged in conversation with another human, a young female of his species. She swished her tail disapprovingly; who was this meddling female? Drishya was Gaurika's boy!

*Get lost, young woman. Let him play his song.*

It was a while before Drishya did that.

# *Drishya*

~

DRISHYA LOOKED CURIOUSLY AT the girl who stood before him. She had appeared out of thin air. No, not thin air. There had been a disturbance in the air first, a shimmering, then she had stepped onto the grass. The shimmering remained in the air behind her for a moment, then winked out.

A portal. She had come through a portal. From another place in Arthaloka.

"Hello, brother."

Her voice was sweet and mellow, with the promise of the husky weight it would carry when she was older. There was something else about her, a maturity that belied her age.

She was like him. Not exactly, not entirely, but close enough to be . . . his sister? Why not? That was as good a word as any. They were siblings in *Auma,* linked by a common connection to the power that controlled, fed, and would ultimately consume the universe.

"Hello, sister," he said pleasantly, setting the flute down and smiling at her.

She was smiling too. Then she surprised him by throwing herself at him and hugging him tightly.

"It is so good to meet you at last!" she said. "Ever since old Vessa told me that you existed, I've been longing to meet you."

Vessa. That was a name he knew. Or rather, a presence in *Auma.* A powerful presence. Not quite a Stone Sage, but . . . close. A Krushan priest and hermit. One who had schooled himself in the arcana of *Auma* sorcery and had become quite good at it. Yes, about as close to a Stone Sage as one could expect in this modern, unempowered age.

"And I you," he replied. Not to be polite but because it was how he felt, he realized. In a sense, he too had been looking forward to meeting her. That was the moment he became aware that he had known of her existence, even without knowing that he knew. Such were the mysteries of *Auma*!

A cow lowed complainingly in the pasture below, and he grinned to himself. Gaurika was jealous. Well, let her be. The mortal girl was pretty, but she was his sister, after all, or at least, his sibling in *Auma*. Gaurika didn't know that; let her stew if she wanted. She had become far too possessive of him anyway. It would do her some good to know he had other friends than the cows!

The girl detached herself from Drishya and smiled up at him with damp eyes. "It is so lonely being the only one with powers. I feel like the weight of the world is on my head. If only I could set it down for just a bit. But I can never do that, because he's always up to something, always finding some way to harass us, to hurt us. It's been years since I've been meaning to come visit you, but every day brings some new challenge."

Looking at her, he saw into her mind and knew at once what she meant. He saw a vast desert of red sand, a caravan of thousands of wooden vehicles similar to uks carts but much larger and covered on top, bearing thousands of people. There had been many more at the start of their journey, but attacks by a number of forces had depleted their numbers. Among the survivors were this young girl and her mother. He saw, in a flash, everything that had happened to her since leaving Aqron, and saw also the cause of her troubles: a tall, snake-thin urrkh-Krushan spawn named Jarsun.

Krushita must have been able to feel him combing through her mind, because she said then, "He is my father." There was sadness in her voice, and it made him feel sad too. He did not want this pretty young woman, his new friend and visitor, his sister, to be sad. "He won't stop until we are dead, or until my mother and I surrender to him."

Drishya nodded and patted her arm. "I understand."

She smiled sadly at him. "I heard you thinking, as you always do, and I thought it was time I visited at last and told you the answer."

He frowned. "The answer?"

"To your question."

"Which question?"

"How did the urrkh Tyrak escape long enough to create a mortal son?

It was my father. Jarsun Krushan released the urrkh's essence. Vessa sensed it and came as quickly as he could, forcing the urrkh back into his eternal prison. But the damage had been done. The mortal Tyrak had been conceived already and the flow of *Auma* altered. That was why you had to be born. To balance the flow and stop Tyrak."

Drishya looked at her for a long moment.

"Of course," he said at last. "Of course. It was the Krushan named Jarsun. He is malicious enough to do such a thing. I didn't know he was powerful enough, though."

Krushita nodded, her brows knitting. "He grows stronger all the time. I feel it. Vessa says so too."

"Vessa is also Krushan?" Drishya shook his head, realizing his mistake at once. "Yes, of course he is. He is the son of Jilana and the sage who was actually a Krushan emperor traveling incognito."

"Jarsun enhances his powers by use of urrkh maya, strengthening himself and learning cruel new tricks he uses to torment others. The way he torments my mother and me, and all the innocent people who were unlucky enough to be on the same wagon train with us."

Krushita's eyes flashed with flecks of fire. Drishya admired her banked power: yes, she was truly his sibling in *Auma.* She had great power, and her powers were multiplied when she was angry. The very thought of Jarsun and her mother enraged her enough to take on an army single-handed. *Which she already has,* he thought, *an army of the undead.* He liked Krushita.

Drishya nodded. "I feel the same way about Tyrak. I would like to end his cruelty. I wish I could do it today." He clenched his fist. "*Now.*"

Krushita touched his taut jaw. "I wish you could too. I would go with you to Arrgodi and end his reign at once. Every day that urrkh monster lives, he causes misery to more and more innocent people. He has to be stopped."

Drishya sighed, opening his fist. "But it is too soon."

"That's what Vessa says!" She shook her head, her long hair moving in the cool autumn breeze. "He keeps saying I must wait until I am old enough, strong enough." She stamped her foot on the grass. "I'm sick and tired of adults saying that all the time!"

Drishya shrugged. "Nobody tells me. I just know. I have to wait until the right time."

"When will it be the right time? It feels like we're waiting centuries."

"I know. But it's only a few more years. They'll pass. And then I will kill him and fulfill the prophecy. Then I can return and resume my eternal rest."

Krushita's eyes widened. "I forgot that you're not like me. I mean, you are like me in some ways, but not every way. For me, killing Jarsun is only a means to an end. I have to do it to stop him from harming and killing so many other people and from trying to hurt my mother. But once it's done, I just want to live with my mother in peace. That's the reason why I have to do it. But you, you have a different goal."

Drishya nodded. "I don't belong to this world. This era. I'm only here to do a job. Once that's over, I will go back to where I came. Just as Tyrak's essence will return to the urrkhlord Tyrak in the otherworld prison. I want nothing else but to complete my given task and return home."

"Except, I don't think you will. I'm sorry if that disappoints you, but you have more work here than just killing Tyrak. I need you too. You see, Drishya, Vessa says that I need your help to confront and defeat my father. It's the only way. Alone, I can hurt him badly, maybe even fatally, but the only way to be sure is with you fighting alongside me. The two of us can best him together, using all our powers, all our strength, and some strategy. Tyrak is one thing: Jarsun Krushan is a whole other kettle of fish."

Drishya frowned. He had never the phrase before: it sounded strange. But he understood her meaning. "I don't know," he said uncertainly, "if I *can* stay once I kill Tyrak."

Krushita smiled. "Don't worry. Vessa will help with that. He's said so already. And you would like to help me, wouldn't you?"

He nodded, smiling back. "And you will help me too. I can feel it. You will be with me in spirit when I face Tyrak and slay him. It is part of the prophecy."

"I will. I promise I will. But now I have to go. I'm the only protection my mother and the rest have back there, and the longer I'm gone, the greater the risk that my father may try something. I'll come see you when I can."

He nodded, but then felt his face forming a sad expression. "I wish I could come help you. You need it badly. But I can't do it. If I leave here for even a day, I think it will upset the whole balance. I feel it."

She sighed and nodded. "I feel it too. It's all right. I'll manage. I'm getting stronger each year. It isn't long now, I know. And we can always speak, no matter the physical distance between us. You know that."

He nodded. "I'd like that. Very much. Bye, Krushita, take care."

She summoned a portal, and it appeared, shimmering in the air. "Call me Krush."

"Bye, Krush."

"Bye, brother Drishya," she said, giving him a quick peck on his cheek and a half hug.

Then she stepped through the portal and was gone.

Drishya was still staring at the empty air when he felt a nudge at his waist and something wet and heavy being pushed against his side.

He turned to see Gaurika, her lips parted to show her teeth, her eyes angry. She mooed at him.

"Yes, yes, my love," he said reassuringly, "I know you're upset. But don't be. That was my sister, Krush."

Gaurika's expression and attitude changed at once. *Sister,* she thought, and he saw her with her sibling calves of different ages, all milling about their mother. *That's all right, then.*

"Yes," Drishya said aloud happily. "That is all right. It's very much all right."

# Part Five

## *A Dark Prince Falls, A Dark Queen Rises*

# *Tyrak*

## 1

JARSUN SAT EASILY ON the throne of Arrgodi. It was the day after the Krushan had restored Tyrak to human form, and they were in court.

He looked relaxed, calm, as if he belonged there and had occupied this very seat of power for years. Arrayed around him were several familiar faces that Tyrak recognized as well. Henus and Malevol were on either side, as always, like pillars framing the royal personage. Bane and Uaraj were there as well, standing behind the throne and off to one side. They avoided meeting Tyrak's gaze, though Henus and Malevol had no compunctions about staring arrogantly back at him. A few others he knew were Trnavarta; Agha; Baka; Dhenuka; his own chief advisor, Shelsis; a woman he recognized as the wife of Pradynor, his new captain of the guards; and of course Bahuka.

His gaze drifted back to the woman, the wife of Pradynor: she was looking at him with an expression that he could not interpret. Was it interest, curiosity, or mere boredom? Perhaps all or none of them.

The woman was very attractive in an intense, menacing way. She was muscled and carried herself like a warrior, yet dressed as a lady, not a soldier. Jarsun had insisted that men be given preference over women in positions of power; as far as the "God-Emperor" was concerned, gender was binary, and men were superior.

Tyrak had had no particular objection to following this diktat, as he had followed all Jarsun's other "suggestions," but he now wondered whether Pradynor's wife might not have made a more suitable captain of the guards than her husband. She certainly looked capable. What was her name again? Ladislew? Yes, that was it. A typically Reygistani name matching her features and appearance.

Bahuka made a sound, drawing Tyrak's attention.

He forced his face not to show the irritation — to put it mildly — that the man's very presence aroused in him. The Tyrak who had usurped his father's throne and imprisoned both his parents would have expanded himself to gargantuan size and crushed the Krushan like the slimy worm he was.

Bahuka's face openly showed his feelings for Tyrak: contempt. He then did exactly what he had been doing these past several months. He told Tyrak what to do.

"Prince Regent Tyrak," he said in a tone loud enough to carry across the sabha hall and be heard by every one of the wealthiest and most powerful nobles of the Arrgodi race, not just of Arrgodi city, assembled there. "Will you not show your allegiance to your benefactor and mentor, who also happens to be your illustrious father-in-law, the Honorable God-Emperor of All Arthaloka?"

Once again the shrewd old tactician had outwitted him. By exhorting him in front of every person whose opinion — and power — mattered in this part of the world, he had compelled Tyrak to adhere to protocol. Not to do so would be seen as being churlish and rebellious, if not outright fatal. Tyrak knew Jarsun's methods too well; tolerating insubordination or insults was not part of the Krushan lord's worldview. He had killed men closer to him than Tyrak for lesser infractions.

Seething inwardly with pent-up frustration and fury, he bent his knee in obeisance. *Bowing before my own throne, here's a royal irony!*

"My lord," he said. That was as much as he was willing to do. If Jarsun expected any more, he could come kiss his royal seat.

Instead, Jarsun surprised him by leaving the seat — the one he was sitting on — and descending the dais steps with outstretched arms in an attitude of dramatic majesty.

"My son!" he cried with redoubtable sincerity. "Tyrak, my eyes have ached to look upon you these past years. Too long have you kept yourself from me. My heart languishes without your youthful exuberance and energy. Come, embrace me."

Tyrak let his former friend and mentor enfold him in the same lean yet whip-taut arms that he recalled from when they first met. Jarsun looked as if he hadn't aged a day since. His grip was powerful enough to snap Tyrak's back easily, and the squeeze he received was clearly a reminder of that fact. He half expected Jarsun to pull him close and whisper some snarling threat that could not be caught by the rest of the sabha. But Jarsun did no such thing. He behaved as if he were genuinely pleased to see Tyrak again after their long separation. Tyrak recalled his wives, Jarsun's daughters, with a vague twinge of not-quite-guilt. It had been a fair time since he had seen them last. Perhaps there was as much of the father-in-law's wrath and reluctant tolerance in Jarsun's attitude as that of a conqueror seeking new territories. It also gave Tyrak a sense of righteous indignation: despite his neglect of Jarsun's daughters, the Krushan should be treating Tyrak with more respect than he was at present!

Jarsun regained his seat upon the throne, gesturing to Tyrak to be seated on a silk-cushioned gilded stool that was quickly brought forward by attendants and placed close to the throne — yet slightly behind it and much lower in height.

"Come, drink and partake of refreshment with me. You must be tired after your tax collecting trip. If you will excuse me, I shall finish dealing with some minor administrative matters."

Tax collecting? Was that where he was to have been? Perhaps he had been expected to collect the manure the horse had dropped on the field — was that the "tax" Jarsun had in mind?

He sat holding a goblet of honey wine as Jarsun issued a few formal proclamations and signed several agreements, armistices, trade deals, and other such "minor administrative matters."

*Go on,* Tyrak thought sourly as he watched over the rim of his brass goblet. *Be comfortable, dearest father-in-law. Consider this your own kingdom.* It was also clear that all these deals and agreements were the culmination of months of diplomacy, negotiations, and tough talk. He studied Bahuka, who was supervising the formalization of each scroll, instructing the munshis, and otherwise overseeing the whole process. Bahuka looked up, grinning broadly. Tyrak turned away, disgusted.

At one point, Jarsun shot him a shrewd, knowing glance. He turned to Bahuka, then Henus and Malevol, and finally included his other cronies and associates in his cryptic gaze. Some silent communication passed between them as they all turned toward Tyrak. Then, as one man, they burst out laughing. Jarsun looked at Tyrak again, his thin lips pursed, eyes half lidded, a faint shadow of a smile sketched on his sharply malevolent features.

Tyrak fought the desire to dash the goblet of wine at the God-Emperor and then throw himself at the man who had reduced him from a king of kings to a mere puppet figure and a laughingstock in his own court.

Jarsun saw the change come across his features and read Tyrak's mood accurately.

"Does something trouble you overmuch, my son?" he asked. He took a sip from his own goblet. "I trust you will not mind my calling you son? After all, a son-in-law is like a second son in our culture."

"Not at all, Father dearest," Tyrak said, seething within but smiling pleasantly. "I was merely wondering what our plans are."

Jarsun nodded in response to some query whispered in his ear by Shelsis, before glancing casually at Tyrak again. "What plans do you refer to, Tyrak?"

"For Arrgodi, of course," said Tyrak, using every ounce of his willpower to keep from shouting and throwing things; with merely mortal strength and body, he would be crushed in a moment. But there were other weapons in his armory. *So if it's talk and public displays you want, let's do it your way, then!*

"Arrgodi is your kingdom, Tyrak," Jarsun said condescendingly. "Surely you know what your own plans are?"

"Of course," Tyrak agreed. "But your overview and grasp of the entire sociopolitical climate is so superior to my own, I would be amiss if I did not ask you to lend your expert mind to the situation."

Jarsun looked out across the lake of upturned faces. The chatter in the sabha hall had risen to a gentle background noise while Jarsun was sealing the treaties and other formalities, but now it had died out. Clearly, the court sensed some animosity between father-in-law and son-in-law and was eager to see what would transpire. There was also the fact that Tyrak's reign of terror had not yet been forgotten, and from the looks he received daily, he knew that everyone was expecting him at any moment to return to that old demoniac form. Perhaps they even thought that this human and vulnerable Tyrak was but a ploy, some tactic designed to appease and lull them. They were rich and powerful, lazy and self-indulgent, but they were not fools. And Jarsun's reputation preceded him across the length and breadth of the civilized world—and beyond. His cruelty was renowned, his demoniac origins legendary. A clash between these two titans would be a sight to see. And the rich always enjoyed spectacles, especially the gory, brutally violent kind. *We have taken the trouble to get dressed and attend court,* the hall full of nobles seemed to be saying through their rapt silence, *now give us a show!*

Tyrak saw from Jarsun's face that his father-in-law had read the room as well and come to the same conclusion. The grey eyes remained cool, the attitude stayed nonchalant. "Perhaps it may be more pertinent if you were to ask me specific questions, so I could answer to the point." He gestured to the chamber at large. "One would not wish to bore the entire nobility of the kingdom."

"Of course," Tyrak said, carefully mirroring rather than mimicking Jarsun's polite coolness. The game was on.

He rose to his feet and stepped a few yards ahead. At once, Jarsun's coterie drew suspicious and alert: from the corners of his eyes, Tyrak glimpsed hands reaching for sword hilts, feet shifting, eyes narrowing. He kept his movements casual and relaxed, even as he walked to and fro before the throne. It was unorthodox in the extreme, could even be considered an affront, but after all, he was the prince regent, was he not? And he was speaking not only to the God-Emperor but also to his father-in-law. The informality could hardly be seen as an insult when Jarsun himself had encouraged the casual attitude and emphasized their personal tie.

"What steps do you intend to take to find this so-called Slayer?" Tyrak asked. It was important to start with a hard-hitting question, to gain the upper hand from the very outset. The collective nobility of the kingdom was watching. He would ram question after question down Jarsun's slender throat, until the so-called God-Emperor's gullet was too full for him to take a breath! Then he would go in for the kill and tear the man's innards out with a single slashing accusation. So much for dear, loving father-in-law. Before this sabha session was ended, he, Tyrak, the rightful king, would be on the throne of the Arrgodi nation once more.

A faint, niggling doubt reared its head in his conscience, suggesting that perhaps he ought to tread carefully here. After all, irrespective of his arrogant treatment, Jarsun was one of the most powerful warlords in the world at present, as well as a harsh and unforgiving enemy. It might perhaps be wise not to antagonize him completely.

But he had already dealt the first punch and now waited to see his opponent reel and rock.

Jarsun frowned and spread his hands. "What Slayer?" he asked with convincing perplexity.

Tyrak resisted the urge to snort. Somehow, without living things dropping from one's nostrils, snorting and sneezing were no longer as much fun. "The prophesied Slayer of Tyrak, of course! The one told of by Sage Vessa so many years past, and whose coming has been awaited by his people for over a decade."

Jarsun chuckled. "Rumors. Gossip. Idle chatter. Nothing more."

Tyrak stared at him, dumbfounded. "You would question the prophecy of a great sage? Vessa himself stated that —"

"Stated to whom?"

Tyrak blinked, unused to being interrupted. "What?"

Jarsun smiled indulgently as if addressing a feeble friend. "You say this Vessa stated this alleged prophecy. To whom did he state it?"

Tyrak looked around, wondering what was happening. "What do you mean, to whom did he state it? Everyone knows about the prophecy. The whole kingdom has been clamoring for the Deliverer to be born, and now they say he has been born and that my days on Arthaloka are numbered! Everyone knows this! Where have you been?"

*Careful, don't get carried away. Winning petty points here won't assure your victory in the final minutes of this game.* This was his inner voice of conscience and good sense, advising him again. He ignored it. It felt far too good to be slapping the great God-Emperor around. His larger, dominating, demoniac side might not be able to display itself through the use of power and force, but it could still unleash some much-needed anger.

Jarsun looked as calm as Tyrak felt angry. "Where have I been? Consolidating a hundred divided tribal principalities and minor kingdoms into a cohesive collective. Building an empire, in other words. Possibly the greatest empire ever assembled in this subcontinent, if not the world." He smiled disarmingly as if embarrassed at the sheer scale of his achievement. "But let's stick to the point, shall we? This Slayer you speak of. Did anyone else see this Vessa when he is said to have made this outrageous claim of a Deliverer being born, etcetera, etcetera? A serving girl, perhaps? Or a charioteer on his way to the stables? A cook, a sentry, an elephant trainer, anyone? Nobody at all? How odd!"

Titters of amusement rippled through the sabha hall.

Tyrak looked around, furious. "Silence when the king speaks!" he roared.

He turned back to Jarsun, arm outstretched, finger pointing accusingly. "Stop trying to twist this around. What difference does it make whether Vessa spoke the prophecy to one man or a hundred thousand? The point is, he prophesied the Slayer would be born, that he would be the eighth son of my sister Kewri by her husband, Vasurava. And that prophecy has in fact come to pass. The Slayer has been born! What I want to know is, what in bleeding hell you intend to do about it! Answer me, father-in-law dearest."

Jarsun sat back on the throne in the attitude of a man who belonged there. It was the look of a man in complete control of his faculties, calmly contemplating before speaking his mind.

Silence prevailed in the sabha hall.

Tyrak realized he had openly confronted Jarsun now. He felt sweat pop from the crown of his head and trickle down his skull. The nape of his neck prickled with a sense of impending threat.

*You've pushed him too far now, you fool,* warned his sensible human side.

*So be it.* The demoniac side laughed scornfully. *Let's have it out right here and now!*

There was little doubt about which side ruled Jarsun. The Krushan replied with unctuous calm, "I intend to do absolutely nothing, son-in-law."

Tyrak laughed. The sound was shockingly hollow in the vastness of the sabha hall. "Nothing! That's all I expected of you!"

"But I expected far more of you, Tyrak," Jarsun went on. Now he stood, slowly and with great dignity, moving with fluid grace to the end of the dais, then pausing to face the rapt audience. "When I sent you here to Arrgodi all those years ago, I expected you to take a very different course of action. Instead, what did you do?"

Tyrak stared up at him, puzzled. What was the man talking about? What was this new ploy? Tyrak had outwitted him by making him admit he could do nothing to stop the Slayer. He had won, damn it! Why wouldn't Jarsun shut up, or at least offer his regrets to Tyrak now? Why couldn't he just let Tyrak lose gracefully?

"You usurped your father's throne, imprisoning the great king Ugraksh, perhaps the greatest ruler of this nation since the great Arrgo himself." Excited murmurs rippled through the court at this unexpected praise of their rightful king. "Then you embarked on a mindless campaign of death and destruction for over a decade, under the pretext of stopping an alleged 'Slayer' that you claimed had been prophesied. And who was this Slayer intended to kill? You, of course! Because as an immature, thoughtless, patricidal and matricidal boy, you assumed that you were the most important person in the whole universe. So you created this myth of a fictional Slayer who would rise one day from your sister's womb and destroy you, and through the perpetuation of this myth, you brought this proud kingdom almost to its knees."

Jarsun gestured with one hand to the audience, as if asking, *Is it not so?* Tyrak glanced around with startled eyes and saw several heads bobbing, faces rapt with admiration. He could not believe this was actually happening.

Jarsun acknowledged his audience's response. For a moment, Tyrak saw his intent set eyes and felt sure that this was the moment when his father-in-law would attack and kill him without compunction. But Jarsun opened his arms in a clear gesture of peace and conciliation as he descended each successive step from the dais, his words carefully chosen and delivered to match his actions in rhythm and pace.

"Now it is time for you to put this mad delusion out of your head, my son. There is no Slayer of Tyrak! It is a product of your own fevered imagination. You were in the grip of demoniac forces all these years, and they worked their will through you. But I have released you from their grip. The results are visible for all to see."

Jarsun reached the bottom of the dais and gestured at Tyrak, showing him off to the court. "What was once monstrous and bestial is once more a man. Celebrate your return to humanity, Tyrak! Once I have fulfilled my promise to your father and completed my work here, I shall leave Mraashk to continue my imperial expansions and consolidation. As it is, I am neglecting my own empire to aid my friends the Arrgodi nations here. I am an outsider and will soon be gone. You, however, are a son of this nation, a lord of this great court, a master of the Mraashk. You are rightful heir to the Arrgodi throne and a potential ruler of all the Arrgodi kingdoms. History is yours for the making. Give up these foolish delusions, these fruitless quests for this mythical Slayer. There is no Slayer! The people desire a Deliverer, that is true. They are weary of the constant rebellions and uprisings by various Arrgodi factions. It is time to complete the great initiative to which your father devoted the last years of his reign and consolidate this great race into one united coalition. The very republic Arrgo envisaged! You can be king of that nation, Tyrak. You can be the Deliverer they desire. Be a man, step up and grasp your future with both hands. The world awaits you."

And in a gesture that Tyrak could never have expected or foreseen had he lived a thousand lifetimes, Jarsun gripped Tyrak's shoulder tightly with one iron fist and gestured up the dais at the Arrgodi throne itself. "Go on, my son. Seat yourself in your rightful place. Yesterday, you were cursed as a demon. Today you are a man again. Now become the king you are destined to be."

The roar of approval that met the end of Jarsun's speech drowned out everything else for the next several minutes.

Jarsun smiled at him, his brow lowered in that peculiar way he had of looking down while looking up at the same time, and between his slightly parted lips, the tip of a divided tongue flickered and snapped as tautly as a whip.

Tyrak stared into the translucent grey eyes of his father-in-law and realized he had only two choices left to him now: to bow gracefully to Jarsun, acknowledge him as the superior man, then accept as a magnanimous "gift" his own throne and crown. Or attack, attempt to kill Jarsun, and most likely die in the attempt. He had only a split second to make the choice, but in a sense it had been made for him the day he went to Morgol in search of the man who would become his guru and guide, replacing his own father in time. The events of today and of the past several months were merely a seal of authority stamped upon that choice. A formalization. It was only his own seething rebelliousness that insisted he could still choose between the two options available to him: Bow. Or be humiliated in certain defeat.

He bowed.

## 2

Tyrak was in a state of shocked bemusement. Shocked because he could not begin to fathom the machinations of Jarsun's politicking; his mind was not built to comprehend such things. Bemused because he didn't know what to expect next. The confrontation in the sabha had turned his head around and spun it like a top until his entire worldview was blurry.

Apart from that, he was experiencing time leaps that further addled his consciousness. He never knew if he would be able to complete a conversation or finish eating a mouthful of food before the next leap took him. The irregular pattern confused him even more. Sometimes he lost months; at other times, a week or three — he would fall sleep one night in spring and wake one morning in summer. Some leaps were only a few minutes or a few hours long, leaving him in a constant state of disorientation and readjustment. During the interim, he would apparently have been talking, eating, drinking, living, breathing as normal, but in fact that was only a drug-induced walking coma. He went through his days feeling as if he had not slept or eaten or rested properly, meeting palace staff who greeted him with condescending familiarity while he had no recollection of ever having met them before, and even the stable dogs, who had always feared and respected him when he was a giant, now barked and curled their lips back to threaten him; one attacked him viciously, mauling his arm as the watching guards only looked on and laughed as he cried out for them to put the damn beast down.

Bahuka ran the day-to-day affairs of the kingdom now, through Chief Minister Shelsis, using Captain Pradynor to maintain law and order and an elaborate hierarchy filled entirely by new faces loyal only to Jarsun. Bahuka was little more than a spare tongue and pair of hands for Jarsun himself. Tyrak meanwhile was barely tolerated as the pale silhouette of a king. Within hours of the end of the sabha session in which Jarsun had so graciously granted Tyrak his own throne, the sham of that show had been obvious. The only faint flicker of relief was the God-Emperor's public announcement that he would be departing shortly and the constant messages that arrived each day for him. Sooner or later, he must leave Mraashk to join his armies and continue his campaign or risk losing the valuable ground he had gained. But until then, each day was agony to Tyrak. The manner in which Jarsun willfully excluded Tyrak from any discussion or decision of importance, while continuing to be patronizing and demonstrating his fatherly affections, was infuriating.

At night, he lay awake on his silken sheets, ripping them apart with frustration as he tried to think of a way out of his predicament. How had he lost so much power so quickly? Or perhaps he had never had the power at all? Perhaps he had always been Jarsun's stooge but hadn't realized it. He had heard of puppet kings and child emperors whose kingdoms were actually run by shrewd ministers, mothers, or preceptors. But a father-in-law? Well, why not? One backroom kingmaker was as likely as any other.

What truly infuriated him was his lack of power.

The old Tyrak would have torn apart buildings and regiments, taken on the Eoch Assassins, or even Jarsun's whole army, rather than stand for this treatment.

But this Tyrak couldn't face Bahuka or Agha or any one of Jarsun's lieutenants or allies, let alone risk incurring the wrath of Jarsun himself in an all-out physical confrontation.

He had no supporters to foment and stoke a revolt or coup of some kind. His years of debauchery and butchery had made him the most reviled ruler of Mraashk — and the most despised and disregarded now. He had no friends left. He had imprisoned his father and mother, placed his own sister and her husband under house arrest, murdered her first seven children, and slaughtered countless other infants in the kingdom. He had even ordered Bane and Uaraj and the rest of his soldiers to kill their own newborns! His desperate quest to prevent the birth of the Slayer had cost him everything; he trusted nobody, allowed no one to come close to him.

And ultimately, as he fretted and fumed and tossed and turned, one thought came to him over and over again.

The Slayer was responsible for all this.

If not for the prophecy, Tyrak would have ruled Arrgodi with an iron hand, would have indulged his every lust and his love of violence, and eventually won the grudging and fearful respect of the people. A dictator was better befriended than antagonized; even he knew that much about politics. He would have been a great dictator, he thought.

In due course, once the Arrgodi were united and in his grasp, he would have allied openly with Jarsun and aided his father-in-law in his campaign of conquest. Together, they could have taken not just the subcontinent but other parts of the world as well. If Jarsun sought to be the God-Emperor, then Tyrak could certainly have been Demigod-Emperor alongside him. Like father-in-law, like son-in-law.

But that damned prophecy had forced him to change his entire list of priorities.

Because of his fear of the Slayer, a fear that wretch Vessa had instilled in his heart, he had devoted most of his reign to the persecution of his sister and brother-in-law and their supporters, leaving him with little time or awareness of anything else. And in the end, what had he accomplished? Nothing! The Slayer had still been born and was out there somewhere. Jarsun could say anything he pleased: Tyrak knew the Slayer existed, was real, and was growing day by day in strength and power. One day, he would be strong enough and powerful enough to come destroy Tyrak. And in this all-too-pitiful mortal state, Tyrak would not stand a chance of survival.

The Slayer was responsible for everything.

The very day he had been born, Tyrak's own decline had begun.

At times, he even wondered if what Jarsun had truly wanted was for the Slayer to be born and to escape unharmed.

Then he dismissed that possibility as absurd. Whatever else Jarsun was, he was no fool.

The Slayer was also the Deliverer. That meant he would champion the rights of the people. And if the people did not want Tyrak to rule them, they desired Jarsun even less. Tyrak knew he was not very shrewd or politic, but of this much he was certain. The Slayer was Jarsun's enemy as much as Tyrak's nemesis. Once he was done with Tyrak, he would go after Jarsun. And if he was powerful enough to escape Tyrak even while yet a newborn, then how much more powerful would he be once he was fully grown?

He had to act soon. Somehow, he must find and assassinate the Slayer before he gained his full power.

But how?

He had no power himself.

**There is a way. But it shall require the assistance of Jarsun.**

Tyrak started from his bed. "Who's there?"

A shadowy figure moved through his darkened bedchamber. He could see the way it cut the faint moonlight that came in through the verandah, but not the person.

**It is I, Vessa.**

"You!" He almost lunged across the chamber in anger. "You ruined my life! Your prophecy —"

**Saved your life. Had I not forewarned you of the coming of the Slayer, you would certainly have been destroyed by now.**

Tyrak reached for a weapon. He had lost confidence to such an extent he no longer bothered wearing a sword or even a dagger. Now he found nothing on the bed or chair and had to grope around on the floor as his fear mounted. In the darkness, he could find only a long wooden object of some kind. He wielded it but did not attack. "What do you mean, *would have been* destroyed? Your prophecy is the reason I am in this state! Stopping the Slayer became my obsession, costing me my throne, my powers, everything. Now I'm little more than a pawn of Jarsun the Krushan!"

**You are wrong. Had you not been so fierce in your efforts those many years, the Slayer would have been able to slay you the very day he was born. You have no reckoning of his powers.**

Tyrak rubbed his eyes, trying to see in the darkness. All he could make out was a faint vertical shadow against the patch of indigo blue sky visible outside the verandah. "Truly?" he asked.

**Have no doubt. I am a seer of the future and the past. I can track the movements of the great Samay Chakra itself, the primordial Wheel of Time. Everything you did served a purpose.**

"But the Slayer escaped anyway!" Tyrak cried. "He is out there . . . somewhere! Waiting to kill me."

**That is why you must act now to stop him.**

Tyrak put down the length of wood. It appeared to be a broom left under his bed by the cleaners. "How?" he asked miserably, sitting again on his bed. "I have no powers left. I cannot even expand myself anymore. And this wretched loss of time I experience . . . Even if I plan to do something, I can never be sure of seeing it through to the end. My life is a living hell!" He buried his face in his hands, on the verge of tears.

**It is all Jarsun's doing.**

Tyrak jerked his head up. "What?"

**He prepared a special compound that his henchman Bahuka puts in your food and drink. It causes the effects of which you speak.**

Tyrak regained his feet, his hands clenched into fists, fingernails digging into his palms hard enough to draw blood. "I WILL KILL HIM!"

**That is quite impossible. Jarsun is beyond your ability to kill. Even the Slayer himself could not harm him if he desired. But I can show you how to regain your powers and take control of your life.**

Tyrak considered this briefly. There was something peculiar about the great sage's offer. "Why?" he asked at last, tilting his head suspiciously. "Why do you assist me thus? What purpose does it serve for you? What do you desire from all this?"

**That is not important. All that matters is that I can help you. And I do not see anyone else willing or able to do that at the present moment. Am I correct?**

Tyrak's shoulders slumped. "Yes. I have no one," he said miserably.

**Then sit quietly and listen while I instruct you.**

Tyrak sat.

And listened.

**There is a woman in your employ. Her name is Ladislew . . .**

## 3

The moon was well risen and halfway across the night sky when Ladislew made her way to Tyrak's palace annex. From the lights still glowing in the main palace residential complex and the fact that Pradynor had not yet returned home, she knew that Jarsun was still sitting with his underlings. There had been a time when Pradynor had been far more than a mere tool of another man; he had desired a command of his own, to be a land owner and to rule and live free. It was one of the things that attracted Ladislew to him at the time. Now he thought the earth and sky and sun and moon of Jarsun, and all his own ambitions had been long forgotten. She had tired of even discussing it with him. There was no point anymore.

She paused outside the high wall. No lights gleamed or flickered on the top floor of Tyrak's annex. She saw that the sentries who ought to be on duty were nowhere to be seen; there were no guards patrolling the grounds either.

She frowned. She was aware of the change in power and stature since she and Pradynor had arrived with Bahuka's entourage. She knew that Tyrak was considered an impotent figurehead now, merely the limp hand holding the royal seal that sanctioned Jarsun's decisions and orders. But she had not thought he was this neglected. To leave a ruler's private quarters thus unguarded, this was beyond negligence. But she knew that Jarsun did not make mistakes of this nature. If he had left Tyrak unguarded, it was because he genuinely wished him dead. And what better way to have it done than by one of his own disgruntled or disaffected citizens! If Tyrak had not yet faced any assassination attempts — or at least, no successful ones — it was probably only because the very presence of the Krushan and his legendary feared associates was enough to make any Arrgodi want to keep his distance from the royal quarter. But it was only a matter of time before Jarsun left; soon Tyrak's many enemies would realize that he was improperly guarded at night.

She wondered if Tyrak himself realized it. He must.

She was mildly disappointed. She had hoped to meet some resistance on the way in. It had been several weeks since her last active mission, and she was itching to engage again. There was also something curiously thrilling about killing her own husband's guards, no doubt handpicked by him to work in this prestigious royal quarter.

But nobody challenged her, called out, or barred her way as she scaled the wall, dropped over the side, and strolled to the darkened portal. Somewhere in the shadows along the wall, a feline meow rose plaintively, and she saw the shadow of a tail flicking back and forth, but apart from that, nothing. There seemed to be no guard dogs around either, judging from the insolent way the cat called out and roved the grounds freely.

She made her way up the stairs, sensing the emptiness of the house. Not a soul stirred, not a sound disturbed the night. This new annex had been built far, far back from the main palace. It was almost an outhouse in terms of the overall layout. She knew that that itself was a sign of Jarsun's obvious campaign to humiliate Tyrak. But its spacious interiors were lavishly decorated and furnished as befitted a prince regent, if not a king. Far more lavishly than the official residence of the captain of the guards.

The bedchamber was larger than her own house, for one thing. And the verandahs were huge, surrounding the room on two sides in a crescent. Gossamer drapes rose and fell on every gust of night wind, and moonlight was the only illumination, silvering anything that reflected or shone or glittered. The sleeping area was a dark morass of shadows. She could not see anyone sitting or lying there. But she could smell him unmistakably. He was there, all right.

"You said moonrise," the voice said out of the darkness.

She shrugged, then realized he might not see the action in this shadowy dimness. "I am here, am I not? What urgent business do you have that you needed to see me alone in your private chambers at night?"

A shadow stirred among the many shadows around the bed. "You chose the place and time, remember? I merely wished to speak with you. You could have elected to meet in the middle of the riding grounds at high noon. Instead you chose here and now. I should be the one asking why."

She grinned. "So you're not as stupid as they say you are — and as you look."

"I'm very stupid. But I learn something new every day."

"What have you learned about me?" she asked, challenging him.

The shadow moved again, and this time she was certain he was standing now, beside the bedpost closest to her. It was still several yards away, but she found herself wondering idly if he was clothed or if, in this warm weather, he slept without garments.

"I have a proposition for you."

She smiled lazily, then shook her hair back off her face, using both hands to sweep it over her shoulders. "There is nothing you have to offer that interests me."

He was silent for a moment. The moonlight streaming through the open verandahs altered slightly, and her eyes had adjusted further to the darkness. She could now make out his silhouette. He was standing by the bed. She could not tell if he was clothed or not, but he was definitely not armed. There was a certain way he would have to stand if he was carrying a weapon, any weapon. She could tell.

"Yet you came," he said after the pause.

She stroked her hair again, running her fingers through it. She had washed it that afternoon and scented it, and it felt sensuous. "I am bored. There is nothing for me to do here in your great city. I was happy for the diversion."

"What I have to offer is a great diversion. If you choose to see it that way."

She walked slowly across the chamber. The floor was cool to her bare feet. She stood before the verandah, enjoying the soft breeze that gusted in waves. Moonlight lit the lower half of her body. It made her fair skin seem milky white. She thought she could feel the moonlight and that it was cool, but of course moonlight had no temperature.

"I think you are mistaking me for my husband," she said, her back to him, to the whole chamber. "He is the captain of your guard. He is under your command, not I."

"Your husband cannot accomplish the task I require. Only you are capable of it."

She turned her head to glance over her shoulder. A smile of contemptuous irony played on her lips. Who did this fellow think he was? What a fool! "Flattery will get your nowhere. Certainly not into your bed. Not if I do not choose to play along. I am my own woman. Ask anyone, they will tell you. Ask Pradynor."

"What I seek is far more than the pleasures of your flesh. Will you not understand that?"

Her smile widened. "The great prince grows impatient. Will you have me bound in chains and whipped now? Decapitated? Thrown into your dungeon and tortured? What terrible punishment will you inflict on me if I refuse your proposition?"

"None. You are free to leave at any time. I will not force you to aid me. I respect you too greatly for that."

She turned around, surprised. "Respect me? You? The legendary Marauder? The Tyrant of Arrgodi? You are a legend in your own time, Tyrak! Your atrocities, brutalities, slaughter, massacres, genocides . . . Even for one of Jarsun's minions, you are extraordinary in your reputation for cruelty. What do you know of respecting women?"

"I respect a Maatri. Especially a Maha-Maatri such as yourself."

She went silent. Of all the things she might have expected, this was not one of them. She looked around, alert, but there was no danger, no threat. Only Tyrak, alone. And she did not fear him. The only one she feared was Jarsun, and he was not near; she would have smelled him a mile away — in fact, she *could* smell him. He was about *half* a mile away, in the main palace complex. This was not some ploy on Tyrak's part. Whatever game he was playing, he was playing it alone.

"I don't know what you mean," she said stiffly. *He's bluffing; he does not know anything. Somehow, he has got hold of some lopsided rumor or idle piece of gossip and is pretending that it means more than it does.*

"I think you do," said Tyrak.

He stepped away from the bed, emerging from the shadows, coming toward the light very slowly, one step every two or three sentences, like a wolf moving toward its prey.

"A well-wisher told me who you really are."

She showed him a look of amusement, careful not to let her concern show. "I am Ladislew, the wife of your captain of guards." Inwardly, she thought, *He knows. I am found out!*

"In Arrgodi, you choose to call yourself Ladislew. But back home in Reygar, from where you hail originally, you were Shinira, one of the High Maatri. The leaders of the matriarchy that governs the cities of the Red Desert that loosely refer to themselves as Reygistan."

She laughed, doing her best to make it sound spontaneous and sincere. "I have never even been to Reygistan. I am a Gwannlander, a foreigner to Arrgodi, but grassland is all I know."

He nodded. "You would, of course, deny it. You left Reygar when Dirrdha laid siege to the city, and came to Gwannland, where you met Pradynor, seduced, and married him. But your ultimate goal was to come here to Arrgodi and await Jarsun's next visit."

She put her hands on her hips, trying for an expression of mockery and derision. "You must be one of those culturally enlightened princes one hears about in the Burnt Empire. The ones who play musical instruments, dance, or compose ballads in their spare time. You definitely have a gift for invention! Since you have created such an elaborate fictional history for me, tell me more. I am amused and entertained. Tell me, why would I have awaited Jarsun's return?"

"Because you wish to assassinate him. That is your goal, your mission. When Dirrdha laid siege to Reygar, it was with the backing of Jarsun. The Krushan seeks to seize control of all Reygistan to form what he calls the Reygistan Empire. *His* Reygistan Empire. Dirrdha alone could never have raised an army or resources sufficient to take Reygar."

She raised an eyebrow. "And who, pray tell, is this person 'Dirrdha'?"

"The brother of Queen Drina of Reygar. He resented the matriarchy, blaming it for all the social ills and injustices of Reygar, and tried to steal the throne from his sister by force. She suppressed the uprising, killed all his supporters, and banished him from Reygar. He turned to banditry, forced to fend for himself by preying on wagon trains on the Red Trail. Until Jarsun found and recruited him as his puppet king of the proposed Reygistan Empire."

Tyrak paused, and said with some bitterness, "Just as he found and recruited me as his puppet for the proposed Arrgodi Empire."

Even in the dim light, she could see that he was ashamed and angry, but was controlling his emotions. She was surprised: the Tyrak about whom she had heard so many stories was not one to control his emotions — or his impulses. Apparently, the years since he had usurped his father's throne had mellowed him. Or more likely, serving under Jarsun for this long had taught him necessary survival instincts. Even predators fear other, much greater and fiercer predators. And as she knew only too well, no living predator matched Jarsun's ferocity and capacity for cruelty. In comparison, even Tyrak's long list of crimes could not compete.

Not the least bit sympathetic — he was still a monster, if only a smaller monster than the one he served — she decided to throw him a bone. He had said enough to earn himself the death penalty from Jarsun; perhaps there was a deal of some kind to be made here tonight, after all.

"And so you believe that I came here incognito and embedded myself in your kingdom, with the mission of assassinating the God-Emperor?"

He did not reply. His silence was assent enough.

She went on. "Then why have I not done so already?"

"The Krushan are not easy to kill. Jarsun, harder than any. Legions of assassins have spent their lives in vain. You wouldn't make it past his henchmen, let alone survive a direct encounter with the man himself." The bitterness was back in his voice. "That is the root of his arrogance. He considers himself invulnerable. Perhaps he is."

She was silent for a long moment. Somewhere in the night, a kole bird sang a mournful series of notes. It received no reply. There had been roast kole served at the feast tonight: it was considered a delicacy in Morgolia and had no doubt been served in Jarsun's honor. Kole birds mated for life. That lonely male out there would receive no response tonight or any other night; its mate was somewhere inside Jarsun's flat belly, being digested.

"Let me play along with your fanciful scenario," she said. "It amuses me. So I am a Maha-Maatri from Reygar, dispatched by the matriarchy on a mission to assassinate the enemy responsible for the wolf at our door. I have successfully infiltrated your court and bided my time until Jarsun's arrival. But even though the Krushan is now here, I dare not attack him because I stand no chance of success. Then what is the point of my being here at all?" Now it was her turn to laugh bitterly. "There's little point in going to all that effort and making such an arduous journey just to sit around and watch the bastard feasting and fornicating to his heart's content, is there? Why would I do that?"

Tyrak walked toward her, stopping a hand's breadth from where she stood. The swath of moonlight had moved again, rising as the moon dipped toward the horizon, and it illuminated him partly. His thighs were muscular and as thick as sala tree trunks. His torso was bare and hairless, layered with slabs of muscle and taut sinew. He was as attractive as she had thought, and then some. He reached out and touched her shoulder. It was a gentle touch. His fingers lingered there, as his eyes looked deep into her own, asking for permission.

"What is it you want of me?" she asked. She was intrigued, aroused, seething with something she had not felt for a very long time. Long before Pradynor, long before any man, back when she had shunned the race of men entirely and had been a creature of the forest and the earth, burning ghats and crossroads, springs and riverbanks, caves and mountain crags. Back when she had been simply Maatri. When all women had been Maatri and there were no other women but Maatri.

He lowered his hand upon her chest. "To begin with, to know if the legend is true."

"Which legend is that?" she said, smiling. "There are so very many, after all. Arthaloka is a land of legend and myth."

A cloud was passing over the moon. She could see the shape and body of the cloud eating away the patch of moonlight that illuminated him and the floor around him. It was moving quickly, consuming him with darkness.

"The legend that your breasts give out poisoned milk, the milk of the Cosmic Churning itself. The Halahala."

She swallowed. Yes, Tyrak knew, then. He must have had contact with someone far more knowledgeable to learn this much. This intrigued her.

There were forces at work here, powerful, unseen forces that suggested a swirling eddy. Perhaps she—and Tyrak—might ride that eddy and overcome Jarsun. It was still a suicide mission, as it had always been, but perhaps there might be a way to knock a chink in the Krushan's impenetrable armor if the two of them joined together.

"And if I say yes?"

"Then I would like to see for myself."

"And how do you propose to do that?"

The cloud began to cover him completely, but in the last patch of moonlight, she could see the white of his teeth gleaming as he smiled. "There is only one way for me to be sure." He paused, eyes glistening at her in the darkness. "If you permit."

She surprised herself by baring her breasts to his mouth, and he bent low, worshipping them.

"You may," she whispered.

The cloud consumed the moon, and the darkness consumed them both.

## 4

Once as a child, Tyrak had tasted a potion being mixed by the royal vaid. He did not know what it was until much later: snake venom in the process of being turned into antivenin. A noxious concoction. He had deliberately consumed it to attract attention to himself. Acting out. His father had been away at another of his endless campaigns of conquest and had returned three days earlier, only to sequester himself within the queen's private chambers. Tyrak did not know exactly what they were doing in there for so many days and nights, but he had an idea, and it infuriated him.

He was even more incensed by the fact that his father had not yet come to him. He felt ignored, unwanted, fatherless. It brought back some ancient memory from his birth, when he arrived into the mortal world aware of his true nature and of the true nature of the creature that had sired him upon his mother. Coupled with that awareness had been the knowledge, terrible in its immutability, that his true father would never spend a single moment with him for as long as he lived. He knew this because that father, the urrkh who had begotten him had told him so, taking cruel pleasure in imparting this heartbreaking piece of information to his just-birthed son.

*You will never see me again, mortal-spawn,* he had sneered derisively. *Live your wretched life in the prison of your mortal flesh!* And he had roared away like the wind, leaving only a dust whorl that spun in the empty courtyard, frightening horses and passing courtiers.

So Tyrak had decided that whenever Ugraksh returned from another battle, or war, or campaign of conquest, or whatever the hell he had gone for and ignored his son yet again, he would do something to make himself seen. He had seen the concoction the royal vaid, his father's own physician, had prepared to give to some unfortunate minister who had stepped on a cobra, and had picked it up and drunk it whole.

He would never forget the unspeakable sensation. The noxious mixture had the consistency of raw egg white and the taste of . . . a taste like nothing he had ever had before or since. And it had scorched his insides going down, like pure rage distilled into liquid form. It had taken him a week to recover from its effects. But to everyone's surprise but his own, it had not killed him. The thrashing he received from his father when he was fully recovered almost did, because back then Ugraksh had been a very different man, *a hard king for hard times,* to quote his own favorite phrase. Tyrak had forgotten the thrashing — one of several he received in his childhood and youth, worsening in intensity and frequency as he grew, until his father's transmogrification to a proponent of *nonviolence* and *nonaggressive governance,* his new favorite phrases. But he vividly remembered drinking the snake venom. And he remembered how it had made him feel after he drank it.

But this, this was far beyond that potency!

This was poison in its highest form. The Halahala itself, if the legend was true. And he had no reason to disbelieve the legend. Vessa had no reason to lie, and even if he had lied, what was the worst that could happen? This fluid that Tyrak was now suckling and swallowing could be mere milk.

He had expected it to be noxious, nauseating, toxic, like the cobra venom.

It was the very opposite.

It was the sweetest, most intoxicatingly delectable thing he had ever consumed in liquid form.

And the instant it touched his lips, tongue, and palate, its potency was undeniable. This was not mere milk. This was magic, sorcery, urrkh maya . . .

It was like drinking liquid power. And as it flowed through his body, he felt himself electrified as if struck by a bolt of lightning.

He cried out, tearing his mouth away and falling back onto the floor. The cloud that had come across the moon, leaving them both in darkness, had passed on, and he could see Ladislew, still standing with her back to the verandah, silhouetted by moonlight.

He felt his senses warp and burn, his nerve endings flaring and firing, his veins and arteries roaring as the Halahala coursed through them, entering his heart, his lungs, his brain, his vital organs . . . He felt the divine poison infiltrate his very bones, his flesh, the cells of his body. He felt it wash through him like a flash flood through a long-dried riverbed. His consciousness exploded and altered. And the world around him blurred into nothingness as he transcended to a different plane of awareness.

## 5

He returned to his senses to find Ladislew standing out on the verandah, leaning on the balustrade and staring at the horizon. The faint light of a new day was visible in the eastern sky, which told him he had been lost to the world for half of the night. He lifted himself on his arms and was surprised at the ease with which he was able to get to his feet. Not merely the ease born of well-exercised muscles, but something else. He felt himself fueled by the power of the Halahala as it continued to work its way within his body, catalyzing enzymes and engendering new growth. This was not like his earlier strengthening. He felt more powerful, yet in a completely different way.

He decided to try to expand himself. He strained for several moments, without success. Damn. He tried again. And again

Ladislew heard his grunting and straining, and turned. She came to the doorway and stood leaning against the jamb, watching him. A faint expression flickered around her mouth. Not quite a smile. Not quite anything.

"The compound Jarsun has had you consume these past months will have altered your metabolism drastically," she said. "I doubt you will be able to regain your earlier powers. Apart from everything else, he is a formidable vaid and knows his herbs and mixtures well. He once gave a pregnant woman —"

Tyrak raised a hand. "Spare me."

She shrugged. "Also, the Halahala is a poison. You did know that before you chose to consume it, didn't you? And the quantity you consumed . . ." She shook her head deprecatingly. "I have killed entire tribes with less than that much, simply by mixing it in the well from which they drew their drinking supply. They were wiped out within the day."

He grunted in response, dropped to the floor, and began pushing it. Frustrated by his inability to expand, he had energy to burn. Two hands proved too easy, so he switched to one, then to a fist, then to the tips of four fingers, three, two, and finally, he was pushing himself on the tip of a single finger, using the pressure caused by the awkward angle to work his abdominal and back muscles as well. He pushed past a hundred count and kept going. He felt as if he could continue this all day and still not be tired.

She watched him speculatively. "On the other hand . . ."

He looked up at her from the floor. "What?" Speaking seemed no harder than it would have had he been seated and talking. He continued pushing. Three hundred . . .

"The very fact that you are still alive and clearly not harmed by its effect . . ."

"Yes?" Three hundred and forty-four . . . forty-five . . . forty-six . . . He was moving faster now, switching to a different finger with every ten count, barely an effort . . .

"Suggests that there is something else going on inside you that even I cannot understand. What exactly was it that you desired when you called me here last night?"

"To consume the Halahala, regain my powers," he said. Four hundred and two, three, four . . . *Faster now, must go faster . . .*

She gestured at him. "Looking at you, I'd say you regained *something*."

He grunted in frustration and pushed himself off the floor, hard. He rose up but instead of merely returning to a standing posture as he had desired, he found himself rising up, up, until his upper back and head struck the ceiling ten yards overhead and broke the plaster coating, sending a shower of white powder and chunks raining down. Returning to the ground, he landed on his feet as easily as if he had just jumped an inch. But the marble slab underfoot cracked with a rending groan and the vibrations seemed to ripple through the entire chamber.

Ladislew looked around, then at the ceiling, which now bore the shape of his skull, then down at the cracked marble floor. "Clearly, there has been some effect."

She walked toward the chamber's entrance. "I shall be taking my leave now, Prince Tyrak. It has been an enlightening and interesting experience. Which is more than I expected. And in case you failed to comprehend the subtext, that is a compliment I rarely pay men."

He was at her side and grasping her shoulder in an eye blink, even though the distance between them had been over fifteen yards. She raised her eyebrows, reacting to his speed but not commenting on it.

"What does it mean, these changes that are happening to me? Where will they end? Will I be restored to my former powers or . . . I beg you, give me some answers before you go."

She shrugged his hand off with surprising ease. He was startled by the power in her limbs, even greater than his newfound (and growing) strength. "I don't know how you learned the truth about me, but I suspect you are not intelligent enough or worldly wise enough to have gained such knowledge on your own. No man is. Therefore it must have been imparted to you by someone of a far superior stature. A stone god or an urrkh devil perhaps, for reasons best known to them. Or a great sage, for it is their job to know such things, and they do love manipulating the affairs of mortals." She paused. "Not that either of us are mere mortals, but compared to them, we may as well be."

She looked at him closely, watching for his reaction. He was careful not to reveal any trace of an expression. Finally, she shrugged.

"In any case, it doesn't matter who it was, or what the purpose. I think it has to do with you rather than me. I was merely a tool serving your purpose in this matter. I've served that purpose. Now I shall go."

She started to move away.

He reached for her again, and she said sharply, "Touch me again, and I break your hand. You may think you're strong, but don't forget where that new strength came from!"

"But Jarsun? Our common cause?"

She shook her head. "Not so fast. You are still Jarsun's lackey, not to mention his son-in-law. I still don't know how much to trust you. You may well be playing a power game here, and I don't want to be the piece that gets sacrificed. If your desire to turn against Jarsun is genuine, then perhaps we may find a way to work together. But if you betray me —"

"You don't understand," he said. "I need you. You are the only way I can regain my strength. Vess —" He broke off. "I was told that imbibing the Halahala venom from your breasts would counter the potion Jarsun has been secretly drugging me with, enabling me to grow strong again. When I am strong enough to face him, I will fight him and kill him."

She laughed then, amazed at his naive arrogance. "Fool you are, if you believe that. You cannot kill Jarsun. He is Krushan. Do you think the Burnt Empire dominates our world out of sheer happenstance? The Krushan are wedded to stonefire, and stonefire is the stuff of which the entire universe was born. Even the stone gods are subject to its power and its laws. The Krushan ascend, they do not die, and they only ascend when they choose. No mortal being can end their lives, no matter how powerful —" She gestured down at her own chest, the garment damp from the excess that had leaked after Tyrak had fed. "Or venomous."

He stared up at her with the look of a boy who had just been denied his greatest desire. "But I was told!"

*Yes, by the great sage Vessa,* she thought. So that's who put us together. Interesting play. I wonder what larger game the sage has planned for us both. And how does the little girl fit into all this — what was her name, Krush? She is powerful too, to have opened that passageway that brought me all the way from Reygar to the grasslands in a few moments. I see a master plan unfolding here, and no doubt I am one of the pieces. So be it. As long as I fulfill my mission, I don't care how it benefits anyone else.

She started toward the door, looking back over her shoulder. "Then ask the person who advised you to call on me. If you do not know, that person surely does. That's why they advised you to do this, isn't it?"

And with that, she left.

## 6

After Ladislew had gone, Tyrak prowled the corridors of his private quarters, growing steadily more agitated. Like a heavy meal eaten late at night, he felt the Halahala still being processed within his body, working its way through a series of transformative stages. He had no idea what the eventual result would be, and that simultaneously excited and frightened him. His frustration, fear, and impatience expressed itself in sudden bursts of energy. Striding up and down the corridors, deserted at this early hour because his personal staff was accustomed to his waking around midmorning or even after noon, he suddenly found himself leaping several yards at a time, then flying through the air fast enough to land feet-first on the opposing wall, propel himself back, and thus go bouncing from one wall to the other, until he lost his balance and crashed into a pillar, breaking it almost in half. He sat in the debris, grinning stupidly at his newfound strength and vigor.

He was suddenly overcome by a great thirst. He felt as if a fire raged within his veins and he must quench it at once. He sought out the pot of water in his bedchamber and lifted it in one hand, emptying it into his mouth, spilling much of it on himself. When it was drained, he tossed it aside to smash against the far wall, then went in search of more. He ended up at the drinking trough by the stables, freshly mucked out and filled with clean water. *Almost* clean, anyway. As clean as one could expect horses to drink. He emptied most of the contents of the trough, then paused. He looked down at himself. His belly wasn't distended, nor did he feel the normal fullness that accompanied the consumption of so much fluid. He patted his abdomen; it felt as flat as ever, the ridged muscles moving beneath his palm. Where had all that water gone?

He sat on the edge of the trough and thought about what to do next. Vessa's advice had been more effective than he had expected. Certainly Ladislew had provided the catalyst he had been desperately seeking. Suddenly he was eager to see if the rest of the sage's advice proved as fruitful.

He needed a place to try out his new abilities. To learn for himself what they entailed. Could he actually fly? Or merely leap higher and higher, only to land with successively more destructive force? He must find out! And his strength. How to measure it, test it to its limit?

He thought of going to the palace akhara, a huge semi-enclosed space where the palace guard and most of the senior military officers exercised between shifts. But he did not wish word of his new powers to spread. At any cost, he must keep this a secret from Jarsun. And since Jarsun had eyes and ears everywhere in Arrgodi . . .

He took a horse from the stables. The old syce, Arrgo, looked at him with his usual unnerving expression when he asked for a mount, but somehow had the wits to bring him the biggest and strongest in the stable, a massive battle charger accustomed to carrying men with full battle armor, shield, and weaponry. It was a choice Tyrak would be glad for before he returned, though he did not know it then. He took the horse, got on in a single leap, and rode off at an instant canter, breaking into a full-fledged gallop in a few dozen paces. The horse seemed glad for the exercise and did not complain or turn its head when he rode it off the training field, up the hill bordering the palace complex, and onward through the woods.

He took himself a good thirty miles out of Arrgodi, far from prying eyes or ears. He found a box canyon deep in the woods, where he had once been as a boy. It had only one point of ingress, and due to the high walls and peculiar acoustics, any rider or pedestrian entering the canyon would be heard long before they came into sight. The forest above the canyon was dense and the overhang too sloping and slippery from the recent rains for anyone to watch from above. Here he could do as he pleased with nobody to witness or report back to Jarsun. Not without him spying the spy himself, in which case he would make sure that the only thing the spy would be fit to report was an alarming descent into annihilation.

He began with some brisk running, warming up to leaping, first off the walls of the canyon. He bounced from one rocky wall to the other, a distance of a hundred feet or more, dislodging rocks at first, then punching holes as his speed and intensity increased. He experienced a great exhilaration as he flew from wall to wall, bouncing like the wooden stick in the popular children's game. As his feet hit the canyon walls, he found the impact to be greater, as if he was growing heavier. When he finally stopped, the high sloping walls, rising a hundred and fifty feet aboveground, were pockmarked with holes left by his pounding feet, some a yard or two deep. Rocks and rock dust lay everywhere; it looked like the aftermath of a landslide.

He tried punching the wall next. He found he could punch his way through solid granite without harming himself. Again, as his efforts and concentration intensified, he felt the same sensation of growing heavier. But each time he checked himself, he found he was still the same size as before.

It took him the better part of the morning to understand: his ability to expand had not returned. But the corresponding increase in weight as he expanded had come back.

Earlier, if he grew ten times his normal six feet to, say, sixty feet tall, his weight would grow proportionately.

Now, it seemed, his weight increased if he concentrated hard, and with that increased weight, he gained the ability to pack much more power in each punch or kick or blow. But he stayed the same height and size.

He examined his fist after punching a large boulder to smithereens. Apart from the red dust of the boulder, it had no other marks.

Apparently, he could increase his weight by concentrating, but not his size. He guessed this was a side effect of the compound Jarsun had had him fed daily for the several months.

As the day wore on, he felt the Halahala continuing to work, changing him from within in ways he could not fathom, but he could see no visible signs of his transformation. He looked the same, remained the same size, and was much the same, apart from the considerably increased muscular strength and density.

But it was enough to start. Yes, more than enough.

In the days that followed, he continued to explore the extent and nature of his newfound abilities. When he adjusted his density correctly, the effect it produced was that of turning his flesh and bone and skin harder, heavier, to the point where bone became like iron, flesh grew solid as stone, blood and muscle and tissue and tendon grew as tough as ironwood, and even his skin became as impenetrable as oak. He practiced turning from normal flesh, blood, and bone to this new state until he could achieve full transformation in moments.

Once transformed, he could not only punch a granite boulder to smithereens, he could drill through it with precision if he desired, or pound an entire hill into dust. The proportional increase in weight was remarkable. It was difficult to estimate exactly how heavy he turned after these transformations. There were no scales designed to weigh such heavy loads, after all! But after several successively higher leaps, he tried jumping off the top of the canyon's highest ridge and found himself boring several yards into the ground, through solid-packed earth and rock.

He had never been very good at numbering, but as he clambered out of the hole, he thought that he must surely weigh as much as several elephants—perhaps even several dozen. He had once seen a dozen-odd war elephants driven off the edge of a cliff, and when they landed below, they did not make a crater this deep or large, merely a wide depression in the ground. He suspected that his greater density and smaller size made the difference. He could see that as his ability to focus his power increased, and over time he was able to punch neat fist-sized holes in even the hardest boulder, all the way to the end of his shoulder, then slowly pull his arm out from the hole, leaving the boulder intact. One particular boulder was left looking like a large fruit into which numerous worms had bored holes.

After each practice, he felt the same desperate thirst. Even two or three water bags, enough to slake a company's thirst for days, were merely a few gulps to him in his newly transformed condition. He went in search of a more plentiful source, and on the second day, he found it. An old well, its mouth half covered by overgrown brambles and bushes, probably forgotten when some trade route changed in the past. The bucket was cracked and leaked out half its load before he could winch it up. Frustrated after three or four such half-bucketloads, he leaped into the well, his thirst making him too desperate to think beyond the immediate need. The water was wonderfully cool and refreshing, somewhat heavy with minerals. That suited him perfectly, because mere river water seemed unable to slake his epic new thirsts. He drank to his heart's content, then found himself easily able to climb up the moss-lined brick walls by the simple expediency of punching his fingers into the brick to create handholds and footholds.

Visiting this well became his routine each day after his practice session in the canyon. Each time, no matter how much he drank, his body seemed to miraculously absorb every drop of the water, leaving him as lean and empty-bellied as when he had leaped into the well. He thought it had something to do with the way his body's muscles and cells grew denser and heavier.

He did not understand the philosophy or science behind such things and did not really care. All that mattered was that he was strong again. Strong enough to fight the Eoch Assassins, or even Jarsun's champions. And soon, someday, he would be strong enough to face the Slayer without fear and destroy him. But first, of course, he must find that elusive foe.

Despite his newfound confidence in his abilities and his burning desire to avenge his humiliations, he was careful to keep his practice secret. What success had been unable to teach him, failure had schooled him in quite effectively. He knew better than to show his hand too soon or at the wrong time and place. Even if he no longer feared confrontations with the Eoch Assassins or the minions of the Krushan, he still knew better than to think he was strong enough to take on Jarsun himself. The God-Emperor's martial skills were more greatly feared because they were largely unknown. The effects of his great slaughter had been witnessed several times, but nobody had actually seen him in full battle mode during one of those legendary massacres. The reason was that Jarsun rarely, if ever, left any survivors to tell the tale.

Because Tyrak was so studiously ignored and neglected, it was easy for him to come and go as he pleased. Rarely did anyone ask after him or bother determining his whereabouts. He suspected that Jarsun's spies watched him closely enough to know he rode out and back each day, and he was shrewd enough to float a rumor that he was visiting a woman. Another man's wife. From the old syce, Arrgo, he learned that they bought the rumor without question, even laughing at the foolish prince, wasting his time on dalliances while Jarsun ruled Arrgodi as he pleased. *Tyrak's* Arrgodi. He gritted his teeth when the old man told him these things in his laconic devil-may-care way, but he knew that so long as they laughed at him, they would not suspect him.

The old man knew, though. Tyrak could see it in his eyes.

"Will there be anything further, my lord?" he asked as he took the frothing horse by the bit. Tyrak had practiced increasing his weight while riding today, to judge from the horse's reactions how heavy he became. When the beast began to snort and whinny in panic, he had stopped, but the animal had never trusted him after that, especially since he tried the same thing several more times. Now it reared, white-eyed, as Tyrak walked past, pulling away from him.

Tyrak paused and glanced at the horse, still bucking in the syce's hands. Arrgo seemed unperturbed. Most men would have been at least a little nervous when a half-ton animal grew this agitated and began lashing out with those deadly hooves. The syce appeared as calm as ever, and not for the first time, Tyrak wondered just how old the man really was and what role he had played in his father's coterie before he retired to this menial job.

"A fresh horse tomorrow," Tyrak said, and turned away without waiting for a response. There would be none in any case. Arrgo spoke only when absolutely necessary. It was one of the reasons Tyrak trusted him.

Tyrak increased his pace as he emerged from the woods northwest of Argodi. This region was unforested land, too barren to farm. The arid ground suddenly gave way to plunging dry gulches here, many of them dangerously steep and narrow. The streams at the bottom of those steep gulches were barely muddy trickles, and most were carpeted with the bones of animals that had fallen to their deaths. They only filled up during the monsoon season and a few weeks thereafter. The area was too hostile for habitation, and as a result, it had been overrun by predators.

Tyrak came here to practice his newfound abilities daily, testing the limits of his transformed body, exploring the possibilities, developing his unusual skills further, finding new ways to use them for combat. There was one particular box canyon he had favored at first. But he had long since reduced it to a heap of collapsed rubble. Later, under Ladislew's supervision, he had developed a regime that catered to his particular abilities and strengths. But today, following a daily regime was the last thing on his mind.

He simply ran, feet pounding up chunks of earth, stomping noisily, leaving a dust trail bigger than that left by a herd of stampeding elephants. The ground shuddered beneath his increasing weight.

He was approaching the edge of a gulch, running too fast to stop. Even if he slowed, his weight and momentum would carry him off the edge anyway. So instead of choosing to stop or slow, he ran faster. He launched himself off the edge of a ravine several hundred feet high. The far side was a good fifty yards away. He flew up into the air, wreathed in a dust cloud, and as he hung suspended over certain death for any mortal flesh, he beat his chest and roared his anguish to the skies.

The sound echoed through the gulch below his flailing feet.

His momentum carried him all the way across to the far ridge. He landed in an explosion of dust and shale, cracking the stony back of the ledge. A small avalanche's worth of debris collapsed behind him into the ravine. But he was already racing away, across dry, almost desert-bare terrain, his body so heavy that his feet were embedded a whole yard deep in the surface of the ground. He tore up earth and rocks and roots and stones the way a chariot's wheels might throw up clods of supple soil. He barely felt his thighs moving through solid ground and stone with greater ease than a metal plow could churn through sodden earth. He felt his power, his strength, his invulnerability. It was a palpable thing, as real as the air pumping in and out of his lungs, the sunlight on his face, the scent of freshly broken earth in his nostrils. He felt the very cells of his body resist the onslaught of stone and earth as he tore through the ground, and at that moment he knew that there were no limits to his power. He needed only to learn how to control his body, to focus long and hard enough to increase his density to the point he desired, and he could punch through stone or withstand any force and survive unharmed.

The only problem was focusing that intensely and holding his concentration long enough. But he would master that as well. He would grow stronger than ever before, stronger than anything else or anyone else upon Arthaloka. He would do it for Ladislew. For himself. To prepare himself for the Slayer, the prophesied Deliverer.

He roared his fury to the skies. Then slowed as he saw something ahead. Something alive and mobile.

He came to a halt. The dust cloud settling slowly around him, the long winding trail of furrowed ground stretching for a mile or more in his wake.

He stared at the moving shapes ahead, milling about in confusion and hostility as they sensed the strange being that had approached so unexpectedly.

It was a herd of rhinoceros.

There were at least a dozen of them. It was unusual for them to be together in such numbers; they were mostly solitary creatures. But he did not think about the why or wherefore. He looked at them, and they stared at him suspiciously, lowering their horns and stamping their feet and snorting threateningly. They had young 'uns. That meant they would fight to the death to protect them.

Tyrak did not care.

All he cared about was the fact that they provided an outlet.

He was angry.

He desired something or someone on which to vent his rage.

Humans were insufficient: there was no sport in being able to smash soft bags of pulpy flesh and brittle bone. It was like a boy mashing insects between his thumb and forefinger — as he himself had done when he was a boy.

He needed real sport. Something that would offer opposition. That could withstand his iron blows and stone flesh.

Rhinoceros. What could be more perfect?

He grinned, an inane smile in a reddened face.

Then he began running straight toward the rhino herd. They snorted in surprise, lowering their horns. Four of them charged him at the same time, all large adult rhinoceros. The two smaller ones stayed back, making sounds of distress, and a large one stayed with them — probably a mother or aunt.

Man-urrkh and rhinos thundered at each other with the fury of creatures supremely confident that nothing could withstand their onslaught.

Tyrak had seen rhinos charge at solid wooden walls inches thick and drive their horns through them like nails through soft wood. He had seen them smash human bodies to mangled pulp in Jarsun's sports arenas. He had seen them knock down elephants and pound stone walls until they cracked and shook. He knew the damage these creatures could inflict when enraged or challenged. By charging straight at them, he was invoking their maximum fury. They would not rest now until he was dead.

Unfortunately for them, the rhinos had no idea of the damage he could inflict.

Two-legged being and four-legged creatures met in a thumping impact.

When the dust cleared, two rhinos were lying on their sides in the dirt, their horns shattered and bleeding profusely. The other two milled about in confusion, unable to fathom what had happened. Never in their lives had they encountered a living creature that could withstand their direct charge.

Tyrak stood facing them, arms on his hips, grinning. He was happy now. Still enraged. But happier than he had been some moments ago. He had killed — or at the very least inflicted mortal wounds upon — living beings. That was the one thing that could always lift his mood. Happiness was an opponent best served dead.

He charged the rhinos again.

And again.

And again.

When all four adults were dead, their armor-plated bodies lying broken and bleeding from a dozen wounds, heads and horns torn and ripped and mangled from the terrible impacts, he turned to the surviving adult female and the two young 'uns. They were bleating in distress but still lowering their horns and stamping their feet, ready to defend themselves. That was the thing about rhinos: they were stubborn to the point of death.

He was happy to oblige them.

He charged again. And again. Until there was not a living rhino left.

# 7

He was startled to see eoch sentries at the perimeter of his palace. They did not deign to give him even the dignity of a sideward glance, merely continued to stare fixedly forward, but he sensed their derision and scorn and felt the urge to crush them like flies. That would get them to notice him again! But he reminded himself how hard it had been to regain even this measure of strength, and what Vessa had said when he told him how to achieve it — and thus knew he must keep his strength a secret until the right time and place.

There were eochs lined up along his corridors, a full force. That could mean only one thing: someone very important had come to see him in his private chambers. Uninvited.

He brushed past the eochs and strode forward with deliberate ease. He was pulling off his gloves and whistling when he entered his bedchamber.

Jarsun was waiting. And with him were his usual cronies: Henus and Malevol on either side. Bane and Uaraj off in the corners, skulking and still avoiding Tyrak's gaze. Bahuka, Agha, Baka, Dhenuka, Trnavarta, and with them was Ladislew as well. Shelsis and Pradynor were there too, but from their positions relative to Jarsun, it was evident that they did not enjoy the same favor as the others within the cherished circle of trust. And finally, there were four of the familiar Eoch Assassins, the toughest and most ruthless of the lot. Tyrak knew them from his days with Jarsun. They had always been the first to go into battle and the last to leave a field; their death count was greater than that of entire regiments. The very fact that they were still alive, despite their many years of service, was testimony to their ability to kill and survive against all odds. They barely glanced at Tyrak; he was nothing to them, not even a hint of a possible future threat. That infuriated him more than anything else, but he kept his self-control. He had gained too much ground, expended too much effort to lose it only because of his weakness of temper.

Jarsun was seated on Tyrak's bed, leaning back like an emperor upon his throne, legs crossed casually. Henus and Malevol lounged, as still as bedposts.

"Come, come, Tyrak," the God-Emperor said. "We have much to discuss."

And behind him, Tyrak heard the sound of the chamber doors being shut and bolted.

# 8

"Tyrak, dear Tyrak," Jarsun said, then clicked his tongue sympathetically several times. "It seems there is a revolution brewing behind your back that you are blissfully unaware of, my son."

He paused and glanced at his cronies. "Although, judging from the way you have been these past months, almost anything could be brewing behind your back, and you would hardly know it!"

A round of derisive laughter greeted this quip. Even Ladislew's lips twitched in a sardonic imitation of a smile.

Tyrak stood, impassive.

Jarsun looked at him, chin lowered in his usual way so that his eyes and brow seemed to merge. Like all natural predators, his eyes were close set and intense, and were most accustomed to focusing on the middle distance. His lips were slightly parted and the tip of his split tongue rested on his lower teeth, barely visible. He flicked it out, licked at his left cheek, then drew it into his mouth. "My spies tell me that your Arrgodi are trying to forge an alliance with the Gwannlanders as well as other nations. They will not succeed, of course. The Gwannlanders are far too wise to align themselves with the wrong faction, but the very attempt is an affront to my sovereignty. This kind of rebelliousness cannot be permitted to continue. It undermines the Reygistan Empire and the power of Arrgodi."

Tyrak asked quietly, so quietly that Jarsun would hear part but not all of what he said, "What do you propose to do?"

Jarsun frowned.

Tyrak knew that the God-Emperor was too proud to ask Tyrak to repeat himself. As he had intended, the Krushan heard enough to presume to have understood him.

Jarsun shrugged: "I propose that you quell this rebellion at once, of course! Find the guilty parties, bring them to book, and mete out such punishment as seems —"

Tyrak held up his hand, palm outward, fingers splayed. In a slightly louder but still calm tone, he said, "I did not ask you what I should do. I hardly need advice on how to manage my own kingdom. I asked you what you propose to do."

There was a moment of shocked silence. Even Jarsun seemed at a loss for words. Out the corner of his eyes, Tyrak saw Ladislew turn her head a fraction and look directly at him. He kept his eyes fixed on Jarsun.

The Krushan sat forward on Tyrak's bed, slowly uncrossing his legs. "I see. So you think you know how to manage your own kingdom, do you? Interesting."

Jarsun stood up, now facing Tyrak directly. He came forward a step at a time, pacing his movement with his words as precisely as ever to produce the effect he desired. "In that case, could you explain to me how these rebels have taken matters this far already? Why haven't you done anything about it yet? Instead of standing here and asking me — me — what I propose to do to help you! Why must you always look to me for help and advice? You are not the young green-eared boy who came to me all those years ago, Tyrak. You are a prince regent now. It's time you started learning to behave like one!"

He stopped less than two yards short of Tyrak.

Tyrak chuckled. He permitted himself merely to make the sound, not to hold the snicker more than a second. It was for effect, too.

"I do not seem to be able to make you understand me, Jarsun," he said. "I am asking for neither advice nor help. I need naught from you. I was asking what you intend to do personally! About your own problems! As I said before, I can handle my matters myself. You're right in saying that I'm not the young boy who came to you seeking alliance and military backing to implement the coup I felt was needed to replace my father's senile administration with a more robust and hard-dealing one of my own. I'm a man now. A king in fact. I was a prince regent, it's true. But I have already made the necessary declarations to proclaim myself king officially at the tribal councils as is the age-old custom. With my father still absent, there will be no opposition. I expect your support of course, as you have already offered it. And your military resources and aid, which you have placed at Arrgodi's disposal per the treaties we have signed.

"But other than those things, I was merely asking about you personally, Jarsun. Since your presence here is fomenting rebellion amongst my people, surely you do realize that it's time you ought to be moving on from here. After all, it's you they want to depose, not me. The Arrgodi have never accepted an outsider governing them and never will. So what I was asking, to put it quite clearly this time in order to avoid any further confusion on your part—"

"How dare you!" said Bahuka, stepping forward, his face red with anger, his whip in hand. "Nobody speaks to the God-Emperor in such a manner!"

Jarsun's hand shot out, surprising Bahuka. Without taking his eyes off Tyrak, Jarsun waved Bahuka back.

"But, my lord, he—"

Jarsun gestured a second time. Everyone who knew him knew there would not be a third time. Bahuka restrained himself with a visible effort and stepped back, lowering his whip but keeping it in hand, ready to use again, and his eyes glowered at Tyrak.

"To repeat it one final time," Tyrak went on, as if he had never been interrupted, "when will you be removing your imperial presence from my capital city and kingdom? That is the question I asked you."

Jarsun put his hands behind his back and continued to examine Tyrak. His head tilted slightly, his gaze unwavering, he remained as still as a coiled cobra, but his very absence of motion was fraught with violence. There was powerful threat and aggression in the very lowering of his brows, the narrowing of his eyes, the pursing of his thin lips. Nobody in the chamber moved, all frozen in time and space, awaiting the next course of action of their master.

"So," Jarsun said at last. "The sleeper awakes."

Tyrak saw from the frowns on the faces of the others that none of them understood the reference. He might have missed it too, had he not overheard the old stable hand Arrgo telling the stable boys the legend of Sia of

Aranya and her epic tragedy. Just the night before, Tyrak had put his horse into her box as usual and was leaving the stables when he heard the old Arrgodi's voice, cracked and rough with age, speaking over the chirring of crickets and cicadas, narrating the tale of the warrior princess Sia and her battles against the urrkhlord Ravenous. Ravenous was renowned for sleeping for a great length of time — some said decades, others said centuries — and then warring and feasting for an equal length of time. Tyrak had paused, leaning against the worn wooden boards of the stable wall, sweat drying on his body, and listened with a fascination he could not explain. Sia's legend was one that every child in Arthaloka knew, but retold in old Arrgo's cracked voice, it came alive in a way it never had before for Tyrak.

"To awaken," he said slowly now, "one has to first be asleep."

Jarsun stared at him intently, eyes narrowing to pinpoints in his straight, perfectly symmetrical face. Then suddenly, he relaxed his scrutiny. "Indeed," he said, and flashed an unexpected smile. "Indeed!"

He barked orders in a foreign tongue at his men, prompting them into action with startling speed.

The language was Morgol. Tyrak had learned enough of it during his time with Jarsun to know that it was a command to attack and kill him at once. Or else Jarsun would kill each one of them and then kill Tyrak himself.

The last part was unnecessary. Bahuka was the first to move. Trnavarta, Baka, Agha, and Dhenuka spread out to avoid conflicting with each other's lines of attack. Even Shelsis and Pradynor moved forward, eyes flicking apologetically to Tyrak. Henus and Malevol stayed back, smiling openly now: they hardly expected that their services would be required. Bane and Uaraj glowered, their faces revealing the long-festering resentment and pent-up hatred they had kept hidden this past year, but waited their turn. Ladislew hung back to one side, neither committing to action nor avoiding it. She kept her eyes studiously averted from Tyrak, though he knew better than to look at her directly anyway.

But it was the four eochs closest to Tyrak who were the first to attack.

He had known that would be the case from the beginning. And every step he had taken while speaking, every gesture he had made, apart from serving its purpose in his speech, also served to position him most favorably to receive their attack.

He had also been increasing his body's density as he spoke, extending his words to give himself time.

Now, when the four eochs moved in to kill him, he was ready.

## 9

Tyrak remained standing with the closed door to the bedchamber behind him and the verandah to his right, not moving an inch. He was exactly where he wished to be. If they wanted him, they would have to come from his left, his fore, and his right, and that was exactly what they did.

One eoch slipped out onto the verandah, around a pillar, approaching from Tyrak's blind spot. Two others came at him from the front and left, with the fourth staying just between and behind them both but approaching at the same pace.

He had seen quads of eochs work in the battlefield using similar formations. The first two would attack in perfect coordination, just far enough apart to make it hard for the target to defend against both simultaneously. In moments, with devastating speed, one would strike a blow that forced the target to leap back or otherwise deflect — and that was when the eoch on the extreme right (or, in an open field attack, the eoch coming from behind) would lunge, strike a single blow, then fall back, and the first two would move aside unexpectedly, leaving room for the fourth to come forward and deal the death blow.

The entire maneuver lasted no more than a few seconds, and it was rare for the quad to need more than two strikes. Even as the first two eochs finished their action, they would move on to the next target. And so on, killing with such precision that the enemy often dropped their weapons and ran helter-skelter. Forces that attempted to fight were slaughtered to the last man.

The men watching the eochs move in glanced at one another knowingly. Tyrak was using his peripheral vision to watch the eochs, and his frontal view was occupied by Bahuka. The grizzled veteran snarled and showed his teeth in a lupine threat.

Tyrak made no response. Later, he was proud of that more than anything else he did in that chamber. He had not let Bahuka provoke him at that crucial moment — which, of course, was precisely what the old dog had intended to do.

Bahuka instantly lost his snarl and frowned. This was not on his list of possible reactions from Tyrak, and it disturbed him. He turned to Jarsun.

Tyrak did not see Jarsun's response. He was now focusing on one thing and one thing only: becoming a weapon.

As everyone in the bedchamber assumed, Tyrak was unarmed.

But he didn't need a weapon.

He *was* the weapon.

The first two eochs made their move, their short curved swords blurring through the air with numbing speed as high-pitched, bloodcurdling shrieks issued forth from throats that had, until that instant, been deathly silent.

## 10

The most dangerous thing about the eochs was not their speed or even their razor-sharp swords.

It was their footwork.

The reason most battlefield combat broke up into small units was because warriors attacking en masse could easily get tangled up with one another. Even a regiment seeking to slaughter only a single warrior still had to approach one or two at a time, and two coming at the same time were more likely to get in each other's way than to finish off the solitary opponent.

This was why most gurus of combat cautioned their overzealous acolytes: two against one meant double the chance of success — for the solo warrior! Unless the pair worked in perfect tandem, like dancers in an elaborately rehearsed performance where the slightest misstep meant death, pairs, trios, and quads against a single fighter rarely had any significant advantage to offer. As the same wise gurus also cautioned, the only way to best a single champion was to send a superior champion against them.

But the eochs had turned this basic notion of Krushan warcraft upon its head. Bonded since birth in a way that ordinary warriors never could be, they followed only the code of the comrade. When two eochs were together, both succeeded or both failed. There was no third option: Jarsun made sure of that. If you were put in a triad, the same applied: three for one, and one for all. And so on through quads, pentads, sextets, and more. Until finally, the entire Eoch Assassins functioned as one organic unit, an army that breathed and lived as a single being, independent only in death.

While the logistics of defeating such an army were mind-boggling, the chances of facing even a pair, triad, or quad and surviving were almost nil. When one army fought another, some quantum of loss of life was acceptable, inevitable even. When one was fighting alone, one had literally only one life.

And in Tyrak's case, with not just the eoch quad but so many other champions also posed against him, he had only one chance. Either he took the upper hand from the outset, or this fight would be over in a moment, with him the loser.

Tyrak watched their feet as the first two eochs came at him, shrieking and whirling like dust devils. Their attack was designed to disorient a standing opponent who was whipping around to try to face both of them at once. The shrieks were coordinated in a rising and falling pattern so that the opponent unconsciously looked at the one on the left, then the one in the center, then back again, becoming so confused and misdirected that it was impossible to attack or defend against either one.

Even if he stayed with one eoch, the other would be able to slip in past his guard and deal the single maiming blow that was all they desired to inflict at first. Just one blow. Sever the biceps muscle, disabling one arm. Hack at the collarbone, disabling one arm and making it impossible to use the other without excruciating pain. Cut at the upper brow, deep enough to hurt badly as face wounds always did, and enough to make blood pour into the eyes, blinding the opponent. Pierce the armpit, slice the triceps muscles . . . There were a dozen other points. None critical or mortal in themselves. But that one disabling cut was all it took to open a man to the next — lethal — strike.

But this strategy depended on the upper body. Hence the leaping and dancing and shrieking to make the opponent look up, swing around, and keep his guard high. As one eoch leaped, scream rising to force the opponent to raise his weapon and line of sight, another slid in to deal the vital blow.

So Tyrak did the one thing they were not prepared for.

Even as they came spinning at him, shrieking like death criers at a king's cremation, he turned and dropped to the floor in one swift motion, thumping on his buttocks, jarring his spine hard enough to feel the impact all the way up to his skull. And he angled his upper body back, lying flat as the eochs leaped and slashed above him. Several feet above him in fact.

In that fraction of an instant, his hand shot out, grasping hold of a single ankle of the eoch who had been on his left, his densely packed body strength making the leaping warrior seem no heavier than a straw in his fist. In the same action, Tyrak slammed the eoch down onto the eoch who had been facing Tyrak's center.

The two eochs crashed into the floor hard enough that the sound of breaking bones and shattering cartilage was loudly audible. Their shrieks ceased abruptly. Two superb dealers of death, who had been leaping through the air in a balletic display of warcraft, now lay crushed and dazed upon the marble floor.

From the position in which he lay, looking back across the room, Tyrak could see the twin coals of Jarsun's eyes glowing. He took another brief instant to flash a grin and drop a lewd wink at the Krushan.

Then, without waiting to see the God-Emperor's response, he regained his feet with a single leap. He had been practicing this move as well and was pleased at his body's response. He landed with a jarring thud that shook the chamber and left spiderwebs of cracks beneath each foot. He was still growing in density even now, but he had other things to concentrate on for the moment. Such as staying alive a few minutes longer.

The third and fourth eochs were still moving in for their attack. Stunned though they were by the unexpected downing of their comrades, they were now deadlier than ever. With two of their comrades crippled, perhaps dying, they were doomed. Even if Tyrak did not kill them now, Jarsun certainly would. They had nothing to lose or gain, except for one thing.

Jarsun barked a single word.

Tyrak knew its meaning well; it was so commonly yelled among Morgol it might well be considered their battle cry: "Avenge!"

The eoch on the verandah touched one short sword to the marble floor, raking it across sharply enough to cleave the soft stone. The other sword was held out in an unusual backhand that Tyrak knew would spring back to pierce at the least expected moment. The fighter came at Tyrak in a low, loping stride. Sparks flew from the point where the deadly sharp blade met the polished stone floor.

The other eoch, the one who had been on Tyrak's right, somersaulted forward once, twice, then kept coming in that fashion. The bedchamber was palatial, but Tyrak knew that a fighter somersaulting in a closed space always held an advantage over one standing still. For one thing, the somersaulting fighter could change trajectory at any time and still strike with considerable force — too much to easily fend off without being thrown off balance. The two eochs had turned Tyrak's geographical advantages against him: pinning him against the closed door and wall, coming from two different directions, and covering both the upper field of attack as well as the lower.

There was no shrieking this time. Just the soft thuds of the somersaulting eoch's brief contact with the ground and the shirring sound of metal scraping stone as the loping eoch's sword threw up a shower of golden flaring sparks.

Tyrak stood his ground.

Had he been any normal warrior, that would have been a mortal error.

The impact of the somersaulting eoch striking him with such momentum would have slammed him back against the wall, and the eoch would have reversed the movement and bounced off, leaving Tyrak momentarily stunned, an easy target for the second eoch, who would swing sideways, slicing upward with the lowered sword, then stabbing deep and hard with the backheld sword. Tyrak would die impaled against the wall.

But he was not a normal warrior. He could not be certain how dense he had been able to make himself, but he was certainly at least nine or ten times denser than his usual weight.

For a somersaulting attacker to strike a man weighing two or three hundred pounds was one thing, but to strike a man weighing a ton or more, with skin like steel, flesh like iron, and bones like alloy . . .

The eoch somersaulted right at Tyrak, body twisting with expert grace in midair to land with feet squarely on Tyrak's chest.

There should have been a loud thud, perhaps the cracking of a few ribs, and then the thump of Tyrak's body hitting the wall.

Instead, the eoch's feet shattered beneath the momentum and force, like dried sticks under a heavily laden wagon's wheels. Legs bent and bent again grotesquely, and the eoch fell in a broken heap to the floor, silent even in this terrible condition, because Jarsun's ruthless discipline had conditioned the fighter not to express pain through sound.

A fraction of a moment later, the second eoch struck, raising the sword from the marble floor and slashing viciously at Tyrak's upper thigh, groin, and lower abdomen at an angle designed to accomplish irreparable damage. Without waiting to see the effect of this first strike, the eoch swung around, dancing in a diagonal turnaround move from one foot to the other, and stabbed the other short sword directly into Tyrak's solar plexus.

Both swords snapped and broke.

The action left the eoch at a sideways angle to Tyrak. The fighter turned, expecting to see Tyrak vomiting blood and dying. Instead, Tyrak was standing exactly as he had been before, and the swords were broken and useless. The eoch raised them, astonished, then snarled and attacked again, stabbing out with the edges of the broken blades. They were still dangerous enough to cut through normal human flesh.

But when they struck Tyrak's skin, they simply broke again.

The eoch stared in disbelief.

Tyrak smiled, reached out, and caught hold of the eoch's bald pate in his left hand. He took hold of it in a grip so tight, the eoch was suspended an inch or two in midair.

The eoch lashed out with swords, feet, every ounce of strength and skill the fighter had left.

Tyrak squeezed, barely exerting more effort than if he had been squeezing a ripe grape.

The effect on the eoch's skull was much the same.

He tossed the body aside, then looked a challenge at the others.

"So let's see if you men fare better than your eoch comrades," he said.

All stared at him. There was hatred in their eyes now, not the superior smug contempt there had been before. Even Jarsun had lowered his chin further, his eyes barely visible beneath his heavy forehead and brow, and was examining the slaughter with a mind expert in strategy and tactics. His split tongue flicked out and back inside.

Nobody said anything for a moment.

Tyrak sighed wearily.

"Come on, then, get a move on. I've got a kingdom to run and things to do."

# *Jarsun*

EVEN THROUGH HIS SURPRISE and rage, Jarsun could not help but feel a certain astonished pride at his protégé. The eponymous urrkh had sired Tyrak, and Ugraksh and Kensura had fostered him to adulthood, but it was Jarsun who had made Tyrak a warrior. Until he met Jarsun, the Arrgodi prince had been little more than a roughhouser, winning fights through brute strength, a disdain for protocol, and sheer arrogance. It was Jarsun's mentorship that had transformed him into a carefully honed weapon of war.

But now it seemed that weapon had grown beyond Jarsun's ability to wield it.

At first, he had assumed that Tyrak's cocky arrogance and high-handed attitude was the final stage of breakdown of the Arrgodi's damaged mind. Now he saw that it was in fact the opposite. Somehow, Tyrak had outsmarted him, if only briefly. He did not know how the Arrgodi had managed to gain such formidable powers or what exactly those powers entailed, nor could he comprehend how the man had managed to overcome the effect of his daily potions. Those potions ought to have been enough to drive Tyrak insane by now or, at the very least, make him the same irritable, frustrated, but otherwise malleable idiot he had been of late. But somehow Tyrak had dodged the arrow and slipped the noose. Then again, perhaps that was the essence of Tyrak's life story. Jarsun recalled his spy's report of how Tyrak had been under the executioner's axe when his urrkh blood first heralded itself in astonishing display. Jarsun had played some part in that as well, secretly feeding Tyrak certain potions in his diet which enhanced his urrkh qualities; it had only been a matter of time before nature took its course then. But the fact that it had taken a near-death experience to transform

Tyrak suggested that perhaps the Arrgodi needed that ultimate level of threat to finally effect his change.

And now again, it seemed, he had done the unthinkable, transforming when faced with certain death. Except that this time he had accomplished it without Jarsun's knowledge, and that intrigued Jarsun. Like any purveyor of violence and power, he was fascinated by any use of it that he could not comprehend.

"Are we going to stand around all day and look at each other's faces?" Tyrak asked with just the right touch of irony.

That was another thing that surprised and greatly interested Jarsun. Not long ago, Tyrak was little more than a loutish, selfish, pleasure-seeking dolt. This wit was something new. This was not the result of a potion or even training; it was a change from within.

Bahuka and the others looked back at Jarsun, waiting eagerly for him to give the command to attack. The fate of the eochs had only angered them, not scared them in the least. Superb fighters though the eochs were, they were still subject to the vagaries and weaknesses of mortal physic. The others, however, had powers that few even knew about, and which were rarely displayed in public. On Jarsun's instructions, they were to be used only on the battlefield and only on his orders. Any unauthorized use would face the same penalty as any other form of disobedience: instant death at Jarsun's own hands. Each wanted desperately to be given the opportunity to put these powers to use now, to teach this impudent Arrgodi a lesson. His last lesson.

Jarsun had no doubt they could do it. Well, perhaps one or three of them would fall too, not quite as quickly as the eochs had, but fall nevertheless. Whatever transformation Tyrak had wrought upon himself, it was no mere muscle-building or special training. There was real power there. Whether or not Tyrak could be overcome would be determined only by an all-out fight to the death. And that would leave either Jarsun's fighters or Tyrak dead or damaged beyond use.

He did not want either to happen. Not now, at any rate.

For one thing, he wished to examine and understand Tyrak better. To know what had wrought his transformation and if it could be repeated.

But more importantly, he was sensing a greater opportunity. The earlier Tyrak, the giant urrkh who all but destroyed his own capital city single-handedly and drove his people to revolt, that Tyrak had been useless as an ally. It was why Jarsun had had to come to Arrgodi himself, step in, and take charge of matters here. He had plans for Arrgodi and Eastern Arthaloka. Long-term plans. It had taken Jarsun the better part of the last year to repair some of the damage, rebuild the city and palace enclave, build ties with the populace, seed future alliances and trade deals, and generally set Arrgodi back on the path of prosperity and growth. An Arrgodi at war with itself, destroyed from within by its own mad ruler, was of no use to him in the long run. A strong Arrgodi with a king who would do his bidding — for a price, of course — and who would rule the powerful and prosperous nation as a proxy for himself . . . well, that king was of great use to him.

This Tyrak just might be capable of being that king. His transformed manner, mind, and physical power added up to a man who was a far cry from the insane rampaging urrkh Tyrak of a year ago, or even the adolescent Marauder who enjoyed slaughter too much to even care who he was killing or why. Neither of those were fit to be kings, let alone rule Mraashk.

This man, on the other hand, facing a chamber full of Jarsun's most lethal fighters, yes, he could rule as Jarsun's proxy.

There was a third, crucial reason why Jarsun did not give the order to attack.

Tyrak was his son-in-law.

And Jarsun loved his daughters dearly.

He wanted them to bear him heirs. And heirs who would inherit the Arrgodi nation would be invaluable in future.

Like any truly wise emperor, Jarsun knew his history. No liege, however strong or empowered with the greatest army, can rule indefinitely by force alone.

Statecraft, kingship, diplomacy . . . or call it simply politics . . . were essential to long-term governance.

Tyrak, as the blood heir to the throne, would ensure that. As would Tyrak's offspring from Jarsun's daughters.

And if Tyrak indeed had come to his senses, acquired formidable new powers, even gained a modicum of wisdom and maturity in the process, well, in that case, he had suddenly removed all reasons for extermination and made himself a desirable son-in-law and ally once more.

It was with this in mind that Jarsun shook his head. His fighters stared back at him in disbelief.

"No," he said aloud, ending any doubt they might have.

Bahuka snarled. "My lord, he has insulted you!"

Jarsun strode across the chamber to where Bahuka stood and slapped the man backhanded across the cheek. Though it was but a casually dealt blow, it was hard enough to split Bahuka's lip and draw blood. "That is for me to decide. Now, stand down!"

He turned to the others as well, meeting each of their gazes in turn, and said loudly, "Stand down!"

They lowered their eyes, knowing better than to challenge him.

Beside him, Bahuka still glowered at Tyrak even as he wiped the trickle of blood from his lip. "It is a bad precedent," he said very softly, just loud enough for Jarsun to hear. "The dog that gets away with a finger may someday bite off a hand."

Jarsun looked up at the ceiling. There was an interesting dent there where something had struck the ceiling hard enough to break a piece of the stone overbeam. It would take considerable force and velocity to do that. He wondered if that was somehow connected to Tyrak's recent transformation; he thought it must be.

"Leave us," he said quietly for Bahuka's benefit. Firmly but not like a command. The old veteran had been with him too long and fought too many wars and conflicts alongside Jarsun to be easily cowed. Beating him down would only end in another unnecessary death. Some flies were more easily drawn with honey than slapped with sticks.

Bahuka went slowly, reluctantly. The others went too, glowering at Tyrak as they passed him by, but none making a move toward him. Other eochs came in once the doors were opened to drag out their fallen comrades. Soon the faint sounds of necks being cracked outside were audible to Jarsun's sharp ears; there was no room for the physically challenged in his army. Being a soldier for Morgolia was in itself a challenge, physically and in every other way. On the battlefield, he himself went around finishing off wounded soldiers. He called it "relieving them of their duties."

When everyone had left and the doors had been shut once more but not bolted this time, Jarsun turned to look at Tyrak shrewdly.

"Tell me everything," he said.

# *Tyrak*

## 1

TYRAK LOOKED AT JARSUN laconically for a moment. "What does that mean, 'everything'?"

"How did this happen? When did it happen?"

Tyrak tore off a silk sheet and used it to wipe himself clean of the blood from the eochs. He also felt the great thirst that came every time he used his powers, but he controlled the urge for the moment. He wanted nothing more than to pick up the oversize water pot he now kept in his chamber, upend it, and drink until it was drained. But he didn't. Any need was a potential weakness, and he did not want Jarsun to know his weakness. Instead, he picked up the pot but merely sipped at it slowly, more as an affectation than an expression of need. "Could you be more specific, Father dear? At least give me some hint what you might be referring to?"

Jarsun smiled wryly. "You have changed completely. I'm tempted to say 'overnight,' but of course that can't be true. This has taken time, effort." Something occurred to him. "And training! I see now. The question I should be asking is who has effected this transformation? Who was it, Tyrak?"

Tyrak took another sip, aching to empty the contents of the pot into his belly, to pour the cold water onto his head, drenching himself. He could almost feel the water splashing on his sweaty, overheated face and torso as he imagined it. But to Jarsun he showed only indifference. "What transformation?"

Jarsun shook his head. "Come now, Tyrak. You are a different man. A new man. With extraordinary new abilities. That does not come on its own, it is acquired somehow. All I wish to know is how and when and from whom."

Tyrak took a third sip and weighed the pot in his hand a moment, thinking. It must weigh well over two hundred pounds, he knew, because it contained twenty-five gallons of water. He felt as if he could drink five of these right now and still want more. He forced the need to the back of his mind and focused on the matter at hand. It was important he make Jarsun understand this the first time, otherwise this process would take weeks or months instead of days to accomplish. And something told him he could not afford a delay. Each day that he dallied here with Jarsun, the Slayer was out there somewhere, growing up, growing stronger, getting ready to attack him. He must be ready when the time came. He must choose the place and manner of the confrontation. It was the only hope he had.

"You are right about the rebellion," he said quietly, being sure to couch his words in calm indifference. Any sign of urgency would only make Jarsun suspicious. "It is led by Rurka, acting on behalf of Vasurava himself."

Jarsun immediately dropped his sardonic smile and came several steps forward. "I knew it! Did you learn this from your spies? What else did they tell you?"

Tyrak waved away the questions. "It does not matter how I know this. All that matters is that it is true. You can verify it with the help of your spies — but if you do, you will run out of time."

Jarsun frowned, lowering his chin again as he was wont to do when he grew suspicious or aggressive. "Is that some kind of threat?"

Tyrak said, "Yes, but not by me. By the Arrgodi. If you do not heed them now, your entire empire may be lost to you forever. Already they have begun to chip away at the edifice, and given time and your continued indifference, they will surely bring you down into the dust sooner than you may think possible."

Jarsun stared at him, then seemed to grow aware of the fact that Tyrak still held the pot of water in one hand, with his elbow crooked, as easily as any man might hold a mug of wine. "You have gained great strength somehow. There are potions that can give you such strength for brief periods, taxing your body to its limits. What they gain you in strength, they cost you in years of life."

Tyrak chuckled. "You think my strength is gained from a potion?" He raised the pot higher. "Can a potion give any man the ability to absorb a hundred liters of water without it showing anywhere on his body?"

And he upended the pot, touching the rim to his lips, and drained it. It took several moments, and he was careful not to spill a drop. He was trying to make it seem as if he was drinking the water to prove a point. When the pot was empty, he tossed it across the room. It flew out the verandah and landed on the ground below with a loud crash. A few voices could be heard, Bahuka's unmistakable among them, expressing their disapproval.

Tyrak raised his vest to reveal his flat, taut belly and ridged abdominal muscles. He thumped his stomach and groin with his fist, hard enough to make a sound like an elephant driving its head against a heavy tree trunk. "You see now? Is this the work of a potion, do you think?"

Jarsun's eyes glittered. He came slowly toward Tyrak, hand outstretched as if longing to touch and see for himself. Tyrak raised a hand in warning. Jarsun's tongue flickered and disappeared again.

"No," he said finally. "This is something else entirely. Something I have never heard of or encountered before. It intrigues me."

*Good. For as long as it intrigues you, you will not try to kill me, I trust.* Aloud, Tyrak said, "About the rebellion, then. The rebels have mounted an army and are attacking your outposts. Those nearest to Arrgodi have already fallen. Now they make their way northward and westward."

Jarsun frowned. "Northwest? But that would take them beyond the borders of the Arrgodi nation!"

Tyrak nodded slowly, waiting for Jarsun to reason it out by himself. "Exactly. There is an old saying among us Arrgodi — when you pour hot lentils onto a plate of rice, never try to eat the middle first."

Jarsun blinked. "What?"

Tyrak gestured to indicate an imaginary plate of rice onto which he poured steaming hot daal as he repeated himself slowly: "Never try to eat the hot rice and lentils from the middle of the plate. You will burn yourself. Instead, start from the outside and work your way in."

Jarsun shook his head, looking irritated now. "Rustic sayings were never my strong suit, son-in-law. If there is wisdom there, it eludes me."

Tyrak sighed. "They want you out of Arrgodi, but rather than defy you here and risk destroying their own capital city and kingdom, they have taken the fight to your territories. That's why they head northwest. They have allied with the kingdoms you have taken over and intend to liberate them, one by one."

Jarsun looked at him, light dawning in his eyes. "Eat the dish from the outside, working their way inward. Arrgodi is the hot center of the plate. I see it now! How quaint, and quite apt. So they think they can unite my principalities against me, do they? How ridiculous!"

"And yet how dangerous. With a few other allies as strong as Hastinaga —"

"Did you say Hastinaga? The Krushan would never align with these foolish rebel factions!"

"Not officially. But unofficially, much can be done. And the Krushan are very powerful indeed. As are the Gwannlanders. And the Harvani. And the Galdees. And who knows who else?"

Jarsun shook his head, lips pursed in the spiteful stubborn way he had when contradicted. "Impossible. The Gwannlanders, perhaps. Not the Harvani and the Galdees. As for Hastinaga. It's true that Vasurava's sister Karni is now wedded to Prince Shvate, so the Krushan have some reason to sympathize with the Mraashk rebels, but these others . . ." His voice trailed off as he thought for a moment. "Unless you mean that the Karni connection alone is sufficient to bring the Krushan into this, not directly, but indirectly as sponsors of the rebels. Yes, I can see this as a stratagem Vrath might concoct. Back the rebels against you, which means against me. Then bide his time until the stage is set for Vrath and the Krushan to enter the theater of battle."

"Yes, that is what I meant, father-in-law. And with Hastinaga's backing, many more will join them in time. This is not a rebellion against me or the throne of Arrgodi. It is a rebellion against you and your empire building. Everything you have worked for is in danger of being lost. Heed my advice. Go now. Leave Arrgodi. Consolidate your empire outside this nation. Leave Mraashk and the Arrgodi to me to manage as was our original understanding. And I shall remain allied with you always. I shall even visit your daughters, my wives, and sire children on them. But if you stay, you risk losing everything."

Jarsun was silent for a very long time.

Tyrak waited patiently.

From below, he could hear the voices and murmurs of many men and the clinking of weapons and snorting of horses. He guessed that the riders bearing the news he had intercepted the previous day had arrived and the news they brought was causing consternation among Jarsun's advisors.

Finally Jarsun nodded once, decisively. "Everything you have said can be easily proven or disproven. I am expecting riders with news from the outposts even now. If what you say is true, I shall do exactly as you advise. I shall leave Arrgodi to you. But if you fail me in any way — whether as an ally, a king, or a son-in-law, I shall return. And the next time I come to Arrgodi, I shall make her mine forever. Do you understand?"

Tyrak smiled. "Arrgodi is already yours. I am merely holding her on your behalf, father-in-law."

## 2

Tyrak had almost finished his exercises when he saw Ladislew approaching. She paused by the wooden stable wall and pretended to watch him as he worked out, as if casually interested in a professional way.

He knew better.

He had been with her only the previous night, and when he had looked out of his verandah and seen her approaching, she had walked quite differently then. There had been an urgency in her step as well as a certain diffidence that he had not known she could possibly feel. Her head had been lowered as if she felt embarrassed at coming in that secretive manner.

Later, after he had drawn on her store of Halahala, concluding their peculiar transaction, when he was filled with an insight that came of their intimacy: he had known then that she was not ashamed or embarrassed because she was a married woman coming to another man's quarters in secret at night. She was ashamed of her own great need to come to him, the hunger that she felt and which he sensed so powerfully within her each time he fed on her poison milk.

He finished his exercises, crushing the last wooden tree trunks that had been set up with the use of elephants for this express purpose each day. The final one he punched so hard, it was pulverized into a cloud of wood dust, a few chips and pieces falling across the acres-large field. His power had grown steadily with use, and the techniques he had picked up from the old syce Arrgo were amazingly effective when used with his newfound ability. Any normal man would have broken every limb in his body by now, no matter how strong or heavily muscled he might be. But for Tyrak, it was the perfect technique and exercise. He felt now as if he could take on Jarsun himself. And in a way, he wished that the last encounter, the one in his bedchamber, had gone on a while longer. He would have relished the chance to test his strength and skill on those minions. For that matter, he would enjoy testing it on them even today, when he knew for certain he would win easily.

"So?" he said as he came up to the fence against which Ladislew leaned with exaggerated casualness. "How is the wife of the captain of my guard?"

She didn't respond to the jibe. He knew she felt no guilt at being a married woman. The marriage itself was a cover, a mere disguise. What she shared with Tyrak was no mere illicit dalliance. It was a matter of her own power being useful. And of their secret alliance someday leading to the downfall of Jarsun.

Still, she said nothing so long as Arrgo was in earshot. The old syce finished rubbing salt into Tyrak's body as he had taken to doing after every practice session. The salt seemed to help him cope with the increasing density of his flesh and bone. Already, he was able to increase his weight a hundredfold. That entailed other side effects, such as the epic thirst — and a corresponding need for salt. It was the old stable hand, now Tyrak's trainer, who had suggested that sometimes salt rubbed into a sweaty body could replenish more readily than when consumed orally. And like every other bit of advice given by the old stalwart, it proved effective.

"What is it?" Tyrak asked, after Arrgo had left them alone in the empty stable.

She looked at him in the fading dusk, and he saw something in her eyes that he had not seen until now. A kind of hunger. It was not pleasant. It was a glimpse of what she had once been and might be again. "I have found the Slayer."

He sprang to his feet, toppling a barrel of cold water the size of a man. The water gurgled out, splashing and spreading across the entire stable. Horses neighed and whinnied in complaint in their boxes. He grabbed Ladislew's shoulders, forgetting that he had not yet reduced his density to its normal proportions.

"Where is he? Take me to him at once!" He spoke through gritted teeth, and as he ground his molars, the sound was loud enough to be heard across the entire stables. Elephants a hundred yards away trumpeted, disturbed by the unusual yet distinctly animal sound.

Ladislew put out her hands, grasped his shoulders, and pushed him off her. As usual, he was surprised at her strength. It took her some effort, but not much. He knew he had grasped her with enough force to crush an oak trunk held sideways between his palms. Yet Ladislew had pushed him off as if he were merely a normal human man and she a normal human woman.

"He is outside your reach. If you go to him now, it will be too soon. Already he is strong and gaining strength each day."

He roared with fury, losing his temper for the first time in almost a year.

"*I am strong!*" he said, and smashed a fist onto the side of the fallen barrel. It splintered into fragments.

"Not strong enough. Not yet." She was calm, unafraid. She had power of her own. She did not fear his strength or his temper.

That calmed him down. What use was it getting angry with her?

He sat down on a nearby bench, basically just a solid iron block. It creaked, and he felt a tiny crack or two appear beneath his thighs. He had unconsciously begun to increase his weight again. "Tell me everything you know."

"He is living with a cowherd named Eshnor and his wife, Alinora, in a place called Goluka. It is a tiny hamlet in —"

"Arghbhoomi. Yes, I know," he said. "I know Eshnor too. He is the chief of Goluka. A popular and powerful local leader. How could his child have escaped my grasp? My soldiers slaughtered every young child in the great purge." A thought struck him. "His delegation came to my court this very morning, to pay Goluka's taxes for the past year. He stood there before me, he even spoke to me! How could this have escaped my knowledge?"

She shrugged. "The Deliverer is no fool. He has means and ways to trick you at every turn. Don't forget, Kewri was under your soldiers' watch, and yet she was able to give birth to him, and Vasurava was able to spirit him out of Arrgodi —"

"Yes, yes," he said impatiently. "But if what you say is true, then I shall go to Goluka at once. I must destroy the Slayer before he grows strong enough to fulfill the prophecy."

She laughed, throwing her head back and flicking her long hair over her shoulders. He scowled up at her, gripping the corners of the iron slab. It yielded beneath his fingers like warm butter. "He is already strong enough, Tyrak!"

He pointed a finger at her in warning, ignoring the iron chips that fell to the ground. "Don't mock me. You may be a Maatr, but I am no mere mortal either."

She lost her grin and nodded. "That is so. And in time, you will be very powerful indeed. Perhaps even more powerful than I, in at least sheer physical strength. I have never seen nor heard of an urrkh who was gifted with the particular power you possess, or the ability to use it in such unusual ways. I suspect that this is all preparation for you to eventually face the Slayer in some manner that will give you the advantage."

Even as he opened his mouth, she held up a hand. "Do not ask me how or when that confrontation will occur. I am not omniscient, merely prescient. But this much I can assure you: if you go to the Slayer now, you will lose. You will die. In a sense, that is what he wants and the reason why he taunted you by coming into your lair today, hoping to tempt you to take this rash step."

He thought about this for a long moment, calming himself using the yogic breathing methods that Arrgo had taught him. The old stable hand was a storehouse of ancient lore and knowledge, and it was amazing just how much Tyrak had learned from him. When Vessa had said that he would provide a guru to guide him through the process of rebuilding his powers so he could face the Slayer, Tyrak had been skeptical. Now he would touch the syce's feet if not for the fact that it would appear laughable to the world and also because Arrgo himself had warned that the day Tyrak acknowledged his guru, Arrgo would vanish from his life forever.

Finally, he said, "Then what do you propose I do?"

"Wait."

He ground his teeth in frustration.

"And test your limits."

He looked at her. "How do you propose I do that?"

She smiled. "Khobadi."

He was about to laugh, then stopped. He thought about it for a moment. "The way it is fought in Mraashk and Gwannland, and rural Arrgodi?"

"And in your own Arrgodi city as well."

He looked at her skeptically.

"Jarsun has built amphitheaters to house large audiences all over the grasslands, has he not?"

Tyrak nodded. The God-Emperor had made a big show of it at court, claiming that he was bringing entertainment within the reach of the masses. He had made it sound like a charitable gesture. Tyrak had resented the resources — men, building materials, prime space in the heart of every city and town across the areas he controlled — but Jarsun had made it clear that this was something he wanted done, and done efficiently and quickly. "I have been to a few entertainments."

"Now it is time for you to fight in one."

"Like a common wrestler? I am Tyrak, Prince of —"

"Of everything except what really matters, your own fate. Take your life into your own hands. Lay it on the line in the pit of the amphitheater. It will prepare you for the coming encounter with the Slayer and earn you the respect of your father-in-law as well."

He considered this. "What do you get out of this?"

She smiled like a cat that had caught a particularly large and vicious rat. "It is part of my plan. Kill the Slayer and cripple Jarsun, both at once."

She explained. He listened.

## 3

When Tyrak felt somewhat calmer and ready for conversation, he sent for Shelsis. The old minister arrived, visibly nervous. He had probably heard the rumors of Tyrak's unusual mood.

The old man had been sidelined by Bahuka, Jarsun's emissary, who had been sent to oversee Tyrak during his most manic period following the birth and escape of the Slayer. Tyrak had been truly out of control then, and in retrospect, he knew that had Jarsun not stepped in and taken measures to bolster up his regency, Arrgodi would have burned in a brutal civil war that would either have left Tyrak without a kingdom to govern or the Arrgodi without a king to oppress them.

It had taken Tyrak months to regain his self-confidence and strength, and it wasn't until the violent encounter with the quad of Jarsun's personal Eoch Assassin bodyguards that he had demonstrated his newfound strength and abilities for the first time to the God-Emperor.

Jarsun had been impressed.

Tyrak had been cautious not to reveal more than was necessary: such as the fact that his powers were growing. What Jarsun had seen was barely half of what he was capable of now. Yet Ladislew had told him that he would take years still to come into his full powers and if he moved too soon, he risked losing everything. It was one thing to smash the skulls of a few eochs; it was another thing altogether to go up against Jarsun himself. Even Tyrak was not impetuous and impatient enough to do that just yet; perhaps he never would be. After all, Jarsun was more useful to him as an ally than as an enemy. It was the knowledge that Jarsun stood behind him that kept civil war from breaking out even now, that forced tens of thousands of Arrgodi to flee into exile rather than stay and fight openly. And it was the same knowledge that kept his Mraashk neighbors from invading and attempting to take over Arrgodi.

But this was a different problem. This was the Slayer. An enemy who was not merely interested in regional politics or imperial ambitions. This was a being prophesied to destroy him. Why? Because he had a great destiny, and all those born with a great destiny are bound to attract powerful enemies. Every great hero has a great villain.

So Tyrak had his Slayer, an infant child born to his own sister under his own roof and who desired to murder his own uncle.

If *patricide* was the word for the killing of one's father, and *matricide* was murder of one's mother, what was murder of an uncle called? If there was one, he did not know it. He had disliked Ashcrit so intensely as a boy, he had tipped his Ashcrit guru out of a high tower window one morning after a particularly grueling session on derivatives.

How could a mere boy be a threat to him, Tyrak, the most powerful being in this part of the world? It was ludicrous. Age notwithstanding, Tyrak would put an end to this right here and now.

Shelsis stood as Tyrak paced, musing on his course of action. Finally, Tyrak turned and looked intently at the chief advisor. The older man blanched, his greying mustaches twitching. Ever since Jarsun's departure, he had lived in perpetual anxiety about his fate.

Tyrak knew that other kings would have had the advisor put to the sword merely for fraternizing with the Krushan emperor acting as de facto king of Arrgodi while Tyrak was unable to govern, but Jarsun was Tyrak's father-in-law, and Arrgodi had sworn allegiance to Morgolia.

So strictly speaking, Shelsis had done no wrong. Even so, the man was never quite at ease around his king, and Tyrak saw no reason to make the man feel at ease. Even if Shelsis had not betrayed him entirely, he had not demonstrated loyalty either. Had Tyrak not withstood the attack of the four eochs in his bedchamber, they would have killed him and Shelsis would have stood by and watched.

So would Pradynor, Ladislew's husband, and for that reason, Tyrak had a bone to pick with him as well. But this was not the urrkh Tyrak, whom they had expected to turn into a festering giant, suddenly raging and rampaging; this was Tyrak the Terrible, as he now liked to think of himself. A king so shrewd he had outwitted the great Jarsun himself, and before his reign was over, he would dethrone his father-in-law as well.

And to achieve such great things, he needed every political support. Shelsis was an experienced advisor with keen knowledge of the Arrgodi tribes and clans, and his spy network was excellent. He was more useful to Tyrak alive than dead. And so long as he remained useful, he would stay alive.

Somehow, the advisor was canny enough to sense this, and he seemed to grow less anxious as Tyrak paced. After all, tyrants who lashed out viciously rarely took such a long time to brood on their actions beforehand. Even so, he was wise enough to gauge Tyrak's agitated state and to know better than to speak before spoken to; that was another reason Tyrak had kept him around after Bahuka's departure. Because of his canny judgment.

Finally, Tyrak turned to him. With offhand casualness, he said, "Goluka-dham."

Shelsis dipped his head to acknowledge that he heard. "What of it, Your Highness?"

"Burn it to the ground. Punishment for the uprising to which they give the lofty term *rebellion*. Goluka is the heart of the unrest. I have it on good authority. Raze the settlement to the ground. Kill everyone living there. Also kill those who stand in the way or express sympathy for the dying."

Shelsis was silent for longer than required. He did not make any sound or gesture to indicate he objected to Tyrak's orders, nor did he utter a simple "yes, sire," and leave to execute his king's orders. This was his diplomatic way of communicating to Tyrak that he disagreed but that it was up to Tyrak to ask him why. Again, another excellent reason why he remained alive when every other minister, advisor, preceptor, and officer of the court had been executed or imprisoned in the past decade.

"Well?" Tyrak asked, his voice echoing in the empty throne chamber. "Since you have not left to do my bidding, I can only presume you wish to offer some objection. Speak!"

"Not an objection, Your Highness. Merely . . . a doubt."

Tyrak gestured impatiently, indicating to him to go on.

Shelsis went on with a mite more confidence, careful to keep his voice low and his gaze unchallenging. "My lord, Goluka-dham is governed by Eshnor."

"So?'

"Eshnor himself is a peaceful man. And he is dearly loved and supported by the Mraashk people."

Tyrak nodded grimly. "And this dearly beloved Eshnor is one of the key troublemakers in this rebellion. All the more reason to teach them a lesson."

"True, my lord. The rebels must be dealt with firmly. But you propose to attack Goluka-dham and harm Eshnor and his people. They are peaceable folk and not directly involved in the rebellion." He added quickly, "Not as far as the people of Mraashk know."

"They must support, encourage, supply the rebels. Otherwise Rurka and the other chieftains would not have been able to sustain themselves for so long and harry our army this effectively," Tyrak said. "Ever since Vasurava and Kewri scurried away like cowards . . ."

He clenched his fist in anger. The thought of his sister and her husband eluding his grasp still rankled; even though ostensibly they had left on a pilgrimage, his spies informed him that their departure had given credence and strength to the growing rebellion within his nation. Rurka, son of Svaalka, was reportedly leading the rebellion, with the cowherds at the fore of the insurrection. Until now, they had only succeeded in harrying his army and defying his authority symbolically, rather than with meaningful military tactics, but any such defiance was a thorny barb in his flesh. "Goluka-dham is the heart of Mraashk territory. It is not possible that this Eshnor and his people do not supply the rebels. Punishing them will send a message to the rebels and curb the menace before it grows into a full-blown insurrection."

Shelsis nodded slowly, unable to ignore the unshakeable logic of this argument. "What you say is true, sire. But attacking a peaceful hamlet such as Goluka-dham and a revered community leader such as Eshnor will also send out a different message, one that you may not wish to send."

Tyrak frowned as he seated himself on the throne. "What do you mean?"

"If we attack Goluka, not the Mraashk alone but all rural Arrgodi will rise up against you. No Arrgodi can bear the slaughter of innocent shepherds and cowherds in the heart of the grasslands."

Tyrak shrugged. "They are already harrying us through forays and petty insubordinations."

"But this would be an all-out rebellion. They would raise up militia under you, with Rurka's Mraashk leading the fray. We are not talking about a small assault or harassment."

Tyrak was still not impressed. "We Arrgodi have fought the Mraashk for decades. We are willing to continue if need be."

Shelsis clearly wished to argue the point, but he took a moment to gather his wits before continuing. "But this time if they rise up, Gwann would support them. He might even join his forces with theirs."

"Gwann? King of Gwannland?" Tyrak snorted. "Why would he risk making an enemy of Arrgodi?"

"Because he is already involved, sire. It is well known that he is sheltering many tens of thousands of refugee Mraashk who have fled to Gwannland. And as you know full well, he has always coveted Arrgodi."

Tyrak could not disagree. "That he has," he admitted reluctantly.

"And if Gwann joins the Mraashk, then Stonecastle will certainly join in as well."

Tyrak raised his head, thinking. "Stonecastle regards Vasurava's sister Karni as his own daughter."

"Indeed, sire, Karni. The name means 'daughter of stone' in Ashcrit." Shelsis was wise enough to see that his liege had caught the thread of the argument and did not need to be prompted further. He waited as Tyrak rose from his throne and paced a few moments, thinking.

"And Karni, Vasurava's sister, is married to that albino king of Hastinaga, what's his name? White-face?"

"Shvate," Shelsis said.

"Yes, Shvate. So if Stonecastle joins in, then there's a possibility of old man

Vrath putting Hastinaga's legions into the alliance as well." Tyrak walked over to a painted map depicting the continent of Arthaloka. He considered the forces that would be aligned against him, jabbing his finger against the heavy canvas as he called out each name. "That would bring the wrath of the Burnt Empire down upon us."

He turned to look at Shelsis, eyes glittering. "Is it a coincidence that all these happen to be territories that have successfully resisted the efforts of Jarsun and remain hostile to the Reygistan Empire that he is building?"

"Nay, sire. It is no coincidence. That is another reason why they are only waiting for an excuse to open a war front with Arrgodi. They regard Arrgodi as a weak . . ." The old advisor bit off his words in midsentence. He was about to say "weak link" but had just realized how that might sound to the ruler of that alleged weak link. "As a possible bargaining tool," he continued, "and hope that by fighting and crushing you, they will force Jarsun to break off his campaign against the other territories and return here to defend you, his son-in-law, as well as Arrgodi, the pride of his empire. Tactically, that would make it impossible for Jarsun to continue his campaign of expansion and consolidation. If Jarsun has to stay and defend Arrgodi on so many fronts"—the advisor gestured at the map which depicted the Sea of Grass surrounded by the territories Tyrak had just pointed out—"it would effectively grind the campaign for the Reygistan Empire to a halt. Through shrewd alliances with the other nations, they would throw Jarsun's forces out from there as well, and push him back to the western frontier provinces, leaving him nowhere to go except the far western lands."

Tyrak thought about this for several moments. He could not find any reason to disagree with anything Shelsis had said. Yet he seethed at the thought of letting the Slayer live in peace another day.

But if the Deliverer was a personal threat to him, then the Burnt Empire was an enemy beyond all imagining. He could not afford to start a fight that would end with Hastinaga declaring war against Arrgodi. Jarsun would kill him for that alone, and if Jarsun didn't, then Vrath certainly would. The prophecy claimed that only the Slayer could kill Tyrak and Deliver the people from his tyranny—he chuckled at the play of words in his own mind—but he would not care to test the powers of either Krushan. Compared to the might of the Burnt Empire, the Sea of Grass was only a minor thorn.

They could pluck it out, crush Tyrak and Arrgodi, and incorporate the grasslands into their already prodigious borders.

He dismissed Shelsis abruptly and sat brooding.

No question, he must find a way to get at the Slayer. But this was not the time nor the way to go about it. Somehow, he must figure out how to destroy him once and for all.

## 4

Tyrak finished oiling his body and dismissed the helper. The boy ran back to the sidelines to join his companions, whispering amongst themselves as they pointed out the players on the field. Tyrak saw some coins exchanging hands and grinned to himself. He wondered whom they were betting on. He felt certain it would be Jarsun's team of champions. Tyrak had been given a choice of playing with Jarsun's team or the opposing army's team. He had deliberately chosen to play with the opposition, knowing that would irk his father-in-law and provoke him into trying harder. Jarsun still believed he was tricking his son-in-law into thinking he would be able to use his powers to demolish his opponents, not knowing that each of Jarsun's players was possessed of their own powers as well. But Tyrak knew this already. The old stable syce had told him so the night before. Not merely told him to warn him, but had prepared him for it as well.

Now Tyrak stepped out on the field and began slapping his muscles to warm them up. He slapped his chest hard several times, then massaged his shoulders, swung his torso around to loosen his back muscles, bent and slapped his inner thighs, outer thighs . . . He felt a shadow approach, looming over him. In the background, the sound of the crowd was a tangible thing, all pervasive, filling the air like rain on water.

"Arrgodi!" said a booming voice. For a moment Tyrak thought he must be hearing an echo caused by the enclosed stadium. Then he looked up into a jaw the size of his own thigh and realized that it was not an echo, merely the natural sound produced by a person of that great size. The man's chest was probably twice as wide as Tyrak's, and Tyrak was not a small man by any standards. He was also a good two heads taller, and his arms hung by his sides like entire sides of meat. His jaw was square and jutted out at an angle, forcing his lower teeth up over his upper teeth. When he spoke, the sound was like someone speaking inside a wooden barrel filled with metal ingots.

"Our master tells me you consider yourself invulnerable," said the grating barrel voice.

Tyrak did not answer. The man's tone made it clear he was more interested in issuing insults than actually conversing. This was a common precursor to games as each team boosted their own spirits by insulting the other team and calling them names. He had expected no less.

The man seemed to realize that an answer was not forthcoming from Tyrak.

"Well, since you consider yourself invulnerable," he said, "I wanted to show you this."

The man drew a sword. It was a fine broadsword, fit for any high lord or even a king in battle, the metal beautifully worked and beaten to a fine perfection. Judging by the size and length, it could probably hack through armor if wielded hard enough; it might take a swing or three but no armor could withstand more than a few direct hits with that weapon. It was what Arrgodi's Marauders used to call a godslayer.

The man with the crooked jaw raised the sword in his hand, then hacked at his own forearm, the inner softer side. The godslayer struck with force enough to cut metal armor. With that much force behind it, it should have parted the limb from his body easily.

Instead, the sword simply struck the forearm with a dull *thunk*.

The man raised his eyes to see if Tyrak had noted this result. Then he raised the sword again and hacked at his own foot, aiming directly for the knee, the weakest part of any man's leg. The sword struck it again with a dull, thumping impact. There was no effect on the man's knee. Even the skin wasn't broken.

The demonstration went on a few moments longer. By the time Crooked Jaw was done, the sword was chipped and cracked in a dozen places, but there was not so much as a blemish upon his person.

Finally, he handed the sword to another of his companions, a broad shorter man with enormous bulging shoulders who grinned to display missing teeth. "That is Maitrey," said Crooked Jaw in his booming nasal voice. "He eats only nails and glass."

Tyrak did not say a word.

Crooked Jaw looked down at him and smiled grimly. "You thought you were the only one, did you not? Well, you were wrong. We are all the same, and we have far more experience and knowledge of our abilities than you, sweet-faced prince. You should go back to your sweet-smelling kingdom and resume prancing with your ponies and princesses. This is no place for you."

Tyrak cleared his throat. "King."

Crooked Jaw frowned.

"I am king of Arrgodi, and of Mraashk."

Crooked Jaw grinned. "I hear your Arrgodi have fled to other kingdoms rather than be ruled by you. Is that why you come here? To grovel at our master's feet in the hope that he will aid you again and give you more of his potions to drink so that you may gain more abilities?" He leaned closer and chuckled. "Or perhaps you needed something to aid you in bed with his daughters? Word is that you have not been able to seed either of them with child for years. Perhaps you require some help? I would be happy to help anytime. As would all my teammates. Just say the word."

Tyrak reached out a hand, indicating the sword.

Crooked Jaw raised an eyebrow, but handed the sword over without comment.

Tyrak took the sword, turned it inward, the point of the blade aimed at his own lower abdomen, gripping the hilt in both hands, and said, "When I am done here on this field today, you and all your teammates will wish you were my wives and could feel the pleasure of mating with me."

Crooked Jaw's eyes narrowed, and his fists clenched.

Tyrak went on. "And if you survive, I would be happy to seed you with child if you wish as well. I have more than enough to seed all your nation's women as well as men."

And he plunged the sword's point into the weakest point of his abdomen, hard enough to pierce wood.

The sword cracked and broke into three pieces.

Tyrak handed the hilt back to Crooked Jaw, who stared at the broken blade. "You can keep this one. I prefer my own."

He smiled to himself as Crooked Jaw flung the pieces of the sword across the field, yelling at his startled teammates as he strode back to his side. Jarsun knew his own words had been bombastic to say the least, but it was the only way to get the point across . . . and then break it off.

# 5

The crowd favored their own men, naturally. The roar of approval that met Crooked Jaw and his team as they took their positions was deafening. Tyrak glanced around the stadium. There had to be a thousandscore soldiers assembled tonight, most of them drunk and battle fogged from the day's fighting. He had seen similar events often before, but never on this scale. All armies needed some way to release the day's frustrations and pain. But what Jarsun had done here was unprecedented. He had sponsored the biggest mass entertainment venue ever heard of, and by centering it around a game involving war stratagems with their own champions, he had made it personal and involving for the men. This must be the highlight of the day for the men gathered here, those that had survived the day's fighting, anyway. He saw any number of men exchanging notes and coins, and understood that betting was not only permitted, it was encouraged. Of course! Jarsun would be managing the betting and profiting from it as well. He was the "house," so to speak. And as Tyrak knew well, whether you won or lost, the house always won. Leave it to Jarsun to find a way to not only boost morale and relieve tension but also profit from it! The consummate merchant and warrior and king and priest, all rolled into one.

Tyrak took stock of his own teammates. They were tough-looking men, of a tribe he had never encountered before nor heard of. From the looks of it, they appeared to be the reserved reticent type — not saying much, not displaying much emotion, but strong and confident. They exchanged looks, gestures, and little touches amongst one another that suggested they had a strong bond. Clearly, they had played before as a team. Jarsun might take pleasure in humiliating him as well as in winning, but he was not fool enough to give Tyrak a useless team. The only point of this sport was for both teams to be evenly matched. Otherwise, it would be a very quick and boring game.

He turned to his teammates, drawing their attention. They regarded him dispassionately, neither displaying subservience nor arrogance. They had understood their condition but not accepted it, he saw. They had something to fight for and were willing to do what they had to, even risk their lives, but not kowtow to the enemy. That pleased him. He could work with this team;

he needed only to be certain that they would accept him and work with him as well.

"I am here to win," he told them. He used elaborate hand gestures to emphasize his words. "If we work together, we will surely succeed."

Then he clenched his fist and pointed it at the sky. "To victory!"

After a brief pause in which they glanced at one another, they raised their clenched fists as well. "To victory!" they said in their dialect. He was relieved to note that he knew the dialect.

Tyrak heard a commotion in the stadium and looked around. He saw two familiar female shapes entering the royal pavilion above the playing field. His wives, Jarsun's daughters. They were dressed in rich robes and bejeweled as queens, and looked as coquettish and alluring as ever. They waved excitedly to Tyrak, calling out his name. He nodded, embarrassed, and saw Jarsun smile down at him. So. His wonderfully considerate father-in-law had decided to add another level of pressure: the prospect of abject humiliation and embarrassment should he lose here today. It was one thing to lose before twenty thousand soldiers; it was unacceptable to lose before one's own wives. At least for Tyrak.

Which was why he would not lose.

He took his position at the fore center of his team's playing area, awaiting the signal to begin the game. Bending over, patting his oiled thighs, he recalled the words of Arrgo the night before:

"Until now, whatever you did was your own madness. I desire no part in that. But the road you're set on now will lead Arrgodi to fall into the hands of the Burnt Empire, and that I will not tolerate. You may not realize this, but Jarsun desires nothing more than to make the Arrgodi nation a part of his greater domain."

"I realize it," Tyrak had replied. "And I will not let it happen."

Arrgo scoffed. "It will happen no matter what you do here. The only way to prevent it is to convince Jarsun that he is better off letting you run Mraashk for him than taking it over himself. He has enough on his field already to manage. There comes a point when an emperor has to delegate and trust his kings to rule their individual kingdoms. Right now, Jarsun is not fully convinced that you are capable of doing so. Your record has been . . . spotty . . . to say the least. But you can prove that you have changed. You can give him confidence in your ability to manage on your own and keep him at bay."

"How?" Tyrak asked, genuinely interested.

"By gaining the respect of your people again," Arrgo said. "You have done bad things, terrible things that can never be forgotten or forgiven. But you are a warrior, and warriors do terrible things. Violence is the wrong path, and yet a warrior has no choice but to walk that path all the way to the end, so that other castes can live their lives peaceably. This is your *Auma.* But the least you can do is balance the scales. Prove to your people that you do what you do for the betterment of Arrgodi, for the future of the Arrgodi. Put the marauding and madness behind you. You have already suppressed your urrkh side admirably. That is why I decided it was worthwhile speaking with you. Now you must rebuild the reputation you lost and become the king Arrgodi needs once more."

Tyrak had only stared at him. It was as if Arrgo had stated his entire life goal in words. There was nothing the old man had said that he did not agree with. He had put his urrkh side behind him, he had turned his back on the madness and marauding. That was the old Tyrak. The Tyrak he was now desired to be a king in the true sense of the word. To command dignity, respect, adulation. Even the respect of his own father-in-law. He craved desperately for Jarsun to acknowledge him as a good king and an equal, not merely a protégé and son-in-law. But how could he achieve such things?

"How?" he asked.

The old man smiled, his thousand-wrinkled face creasing like a crumpled leather map that had been folded and refolded too many times. "By winning."

Now Tyrak returned to the present moment, to the stadium in Jarsun's war camp, where he stood with nineteen other team members, awaiting the signal for the game to begin. Out the corner of his eye, he saw Jarsun raise his hand, assenting. Below, the game referee blew a long, sharp burst on his carved bone horn, indicating the start of the game.

The two team captains stepped forward. Tyrak and Crooked Jaw faced each other across the line that separated their two "kingdoms."

Crooked Jaw glared down at him. "We will tear you apart limb from limb."

Tyrak grinned.

Crooked Jaw had been expecting like threats and bombastic claims from Tyrak, not a congenial smile. He frowned, confused. Tyrak added to his confusion by dropping one eyelid in a mocking wink. Crooked Jaw snarled and shook his fist, almost striking the referee.

The man in question shouted to be heard above the hubbub of the spectators, eager for the game to begin.

"God-Emperor Jarsun has declared that there will be no restrictions on body blows and strikes. All moves are acceptable. However, there will be no replacements either. If you lose a man, you play with what you have left. The last team standing wins! Jarsun has also declared that since the Krushan team won their last match, they have the honor of starting today."

And with that he stepped back hurriedly, eager to be out of reach of the opponents, and blew a sharp, short burst on his bone horn.

At once, Crooked Jaw leaped across the line, choosing to send himself into the fray as the first invader.

The game was on.

## 6

Crooked Jaw lunged forward. Tyrak's teammates were spread out in a semicircle surrounding the intruder, blocking his way, ready to grasp hold of him if he tried to make a rush at their home line, but also wary of coming within his clutches. His goal was to try to reach their home line, while theirs was to stop him from doing so. It was basic war strategy: the enemy attempted to take your prime city; your army attempted to stop them.

The game required the intruder to constantly chant a single word. It could be anything the player or team wished, so long as it was chanted constantly without pause. The effect was to prevent the intruder from drawing breath too easily and make him tire much faster, thereby pressuring him to either achieve the enemy's home line or "perish." The Krushan team's word was, predictably, *Morgolia,* and Crooked Jaw repeated it over and over again — "Morgolia, Morgolia, Morgolia, Morgolia" — as he feinted this way, then that. Among other things, the referee's task was to ensure that all players chanted their word without pause or respite, failing which, they would be deemed to have perished and be removed to the sidelines.

Crooked Jaw's huge barrel chest was probably the reason why the giant could continue his feinting and chanting without tiring for several moments.

The crowd kept cheering him on, certain of their team's victory. Tyrak assumed that the home team almost always won these games, because if they lost, even if some survived the game itself, they would not survive Jarsun's disapproval afterward. That was strong motivation to win, and it showed on the larger man's face as he danced with surprising agility from one end of the field to the other, sending Tyrak's teammates rippling this way, then that, in order to maintain a solid wall.

Finally, Crooked Jaw made his move. Feinting right, he lunged left, then dodged the other way, waited till Tyrak's teammates rushed to block that side, then turned around and ran the same way but got past the first wall of players.

The player he had successfully dodged lunged at him and grabbed his torso with both hands, attempting to knock him off his feet.

It was a serious mistake.

Once a player made contact, the intruder was free to use whatever force necessary to free himself. Other players could join in, but if the intruder then crossed the line of the area they were guarding, they would be out of the game instantly. The player who attacked Crooked Jaw had to either stop him now or forfeit his own part in the game.

But that was the least of his problems.

Crooked Jaw roared with delight, pleased rather than angry. "Morgolia, Morgolia, Morgolia!" he chanted loudly.

And the crowd, smelling first blood, roared in response: "MORGOLIA! MORGOLIA! MORGOLIA!"

Tyrak's teammate held his grip around Crooked Jaw's torso. Crooked Jaw raised his elbow and brought it down on the other man's back in a stabbing motion. Now, with an ordinary man, this would hurt a little, depending on how much muscle and self-discipline he had accumulated. But with the special powers Crooked Jaw possessed, the effect was devastating.

The elbow struck the man's back and broke through it. Blood spattered in a great splash, falling on the dusty ground in globules. Crooked Jaw's elbow pierced the man's backbone, ribs, and lungs, and exposed his entire inner workings. He screamed as the last breath left his body, and Crooked Jaw tossed him to the ground like a sack of yams.

That was why Morgolia's team always won: each player was empowered by Jarsun through the use of his special potions, designed after he had seen the unexpected effects they had had on his son-in-law. Tyrak had thought himself to be the only one possessed of such an ability, but clearly that was no longer the case, if it had ever been. Jarsun had found a way to create more men with the same ability, and logically, the bigger and stronger and tougher the man was to begin with, the more formidable he would be after empowerment. Like Crooked Jaw. Or the rest of his teammates, all of whom were taller and wider and improbably stronger than Tyrak.

But Tyrak had also benefited from Ladislew's poison milk which had given him his ability to increase his density, apart from the fact that he was part-urrkh by birth. The other teams were ordinary mortal men, with all the weaknesses that normal mortal flesh was subject to. Like the man with the shattered chest who lay at Crooked Jaw's feet now.

Crooked Jaw turned and flashed Tyrak a smile, before crossing to the second block.

Tyrak's teammates were agitated for the first time. Whatever they had thought or heard of the Krushan, they had not been prepared for this. Even the earlier demonstration with the sword they had assumed to be some kind of trickery done with a wooden sword or the like. Now they were coming to terms with the realization that these were men whose skin truly was tough enough to resist the sharpest blade and who were possessed of greater strength than any normal man, and it was too much. They screamed at each other and cried out, unsure what to do.

"Hold the line!" Tyrak shouted over their cries.

They ignored him.

"Hold! The! Line!" he yelled, louder this time.

This time they heard him but looked at him as if he was insane.

But those on the second row understood and did as he bid.

They held their line, blocking Crooked Jaw's way.

Perhaps they thought that, despite his superior strength and ability, they might still block him by skill. The game was played in different variations everywhere, Tyrak knew, and every soldier who played it took pride in his skill. The best champions of the sport were often celebrated in their armies and admired by all.

Tyrak shouted instructions to his mates as Crooked Jaw continued his muttered chant, dodging the second wall of defenders now, seeking a way to get past them without making physical contact. Again, as was obvious, it was not that the intruder feared the contact itself, but that he feared being disqualified.

He dodged and feinted and dodged again. But this time the players followed Tyrak's instructions and simply held their positions, not moving an inch. Nobody responded to Crooked Jaw's feints and dodges, and after several tries, the giant grew frustrated.

"Morgolia!" he cried and charged headlong at the space between two of his opponents. He meant to barrel through them and run all the way to the home line, Tyrak knew. And with his superior size and ability, he would be able to achieve just that. Any of Tyrak's players who touched him to try to stop him would be taken out of the game, one way or another.

Tyrak was expecting that; it was the reason he had ordered the second line to stay still and force the Morgol's hand.

Now he leaped after the Morgol himself. Even though he was front and center, there was nothing to stop him from going after an intruder from behind, except the fact that if the intruder crossed the second line while still in contact with Tyrak, then Tyrak would be disqualified.

But Tyrak had no intention of letting him reach the second line.

He'd started running the instant Crooked Jaw began moving forward. Lighter on his feet, he was able to move much faster, and he was not burdened with having to chant a word constantly and deplete his breath. He pounded in an arc, sprinting at an angle that brought him in direct contact with Crooked Jaw, and slammed into the Morgol's right side, taking him by surprise. Had any of his teammates attempted this same maneuver, the result would have been akin to a child running into the side of an elephant. But Tyrak had hardened his body density to the maximum, and he was as tough as granite itself. He struck the Morgol with enough force to rattle him and throw him off his course. Once Crooked Jaw was turned aside, his own momentum carried him the rest of the way.

Crooked Jaw tumbled, rolling over once before coming to a halt with a heavy thud. Tyrak felt the impact through the ground, far greater than the impact of his own shoulder hitting the ground. Tyrak looked up and checked his position: he had fallen safe, within the chalk line of his "kingdom's" boundary.

Crooked Jaw, on the other hand, was just over the line.

Which meant he would have to go to the sidelines and wait until one of his teammates crossed to the home line and brought him back into the game.

The bone horn blew a short, sharp burst, indicating that Crooked Jaw was out for the moment, and the referee pointed to the sideline. Crooked Jaw looked as if he would like to wring the man's neck, but he rose to his feet and went silently to the sideline. From there, he glared pointedly at Tyrak.

Tyrak grinned. If he wanted, Crooked Jaw could demolish the entire enemy team single-handedly in a moment. He must demolish scores of them each day during battle. But this was different. This was a sport, and there were rules and tens of thousands of his admirers watching. He would want to win within the bounds of the rules, not by breaking them. That was the fact Tyrak had counted on. And that Arrgo had reminded him of. "The limitations that you find frustrating are also your greatest advantage. Use them against your opponent. In war, as in sport, the goal is the same. Use what you are given in unexpected yet effective ways. He who does so most shrewdly wins on both fields."

That was what the old man had taught him the night before: how to win at this game. For he had known that Jarsun would send for Tyrak soon and that he would use this very game to try to humiliate and undermine him as a precursor to justifying taking control of Arrgodi. How Arrgo had known this, Tyrak did not know. It hardly mattered. He had listened and trained intently all night, eager to learn as much as he could in those short hours. It helped that he had played the same game often before as a boy and a youth, although in a much milder form without such violence, and that he had actually been quite good at it.

Now he grinned at Crooked Jaw, savoring his first victory of the game.

His teammates were ecstatic but reserved.

"He is out for now," one said to Tyrak. "But when he returns . . ."

"And what of his teammates?" asked another troubled voice. "If they are all as invulnerable as he is, what chance do we have?"

Tyrak smiled. "We take the battle to them."

Then he turned to the referee and indicated himself. The referee nodded and came forward to point at Tyrak, blowing his horn again to indicate that the captain of the enemy team was now using his turn to send himself into the Krushan domain.

Tyrak glanced up. Jarsun was watching with a deceptively genial expression. His daughters waved excitedly, pleased to see their husband achieve his first moment of victory and cheer him on. *Perhaps after I win this game, I will go to them tonight,* Tyrak thought. *In their father's own tent.*

He grinned at the prospect and leaped forward into the enemy quadrant, slapping his thighs and chanting the word he had chosen as his team's mantra. "Arrgodi, Arrgodi, Arrgodi . . ."

## 7

Four of them came at him at the same time.

Crooked Jaw's teammates did not have any reason to hold back. They knew what they were capable of, and after enduring the ignominy of watching their captain being sent to the sidelines by Tyrak, they wanted revenge. They were all bigger and tougher than he was and felt confident they could destroy him easily, even in one-on-one combat.

But just to be sure, they advanced together, their intention not merely to knock him out of the game but to kill him. He had no way of knowing if this was on Jarsun's orders or merely their own death wish for him, but dying was dying, whether it was done on orders or not.

They were smart, he had to give them that much. And they were experienced warriors, so they didn't approach from the front, giving him a chance to flail out at them. Two came at him from either side at the same time, forcing him to choose whether to strike this way or that. The other two attacked from behind, also at the same time, one going high, the other low. They intended to ram him and crush him, breaking his bones and smashing his vital organs.

He stood still and let them try.

They struck with the combined force of four chariots in a head-on collision. Usually, when his body was this hardened, he would sense the superficial impact — the vibrations, shuddering — and hear the sound of something thudding against his petrified flesh. But not actually feel anything.

This time, he felt it.

Felt the massive weight of their combined tonnage hitting him. Felt it through his flesh as rigid as iron, his bones as solid as granite, right into the core of his being. They must have struck him with a combined force of at least a ton of weight. Enough to pulverize almost anything.

He withstood it.

It was the densest he had ever made his body. He had compacted himself so much he could feel his heart pumping only once every several seconds, the blood barely trickling through his hardened veins. He was almost a block of stone.

They had not been expecting that. They had expected him to move, to lash out, to try to dodge or escape the impact. They had moved fast, in order to strike unexpectedly as well as to coordinate their actions and hit at exactly the same time. This meant that they had only partially hardened their bodies, more than enough to crush him, but not so much that they could not move or control their limbs.

So instead of them crushing him, he crushed them.

The same force of impact that they inflicted upon him rebounded on themselves.

It was like hitting a stone wall with an iron fist.

It was a contest between which was denser, stronger.

As it turned out, he was the smarter one.

He saw the two who rammed his shoulders break their own on impact — their arms crumpled and cracked open. He saw the petrified flesh and blood within exposed like an iced corpse cut open, marbled veins and gelatinous blood. He saw the white of their bones snapping, breaking, showing jagged edges.

The ones who struck him from behind he could not see, of course.

It took him an instant of concentration to reduce his density enough that he could move. At once he felt the piercing thirst that always accompanied severe densification. He was parched, felt like he could drink a barrel or three right now.

*Later,* he promised himself. *Time enough for food, drink, and celebration.*

He stepped out of the tangle of bodies, turned, and examined the results.

All four of his attackers lay on the ground, two with shoulders split open, one with his collarbone shattered, the fourth with chest and rib cage and lower jaw broken in several places. All the points where their bodies had impacted with his own. Simply because they had sought to rush him fast, and he had stood stone still. Literally stone still.

"Arrgodi, Arrgodi, Arrgodi . . ."

The words continued from his barely parted lips. It was the only thing he had kept up unceasingly through the scant seconds of the attack.

He looked at the enemy team. They were staring at him with gaping mouths. Never before had anyone downed four of their teammates at one go. Then again, they had never faced anyone like Tyrak ever before.

He had taken out the entire frontline in a single move.

Now he moved across the first border to the second section.

"Arrgodi, Arrgodi, Arrgodi . . ."

He realized the crowd had gone quiet. It was as if the lid of a heavy box had been shut suddenly, blocking off the sound within. The utter silence was deafening. The crowd had probably been watching these games for years. They were so accustomed to seeing their home team win they probably had no conception that it was even possible for them to lose.

He would show them it was possible.

The other team members had recovered from the shock of their teammates' failure.

Six of them made a wall across the second quadrant, blocking his way effectively. Two more lurked on the edges, as a backup measure.

This time none of them made a move to rush him. Instead, they watched him warily, stepping this way, then that to keep the wall tight yet mobile, showing him that they could match any move he made and block him.

Which was what he had expected.

He turned sharp right and sprinted to the side of the quadrant. Because they had all held the line tight to block his way, there was a gap of about three yards at that end. It was unusual for anyone to run fast in the game because of the risk of failing to catch one's breath with the constant chanting, but he was willing to take that risk. He sprinted to the side of the quadrant, where the referee stood with his bone horn, saw the look of surprise on the man's eyes — surprise mingled with more than a little fear, for the man had already seen what he was capable of — then swung sharply left, through the gap.

The instant he'd started sprinting, his opponents had guessed what he was up to and the players on this side had begun moving to block the gap. But they were slower than he was, and only two made it in time.

He barreled straight into them, aiming for their arms, which they had made the mistake of linking together in a foolish bid to block him more effectively.

He tore their arms from their sockets. The cracking and ripping sounds of the limbs being wrenched from the hardened bodies was very loud in the stadium. He threw the torn appendages aside and continued at the same sprinting pace.

"Arrgodi, Arrgodi, Arrgodi," he chanted nonstop.

There were ten players holding the last quadrant. All had begun rushing toward this end of the quadrant the moment he moved to this side. But he dodged this way and that, making them unsure which way he would go. As a result, their line was ragged, and each player was separated from the others by a yard or three.

He ran straight at the nearest player and grabbed hold of him.

The man was not expecting a direct assault. But he wasn't wholly unprepared.

He reacted by grasping Tyrak as well.

Tyrak had the man's head in a vise grip and now, as the man struggled, began to choke him while pushing his head backward. The man in turn had his arms around Tyrak's torso and was attempting to crush his softer rear organs on the sides.

Tyrak hardened his body instantly and shoved with all his strength.

The man tried to harden his body but was a fraction of an instant too late.

Tyrak heard the sound of the iron-hard neck cracking and saw the Krushan player's head topple backward, until it touched his shoulder blade.

Tyrak let the body drop. It fell with a dull thud to the dust of the ground.

He charged at the next player.

This man too was somewhat surprised at the assault. It was usual for the defending team to attack the intruder, not for the intruder to do so to the defenders!

Also, once body contact was made, the two players had to either wrestle one another to the ground till one yielded or push one another across the border lines.

Tyrak wrestled the man. The man was very wide across, with a thick middle, so Tyrak had gone for his thigh instead. Grasping hold of it, he threw his own body backward, knocking both of them off their feet. The man landed heavily on his back. Tyrak had less far to fall and was the one doing the throwing, so he could land less impactfully. Still, it was an effort to keep the chant going and exert pressure on the man's thigh. He climbed atop the man at an angle, grabbing his langot and pulling it to gain purchase. With ordinary wrestlers, pulling the langot was an effective move because it exerted pressure on a man's most sensitive parts. But with these men, it made little difference. What it did achieve was giving Tyrak a handhold.

Using the langot to turn around, Tyrak caught hold of the man's arm and then his thigh again.

Then he stood up.

Straining, he heaved the man up like a sack of bricks — or iron ingots, from the feel of him — and flung him across the border line.

The man roared in fury as he realized his mistake. But by then he was already thudding down . . . across the border line and out of the game. He slammed his fist on the ground in frustration, hurling abuses at Tyrak. He would have gotten to his feet and run back into the quadrant, but the referee was standing by and blew his bone horn at once.

Tyrak turned and saw that the others had no intention of waiting for him to work his wiles on them as well.

Two of them came at him, taking hold of his upper and lower body respectively. Their intention was probably to twist in different directions, either tearing him in two or contorting him enough to injure him severely.

Tyrak rolled over the head of the man holding his lower body, kicking out at the face of the higher player at the same time.

The move was not sufficient to break him free of their grasp, but it was enough to cause them to lose their balance. As each was pulling in a different direction, they tumbled together, their grip on Tyrak loosening slightly.

Just enough for him to grasp hold of their arms and twist — he spun like a corkscrew in midair, using his purchase on their own bodies against them.

Both arms twisted at impossible angles, then turned like wet rags being wrung out to dry.

The men screamed in pain and shock — even though their bodies were hardened, they were still mobile enough to feel such severe trauma. Blood spattered Tyrak from both sides, splashing his chest and back. It was cooler than normal blood would have been because of the hardening. The more sluggish their bodies became, the cooler the blood temperature, the slower the flow.

Tyrak landed on his feet again and turned to the next opponent.

He circled three or four of the enemy players as they watched him warily.

By now, Crooked Jaw was yelling orders from the sideline, frustrated at watching his team being destroyed by a single man.

Tyrak grinned at them and waved to Crooked Jaw who, even more infuriated, began hurling curses.

"Arrgodi, Arrgodi, Arrgodi . . ." Tyrak muttered.

He wrestled his way through the rest of the team. It was hard but satisfying work. Every one of the moves Arrgo had shown him worked perfectly. It was as if the old Arrgodi had known precisely how his enemies would attack or respond. He supposed that was true in a sense: there were only so many ways a man could wrestle or physically block another man. And of those ways, even fewer were effective in this game.

Every move Arrgo taught him came in useful. Including the more complex, hand-foot combinations that required considerable agility and effort.

When at last he crossed the enemy team's home line, the crowd erupted in a huge wave of reluctant admiration and applause. Never before had they seen such a thing done, he learned later. Well, not precisely. They had seen it done only once before, when Crooked Jaw came to play for the Morgol team. An enemy chieftain — like all the members of the Morgol team — he had worked his way through Jarsun's entire squad of champions just as Tyrak had done today, making mincemeat of them all. It had been even more formidable because he had not possessed the power to densify his body back then. On the other hand, neither had the others. This new level of bodily prowess was a relatively recent development.

But Tyrak had faced an entire team of empowered Morgol and demolished them. And that must surely count as a greater achievement.

As he raised his clenched fist, surrounded by his ecstatic teammates, all of whom would now be freed along with their tribes, Tyrak saw Crooked Jaw coming toward him, his ugly face dark and furrowed with anger.

He turned to face him, his teammates moving aside to make way for the giant.

Tyrak hardened his body, prepared for attack. The contest was officially over, but he knew that sometimes the real fighting began after the game was ended. Especially in army camps.

Crooked Jaw stopped a yard short of him.

He glared down at Tyrak for a long moment.

"Arrgodi!" he roared, making the word sound like an insult.

Tyrak waited.

"You demolished my team!" Crooked Jaw shouted.

Tyrak said nothing.

Crooked Jaw raised a clenched fist.

Tyrak braced himself.

Crooked Jaw raised the other fist, also clenched.

Tyrak waited warily.

Crooked Jaw opened both fists and joined the palms together in a gesture of namas. "I bow to you in grace," he said gruffly.

Tyrak stared at him a moment, then realized what had happened and felt a surge of laughter bubble up. The giant was acknowledging his victory! It was the highest compliment one sportsman could pay another — or one warrior.

Tyrak clasped the man's joined palms with his own hands. "Well met, warrior. What is your name?" If they were about to become friends, he could hardly continue to think of him as Crooked Jaw. And he had a feeling that the man might not take kindly to the name being used aloud either.

"I am Musthika," said the giant with the crooked jaw. "And from this day henceforth, we shall be friends and fellow sporting partners."

Tyrak grinned. "So be it."

# 8

The crowd roared with adulation. People even threw money and items of food — anything they had to hand — perhaps not realizing that Tyrak did not fight for money. He fought for glory. And in the year since his first match, he had amassed a great deal of it.

This showed in the way he was greeted by even the aristocrats, nobles, and kings in Jarsun's pavilion as he entered. All Morgolia loved him. A record number had turned out to watch the Champion of Arrgodi play, and before the game began, one of his men had whispered in his ear the figure rumored to be the total value of the bets placed on today's game alone. It was a king's ransom.

Tyrak slapped the backs and shoulders of his men as they parted ways. All his teammates had become his dear friends and mates in life as well. Musthika, Sala, Kuta, Tosalaka, and Chanura were the closest to him, and he treasured the time spent training and practicing with them. His participation in this sport had changed his life, just as Arrgo had predicted. "There are only three things in life that drive a man forward," the old man said once to Tyrak during a particularly grueling training session. "Someone to care for who cares about you, something you love to do, and something to aspire to. Without these three things, nothing else is worth anything."

Tyrak glanced at the stands and saw the person he cared about seated there, watching. Ladislew. She acknowledged his glance with her usual sardonic smile. Her husband's seat was empty beside her. Tyrak didn't know whether she cared about him as well, but at least they shared a common purpose. That was good enough.

The other two items on that short list had never been his to enjoy. He had never found out what it was he truly loved doing, nor did he aspire to anything in particular. When young, he had desired to be what his father was, a great and powerful king of Arrgodi. But after he had achieved that goal and lived the life of a king for a decade or more, it began to seem meaningless and empty. Was this all there was to kingship? He did not love doing it. What next? He had found nothing else to aspire to apart from that. For so much of his life he had barely dared hope he would achieve his first goal, of replacing his father. He had never been able to think beyond that.

But after he had begun playing this sport, he had discovered two important things. One was that achievement and success changed everyone. It didn't matter that he was king of Arrgodi. A king could simply inherit his throne. In a sense, Tyrak had inherited his, after all. But a champion at a certain sport could only attain that position through talent, effort, achievement. Tyrak had excelled at this sport to an extent that nobody could have believed possible. But more than simply excelling, he had made the sport itself a national pastime. Nay, an international pastime! For now they were planning an interkingdom tournament with rounds eliminating teams until only the two or three best were left for the final day.

After all, they were not just a kingdom now, they were part of an empire. And an empire needed something to bind its diverse cultures and peoples together. Jarsun had seen his soldiers playing the game behind their tents one night several years ago and had co-opted the idea, sponsoring larger and larger games until finally, each time his army camped even for a week, they set up a stadium overnight and held games for all to watch. Jarsun had intended it to be a means of alleviating the stresses of battle and the intertribal rivalries and enmities that often led to late-night daggers in the back and gang fights. Tyrak had taken the same sport and transformed it into a national pastime. With himself its national champion.

Now he had queens fawning over him, princesses eager to give their virginity, lords and merchants placing huge wagers on him and eager to be seen by and with him for their own reasons. He had the respect and admiration of his wives. But above all, he had the grudging but unmitigated admiration of Jarsun himself.

The God-Emperor rose from this throne as Tyrak entered the main pavilion. "All rise for the champion," said his father-in-law in his piercing voice. Every last person in the large tent rose and bowed and congratulated Tyrak. Girls ran up and hung flower garlands around his neck until he began to feel like a living garden. Oily-looking men with curled mustaches made thinly veiled offers to have Tyrak wed their daughters, sisters, aunts, nieces.

When all the hubbub was over, he sat with Jarsun on the throne dais. Entertainments continued in the hall, but the Krushan's attention was barely on the nubile dancers or exotic music, said to be from some far western nation named Gyptos.

"You have done well," Jarsun said. "I am genuinely impressed."

Tyrak felt a flush of pleasure. He did not know why he should feel such a great satisfaction at hearing Jarsun praise him. He knew it had something to do with the fact his own father had never praised him much as a child, and once he had imprisoned the old king, he had taken away any reason to be praised forever. In Ashcrit, there was no separate word for *father-in-law.* The term was simply *father.* And he supposed that Jarsun had come to represent a fatherlike figure in his life. He had molded him, prepared him, awakened his urrkh nature, taken that power from him, transformed him into something else, albeit unwittingly. At all the major turning points in his life Jarsun had been present, moving him this way, then that, like a piece in a chaupat game. Even this most recent change was Jarsun's doing. Arrgo had somehow known Jarsun would present Tyrak with this challenge and would expect him to perform or die, but it was Jarsun who had put him into the stadium and told him to play. And even now, it was Jarsun whose opinion mattered to him more than all those screaming crowds and fawning nobles.

"Someday, we should have a bout or two," Jarsun added.

Tyrak felt a thrill of elation. Jarsun prized the sport of wrestling even more than the game of Khobadi. He was reputed to be a master wrestler, perhaps the greatest who had ever lived. For him to invite Tyrak to spar with him was a great honor and privilege. It didn't matter if he won or lost; Tyrak would have given his front teeth just to be able to lock heads with his father-in-law and show him firsthand what he was capable of.

Perhaps that was just what Jarsun desired as well.

## 9

War was an art.

Tyrak was a master of the art.

Now that he had mastered the use of his newfound powers, Jarsun wished to see his protégé deployed in actual combat. "What use a weapon if kept sheathed and only used in practice?" the God-Emperor had mused, then clapped his bony hand on Tyrak's granite back. "Time to put the bull among the sheep."

He charged through the enemy ranks, flailing, pounding, battering, bludgeoning, hammering . . . Though he used swords and sharpened blades in every form, size, and shape, his new method of attack relied more on brute force than technique or finesse. Under Jarsun's guidance and aided secretly by Ladislew's potent elixir, his body had grown even harder and become more invulnerable than before. Finely honed steel blunted when in contact with his skin, a razor-point javelin thrown by a bull-strong giant shattered without leaving the tiniest scratch, and even arrows with special steel heads designed to punch through armor splintered on impact.

But more amazing than his ability to withstand damage was his ability to inflict it.

As he was demonstrating so ably right now.

He was working his way through a throng of enemy foot soldiers. There had been perhaps four or five hundred when he had made first contact. Twoscore or more had been killed at that instant, bodies crushed and smashed like ripe berries under the impact of his weight and forward momentum. The huddled mass of the remainder, no doubt believing that by concentrating their strength they might resist him, swayed for a moment, then held their line like a hemp rope strung taut between trees. Perhaps half a score more were then crushed between their own comrades behind them and Tyrak when he pushed forward. He saw men wheeze bloody spray from their mouths and nostrils as their lungs collapsed or were punctured in the killing crush. He heard bodies crumple as he exerted strength. Others exploded like bulging wine bags bursting under an elephant's foot, spraying bloody remains everywhere.

He was coated in blood and guts and bone chips and offal.

It stank of victory to his flaring nostrils.

He roared and heard his own voice resonate, the increased density of his body somehow altering the sound to something lower-pitched, guttural, hard enough to assault those unfortunate enough to be in his proximity and cause physical pain: he saw men clutch at their ears and blood ooze from their orifices.

He spread his arms, bent forward in a bull's charging stance, locked his knees, and shoved on with a mighty effort.

The ranks of enemy soldiers rippled like grass before wind. At the back of the huddle, men were thrown yards away, tumbling madly.

He heaved again, then pushed, feeling his feet sink into the hard-packed earth, the ground crumbling beneath his weight and force.

The entire battalion of enemy soldiers flew as if struck by a battering ram. Soldiers at the edges and rear went in all directions, bodies flung through the air like straw scarecrows in a gale.

Tyrak grasped hold of as many of the nearest unfortunates as he could, perhaps a score of enemy soldiers, picked the whole mass up bodily, and shoved them to the left, then to the right. The soldiers caught in his actual grasp were crushed like ripe grapes, their organs and bodies spattering in his iron grip. The combined mass of their bodies served as a cudgel with which he bludgeoned the battalion itself. He shoved this way then that, pushing until the whole mass began to yield like a laden wagon once inertia is overcome, and he walked slowly, steadily, step by step, shoving five hundred massed men backward.

At the rear of the enemy battalion, men were being trampled underfoot by their own comrades as they were pushed back by the power of Tyrak's onward momentum. Some were pressed brutally hard against each other, some pierced or penetrated by their comrades' weapons or armor, others merely caught in the press and crushed to death.

It was a grape press, and Tyrak the vintner pressing living men into blood-wine.

By the time he had pushed ahead a hundred yards, every last man in the battalion was dead or dying from fatal wounds. Not a man remained whole. Tyrak stopped and let go of the men he had been holding on to. They fell like wet sacks to the bloodied ground. Ahead of him, the mass that had been an assembled battalion of some five hundred enemy soldiers, clad in gleaming armor, had been reduced to half a thousand pulped and mangled corpses.

He glanced back and saw the gory trail of his death walk: a hundred yards of the battlefield painted crimson with blood, gore, and offal. It reminded him of a freshly plowed field, the dark just-turned earth contrasting with the unturned side. Except that what he had done here was better compared to reaping, not sowing. He had reaped lives as if cutting wheat with a harvest blade.

He looked around the field. The battle was continuing to either side of his position. But not a single other enemy soldier approached him or dared to attack. He stood alone, alive, in a clearing of corpses within a forest of battle.

He grinned and thumped his chest twice to mark his victory.

The sound resonated across the field, louder even than the mangled screams and clash of weaponry, like a giant drumbeat tolling the defeat of the enemy.

A movement out the corner of his eye caught his attention. It was a single warrior, racing toward him on foot, sword held up like a javelin. It was a senapati of the enemy army, probably the commander of the battalion he had just threshed like maize. The man had to know that he stood no chance, yet he came straight at Tyrak, striking down diagonally as if dealing with any normal human opponent. The sword raked Tyrak's waist, the blade crumpling like tin, and with his other hand, the man tried to stab Tyrak with a dagger, aiming for his throat. Tyrak was impressed by the man's courage and permitted him his attempt. When the blade point shattered and then shattered again with each successive stab, the man was left with no weapon and no hope of success. Still, he hammered at Tyrak's iron body with his fists, kicked out, jabbed, and slapped, breaking his ankle, his wrists, his forearm, and dislocating his shoulders. And yet he fought on, audaciously, hopelessly, pitifully.

Tyrak grasped hold of him with a single hand, raising him up by the throat, the broken body still flailing desperately. Tyrak was curious. "Why did you throw your life away? You knew you could not best me."

The man stared down at Tyrak with hate burning in his black pupils. "You slaughtered my entire tribe today, Childslayer. What is a chieftain without a tribe? Kill me now, and let me die with honor like my kith and kin!"

Tyrak cocked his head, glancing sideways at the grape-pressed bodies of the men he had killed. An entire tribe? Had he really done that? In just a short while, no more time than it might take him to eat a meal or quaff a goblet or three.

"Fight me now, Monster of Arrgodi!" the chieftain cried hoarsely. "Fight me or die!"

*Fight me or die?* Tyrak almost smiled at that absurd threat.

Then, without even looking at the man, he closed his fist around the man's throat, feeling his fingers meet as the bones and tendons and flesh crumpled in his fist. The flailing and threats ceased at once. Tyrak let the corpse drop to the ground heavily, blood spurting from the severed throat.

He did not like that phrase, though he had heard it often before and knew he would hear it again. Not the first one: *Childslayer.* That one he did not mind, for he had indeed slain many children and had no regrets. He didn't mind being called what he truly was, after all.

It was the second name he didn't care for.

*Monster of Arrgodi.*

He was no monster.

He was Tyrak, king of the Arrgodi nation.

Lord of Arrgodi.

When would the world accept him as such?

# Jarsun

JARSUN WAS PLEASED. WATCHING the battle from a high promontory, he viewed Tyrak's rout of the enemy with pride and pleasure.

His protégé had come a long way.

Tyrak had done him proud.

His prowess on the battlefield today and in the preceding months had been nothing short of formidable.

No other fighter in his ranks matched the power and ferocity of Tyrak. Certainly none matched his tally of kills to date. The king of Arrgodi took lives like a force of nature. Even Jarsun sometimes found reason to marvel at his accomplishments. Tyrak had already become a legend in the ranks of the Krushan army. Once written off as a mere stripling Arrgodi capable of being taken down by a handful of Eoch Assassins, the son of Ugraksh and Kensura had now earned the respect of even Jarsun's most renowned champions. Almost all had come to accept and befriend him, some more closely than others. A few, very few indeed, had made the mistake of antagonizing or opposing him and had suffered the price for their folly: mostly on the akhara, the wrestling field, which was the only place Jarsun permitted his soldiers to resolve their internal differences. There, as on the battlefield, Tyrak fought with a ferocious single-mindedness that was unmatched, dispatching those foolish enough to oppose him with mortal blows or crippling injuries. Those who played against him sportingly, he dismissed from the game with a mere broken limb or two.

From a stripling of a boy unable to overcome his own base desires and lusts to a true warrior and leader of armies, Tyrak had come a long way.

Even his governance of Arrgodi had improved considerably. While the resentment remained and pockets of resistance continued to defy his claim to the throne, the overall situation had calmed down. No more open defiance and challenging of his authority. No more martyrdom and suicidal frontal assaults on his soldiers or himself. Political backbiting and character vilification were not things that troubled Jarsun overmuch: they were a part of public life, and even he knew how bitterly the people of his dominions must speak of him behind closed doors. So long as that bitterness was restricted to backdoor gossip and mere talk, it did not bother him. If anything, it only proved that Tyrak was maturing as a politician and statesman: every successful ruler had people who resented him. It was only when that resentment boiled over into open violence that it became a cause for concern.

Jarsun regained his seat, gesturing to his lackeys to fetch him choice sweetmeats. He always enjoyed sampling the local specialties of each region he conquered. Somehow, eating their food made the conquest real and memorable. The fact that he literally ate choice portions of meat carved from the bodies of victims in each region, prepared by their own cooks in the style of the region, lent a new meaning to the term "sweetmeat." It also added to his awe-inspiring reputation as the "eater of nations."

As he snacked on some delicious spiced cuts taken from the living body of the chief of chiefs of the region he had just invaded and was in the process of conquering, Jarsun considered Tyrak again.

He knew that the main cause of the change that had overcome his son-in-law stemmed from diverting Tyrak's urrkh predilection for violence and lustful living into more manageable diversions. Cooped up in Arrgodi all year long, Tyrak had taken to unleashing his appetites on his own people. That was not an advisable course of action for a long-sitting monarch. The old Arrgodi who had trained him in the use of his newfound abilities had clearly understood this and had successfully showed Tyrak how to divert his considerable power and strength into more sporting pastimes. Jarsun had then taken Tyrak to the next level: turning him into a yoddha in his own ranks, using him as a tool of conquest and expansion, while providing a natural outlet for his aggression. Better that Tyrak batter the brains of enemies in the battlefield than the heads of his own citizens in the streets of Arrgodi.

Thus far, the plan had succeeded magnificently. Tyrak had performed brilliantly, and Arrgodi had settled into the routine of bureaucratic torpor that was the usual condition of most capital city-states.

Jarsun ensured that Tyrak returned to Arrgodi regularly enough to establish his dominance and leave no doubt about his kingship.

He watched now as the familiar chariot wound its way up the hillside, bringing Tyrak to him.

Moments later, Tyrak stepped off the chariot and bowed, grinning as he presented his father-in-law and emperor with the severed head of the chieftain he had just defeated. "My emperor," he said. "A little something for your stew tonight!"

Jarsun chuckled. "Well done, my son. Come, sit with me. You have done well today."

Tyrak inclined his head graciously. Along with other graces, he had come to accept his position vis-à-vis Jarsun, which was also pleasing to the Krushan. "By your grace, Father."

Jarsun was silent awhile. Then he broached the subject that truly concerned him. The one problem that Tyrak and he had yet to conquer. "I wish to speak with you about the Deliverer."

Tyrak nodded, his grin vanishing and face hardening at the mention of his archenemy. He clenched his fist, crushing the goblet he had just drunk from without realizing he was doing so. The metal crumpled like paper, blood-red wine spilling between his fingers and dripping to the ground. "If only I could face him once, myself. I would—"

"You will," Jarsun said.

Jarsun carefully selected a choice item from the platter beside him, a delicacy left almost raw. He inserted it into his mouth and chewed slowly, savoring the exotic flavor. A trickle of blood escaped from the corner of his mouth and wound its way slowly down his chin. His tongue shot out, cleaning the trail, the tip of the extended organ lingering around his jaw and neck for a moment before retracting into his mouth with a slurping sound.

Tyrak frowned.

"I will what?" he asked.

"Face him."

Tyrak was silent for a spell. Talking to Jarsun made him feel like he was having half a dozen conversations at the same time in as many languages, none of which he was fluent in. Until now, whenever he mentioned the Deliverer, Jarsun had dismissed his concerns out of hand or failed to take them seriously. This was the first time he was actually agreeing that Tyrak should face him. Tyrak searched for hidden meanings. Was the Krushan trying to say something other than what he was putting into words? Finally, he decided to stick to the literal meaning. That was always safest where Jarsun was concerned.

"When?" he asked.

Jarsun wiped his mouth and looked at Tyrak with a smile.

"Will it be soon?" Tyrak asked hopefully.

Jarsun continued smiling. "Tomorrow," he replied. "You will face the Deliverer, your prophesied Slayer, *tomorrow.*"

Tyrak stared at him. "Where?"

"Here in Arrgodi. In the Khabodi arena. In a special tournament. Mraashk versus Arrgodi."

Tyrak was at a loss for words.

# *Tyrak*

## 1

"ARE YOU NOT PLEASED?" Ladislew asked, watching Tyrak's face.

Tyrak sat up in bed. Ladislew was already sitting, the bedcovers fallen around her waist carelessly, her body lit by the flickering light of the lamps. Tyrak stood and walked across the floor to the window. He leaned on the sill, staring out into the darkness. It was a moonless night.

"I have been awaiting this day for half my life," he said.

"That is not an answer."

He turned and looked at her. She was standing by the bed, her slender form moving with a graceful ease that he admired.

"What I feel right now cannot be described in a single word. I do not know if there is a word for it. Clever speech was never my strength."

She pressed her palm against his abdomen. "Your strength is your strength. That is enough. You are ready."

He felt a surge of relief. Jarsun had given his blessing by saying that he looked forward to Tyrak facing the Slayer on the morrow. But somehow Ladislew's approval mattered a great deal more to him.

"I have worked hard, I have trained, I have tested myself, I have tried to push myself to the limits, and each time I found I had no limit. None that I have yet encountered."

She moved her hand up to his mouth, covering it. "You are ready. You will fight him tomorrow. You will win."

He felt a thrill course through his body. Something far more pleasurable than the thrill of arousal or appetite. Something deeper. As a boy, he had longed for such approval, such confident support from his father, his mother, everyone around him; he had not found it. Instead, he had found contempt, disgust, revulsion: at everything he did. Even the most harmless things such as killing and cutting open little creatures to see what lay inside them. It felt like nobody truly understood him or even *wanted* to understand him. Now he had Ladislew. She understood. She cared. She supported him. That was a great thing, a great feeling.

"Yes," he said, believing it for the first time.

She smiled and pressed herself against him. "Come," she said, leading him back to the bed. "Feed some more, build your strength even further. And then I will feed too. On you."

## 2

Twenty-three years had passed since Tyrak usurped his father Ugraksh's throne, fifteen since the birth of Drishya. In that period, tens of thousands of Arrgodi had fled the city-state and chosen exile over life under the yoke of tyranny. Others had joined the rebellion, either openly taking up arms against the Usurper and harrying his armies on the borders and other vulnerable areas, or choosing to join the forces of those who resisted Jarsun's armies and the onslaught of the Krushan imperial juggernaut; they preferred to die fighting their mutual enemy rather than in an Arrgodi army led by Tyrak.

The internal campaign had been led by Rurka, who functioned as a militia commander as well as ambassador of sorts. Over time, politics makes bedfellows of everyone, and even Tyrak had dealings with Rurka, sometimes to resolve disputes to achieve a mutual interest, at other times to parley settlements. Tyrak had gradually acquired the art of diplomacy from Jarsun, learning when to use words rather than swords — and vice versa. He used Rurka when it was worth his while, never making the mistake of trusting the friend of Vasurava nor expecting trust in return.

Once Vasurava and Kewri had embarked on their pilgrimage, it was easy enough to extend it indefinitely. There was no shortage of sacred sites to visit, and they managed to stay away from Arrgodi and out of their tormentor's reach. More than once, Kewri wished to return, if only to be within visiting distance of her beloved Drishya. But Rurka convinced her that it would be too dangerous. Not only might Tyrak harm her and Vasurava directly, Jarsun would certainly use them as pawns in his larger game of empire building. Besides, once the Mraashk themselves went into exile, there was no way Drishya could risk leaving Mraashk to meet her, nor could Vasurava and she chance going to Mraashk themselves. Tyrak's spies were everywhere, watching and reporting back to Arrgodi, and so were Jarsun's spies, watching and reporting back to Morgolia. It was a dangerous era, and alliances were constantly being made and unmade.

Complicating matters further were the growing disputes over ascension in the great empire of the Krushan, the ancestral home of Arrgo, forebear of the Arrgodi and Mraashk lines. Hastinaga, the legendary capital, was at the epicenter of a great game of succession raging between two lines of the Krushan dynasty. Both lines claimed the throne and dynasty; each disputed the other's birthright. The issue was complex and required an understanding of Krushan history, but the basic facts were simple enough: one hundred and one children of Adri versus five children of Shvate. The great patriarch of the dynasty, Prince Regent Vrath, and Dowager Empress Jilana were both said to be keeping silent on the issue — although other rumors claimed that each had a favorite and it was their backing that fueled the dispute. As with all such matters, rumors and gossip dominated over hard truths, and all news was to be instantly distrusted and preferably discarded.

The only thing that seemed certain was that war was inevitable. It was only a matter of time before the dispute spiraled into open civil war between the forces of the children of Shvate and of Adri.

Vasurava's relationship with the Krushan ranged back decades, stemming from the fact that his own sister Karni had married the albino prince, Shvate the White, which made the five Krushan heirs Vasurava's nephews. Naturally, his loyalty lay with his sister's offspring. If and when Vasurava returned to the throne of Arrgodi, as everyone assumed would happen inevitably, then there was little doubt that Arrgodi forces would fight on the side of his sister's children. For this reason, Tyrak's resentment of Vasurava drove him to show hostility toward Karni and her children and to espouse the claim of Adri's offspring instead. A warmonger to the core, Tyrak actively encouraged Dhuryo, the eldest of Adri's children, and assured him of full military support in the event of a civil war.

Interestingly, Jarsun remained aloof in this matter, biding his time. Observers of politics compared his role to that of the carrion crow who waited for the battle to end to pick at the spoils. It mattered little to Jarsun who won, only how it affected his own plan of imperial expansion.

But on the day of the great wrestling tournament, even mighty Hastinaga was less concerned with their own internecine disputes than with the events unfolding in distant Arrgodi. Across the length and breadth of the civilized world, people debated the possible outcomes. Many favored Tyrak's chances of survival. The son of Ugraksh had surprised many by his longevity and unexpected ability to change from a demonic tyrant into a ruthless but efficient ruler. An urrkh he was, no doubt, and tales of his legendary appetites for violence and cruelty sent shivers up the spines of all who heard them, but many believed that sometimes it was better to have a urrkh as ruler than a weakling. Besides, war was a way of life to most, and Tyrak never shied away from war or from settling his disputes through violence, as even his success and fame at the sport of Arrgodi-style wrestling had demonstrated. Ugraksh had been old and too weak to go to war anymore, and Vasurava was regarded as too ineffectual to rule. People were loath to respect any king who permitted his newborn infants to be slain rather than fight back.

But these were the politicians speaking.

The people loved Vasurava, missed Ugraksh, hated Tyrak, and longed for Drishya to save them.

Drishya, the eighth child of the prophecy.

The Deliverer of the Arrgodi people.

Savior of the Mraashk.

Slayer of Tyrak.

Every time a new wave of atrocities had swept across the land, the people had consoled themselves with the knowledge that one day the Deliverer would rise and avenge them.

And finally, after twenty-three long years of suffering and faith, that day had come.

Not since the peace accord of Ugraksh and Vasurava had Arrgodi seen such a turnout. Every citizen came out of doors to view the arrival of the Deliverer. People who had been in exile returned home, preferring to risk their lives rather than miss this once-in-a-lifetime opportunity. Wanted men, entire factions of banned political groups, armed militia and civil rebels, outlaws and fringe collectives, every imaginable group in the Arrgodi nation drifted into the city to view the long-awaited conclusion of the prophecy.

Tyrak enlisted the aid of Jarsun's Eoch Assassins to help maintain law and order, and the bald gleaming pates shone at every street corner, as wickedly curved weapons and armor warned against any attempt to turn the day's sporting event into a political uprising. The Arrgodi army was out in full force as well, the soldiers helmed and armored as if for battle, armored elephants and horses and chariots arrayed at every square. Arrgodi had grown accustomed to being a military state, but where there had been simmering resentment or outright hostility toward the oppressor's army before, today there was an atmosphere of ridicule and laughter.

Even little children made funny faces and boldly knocked on armor plates, warning, "The Deliverer is coming to get you!" Even more unusual, the soldiers themselves seemed reluctant to suppress this insolence and tolerated even the most humiliating insults and behavior rather than resort to their usual crowd control methods.

There was a mood in the city this morning.

And it did not favor Tyrak.

It favored his opponent.

Everyone knew this and saw it.

Except Tyrak himself.

## 3

Tyrak woke early that morning. He had slept well, better than he had slept in weeks. He was in excellent form physically, and he thought he might have achieved the peak of his abilities. He could not see how he could be more powerful or destructive. He was now able to turn himself into the human equivalent of an iron ramrod, and there was nothing made of flesh that could withstand his combination of power and technique. He was the undisputed master of the wrestling field, and his team comprised the most dreaded champions across the civilized world.

He had spent the night enjoying the company of both his wives at once and felt confident that either or both would conceive from that joining. Which would be welcome timing. Jarsun was impatient for a grandchild and Tyrak himself now felt the need for an heir. Not because he desired a son or daughter, but because it was politically useful. Such was the game of kings.

He was leaving his chambers when he noticed the old minister Shelsis waiting silently outside. The aging mantri was in ill health and seemed half decrepit already. He jerked to alertness as Tyrak emerged. "Sire."

"What is it?" Tyrak asked, less sharply than usual. It was a fine day, and he was feeling fine too.

"My lord," the minister said, "the old syce is dead."

Tyrak frowned. "Who?"

Shelsis looked startled. "The old master of stables. I believe he was your friend and guru for a while. I thought you would want to be informed."

Tyrak realized whom he meant. "Oh, that old relic."

"Aye, sire. His name was Arrgo. Nobody seems to know exactly how old he was, and for some reason, nobody knows of any immediate family or relatives he left behind. The rumor is that he migrated here from another country a long time ago and outlived all his family."

Tyrak shrugged. "Why tell me all this?"

"Would you like to pay for his last rites, sire?" Shelsis asked nervously.

Tyrak laughed. "Burn him and throw the ashes into the nearest ditch."

He walked away without bothering to glance back at Shelsis. The nerve of the fellow, expecting him to care about some old idiot. Even if the man was *the* Arrgo, actual forebear of the Arrgodi dynasty, Tyrak couldn't care less how he was cremated. So what if the old syce had trained him and mentored him? He'd been paid to do that, hadn't he? Guru? Pah. Tyrak was the one with the strength, the one who would slay the Slayer, deliver the Deliverer, and it was his day of triumph. Nobody else mattered.

# *Drishya*

THE MRAASHK PROCESSION REACHED the top of the hill overlooking the Jeel and paused. Eshnor was driving the uks cart himself. He reined in the beasts, and for a moment, they all gazed down at the vista, enraptured.

Drishya was seeing Mother Jeel for the first time since the night of his birth. Yet he recalled her color, her fragrance, and the sound of her voice as only a child can recall his mother. He recalled the parting of the waters and the peculiar fish smell of the riverbed as his father Vasurava carried him across. He remembered the sight of fish and crustaceans trapped in the parted waters, still alive and swimming, and gawking at the Slayer newborn. He recalled wishing he could swim and play with them.

He remembered his first days in Mraashk, the milky sweet smell of his mother Alinora, how green and blue and beautiful the trees and sky were, and how he loved this new world and wanted nothing more than to frolic and play and explore it. He had never stopped feeling those things, and a part of him still wished the fighting and warring and crises could just end, once and for all, and all beings live in peace, enjoying the fruits and repast of their shared world.

Why was it so hard for living beings to understand that together they were one whole being symbiotically interlinked through food, weather, biology, and a thousand other intricate interdependent systems, while individually they were nothing but strays, incapable of sustaining or surviving?

Why did beings like Tyrak even exist? Why had they been created? Why was it necessary for a Slayer to be born at all? Why could the Creator not avoid creating cruelty and pain and violence and war? Why could the gods, in whose category he himself was included, not rid the world of such things forever?

But these were questions for other days, other incarnations, other lives.

Today, here, he was Drishya, Slayer of Tyrak, come to face his nemesis at last.

An entire nation looked to him to deliver them from evil.

A world watched, holding its breath as it waited to see if the stone gods still held sway over the mortal realm or if they had finally surrendered it to the urrkh, abandoning their creations and children.

*Drishya,* said a voice inside his head.

Drishya smiled to himself. *Hello, my sister.* He knew she was not his sister in flesh, but he had come to know her so well of late, she felt as close to him as a sibling.

*I am here with you,* she said. *I know you will fulfill your destiny today.*

*Thank you, sister. Your presence and support matter to me.*

*Remember, I am with you. My strength is part of your strength. Together, we are as one.*

*Yes, sister. I need you with me, to end the wicked reign of the tyrant usurper.*

*You have me. We will prevail. And when we have killed Tyrak, we will end the evil reign of his master, the Krushan.*

*It is a good day,* Drishya replied. *We will rid the world of two great evildoers.*

*I leave you now very briefly, but I will return when you need me. Summon me, and I will be with you in an instant.*

*Yes, sister.*

And then he felt the prickle of her presence inside his mind fade as she drew back into her own body, many miles distant.

He touched his father's arm. "Come, Father," he said. "Let us go meet the Usurper and end his story."

Eshnor wiped his face roughly in the manner of a man who is not accustomed to crying openly or showing much emotion. He nodded silently and restarted the uks wagon, urging the animals to move forward, down the long, trundling path that led to the ferry that would bear them across the Jeel. Behind them, the procession of wagons and carts bearing the entire Mraashk clan followed.

# *Krushita*

KRUSHITA CAME BACK INTO herself with a drawn breath. She was lying on the bed of her wagon, and she sat up now, smiling. The moment of deliverance was at hand. Soon the cruel Tyrak would be dead. And after he was finished, it would be the turn of an even more evil monster. Jarsun Krushan.

She was ready. She had regained her strength these past years, knowing she would need it for the final confrontation. She had eaten even when she didn't want to eat any more, run and jumped and played all the games that Afranus and the other young people played.

But she was no longer a child. She was a young woman. Even her mother said so. At fifteen, she was of an age when most young men and women in Arthaloka married and had children of their own. Even younger, in some places. That was not the case in Aqron, where the legally permissible age of marriage was seventeen, but here in Reygar, there was no minimum age. One did as one pleased, so long as all parties consented.

Then, her joy diminished a little, as she reminded herself, *We are not in Renshor.*

*Not yet.*

She realized then that the wagon had stopped. The train had been on the move when she came inside and lay down to commune with Drishya. Why had they stopped?

She parted the canvas flaps that helped keep most of the sand out, and stepped out onto the "porch," as they called it. It was only the raised shelf which served as the backrest for the wagon driver, but she was still small enough to stand on it. She had always been a delicately built child, and that had not changed — much. She was still petite in body, but inside, it was another matter.

What was that line from that old Vanjhani song Bulan and her mother sang together sometimes?

*"The souls of men grow older than their faces . . ."*

That described her to perfection.

On the outside, she was fifteen.

Inside, she felt a hundred years old.

Then she registered the reason for the train stopping and snapped back into herself.

The train was still spread out in its usual traveling pattern. But instead of open desert on all sides as she had seen before she had gone into the wagon, there was a sand cloud in the distance.

She turned and looked around, to the left, then to the right. The sand cloud surrounded them on all sides.

She froze in horror.

"Not now," she said to herself. "Not! Now!"

# *Bulan*

~

BULAN AND AQREEN WATCHED grimly. The Vanjhani had angled each of their heads to be able to see almost completely around themself. Not a Perfect Circle, but close enough.

On every side, they saw the same thing: A sand cloud so high, it could only be raised by a sandstorm or a massed force moving at great speed.

They already knew it wasn't a sandstorm.

No sandstorm formed a giant circle, then closed in on its center.

That left only a massed force.

But a force large enough to surround the entire length of the train, with miles to spare on every side would have to be . . . Bulan couldn't even begin to calculate how many dromads and mortal bodies it would take to make a force that enormous.

Millions? Tens of millions?

Whatever the size of the force, it was impossible to think of any viable defense.

"Shall we form a Perfect Circle, Train Master?" Aqreen asked with a clipped tone that spoke more to her militia training and self-discipline than a genuine desire to execute the maneuver.

Bulan turned one head to look at her. The face smiled sadly at her.

"My lady, you know as well as we do that it takes us, even with so many years of experience on the trail, several hours to form the Perfect Circle. And even if we do so before that force reaches us, what then? No circle, perfect or otherwise, could fight a force that huge. We would only be expending our energy and wasting valuable time."

Her chin quivered briefly, betraying her acceptance of what she had also known. “Then what shall we do?” she asked in a soft, pleading voice, totally unlike the strong, powerful woman Bulan had come to know, to respect, and yes, they could admit it to themself at last, love.

Not the love of a lover, perhaps, because they would never admit their feelings to a woman who was still living in the shadow of a cruel monster of a husband and complicate her already troubled life further, but the love of a dear friend, one who had fought and bled alongside Aqreen and loved her and her daughter as dearly as if they were Bulan’s own family. They *were* Bulan’s family. Every single person on this train was, as well, but Aqreen and Krush were the ones closest to Bulan’s hearts.

“I have an idea,” Bulan said. They turned one head to look in the direction of Aqreen’s wagon. They had noticed Krush going inside a while ago. They understood implicitly the reason for Krush disappearing into her wagon at unexpected times. Not to lie down and “take a rest” as she told her friend Afranus, but to keep her body safe while she roamed the highways of the spaces between places and times. Bulan themself had advised it after the Battle Against the Deadwalkers, and Krush had seen the logic in it. On every occasion thereafter, she had done the same. That way, at least Bulan and Aqreen didn’t have to worry that her body might be harmed while her spirit was away from it.

Aqreen saw the direction of Bulan’s gaze.

“No, not little Krush,” she said wearily, “not again.”

Bulan put a hand on Aqreen’s shoulder, reassuring her. “She is not little anymore, my lady. She is of age, and old enough to take care of herself. She has proven that on ample occasions. These last few years, when we turned away from Reygar, we could never have survived without her powers to aid us.”

Not being able to go into Reygar had been a crushing disappointment to everyone on the train. After coming all this way and enduring so many hardships, it had seemed inconceivable that they could not enter it when they were only a little more than a hundred miles short. But the Maatri scouts posted by the matriarchs had been crystal clear: *Reygar is under siege and can accept no visitors.*

After the unexpected encounter with the Maha-Maatri Ladislew and her departure, they had learned that the traitor Dirrdha’s army had laid siege to the city. It was an odd siege, since the army wasn’t actually within sight of Reygar but was camped some one hundred and fifty miles north of it.

Yet it was a siege all the same. Dirrdha possessed enough numbers to effectively box in the city, cutting off all the major routes. Lone riders could still try to break free, but Reygar had tried, and each time, the escapees had been killed before they could get very far.

Besides, where did one go from Reygar? The other cities of Reygistan were anywhere from a thousand to five thousand miles away. They looked to Reygar for help in times of trouble.

In any case, the point was moot. The matriarchs would rather die than leave Reygar. They had spent ten thousand years building the city, and they had stood against too many enemies before to simply pull up roots and leave.

So the Maatri remained, and so long as they remained, almost the entire population of Reygar would not dream of leaving. This was the safest place to be.

Besides, what would Dirrdha do? He could surround the city, lay siege, attack the walls a thousand times in a thousand years, and he would never take it.

Reygar could not be taken.

It was not a city built upon a mountain.

It was a city built *from* a mountain. The very walls and structures of the houses that rose in concentric spiraling circles from the bottom to the top were carved out of solid rock. Inside the heart of the mountain was a labyrinth of tunnels that led to deep underground caverns where a network of lakes and ponds lay. The city had the greatest water supply in the entire Red Desert, enough to keep the population well hydrated for ten thousand years so far. Water meant the ability to grow food, to water cattle and fowl and other livestock. What else did a people need to survive?

Reygar would stand eternally, and the Maatri would hold Dirrdha at bay while he and his enormous army would starve and die of thirst out on the red sands. In everyone's opinion, Dirrdha had the worst part of the bargain.

Yet, defying all odds, all logic, Dirrdha's encirclement of Reygar remained, month after month, year after year.

Somehow, impossible though it seemed, his soldiers were able to get food and water even out in the wasteland of the Red Desert.

In fact, he seemed to be in no hurry whatsoever to take Reygar.

In the two years before the wagon train's arrival, he had attacked the city only once, at the very outset. Casualties had been light on both sides as the Maatri had seen the invading force coming from hundreds of miles away and had been prepared. For his part, Dirrdha appeared only to want to press home the point that he was there and wanted Reygar. Once the point was made, he withdrew his forces to a distance of some few hundred miles, and there he stayed to this day.

Or had stayed, till some weeks ago, which was the last time Bulan had received news from Reygar.

With entry into Reygar refused to the train, Bulan had had no choice.

They had been forced to change course for the next Reygistani city. The much smaller, much less desirable — from a trade as well as a living point of view — city of Renshor. That was a journey of another two thousand miles.

The travelers had not wanted to extend their journey, which all agreed had been too long and too arduous already. But by this time, they were unified. They knew Bulan could do nothing else. Waiting out in the desert for the siege to end was no solution. If Dirrdha won, they would risk their lives and all their precious cargo — a lifetime's worth of wealth in the form of goods to most. And camping outside Reygar in the hopes that the matriarchs would win could mean waiting an untold number of years.

No, there was no help for it.

They turned toward Renshor with heavy hearts and weary bodies, bracing themselves for another long leg of thankless travel.

And now, when they were only a few hundred miles from their destination, *this* was happening.

What this was exactly and how or why it was happening, Bulan did not know.

The only force this enormous in the Red Desert was that of Dirrdha's invaders. But why would Dirrdha leave his prime target, Reygar, to come after a wagon train carrying goods?

The question would baffle many, but not the three people who knew the answer.

Bulan, Aqreen, and Krushita knew that whether this was Dirrdha's army or some other prodigious force, the sole malefactor behind this was Jarsun. It seemed the Krushan had decided to finally end this game once and for all.

A force of such a size would roll over the train like a firestorm, wiping them all out within minutes. Even if all the travelers had been Vanjhani, Bulan could not have expected a single one to survive. This was no less than the deadwalkers. Perhaps even worse in some ways. The deadwalkers were mindless killing things, laying waste to everything in their path. If these were Dirrdha's soldiers, they were *Jarsun's* soldiers. And Jarsun might not consider death a hard enough end for some of them. He might want to keep them alive for torture, abuse, or slavery — who knew what foul fates he had in mind for the hapless survivors? And he would get what he truly wanted at last: Krushita. And with her, the key to the Burning Throne and the Burnt Empire. And then the world entire.

Unless.

Unless Krushita could use her powers once again.

Bulan hurried to the wagon where Krushita still stood, staring in furious disbelief at the approaching sand clouds. Aqreen was by their side, and she went to her daughter first.

Krushita cried out at the sight of her mother and fell into her arms. Aqreen caught her, and both mother and daughter hugged fiercely, tears flowing down their cheeks.

"Why did he have to do this *now?*" Krushita said plaintively. She sounded angrier than Bulan had ever seen her before. "I only needed a little more time to end it. He must know. It's the only thing that makes sense."

Aqreen stepped back and looked at her daughter. "What are you talking about? Who is *he?*"

Krushita shook her head impatiently. "There's no time to explain now, Ma."

Aqreen caught her daughter by the shoulders. "What are you not telling me, Krush?"

Krushita sighed. "Who else?"

Aqreen's face changed.

Bulan saw it. The expression that came over her was a sadly familiar one. One that conveyed all the years of pain, suffering, anxiety, and more that could not even be comprehended fully by anyone else. They suspected Krush knew what Aqreen felt at such moments; she could slip into and out of anyone's mind as she pleased. They even thought she might be coming and going in and out of Bulan's mind at times, though Bulan had never been able to catch her red-handed. Yet there were times when they felt a whisper-soft touch, like a hint of a breeze not on one's own skin but somewhere nearby.

"Your father," Aqreen said in a resigned tone. "Of course. But what did you mean, you needed more time to end it? End what? What does he know that I don't know?"

Krush shook her head. "It's not something I can explain. It has to do with portals and stopping him once and for all."

"You mean by stopping *that*?" Aqreen gestured at the distant sand clouds.

Bulan was not surprised to see that they were a little closer now, and approaching at the same relentless pace. How long would it take to reach the train? A half hour? An hour? It was difficult to tell for sure, but not more than an hour. It could be a whole lot sooner. Too soon for anyone to do anything — except Krush.

"No," Krush said angrily. "I didn't expect that. He's doing that deliberately because he knows I was doing something to help end him for good. This is his way of trying to stop me before I can stop him."

Aqreen raised both her hands, clutching her head. "I can't make sense of what you're saying, Krush. I know it makes perfect sense to you, but not to me."

Krush raised herself on her toes and kissed her mother on the cheek. "I will tell you everything afterward, but right now, I need to think. I need to figure out how to handle this." She frowned, her mind already drifting inward. "Maybe *he* can help me here. He's more powerful than either of us. He has to!"

Aqreen looked at Bulan in despair. Then, finding no answer in their two faces, looked back at her daughter. "I hope you don't mean your father? Because asking him for help is like asking the fire not to burn. You wouldn't make that mistake, would you, Krush?"

Krush looked at Bulan. "Bulan, please take care of her. I need to go away. Inside. You understand."

Bulan nodded grimly. "I do, Krush. You do what you must, what you can. I'll take care of her and you as well. It's best if you go into the wagon. You're safest there."

Krushita started climbing the wooden ladder again. Suddenly, she leaned over and kissed her mother on the top of her head. "I'll be back quickly, I promise. I'll explain everything. This will all be over soon. I will stop him this time and end it for good. I know I can. I will."

And then she was up the ladder, at the top, and through the flaps.

Aqreen turned to Bulan, her forehead crisscrossed with worry lines.

"What will we do now, Bulan? This is bad, really bad. I have a terrible feeling about it."

Bulan surprised themself by putting their arms around Aqreen, embracing her gently. They were careful not to use too much pressure. Their arms just reached low enough to encircle her upper back, and their biceps bulged out over Aqreen's head by several inches.

Aqreen reacted by stiffening for a moment, instinctively, then relaxed and hugged Bulan back as best as she could. Both her outstretched arms barely went around one side of them, but that was sufficient. She pressed her head against Bulan's muscled bulk, and they felt her shudder.

She was afraid.

Bulan was afraid too.

# *Bane*

"SENAPATI BANE, THE MRAASHK are entering Arrgodi," cried the captain of the outer gate.

General Bane of the Imperial Arrgodi Army already knew the Mraashk had entered the city. He could hear the roaring of the crowds. The sound was so immense, it seemed to come from everywhere, from all around the world. Even on this narrow street, people had filled the houses overlooking the way that the procession would pass, had crowded the rooftops, and were leaning out of windows, eager for a glimpse. In all his years, he had not seen Arrgodi so excited and happy. Not even the day of the peace accord had witnessed such a turnout or such adulation.

The Deliverer was here.

The same child who had been born in this very city, under lock and guard, heavy sentry watch, surrounded by a hostile army and a demoniac king who had killed his older brothers.

He had returned now to wreak his vengeance and fulfill the prophecy.

Bane felt the stirring of emotion in his own heart as well. He had never failed to feel it each time he heard the people speak of the Deliverer. He had felt it when a condemned man prayed to the Deliverer at the moment before his execution, when a child had died of yellow fever with the name Drishya on her lips, when he saw the misery and suffering and pain inflicted by Tyrak and all those who had served him these past twenty-three years.

The day the Deliverer had escaped Tyrak's grasp was as fresh in Bane's memory as if it had happened this very day. For that was also the day Tyrak had compelled Bane to put his own newborn twin sons to death, before his pleading, sobbing wife. And then, because he knew she would never forgive him and, more importantly, he would never forgive himself so long as she lived to remind him of his unforgivable crime, he had killed her as well. Slaughtered his own family with the same sword he carried in his sheath even today.

All for what? To serve a master who was more urrkh than human? Who cared for nobody, respected nothing? For *Auma*? He could almost spit into the dust of the street at the sound of that word spoken. *Auma!* It was not his *Auma* to slay his own loved ones. If that was *Auma,* then the concept itself was wrong, twisted, insane. No act of violence could be justified or condoned by *Auma* or any religious precept, however rigorous the argument. Murder was murder, plain and simple, no exceptions, and he had murdered his family only because he feared Tyrak's wrath.

And it had all been for nothing. All those newborns slain, other children slaughtered, so many more innocents killed . . . for what? To slake the bloodlust of a demon king. To protect a powerful urrkh from the divine vengeance that was due to him. To try to delay the judgment the gods had pronounced on Tyrak for his many, many crimes on earth.

And he, Bane, was a part of those crimes.

He deserved the punishment of the gods almost as much as Tyrak did. For he had done the evil overlord's bidding. And in doing so, he shared equal blame and responsibility.

But perhaps today, he would find some way to redress that long history of wrongdoing. If not redeem himself entirely, at least he might seek to balance the scales a little.

He turned his horse into a side alley. The roaring of the crowds were muffled by the close walls of the two houses that stood next to one another. Waiting in the alley was a man with his face cloaked, despite the warmth of the day. He watched as Bane approached and dismounted at the point where the houses stood too close together to ride through.

Bane walked the rest of the way, admiring the choice of location for this tryst. Only one man could pass through here at a time, and that slowly, or else he might dislocate both shoulders.

But then, Rurka was a clever man. Years of leading the Arrgodi rebellion against the Usurper had seasoned him into a shrewd and effective leader. In a way, Bane understood Rurka better than Vasurava. He could never fathom Vasurava's principles of self-denial and pacificism. How could you fight beings like Tyrak and Jarsun without resorting to violence? He respected Vasurava greatly, but he felt that such times demanded men like Rurka.

He stopped at the place where the houses were closest together. Rurka stood on the other side. Between them was a narrow gap large enough to see one another, but not enough for a grown man to pass through, even slipping sideways. Bane wondered idly if the builders had deliberately designed these two residences to serve this very purpose. Why else would these walls curve this way?

"It is arranged," he said curtly. "All the men loyal to me in the Arrgodi army will lay down their arms and surrender to Drishya if he defeats Tyrak in the tournament. It will be up to you and your supporters to ask for Drishya to be declared king."

Rurka nodded. "We will take care of our part. You take care of yours. What of those not loyal to you?"

Bane shrugged. "Who can say? There may be some fighting. I'm sure you have the stomach for that."

Rurka was silent a moment. "If it is the only way, yes. How will my people know which soldiers are loyal to Drishya and which are not?"

"They will not. You will just have to wait and see the outcome."

"What of the Eoch Assassins? There are few of them, but they are each deadlier than a dozen of your men."

Bane bristled at the comparison but knew he could not argue the point. "I cannot speak for them. Or for the Morgol forces encamped within a day's ride from Arrgodi. If Jarsun chooses to make his move and assert his claim on the city as an imperial holding, even our army and your militia combined will not be able to hold him back."

Rurka frowned. Now it seemed it was his turn to bristle at the comparison. "I think you overestimate the power of Morgolia —" he began.

"I think you *under*estimate it," Bane said curtly. He glanced back. "I must return to my post. The procession will come this way very shortly. May our great ancestor Arrgo look over you."

"And you," Rurka replied.

# *Drishya*

## 1

THE CROWD WAS ENORMOUS, the mood jubilant, the atmosphere electric with anticipation. Out of the press of people, a young man and a hunchbacked older woman came forward, clearly eager to have closer contact with Drishya. The hunchbacked woman was too stooped to even look up at his wagon properly. Drishya saw her plight and leaped down from the wagon. He strode to where the lady stood and took her by the shoulders gently.

"Mother," he said, "you wish to meet me?"

To his surprise, the woman straightened up, up, up until she was standing normally, her back upright, her hunch gone. She looked around, surprised, feeling for her hunch with her hands by reaching around. Beside her, the younger man exclaimed and reacted. "It is a miracle! My mother's hunchback is gone!" Others around him agreed and shouted their amazement.

At once the cry rose from the crowd. "Drishya cured the old woman!"

Tears were streaming down the woman's face. "My life ambition is fulfilled," she said. "I have seen the stone god with my own eyes."

Drishya embraced her warmly. "And he has embraced you, Mother. Go in peace."

When he returned to the cart, Alinora said, "That was a wonderful gesture, Drishya. Curing the old woman's affliction. It was truly a miracle." Her sisters, Drishya's aunts, all agreed vociferously.

"Mother, to be honest, all I meant to do was help her stand straighter so she could see me clearly as she wanted. The rest was the result of her own faith and inner conviction. I had nothing to do with it whatsoever!"

And it was the truth.

It was always the person's own faith that caused the cure, not some divine application of *Auma* by Drishya. All he had to do was be there, and it was enough.

They continued through the city at snail's pace, the wagon constantly crowded by people crying out, laughing, shouting, going into paroxysms of ecstasy at the sight of Drishya. Many incidents such as the curing of the old woman occurred, too many to count or recount. Finally, one of their Arrgodi friends who was helping clear the way for the procession announced that they would reach the wrestling fields soon.

Suddenly, a loud roar of dismay rose from the crowds ahead. Drishya saw people running away, past the wagon and back the way they had just come. They looked over their shoulders fearfully as they ran, clearly fleeing from something or someone. The Arrgodi guiding the procession shouted agitatedly to one another. Finally, the Arrgodi in front of their wagon turned and looked up at Drishya and Eshnor.

"My lords, it is Eredon, the dreaded demon elephant belonging to Tyrak. He has gone mad, they say, and is attacking and killing everyone in sight. We must turn the wagon around at once."

"We shall do nothing of the sort," Drishya said. "It would not be right to turn back just as we are reaching the contest grounds. It would seem unsporting and cowardly. Ride on, Father."

Eshnor did as Drishya bid.

They went a few yards further. By now, the street had cleared, and only the empty road wound ahead, hemmed in on either side by the walls bounding the military cantonment. They came around a winding turn into a straight stretch, and there they saw it, waiting about twenty or thirty yards ahead.

Drishya dismounted from the wagon. "Father, stay here. I will go take care of this."

"Drishya, be careful," Alinora cried out.

Drishya walked toward the elephant.

## 2

It was a giant among elephants, a great white beast. It was old too, its eyes rheumy and heavily wrinkled. Its hide was scored in a hundred places with scars of old battles in which it had fought: spear marks, lance gashes, sword cuts, javelin wounds, arrow punctures . . . It was impressive that the beast still lived, let alone had such energy and strength.

It moved with the ponderous gait of a large, heavy beast, and Drishya estimated it must weigh twice or thrice as much as most local bull elephants. Its enormous ears flapped like the fans held by royal servants attending a king. Its eyes were red and blazing with feverish rage, its mouth slobbering, its enormous tusks yellowed with age but still whole, still sharp enough to gore and kill.

Several dead Arrgodi lay around it, and their blood was smeared on its tusks and armor. The armor itself was designed to drive fear into the hearts of its enemy and bristled with jagged metal points and edges. Clearly, even friendly soldiers must stay far from this beast in battle, or else risk being cut to ribbons on its armor. Drishya could easily imagine Tyrak riding atop this monster, matching its destructive power with his own killing rage.

The elephant raised its trunk and trumpeted at the sight of Drishya approaching. The sound rang out across the city like a war horn announcing the start of battle. The immense crowds that had thronged the streets to greet the procession had fallen silent as news of the mad elephant traveled through the city. Drishya knew that people were watching from behind him and that every detail of what happened next would be spread by word of mouth like wildfire.

Eredon reared up and thudded back to earth with a force that Drishya felt, even ten yards away. It made the ground underfoot shake, and plaster dust fell from the walls that hemmed them in. He understood that Tyrak had chosen this spot because it afforded no place to run sideways. Either Drishya had to come forward and face the elephant or turn back and be seen retreating.

There was no question of retreating.

He came forward slowly, as if he were walking in Mraashk by the lake, along the pastures, overseeing his father's herd.

The elephant trumpeted its displeasure at this insolence, lowered its head, and charged.

Drishya stopped and faced the elephant. Behind him, he could hear Alinora and his aunts and uncles all voicing their concern. After all, even if he was a god and would eventually triumph, he did feel pain and trauma, he had come close to having his mortal form destroyed — everyone understood this now and knew that *invulnerable* was only a word used by those ignorant of the laws of nature. All that was born must die. All that was created could be destroyed.

The demon elephant bellowed like a bull as it charged, head lowered to aim its deadly tusks at man level. Its feet pounded the dirt road, raising a cloud of dust. Its fury was prodigious.

Drishya neither moved nor budged. He stood his ground and let the elephant charge directly at him. Every pair of eyes in Arrgodi was watching. It was important to send a message loud and clear. Drishya would not be intimidated or turn away from threat. He was here to make a stand.

The elephant's pounding caused the ground beneath his feet to shudder as if in the grip of a tremblor. The great white body loomed before him, moving at the speed of a horse's fastest gallop, and those massive deadly tusks pointed straight at his belly and vitals.

Man and beast met in a head-on collision.

# *Alinora*

ALINORA SUPPRESSED A SCREAM by stuffing her fist into her open mouth. She bit down on the knuckle hard enough to draw blood. Around her in the wagon, everyone reacted in similar ways. All down the road, those watching were shaken by the sight of a man standing still before a charging elephant until—

The great white bull elephant rammed straight into Drishya with all the strength and power it could muster.

And Drishya remained standing exactly where he was, unmoved. He did not budge an inch, not even when one of the elephant's tusks struck his abdomen with a force enough to punch through a solid brick wall. Instead, the tusk itself broke off with a resounding crack that could be heard several streets away. People exclaimed with wonderment.

The elephant's body shuddered at the moment of impact, as if it had indeed struck a brick wall, but one so thick that even its formidable weight and power in that headlong rush could not overcome it. The elephant uttered a bleating sound, almost like a dog's yelp, and backed away, shaking its head and rolling its eyes. Nothing in its long life had prepared it for such an experience.

After a moment, it turned around, clearly too stunned to walk straight, then sat down on its hind legs and bleated again. The loss of its tusk had evidently caused it distress, for it kept rolling its head and waving its trunk, seeking out the missing tusk.

The tusk itself had snapped off cleanly almost at the point where the root emerged from the elephant's body. Barely a few inches of its base were left on the animal. The entire length of it, all one dozen or more feet of ivory tusk as thick as a wrestler's thigh, now lay in Drishya's hands.

Drishya held the tusk up and waved it, showing the elephant that he now possessed a part of its body.

The elephant remained seated on its hind legs, resembling a dog that had received a sudden blow to the tip of its nose. Its eyes watered profusely, issuing a whitish gummy substance that Alinora thought might be musth or something similar.

Drishya stepped forward, walking over to where the elephant sat. Alinora held her breath as she watched. The elephant reacted at once: seeing its intended prey still alive, still hale and hearty, approaching, it rose up, shaking off the stupefaction that had overcome it, trumpeted once again — although nowhere near as confidently as before — and reared up on its hind legs, bringing the mighty forelegs and the weight of its upper body down on Drishya with bone-powdering force.

Drishya raised a hand and took the weight of one elephant foot entirely on that hand.

The foot bent and broke.

The sound was unmistakable, the sight distinct.

The elephant bleated in distress, then fell back at once, breathing heavily.

It hopped on three feet, trying to put the fourth foot down and whining at the pain.

Drishya looked up at the elephant and spoke. Alinora was too far away to hear what he said, but it sounded more like a gentle conversation than an angry threat. What could Drishya possibly be saying?

After a moment, the elephant trumpeted at Drishya, clearly rejecting his offer. It attempted to use its trunk to strike at him, then waved its head to try to stab him with its whole tusk. Drishya stood his ground, neither avoiding nor fending off the blows. This went on for several more moments, during which the elephant seemed to force itself to overcome the agony of the injured foot and stomped about on all four feet again, trying its best to smash, crush, and gore Drishya.

# *Drishya*

DRISHYA SMELLED THE MADNESS in the demon elephant's blood and sweat and knew that the creature was in torment. He reached out a hand, not actually touching its hide but making a gentle stroking movement to show he meant it no harm.

"I know you," he said softly. "Your true name is Kuvalone. You were reborn in this form against your will to serve Tyrak. Your rage and violent temperament stem from your desire to be killed quickly and be rid of this chore you did not desire."

The elephant listened with suspicion in its eyes.

"He treats you cruelly, so that you may treat his enemies cruelly as well. That is a tyrant's way, the urrkh way. Even though you are an urrkh now, you were not one always. You resent being forced to enact this violent behavior. You seek to return to your old peaceful way of life. Like an elephant in the wild, you are not violent in spirit and wish only to feed and love and live out your life in serenity. I can free you from this cycle of misery. I can liberate your soul so you will return to the great grasslands of your true home. Is this what you desire?"

The elephant had raised his trunk and curled it, reaching out toward Drishya's face. It snuffed at Drishya, pushing out a blast of rancid breath. Drishya didn't wince or grimace, even though the smell was awful. He understood that this was Eredon's way of replying in the affirmative.

"Then rise up and attack me one last time so that you may die with honor in this life. Attack me with all your might and prepare to be liberated from the cycle of birth, death, and rebirth forever."

At once, the great white bull rose up, standing on all fours as if his injury did not matter, and attacked Drishya.

Drishya permitted the beast to strike at him several times, then, when the opportune moment came, he raised the elephant's own broken tusk and stabbed it beneath the forelegs, hard enough to punch through the tough hide and formidable breastplate, piercing its aging heart. The animal released a sigh of deep relief, then sank to the ground, blood spreading from its fatal wound and dampening the dust. It lay on its side and died in moments, eyes turned to Drishya in baleful apology.

"I understand," Drishya said. "You are forgiven for all the lives you destroyed. Now go. Take liberation from this form and be free eternally."

The elephant's trunk curled around Drishya's wrist weakly, releasing one final puff of rancid air. Then it lay still.

Drishya rose to his feet and began walking past the dead elephant, toward the place where the walled-in road opened to reveal a great wide field. This was where the wrestling tournament was being held. This was the reason why he had come to Arrgodi.

Time for Tyrak to face his Slayer.

He felt inside his mind for his sibling spirit.

*Krush? It is time. I go now to face the Childslayer and end his tyranny.*

But there was no answer.

# *Krushita*

*Vessa!*

She raced through portal after portal at impossible speeds, worlds flowing past like debris in a gale.

There was no trace of the sage anywhere.

*Krush.*

As if from a great distance — a spiritual distance, not merely the physical divide between them — she heard Drishya call her.

It was time to face the tyrant, the one that Drishya had been born to kill.

This was what she had been preparing for the past few years, training for under Vessa's tutelage, building her strength for, waiting for.

The time to end her father's evildoing once and for all.

Where was Vessa now when she needed him most?

*Guruji,* she cried, *please tell me what to do!*

There was no answer.

She clenched her fists in frustration back in the wagon. She was mad enough to scream and did so. Here in the portals, the action reflected as a storm of worlds, swirling and spinning around her. As chaos in some distant universe.

*Vessa!*

But he was nowhere to be found, or sensed. Not so much as a scent trail.

She came to terms with the fact that she was alone. Not entirely alone, because she still had Drishya, but he could not do what she could. His goal was singular: to kill Tyrak. But he was a being of great power, an actual avatar of some mysterious stone god. Perhaps he could help?

She raced back toward him.

Him, she found easily enough.

*Brother,* she cried out, *I need your help.*

He paused a fraction before replying, *And I yours, sister. I am already face-to-face with my quarry. I cannot leave off now.*

*My mother, my family, everyone I love is in grave danger. I cannot face the threat alone. I need your strength combined with mine.*

Another long pause, during which she could sense the approaching dust clouds, almost feel the thrumming of the wagon beneath her supine body as the attacking army came closer, the hooves of a million dromads drumming the desert floor like a battalion of war drums.

Then he replied with a tone so full of sadness that Krush knew he wanted dearly to help her but had no choice:

*I must fulfill my destiny first. It is my* Auma.

Krush cried out in despair.

*Do what you can, sister. I will join you as soon as I am able. If I am able.*

And then he was gone.

Krush hung in darkness, spinning around as she tried to think of something, anything.

Finally, she knew there was no other way, she had no choice.

She would have to do as she had done in the earlier instance, against the deadwalkers.

She would have to fight the attacking army herself. Alone.

She tightened her jaw, held up her clenched fists, and flew toward it.

# *Tyrak*

TYRAK SLAPPED HIS THIGHS and rubbed his palms over his well-oiled body. He raised his hand, rubbing the excess oil on his finely twirled mustaches, stroking the ends till they extended far outward from his face. The crowd had been bustling with noise, like an ocean roaring near a rocky shore, then had suddenly fallen deathly quiet. Nobody spoke a word. Jarsun, watching from the front row on Tyrak's side, did not smile his usual half-faced smile. The eochs flanking him on either side were as impassive as ever.

On the Mraashk side, though, there were visible emotions on display. Tyrak was pleased to see the obvious concern and anxiety on the faces of Drishya's adoptive mother and father and other relatives.

If he won, he would be taking everything the Mraashk possessed, starting with the lives of Drishya's entire family, down to the last remote cousin and his dogs and dogs' whelps.

But that was a matter for later.

Right now he had to fight.

And to slay a Slayer.

Time to end the cloud of fear he had lived under for so many years.

Time to deliver death to the Deliverer.

Tyrak slapped his chest and stood up in his corner of the wrestling rectangle, legs apart, arms open wide, welcoming. He felt better than he had in his entire life. He was stronger than he had ever imagined he could become. He felt indomitable, indestructible, invulnerable. He was certain of victory.

All that remained were the details: how he would maim and make his opponent suffer before finally killing him. How he would deliver the ultimate killing blow. He had a myriad of ways thought out, any one of which would be agonizing and cause the strongest-willed men to depart this world screaming and voiding their bowels. He had used every one of those holds and blows umpteen times. This would be the first time he did so to a god.

He imagined it would not be very different. After all, he was not much less than a god himself, Jarsun had repeatedly assured him. Nobody could withstand him now.

Certainly not this slip of a boy, his body so slender, his arms and legs so lean, no visible slabs of muscle, no excess padding, nothing to cushion the opponent's blows or provide strength for the powerful holds and grips and blows that were essential to victory in this rectangle.

Drishya looked so out of place in this wrestling ring, it was difficult to believe that this was the Slayer himself. The one Tyrak had been dreading for twenty-three years. The prophesied Deliverer of the Arrgodi people!

He moved forward, ready to prove the prophecy wrong.

# *Krushita*

~

THE INSTANT KRUSH MADE contact, she knew something was different.

She could sense the minds of the dromads racing across the desert on their long legs, worked up to a frenzy, spittle dribbling down the sides of their open mouths. She sensed the minds of the soldiers that rode the dromads, their battle-hardened brains intent on only one thing: killing. She even sensed the mind of Dirrdha at the back of the attacking army, evil and wicked.

But there was something else here. Something she had not expected. Not this time.

Or rather, some*one* else.

**Daughter.**

*You? You are here?*

**Where else would I be? I came to see you. It has been a very long time since I last visited, hasn't it? I apologize. I have been occupied with pressing matters that required my presence elsewhere. But you, my daughter, have never left my thoughts, not even for an instant. I am here now. Finally, you and I will be together. We will be a family again.**

*Never! We can never be a family. You saw to that. You tried to kill my mother.*

**That is true, and I regret that profoundly, daughter. That was a long time ago, and I was a different person then. I have changed.**

*You have not changed one iota. You have never stopped trying to kill her. You killed so many innocents during the deadwalker attack. And in the years before and after. You prevented us from reaching Reygar when we were so close. I know everything, you cannot deceive me with your sweet lies. Even now you are trying to wipe us out with this attack. And you dare to talk of family!*

**I can prove it to you. I can stop this attack right now. I can turn this entire army around and march them back to Reygar. Or even farther into the desert. I can abandon them all there to die. They don't matter to me. Only you matter. Say the word, and I will call off this attack, and we will be reunited as a family.**

*You expect me to believe you? It's all a lie, like every word out of your mouth!*

Suddenly, something happened. She sensed his power going out, rippling through the air. The charging dromads slowed, faltered, then as one being with a common consciousness, the entire charging army stopped its forward momentum.

Krushita stared down at the train from above.

The encircling army had come to a halt a few miles short of the train.

Down below, she could sense her mother, Bulan, and everyone else looking around in disbelief, still afraid, trying to understand why their attackers had stopped, yet terrified as the sand clouds began to settle slowly and they could see the sheer size of the force arrayed around them.

**Do you believe me now? I show you good faith by doing what I said I would do. Now it is your turn, Krushita.**

*What do you expect me to do?*

**Give me another chance. Bring me to your mother and let me talk to her. Then all three of us shall go away together and restart our lives.**

*You expect me to just . . . trust you? After all the havoc you've caused? All the pain you have brought us? The many deaths on your hands?*

**We are still family. You are still my daughter. Nothing you do can change that. I have come to terms with our differences. I cannot promise that your mother and I will be able to rekindle our old fire once again. In all likelihood we will not. But I will not harm her. She will live out the rest of her days in comfort and safety, as she deserves and desires. She will never want for anything. I can offer her that much at least. And she will never fear anything else ever again.**

*And in exchange you want . . . what?*

**You know what I want, Krushita.**

*The Burning Throne. You want me to claim it so you can rule the Burnt Empire, and then the whole world.*

**Perhaps more than one world. What difference does it make to you? Your mother will be alive, and safe, and you will be queen of everything**

**that exists. The fairest queen in all creation. What could be more desirable than that, my child?**

*And if I refuse?*

**The wolf is still at the door. Dirrdha's army can continue their attack, and will on my command.**

She tried to think, but she also knew she had to be careful. Jarsun could see her thoughts. She tried to follow her guru's instructions, to shield her mind as effectively as possible, make a tiny space for herself to mull on the problem privately.

He has to know about the Deliverer and me, she thought. That is why he is here now, at this very moment. He knows that by separating us, he takes away the advantage that Drishya has.

But she also knew that Drishya was strong in himself. He was an avatar, after all. He could probably kill Tyrak without her help. After all, he was the Slayer that the prophecy foretold. He had been born for this purpose. And it was not Tyrak she cared about right now. There were a thousand tyrants in the world she could not simply go about killing and stopping. Not while she had family of her own to care for and protect. If she only had to choose between helping Drishya kill Tyrak or saving her mother and friends, it was an easy choice. She had already made that choice. And for the moment, she had stopped the attack on the train.

No. This was about what she had intended to do after Drishya killed Tyrak.

It was about ending Jarsun himself.

That was the bargain.

Drishya would kill Tyrak, then challenge Jarsun in the same arena.

And Jarsun would accept the challenge and fight Drishya.

And Krush would join her strength with Drishya's, and together they would slay the greater tyrant, he who created a thousand Tyraks. Jarsun Krushan.

She had to go through with that plan. It was the only way, her only chance of ending her father's evil once and for all.

Why?

Because Vessa said so?

*Where is Vessa now, when you need him most?*

*He isn't even here.*

This time, it wasn't Jarsun who fled like a coward, it was Vessa.

Somehow, he knew that his plan had been found out, that Jarsun had seen through his stratagem, and he went and hid away. Where Krushita couldn't find him.

Vessa had betrayed her. That was the only way she could see it right now. He had betrayed and abandoned her.

And now she had to face this on her own.

She came to a decision.

It was not the decision she wanted to make, or even one she had ever dreamed of making, but it was the only one she could make in that moment.

She came back to where Jarsun's consciousness waited.

*Very well, Father,* she said. It hurt her brain to even form those words, but she made herself say them. *I will bring you to Mother and let you speak words with her. But if she refuses your offer, if she tells you to go to hell, as I am sure she will, then you will not harm her. This you must promise me. Only if and when you let her do as she wishes — not as you wish — will I consider the next step. But I am not speaking of moments or hours, or even days, weeks, months. I am speaking of years. Let Mother live out her life in peace and safety. Then, when she has passed away in the way of all mortals and I have laid her to her final rest and grieved for her, I will go to Hastinaga and I will claim the Burning Throne.*

**That is not what I asked for.**

*That is all you're going to get from me. Take it or leave it.*

**What if I wait all those years, and after your mother's passing, you refuse to honor your part of the bargain? I will have no hold over you, nothing to bargain with. I know that once your mother is gone, you will not listen to anything I have to say.**

*Unlike you, Father dearest, I have a sense of honor. I honor my promises once I make them. It may surprise you or even shock you, but most people in this world are honorable and keep their word. Not everyone is a lying, murdering, genocidal monster like yourself.*

**I see. Well. Is that your final word?**

*It is. Take it or leave it. You will not get anything else from me.*

**In that case, I will take it.**

# *Drishya*

DRISHYA FELT NOTHING AS he stepped forward to meet Tyrak's first attack. Not fear, not doubt, not confidence, not anger . . . nothing. There was only a blankness in his mind that he felt certain nothing could possibly fill. An emptiness, a void, into which he could pour anything, create an entire world if he desired. This moment was a blank slate on which any future could be written.

He sensed Tyrak's great self-confidence. The Childslayer clearly felt certain of victory. It was writ large on his fair features, in the way he took his time stepping around the wrestling square, in no hurry to attack, yet showing no concern at the outcome. He grinned at Drishya, and the grin was more a leer, promising pain and agony and a slow, torturous, humiliating death.

Then Tyrak charged.

It was exactly like the elephant's charge.

Drishya simply stood his ground.

Tyrak slammed into the slender boy with enough force to shatter a stone wall. Even the demon elephant was nothing compared to Tyrak in his present state. The elephant was mortal, merely stronger and bigger and better armored than most of its kind. Tyrak, on the other hand, had been built into a juggernaut through decades of drug consumption and training. He was a finely honed killing machine.

Yet Drishya was a stone wall mighty enough to withstand even his greatest force.

The shoulder that had pulverized boulders the size of a house struck Drishya's chest and chin and was shattered.

The back that had provided power enough to lift entire quarries of stone and heave them scores of yards away now cracked and broke under the impact.

The arms broke, the joints gave way, the heavy bones of the legs and hip shattered, the muscle that was harder than iron was pulped and turned to bloody mash.

Tyrak bounced off Drishya and collapsed in a heap on the dusty ground of the wrestling square.

A roar of exultation rose from the Mraashk ranks.

# *Tyrak*

ON TYRAK'S SIDE, EVERYONE looked on in stunned silence.

Tyrak moaned. For the first time in a decade or more, he felt pain. Not mere pain, but agony. Blinding, piercing, shooting pain in every joint, bone, and muscle group. So intense, he broke out sweating all over his body.

Somehow, impossibly, he forced himself to regain his feet. He himself hardly knew how he accomplished it, but he was aware that he could not remain supine. Staying down itself constituted defeat, and he would not be defeated.

He *could not* be defeated.

He was Tyrak.

Lord of Arrgodi.

King today, emperor tomorrow.

He rose, staggering and blinking at the shock of the pain coursing through his nerves. He had never thought such agony was even possible, let alone that he could experience it.

He willed his injured bones to knit, his damaged flesh to heal, his body to grow denser than ever before. And he succeeded: the injuries reversed themselves, the healing was astonishingly rapid, and the body that had been like iron now became even denser and stronger.

He faced his opponent again. "I will—" he snarled.

Before he could finish the threat, Drishya came at him.

The boy leaped at him, grabbing hold of his head in the triangular space of his left arm, throwing Tyrak backward.

The boy was but a stripling, yet Tyrak was thrown back in a crashing fall, landing with a punishing thud on his spine.

Drishya's arm was in a chokehold on Tyrak's throat.

Tyrak felt he could break free of the chokehold easily. All he had to do was—

. . . was . . .

. . . was . . .

He felt the world fade, the day grow dark, all thought, vision, touch, smell, sound, recede to a distant point.

Then he heard his own neck break. It was an impossible sound. Even the strongest wrestlers in the world, bodies enhanced just as his own, had tried and failed to break that neck. To break that neck would require a force greater than that required to move a mountain.

Yet he heard it distinctly.

The world spun around him. He saw the arena, the thousands of staring faces. Somewhere among them were two that mattered to him: Ladislew. And Jarsun. He had glanced in their direction before he went to fight the Slayer. They were sitting in the same block, the royal pavilion. Jarsun on the throne that was Tyrak's by rights, and Ladislew several rows lower, with the retinue of advisors and officers serving the throne. She was seated beside her husband, dressed in a fine gown that showed off her beauty quite fetchingly.

He tried to look in that direction, to find her in that crowd of faces.

His head would not do as he bid. His neck would not turn.

He lay in the dust, the sky spinning overhead.

He tried to see out the corners of his eyes.

There.

He could just about make out the royal pavilion. Unmistakable with its bright colors and pageantry. The royal throne shone in the sunlight, the gold catching the rays and reflecting them. They glittered at the edges of his vision. He thought he could see Jarsun there, and imagined he could see Ladislew too. What were they thinking right now?

Suddenly, he knew.

Ladislew had moved to join Jarsun, and was seated close to him now, leaning over and speaking. Through blurring vision, Tyrak saw Jarsun tilt his thin, long face and say something in response, to which Ladislew laughed loudly. They seemed to be enjoying the spectacle of Tyrak's last moments. He knew then that she had misled him from the very start; all that she had done, she had done with an ulterior motive. Why else should she have given him the antidote to the debilitating concoction that Jarsun had drugged him with? What, then, of her story of seeking vengeance on Jarsun for the slaughter of her sister Maatri back in Reygistan? Tyrak was too far gone to even attempt to understand all the devious twists and turns of her endgame. All that mattered to him right now was that she had gained his trust — his friendship! — and had betrayed him in the end. Far from assassinating Jarsun, she was allied with him now.

As for the Krushan, his mentor, his benefactor, his guru, his emperor, his father-in-law, Jarsun's mind was the easiest of all to read.

Jarsun simply didn't care. He could raise a thousand Tyraks and probably had. His goal was a far bigger one than merely the future of Arrgodi. Even if he lost Arrgodi, lost the entire grassland, he would find a way to wrest it back eventually. His target was the Burnt Empire. The Burning Throne was the throne he really wanted to sit upon, not this one. In fact, now that Tyrak thought about it with the clear mind of a dying man, he wondered why Jarsun had chosen him at all. What part had he played in the Krushan's great game? Had he served his purpose? Was that why he was dying now? Yes, that must be it. Jarsun had done all this, played this long hand over so many years, only to achieve some other goal, something Tyrak would probably die never knowing. All the lives expended here, including Tyrak's, were meaningless to Jarsun. They were insignificant pawns in the great game and his part had been played.

He too had been played.

Tyrak closed his eyes, ending his own part in this monstrous game.

# *Drishya*

DRISHYA ROSE TO HIS feet, standing over Tyrak's broken body. The sound of Tyrak's neck breaking had been loud enough to carry to the ends of the crowd thronging the wrestling field, several score yards away. The thousands-strong audience were dead silent for another breathless moment, then, as one, they rose to their feet and let forth a roar of such exultation that the entire city of Arrgodi heard it and responded with echoing cries and roars and cheers.

Sitting astride his horse in the cantonment, General Bane heard the roar and knew that it was over at last. He signaled to his men to do what had been agreed. They did so without question: like himself, they had all seen too much bloodshed and suffering, much of it inflicted by themselves acting under Tyrak's orders. They laid down their weapons gladly and with hearts filled with relief and hope. As one man, the entire Arrgodi Imperial Army disbanded and disarmed itself. The people surged forth, no longer under curfew, no longer restricted. They danced in the streets. They sang the praises of Drishya. They celebrated.

To Drishya's surprise, Jarsun's entourage rode out of the arena. They did not look like they intended to fight.

He watched with amazement as Jarsun rode right past him, down the long avenue, to the gates of the city, and out of Arrgodi.

# Aqreen

AQREEN STARED IN DISBELIEF at the tall figure that dismounted from the dromad and strode toward her.

Her hand flew to her mouth. She turned to stare at the wagon where Krushita had lain for the past hour.

Krushita descended the ladder and came toward Aqreen. She had an expression on her face that Aqreen could not read.

"Krush?" Aqreen said. "Look."

Krushita kept her eyes on her mother. "I know, Mother. He wants only to talk."

"Talk?" Aqreen stared at her. "What is there to talk about?"

"I understand. But that is the bargain I made with him."

Aqreen's mind reeled. *"Bargain? With him?"*

"I had no choice, Mother. It was the only way to save us. He will not harm you. He wants to talk. You don't have to agree to anything he says. Refuse him, reject him, abuse him all you want. Then he will go away and leave us alone. And we will live out our lives —"

"Leave us alone? You really believe that? After all he has done?"

"Please, let me finish. We will live out our lives in peace, and he will never trouble us again. That is the bargain I made."

Aqreen searched her daughter's face, unable to believe that these words were coming from Krushita's mouth. "You cannot expect him to keep his promises, Krush. Whatever he promised you, this so-called bargain, it is meaningless. He will never change, he cannot change. He is Krushan. He is like stonefire itself. Forever evil. I should have known that at the outset, but I was gulled by his sincerity and blinded by my own youth and naiveté.

Don't fall for his lies, Krush. Fight him if you can, fight him now. We will die fighting him together. Better that than any bargain with the devil!"

But Krushita had the look in her eyes that she always got when she was determined to do something and nothing Aqreen or Bulan or anyone else said would change her mind. Aqreen knew that look all too well. She had seen it in mirrors when she was young too. And in her father's eyes before herself. It was a stubborn streak they all shared. The sense of conviction in something, no matter how impossible.

"It is the only way, Mother. I had no choice."

"You always have a choice. Do it now. Fight him. Please, Krush. Do it. You are stronger than you know. You are powerful in yourself. Destroy him if you can, or let us both die fighting him. But don't give in!"

A shadow fell over Krushita's face. Aqreen felt his malevolent presence without even needing to turn her head.

"Hello, Aqreen," Jarsun said.

She forced herself to turn and looked at him briefly.

The sight of that thin, long face and those piercing eyes disgusted her so much, she thought she would lose the contents of her stomach right there. She couldn't believe that Krushita had agreed to this . . . whatever it was.

"Go away," she heard herself say, faintly. Too faintly to be heard.

She felt a hand on her back, supporting her, and realized she was on the verge of fainting. The hand was Bulan's, she could make out from the fact it was large enough to cover her entire back. She breathed in, fighting the nausea and panic that warred within her.

"Go away," she said, louder now. "Whatever you agreed with Krushita, I was not part of the bargain. I don't want to see you, to hear you, to hear anything you have to say. Go away now."

He began to speak again.

She screamed at him, unable to help herself. "GO AWAY, YOU MONSTER!"

She felt Bulan holding her shoulders now, holding her back, and realized she was lunging forward, trying to drive her weapon at him, to spear him, to kill him. Jarsun.

She heard the bastard Krushan's voice saying something. It was barely a murmur, hardly audible over the roaring of her blood and the rage that filled her being.

**It didn't have to be this way. I offered you the world. All you had to do was take it. Remember that.**

And suddenly, she felt something, a sharp pricking at her throat. It was so minute, she thought it must be an insect, some desert mite. But then she felt the trickle of blood roll down her neck and knew.

"You . . . stung me," she said incredulously.

She looked at Krushita, who was staring at her in horror.

"He . . ." Aqreen said.

Then felt herself falling.

Bulan caught her in their enormous hands, bellowing with fury. Around her, pandemonium erupted as everyone tried to make sense of what was happening.

Then Krushita screamed in rage and something, a great ball of power stronger than any force Aqreen had felt in her life, blasted out from her daughter and struck the place where Jarsun was standing.

But instead of hitting flesh and blood, it struck something that burst into a shower of sand.

The wind caught the sand grains and blew them away.

Only his laughter hung in the air, lingering.

**Too late, little one. Remember. You are powerful. But I am still your father.**

The laughter rang in Aqreen's ears as she felt her life leaving her.

Her last thought was, *Krush!*

# *Krushita*

KRUSHITA HOWLED IN AGONY. Her grief was beyond her limits to endure.

She held her mother's corpse in her hands.

"Ma," she cried, tears dripping from her cheeks, "he tricked me. It was all a ruse to get close enough to you. He used me to get to you. I am so, so, so sorry! I didn't know what to do. I made a choice. It was the only choice."

**Little one.**

Krushita raised her head, tilting it slightly as she stared up at the sky. The same sky that her mother had stood under only moments ago, alive. "You! Where were you when I needed you most? This is all your fault!"

**I understand your anger. I feel your grief. But this is all his doing. He outwitted us.**

"I don't care!" Krushita shouted to the wind that had suddenly sprung up from nowhere and was whipping through the wagon train. "You could have helped me. I needed you. I didn't know what to do, and now my mother is dead. Dead!" Fresh tears rushed down her face, spilling onto the red sand.

**He is a great adversary. He knew you were listening in the unspace. He knew of my plan. Of the Slayer and you. He wanted you to be divided and confused. He planned it all, outmaneuvering me.**

"Why are you praising him?" she yelled. "He killed my mother. I don't care about anything else now. Help me find him. Help me kill him."

**That is why I am here. I hoped to arrive in time to stop him, but he knew I would break free, and he made his move, perhaps sooner than expected.**

Krushita felt the sand shift and shiver under her knees. She heard a deep rumbling.

She heard Bulan shouting, then other Vanjhani shouting, their deep voices booming across the train. She registered people rushing to and fro, carrying weapons. And the thrumming beneath her folded feet grew to a rumbling thunder.

**Yes. Dirrdha's army is attacking. He intends to wipe out everyone you care about. This was all his plan. He used you to get close enough to kill your mother himself. He wanted the satisfaction of killing her with his own venom.**

She wept. She was holding her mother's body in her arms, and she still couldn't wrap her mind around it. Her heart felt as if it had exploded and lay in pieces. The world was meaningless.

**There is only one way left. A desperate, insane way. But that may be the only way to outwit and overcome Jarsun.**

Through her grief, she understood one thing only: Vessa was offering her a way to avenge her mother's murder. To kill Jarsun.

"Tell me," she said, forcing herself to listen.

Vessa spoke to her mind.

All the while, the thunder grew, the attacking army drew closer and closer, until she could see the dromads racing madly at the train, the warriors mounted on their humped backs raising their long weapons in readiness to hurl them. A million attackers, a paltry few thousand defenders. It was no battle at all.

She considered Vessa's suggestion.

She had only a few moments.

She needed less than that.

"Yes," she said aloud. "I will do it."

**Good. I will be there when you come through, to welcome you.**

"You had better be," she said grimly.

She bent low and kissed Aqreen on her forehead, then on her cheek, then once more on her other cheek.

"I will see you soon, Mother," she said.

She set her mother down gently.

And rose to her feet.

She saw the dromads charging straight at her, thousands upon thousands, and more like them all around the train. Too many to stop in time. Too many to kill.

Or perhaps not.

She summoned all the power she had within her, building it, accelerating it.

*Sister, I am here now. I regret I could not be with you before, to help stave off the tragedy. But I am here for you now. I am ready to join you in your task.*

*Thank you, brother. Congratulations on your success. You have completed your given task. The purpose of your life in this avatar is ended. I ask you now to give me your next life.*

*I know what you need, and I am ready to do all that is required. Vessa has told me everything. I am joining my power with you now.*

She felt a massive surge as Drishya's power combined with hers. It lifted her body up a thousand feet above the wagon train. She hung suspended in midair, held by a force greater than anything she had experienced before. She had never known such power could exist in the universe.

Then she and Drishya became one.

# *Bulan*

BULAN STARED UP IN confusion.

Krushita hung in midair, high above the wagon train. Her body pulsed with energy, great snaking bolts and jagged edges like shards of blue lightning. They felt their skin prickle with the sensation. The energy was like something in the old tales.

They turned to look at the charging dromad lines. They were only a few hundred yards from the wagon train now. In moments, they would be in throwing range, and it would be the beginning of the end. Bulan was not afraid of dying. They were a warrior born and bred; dying while facing impossible odds was an honorable end. They regretted that Krushita had lost her mother so horribly, that she had not been given a chance to avenge that death. That was unbearable. Bulan had come to love the woman in a way that could not easily be expressed in either Vanjhani or Aqrish, something more than friendly affection and perhaps just short of romantic love. They felt the pain of her loss keenly, almost as keenly as they had once felt the anguish of losing their own mate and offspring.

Suddenly the energy in the sky grew deafeningly loud. It boomed and vibrated like a living thing.

The dromad lines were slowing, despite the forward momentum of their charge. They would not stop in time before they reached the wagons, but the dromads were unsettled, scared by the unaccustomed energy building in the sky.

Bulan felt their ears throbbing, their bones screaming with sensation.

They tried to look up.

Krushita was enveloped in a cloud of blue light so intense, so bright, it was a miniature sun.

Bulan blinked as they tried to see clearly.

They thought they could make out the silhouette of another person in that cloud, beside Krushita, holding hands with her.

A man.

That was impossible.

Or was it?

Whatever was happening here was the stuff of legends and myths. Fit for a campfire tale. A good one.

Bulan watched the sky, no longer caring about the charging army or the sharp-edged steel that they expected to feel tearing their flesh at any moment. The only thing that mattered was what Krushita was doing. Krushita and whoever the other person was who was aiding her.

Then the desert was blanketed by a blinding flash so intense that Bulan felt their vision go completely dark.

Blinded, they sat down. Their hands opened, and their weapons fell out.

That had never happened before.

They felt stunned, bludgeoned by the explosion.

Not one caused by fire or conflagrating oil in barrels.

But an explosion of pure power.

Eventually, their vision and hearing returned, and Bulan saw two things. There were many more things to be seen: such as the fact that the entire wagon train was still intact and everyone still alive. But that was beside the point, to Bulan at least, although probably not to Krushita. It was a happy consequence of what she had done.

The two things that were to the point:

Dirrdha's army had vanished completely. Not a single dromad or warrior remained. Only the fading sand cloud and a broad hoof-churned expanse of hoofprints that marked the charge of the army up to a point several dozen yards from the wagon train.

Krushita was gone too.

As was the silhouette Bulan had seen beside her in the sky.

# EPILOGUE, PROLOGUE

## *The Given Avatars*

YEAR 207 OF CHAKRA 58

# *Krushni*

~

**LITTLE ONE.**

Krushni smiled even as she turned her head.

The portal opened by Vessa as he came through from unknown realms shimmered like a heat mirage in a roughly circular shape. Beyond him, she glimpsed a desolate volcanic landscape, blighted by ruptured ground and bright with flowing rivers of lava. Then, at a word spoken in Ashcrit by the seer-mage, the portal winked shut.

There he stood, as tall, dark, and fierce-looking as his persona in the portals and unspace. Vessa. Finally in the flesh.

"Welcome," he said aloud, joining his palms together in a namas of greeting.

Around him, King Gwann, his queen, his priests, and other people all gaped and murmured in amazement. Those felled by the stonefire still lay scattered around, their bodies reduced to ashes that stirred uneasily in a soft wind.

"Well met, sage," Krushni said, moving toward Vessa. "It worked, then."

He inclined his head silently. "I regret the loss of your mother," he said. "Nothing I do can ever make up for that loss. But you made the right choice. By assuming a new avatar, you remove yourself permanently from Jarsun's game. Now your life is your own to do with as you desire."

He turned his head to greet the young man beside her. "Welcome, Drishya. It is an honor to meet the Slayer of Tyrak."

Drishya said nothing. But he lowered his head to acknowledge the sage's greeting.

Krushni said to Vessa, "I only desire one thing from this life, and one thing alone."

Vessa looked at her. Drishya looked at her too. King Gwann, the queen, everyone looked at her.

She smiled, feeling the power within her. She was stronger. Much, much stronger. And she would grow stronger yet. And with Drishya beside her, she would be unstoppable. She would accomplish in this life what she could not in her last. The only thing that mattered to her anymore.

"To kill Jarsun Krushan," she said.

And thousands of miles distant, in the Burnt Empire, in the capital city of Hastinaga, in the great throne hall, the dark, malevolent force uncoiled and awoke, its black sentience responding to the rage, power, and determination in her, and the Burning Throne spoke in a voice of flame:

*Hail the Dark Queen risen.*

And with a burst of fury that shocked the dozen-odd hapless sentries and servants within the vast chamber, stonefire ignited, impossibly long tentacles of hot rage lashing out to incinerate every last one of them to piles of ashes and blackened bone.

*Burn,* it said in gleeful adoration.

*Yes,* Krushni replied. *Burn.*

# Acknowledgments

Once again, John Joseph Adams, without whom the book you hold in your hands and its predecessor would not exist. He believed in me, in this story and these amazing characters, and has been a pillar of support. By far the finest editor I have had the pleasure of working with over a long career. Looking forward to many more books together, John!

The rest of the team at HMH has been awesome. It takes a publishing village to raise a book as beautiful as this one, and I can't thank them enough for their support and enthusiasm.

Hubris is what it takes to attempt a series this ambitious and complex.

Humility is what's required to carry it from idea to final publication.

Everything I do, alone at a computer for long hours over long days and even longer months and years, is only the beginning of the process by which a book goes from my hands to yours. There are literally hundreds of people involved along the way, and every single one of you deserves my thanks. This is the best job in the world, and it wouldn't be possible without you. Thank you for doing what you do to make books reach their readers. You are special, you matter, you are wonderful. Please keep doing what you doing!

My family is the foundation of my life, and I am only one small part of that matrix of love and solidarity. Unlike the cruel, often barbaric world of the Burnt Empire and its power-greedy demagogues, we are not supporters of patriarchal structures. I'd like to think that Krushita — or Krushni, or even simply Krush — better represents my true self, the self that lives with my wonderful, endlessly supportive, and giving family. They are my real world, my reality. The only reason I can vanish into the secondary world of an epic fantasy series for hours each day for decades is because I have them to return home to at the end. They make it all possible by making me possible.

Thank you, Biki, Yashka, Yoda, Helene, and the littlest one of us all, Leia. Love and only love forever. We go on.

Ashok Kumar Banker
Mumbai, India / Los Angeles, USA
December 31, 2019